RED CARPET BLACK

NOLON KING

STERLING & STONE

RED CARPET BLACK

<h1 align="center">Chapter One</h1>

Taking inventory at Provisions was killing Orson Beck one box at a time.

There'd been a certain entertainment value when he'd first started working at the high-end grocery store, watching well-coifed wives wandering the aisles on their safaris for organic, cruelty-free, gluten-free, and perspective-free fuckery, from chia seeds to guakalemole.

Orson hated the guy or gal who'd thought this up, and double hated them if they were also the person who brought the abomination to market. He also hated every customer willing to pay for perfectly good guac to get ruined by kale. Orson hated kale, and everything it touched. Especially — he could rant about this one for hours — *ice cream*, which had several flavors destroyed by the bitter, chewy vegetable over in Aisle 9.

Inventory would have been the devil's work regardless, but Orson found it an order of magnitude even more demoralizing, handling ice cream that cost more per pint than what he made each hour, and almond butter that ran twice that. Watching the wealthy, well-put-together people piling their carts with overpriced sundries because, for them, cash wasn't too different from Kleenex, was like watching beautiful people dancing all over his dreams. It was a wonder that the checkout lines weren't all 'ten items or less' because who could afford to get more than that in a single go?

The people in this fucking town, that's who.

Orson used to find it inspiring. It's why he'd picked this job. He'd seen a flyer in the coffee shop across the street, the Hill of Beans, advertising the job opening in the grocery store. It felt like a guiding light at the time. He'd waited with a pounding heart for the red light to turn green, knowing that he'd get the job and that somehow that would lead to him being in the right place at the right time and becoming the next big Hollywood success story, the kind that everyone loved to read about. He had been dreaming of living forever.

But that was stupid, and he was an idiot for thinking it.

Now Orson was dying, box by box, because every day shoved him further away from the life he had always believed would eventually find him, despite the terrible odds. Fresh prospects showed up in the city every day. That's how it had been for a century, and how it would be forever. Hollywood held the promise of unlimited everything. Fame, fortune, and an eventual refuge from failure. After you made it.

But how many people would? Once Orson had been certain he'd be one of the lucky few to ooze through the cracks. Saw it as a reality waiting to happen. But that reality had turned to a fantasy, and now it was settling into a lie. Soon his son would know exactly how big a loser he was.

At least work was a reprieve from Alexis. That was the

only thing making his day tolerable. He didn't have to ignore her calls when he was legitimately at work.

Orson shook his head as he finished inventory on the hand-milled, gluten-free soap. Then he turned and--oh shit, there was Bobby Winchester.

Bobby was smiling, but Orson already wanted to be anywhere else. He'd had nothing against Bobby five minutes ago, but right now he hated the guy. Sauntering up with his little hand basket. How could he afford to shop here? They were in the same acting class. Or at least they used to be, until Orson stopped going to that one. These days, it was over his budget by a little more than a hundred percent of its price.

"What up, brother?" Bobby said, reaching out for a high-five.

Orson returned it, smiling wide. "Hey man, what are you doing?" He glanced in Bobby's basket and saw a six-pack of Flying Dog K9 Cruiser, some of that twenty-four dollar almond butter — *what the actual fuck?* — and a nineteen dollar box of sustainably sourced condoms. He nodded approvingly. "Looks like a party."

Bobby laughed. "So how have things been going?"

This was the part where Orson either made a bunch of shit up or admitted defeat.

He shrugged, then gestured around the store. "Living the dream. You?"

Orson didn't want to know. Okay, not true. He was dying to. A twenty dollar box of condoms? His neighbor Lacy charged less than that for a blow job. Not that Orson had ever partaken, but Lacy used her mouth for a lot of things, including talking about all the things she used her mouth for.

"Great, actually." Bobby's smile looked genuinely bash-ful. Fucking actors. "I got it."

"Got what?"

Orson had heard that he was up for playing Cobain in the biopic, but he couldn't see him in that role. At all.

Bobby leaned forward, and in a decibel more than a whisper, said, "*It.* A ticket to the Onyx List."

Fuck him, of course he did.

"Wow!" Orson said. "That's amazing."

"Yeah." Bobby nodded, grinning ear to ear. "I still can't believe it."

Neither could Orson. Except that he could. This shit always happened to him.

Every. Fucking. Year.

"It came in the mail yesterday."

Orson already knew, but he asked anyway. "What did it look like?"

He forced himself to smile his way through Bobby's description. Every actor who'd made it in told the same story, because even though the Onyx List had only been around for a few years now, it was already the stuff of legends.

Orson worked hard to forget about the invitations. Until now, he'd been doing a decent enough job of keeping those thoughts in the black. But now here they were again, turning him green. They always came out in November, just before the year's Oscar bait hit theaters, when the city was feeling especially fancy. It had to happen to someone he knew sooner or later. Might as well be Bobby.

"That's really fucking cool, man," Orson said, and he really did mean it, even though it hurt.

"It's not like anything is guaranteed," Bobby said, self-effacing.

"But it's a helluva head start."

And it was. Not everyone who made it onto the Onyx List became instant Hollywood royalty, but it had been a shortcut for so many. It was the most important invitation in the most important city in the most important country in the world. Orson would die to trade places with Bobby Winchester.

"Any idea why they picked you? All respect, man. We shared a class. I know what you can do. But this town …"

"I don't really know, honestly. I was up for the lead in Cobain, but even I thought I was wrong for the part." He slapped Orson on the shoulder. "Dude, I've seen you too. Hopefully whoever makes the List has seen what you can do."

"*F the '90s* was a while ago. I'm not sure anyone even remembers that show."

A long silence, because they both knew he was right.

Bobby broke it. "How is Alexis?"

Orson opened his mouth to explain *that* failure, but before he could, the universe intervened.

It made sense, in a town built around stories, where the biggest rule was putting *show* over *tell*, that Alexis was marching right toward them, dragging his son behind her.

Chapter Two

After a machine gun greeting and Bobby's retreat, Alexis was immediately in his face.

"I've asked you a million times not to just show up with Connor while I'm working." Orson looked at his son with apologetic eyes, not wanting him to think that any of this was his fault.

"Ohh, a million times? Is that right? Because I've really come down here a million times, and you've had to tell me every one of them. I'm that stupid. *Three times,* Orson. That's how many times I've showed up here. And all of them were only because you did what you're still doing, ignoring my calls. You know how much that pisses me off."

"To be fair, everything pisses you off."

"I don't like being ignored."

"I'm working."

"You weren't working during any of the times I called you in the morning."

"I already know what you want."

"Oh, and what's that, Orson? What do I want?"

Why was she making him do this?

Especially here?

Orson leaned in, then in a low voice he said, "Because you want this month's child support."

But Alexis couldn't pass up the chance to trample on his dignity. She half-yelled, "Because I want you to pay your child support?"

"Stop it," he growled.

"You're the one who wouldn't answer my calls. This is your fault."

"Isn't everything?" Orson looked down at Connor, who stood there mute, observing their quarrel in silence, like always. "Do we have to do this now? Or here?"

"Maybe next time you'll answer my calls."

"Yes, Alexis. Next time I promise to answer your calls. Your many, many calls. Now can you please go so I can get back to work and we can talk about this later?"

Orson had already surrendered. She didn't have to beat him down. But Alexis was all riled up. "I just hope you appreciate how lucky we are that our son has a model example at home, and that that can give him the right impression of what a father should be."

He rolled his eyes. Orson would rather get caught beating off in public than to hear another word about Alexis' magical fiancé, Tyler Crane. He'd landed a role on a show about a hipster grocery store — Greens — which was almost exactly like Provisions. And Tyler's character was a fucking clerk, just like Orson had been when he started working here. The irony was as unbelievable as it was infuriating. The man who mocked his existence in front of millions of viewers was also raising Orson's son and fucking his ex-wife.

"I am so very lucky," Orson said to Alexis. And to Connor, "Sorry about this, buddy."

"Don't do that."

"Do what?" Orson asked.

"You know what. Apologizing to him, like this is my fault."

Orson controlled his breathing, careful not to yell. "You're the one who put him in the Prius and came over here."

"We're not in the Prius," Alexis announced, glowing. "Tyler wanted a new Tesla, so we're in his old one."

"I can totally see how my late child support is an emergency."

"It doesn't have to be an emergency, Orson. It's your responsibility. So just be a man and take care of it. Tyler has a job and he's well-compensated, but it isn't his job to provide for *our* kid."

Orson was boiling. It wasn't that Tyler had so many of the things that he would give anything to get, it was that the asshole didn't deserve them. Tyler was one of those guys who was *just* talented enough, *just* good looking enough, and *just* lucky enough to stumble into one fortunate circumstance after another.

Orson worked hard for everything. Even if Alexis thought his dream was dead, he definitely didn't. He'd been working fewer hours to attend some of the more affordable acting classes, and to show up for auditions as often as he could. He wasn't about to tell Alexis that because she'd see it as an excuse at best and pathetic at worst.

He looked at Alexis, not wanting to fight. He needed to get her out of Provisions before Lester came over and chastised him for taking personal time on the company dollar.

"You're right. I'm sorry. Things are really tight right now, and—"

"Why are they tight? Your place is a piece of shit and you don't even drive."

"Can you *please* not curse around him?"

"We've had this conversation. It's dishonest. He already knows all the words, and that we use them."

Goddammit, Alexis.

Orson gave her his most charming smile. He reached out and touched her shoulder. Then in his best gentleman's voice, he said, "I'll take care of this as soon as I can. I promise."

He wondered how many eyes were on him. It felt like hundreds.

He couldn't have hated this more, but still he gave Alexis a smile that was really for Connor. Bobby was at the edge of his peripheral vision, pretending not to watch the show. Lester was watching and waiting.

Orson fixed her with his best smile and held it. "We good?"

"We're good." She finally smiled back. "I'm not trying to be a bitch. But you can't ignore my calls. We had a deal."

We had a deal.

She might as well get it as a tattoo. That's what she always told him, *We had a deal,* whether that deal was explicit or not. It was her way of making the rules, of designing an argument that couldn't be won. Orson wasn't the piece of shit that she thought he was. She spent too much of her life pissed that he didn't turn out to be who she'd imagined he would one day be. And now she was stuck with his kid. Who she — and the courts — would only allow him to see every other weekend. Orson felt like his son's favorite stranger. They always had fun, but they were sort of starting over each and every time.

"You're right. We had a deal." Orson held two fingers in front of him. "Scout's Honor, I'll have it to you soon. Okay?"

"Okay."

They hugged it out because that was how they always did it. Then Connor began to tell Orson about what had happened on the last episode of *Crazy Town*, because Dr. Nanobot had taken control of the *entire Voltrosphere* and now all the sharks were in trouble. It all came out in the space of a cough. Orson had to cut him off before he started the next sentence because Lester was marching over.

"I can't wait to see you on Saturday!" He kissed Connor on his head.

His wife and son were seven steps away when Lester began to berate him. "We've talked about this, Orson."

Lester would be lucky if he was *only* seen as a loser. The guy was twenty-five, two years younger than Orson, and he acted like managing a Provisions was his life's dream. It was ridiculous. So was he.

But Orson still nodded and smiled as his boss gave him the Personal Time Lecture.

If someone from the Onyx List had been peeking around the endcap to watch Orson right now, they'd have to hand him an invitation. He got more use out of his acting classes at work than he did in auditions.

"You're right," Orson said. "We haven't just talked about it, we've talked about it four times. You shouldn't have to remind me that I can't put personal time on the company dollar. I didn't know that Alexis was going to come by like that, and I didn't invite her, so I didn't have time to clock out. Since of course I would have, if she'd given me a chance."

Lester's shoulders relaxed. "It's fine. Just tell her she can't do that."

Yeah, that'll work. "I'll tell her again."

Lester left him alone after Orson made extra nice by

agreeing to take Krystal's register shift so she could pick up her sick kid from school.

This was all his fault, Orson thought as he logged into the register. He could have finished college. He *should have* finished. Orson had no excuse.

College should have been the best years of his life. He worked his ass off to get there, with the help of his supportive parents. But his confidence took a massive blow just three weeks in. For the first time in his life, Orson wasn't chosen to be the lead, and he'd lost the role to Aaron Roberson, who wasn't nearly as good an actor.

His teachers clearly didn't know shit. That's why they were clinging to the tails of their failed careers, rather than walking the red carpets. College was an artificial environment filled with bullshit hoops to jump through.

Orson had gone from being a big fish in a small pond, to a little fish in an ocean of talent. And so, like an asshole, he dropped out of college. His parents were devastated, and his brother Samuel was *pissed.*

You've always been selfish, but until now it was never your defining personality trait.

Ever since he'd said that, Orson and Samuel only spoke when they had to, each one waiting for the other to apologize.

Now he had to hear his parents' disappointment every time they talked. A hum as they spoke then a ringing in his ears after they hung up. The conversations were always the same. Them mentioning all the job offerings closer to home, asking about Connor over and over, each time with a mention that they didn't get to see him nearly enough, reminding him on repeat that they shouldn't have to come all the way out to *that California hellhole just to see our grandchild.*

But Orson couldn't go home yet. He wasn't ready to

give up. He would continue to work hard, both at his day job and at his dream in the meantime. But his customers weren't making it easy.

At the tail end of what felt like a relentless parade of entitlement and lunacy, things slowed down enough that he could close down his register after just three more customers.

The first was a woman who added items to the belt one by one, looking at the price of each item as she did and giving Orson detailed commentary on what she thought about the price. All of them she deemed very expensive, in a varied number of ways. The second to last customer tried to quick change him.

"Oh, wait," the man said, as though he were perfectly scattered. But Orson knew a performance when he saw one. "I didn't mean to give you that ten. I had a five. Can I just get my ten back and give you this five?"

"Sorry, sir. You just gave me a single."

"No, that's not possible. Just open the drawer, hand me the ten I accidentally gave you, then you can have the five."

Orson gave the man a look: *Come on, man, what do you want me to do?*

"Oh never mind. I have a twenty. Just give me two tens and a five for the twenty and we'll be even."

Orson did what he always did, thinking of Connor instead of tearing off his apron and quitting.

But the last customer in line nearly pushed him over the edge, threatening to call the police after Orson refused to allow him to return a bag of apples that clearly wasn't from Provisions.

How did things turn out like this?

Orson Beck was supposed to be somebody, but the world seemed determined to prove that he was a nobody.

Chapter Three

Orson walked the few miles home rather than pay for a FASTr.

Alexis, Connor, his career.

What the fuck was he doing?

Orson was living with leftovers. Stuck in the unfortunate shambles of what was not all that long ago a promising life.

By the time he ascended the steps to his building, Orson felt like a bucket of nothing and hoped he wouldn't run into any of his friends on the way to his sixth-floor apartment.

The Brick was a six-story behemoth and the street's tallest building when it was brand new in 1921. Now the shithole was a borderline crack den, cowering in the shadows of the newer buildings everywhere around it. Most were taller, and every one immeasurably better. The boiler was broken more often than not; the elevator was a rickety coffin that worked approximately twenty percent of the time; and a healthy share of dealers, drifters, and prostitutes of both sexes wandered the hallways.

The plaque on the front read *The Regency*, but everyone called it the Brick. Rent was cheap, and even better, the place was close to auditions and work.

Orson went inside and opened his mailbox while making small talk with Angus, the thousand-year-old man who claimed to have been living here in the Brick since 1942, when the place apparently wasn't a dump.

He looked at Orson and said, "You know that right now, at this very second, is the oldest I've ever been?"

Angus had a few dozen such questions and answers in constant rotation. His favorite was, *So, how are you this fine afternoon?*, but this one was in the old man's top five for sure.

"Me too," Orson said, stuffing a small stack of bills and bullshit into his backpack.

"Are you thirty yet?"

"Not yet."

"You will be."

"I'm definitely planning on it."

Orson wondered what random thing Angus might say. There would be something for sure.

"It's true. Looking eighty is great if you're a hundred." Angus winked.

Orson thought he looked twice that, at least. He had asked the old man his age many times. So far Angus had admitted to being over a century, seventy-four, eighty-nine, and ninety-three. Orson planned to change his bet in the pool.

Mostly, Angus just needed someone to talk to. So Orson always talked to him for as long as he could handle it, which was usually around five minutes. But every minute after that stretched to four or five times its natural length. Orson figured that he had made it deep into minute six by the time he excused himself.

"There's juice in the icebox if you're thirsty," Angus called out behind him.

As if Orson was his grandkid, coming home from school and wanting a snack.

He eyed the elevator, but he still hadn't burned off all his post-shift annoyance. *Stairs it is.*

Six flights later, he rounded the corner, smiling at the sight of his two closest friends. Sure, the Brick was a shit-hole, but when it came to neighbors, Orson had really lucked out.

"Come to join the party?" Ellis called.

"Been waiting all day." Orson dropped his backpack on the landing floor and nodded at Jess. His heart skipped a beat because that first one was always lost on her.

Living on the top floor gave them a needed reprieve from the summer heat in an old beat-to-hell building that seemed to sweat from its pores. But now that it was November they were hanging out on the landing just because.

"Worst customer?" Ellis prompted.

A born reporter. Ellis lived behind his keyboard and was addicted to questions.

Orson thought about it then told them about his last customer of the day.

"How do you know the apples weren't from Provisions?" Jess asked.

"Because they looked like they came from his backyard. Or someone's backyard. Or some crappy bodega. But they didn't come from Provisions. Our apples look like props. God couldn't even have blamed Eve for wanting to eat one of ours."

"And he threatened you with the cops." Ellis laughed. "I love it."

"How much longer do you think you'll stick it out there?" Jess asked.

Orson wondered the same thing at the beginning, middle, and end of every shift.

"I don't know. Half the time I'm working, I'm sure that I'm minutes from telling Lester to fuck off. But the rest of me is scared that I'll end up working there forever."

Ellis shook his head. "No way you're there at the end of this year."

"I'm with Ellis," Jess added. "You hate that place too much. You'll find something else that doesn't kill you inside, or at least kills you less. Just because you don't have a dream job doesn't mean it has to be a nightmare."

"It's not a nightmare," Orson said, now feeling guilty for all his complaining. "First-world problems, right? But I'm not ready to give up on the dream."

Ellis stood there with a half-smile. He didn't have to say a word for Orson to know what he was thinking.

"You think I should just quit Provisions now and get on with it."

Ellis shrugged. "You do you, man. But you gave the game a fair shake. It didn't pan out. Stop working yourself sick. No way you would be working at Provisions if you weren't waiting around for the real gig. Maybe look for something you love instead of waking up every day to do something you hate."

They'd had this conversation before. Ellis was one of the best humans Orson knew, but his perspective was skewed on a few things. First of all, the guy didn't have a reasonable outlook on work. He spent all day writing his blog and doing God knows what else online and seemed to make enough doing it to buy coffee and beer.

Second, Ellis hated Hollywood.

But he was the person that Orson had come to count

on the most, always willing to help in a pinch with Connor when Orson couldn't switch shifts. So Orson took his gentle discouragement as the sentiment of a friend watching out for him.

Orson looked to Jess, wanting to hear what she would say, even though he knew that too. Right now she looked like her skin had just shrunk and she desperately wanted out of it.

"He's not wrong," she said.

Then there was quiet among them. They would need a change of topic now that this one had stalled. Orson was too deep in his dream to release it, and there was baggage between Ellis and Jess around all of this stuff. They rarely opened it in front of him.

In Hollywood terms, their friendship was ancient. They'd known each other in high school, back when they both lived in Skokie, Illinois. Orson and Jess had never discussed it directly because it was apparently part of her past that she wanted to leave behind her forever, but she had been through the Hollywood ringer, not too long after first setting foot on Sunset. She'd been on a highly promoted show on a major network that lasted exactly half a season. During the lead-up to the fall release and through the first few episodes, the town was whispering that Jess Lindley might be the next big thing.

But then her party girl ways got the best of her and ripped the dream away.

Orson wished he'd paid better attention when the story was happening in real time, but he only vaguely remembered the tabloid attention. He'd been recovering from his own fall from grace.

He wondered what that would be like, to look the end of your dream in the eye. Jess would never get a second chance because in this town that was the only thing harder to get than a first chance.

Even though he didn't want to believe it, Orson knew he was nearing the edge of his own surrender. It grew harder by the day to maintain his faith. He wasn't a child, but he had one to raise. He owed Connor more than he had managed to give him so far.

Orson asked Jess what he had never dared before. "So, you wouldn't ever want to go back to acting, no matter what?"

Jess looked distant and uncomfortable, her eyes widening as her lips thinned. She finally said, "It was an adventure, and I'm glad I had it. But no, I would never want to go through that ever again."

"Sorry," he said, wanting to reach out and touch her but lacking the courage.

"Don't worry about it." Jess smiled. "I wonder sometimes what would have happened if I'd never left USC freshman year to work on the show. But that's all behind me now. I love my job and ..."

She didn't have to finish. They all knew the end of that sentence.

And I'm clean.

Ellis had told Orson that quitting coke had been the hardest thing Jess had ever done.

Orson respected that. But at the same time, he couldn't help thinking, *I wouldn't make that mistake.*

I wouldn't let success ruin me.

If someone would just give me a chance, I'll show everyone who Orson Beck really is.

"So are we gonna hang out here all night, or do you wanna go inside?" Ellis nodded toward his apartment, the door slightly ajar. "I've got some Green Unicorn."

Tempting. Ellis was a weed snob and refused to buy his

herb from any of the local dispensaries, no matter their ratings on Yelp. He bought everything off the dark web, farm-direct. The best that Orson had ever smoked, and Green Unicorn was his favorite among them. According to Ellis, the strain was several generations old and could be dated all the way back to Humboldt in the early '70s, when the marijuana revolution was just beginning.

Normally a bowl made the bullshit better. But right now, looking at Jess, knowing how much he wanted her and feeling how much she probably wanted him, Orson knew that would be a mistake.

There had been something floating between them for a while. There wasn't a girl in the world that he could imagine wanting more. But he had to wait because he wasn't willing to ruin anything else.

His bank account was empty. He owed Alexis child support, and he had little time between his classes, auditions, work schedule, and his scant hours with Connor. What could he possibly offer Jess?

He would fuck it up just like he fucked everything else, and Orson couldn't deal with another failed relationship or another screeching harpy constantly on his ass. So yes, he would love to sit on Ellis' couch and pass the peace pipe, but he didn't feel like sitting next to Jess for another several hours, staring at something else he couldn't have.

"I'd love to, but I'm beat to shit. Rain check?"

Ellis grinned, then held two closed fists in front of Orson. "Which hand?"

Orson pointed to his right with a smile. "That one."

Ellis opened his hand, and there on his palm was a beautiful nug of Green Unicorn. "Enjoy your bubble bath."

"You really are a prince among men," Orson said, accepting the gift.

Orson said his goodbyes, then headed out to his balcony. His apartment was shit, but the vista was worth the millions people paid to see the same thing from slightly farther away. He packed his pipe, flicked the lighter, inhaled, and held it, then did his best to forget.

His phone rang and Orson wanted to ignore it. But curiosity got the better of him and he checked the screen. Another missed call from his lawyer. No mystery there. The lawyer and Alexis had that in common — they both wanted him to take care of his child support.

Bowl smoked, Orson went back inside, wishing he felt better than he did, but knowing that this was par for the course until he found a way out.

Most of the sick in his stomach was coming from the unknown, so he might as well tackle it now. Maybe then he could manage to fall asleep.

Who am I kidding?

He pulled his pile of mail from the backpack and began to sort it on the kitchen counter. No surprises. Bills for acting classes that he needed to keep his dream alive, credit cards that covered the cost of his unfortunate choices, utilities and child support, lawyer fees, and *FUCK.*

It seemed to get worse every month.

The pile was hopeless.

Until he saw it.

Desire displayed all in black.

Gold lettering that promised a better life immediately.

A logo and the words *The Onyx List* in a regal font.

And at the very bottom, words that Orson had been longing to read for years.

You're invited …

Chapter Four

Orson reached for the envelope, but didn't dare to rip it open.

He had to be careful, seeing as his fingers had never been more excited.

Should he go and get Ellis or Jess to share the moment? No, something about this felt so deliciously private.

Dreams were usually better in his head, but even the envelope's weight felt more substantial in his hand than Orson could ever have imagined. The invitation wasn't just beautiful, it was mesmerizing. The insignia was embossed in gold. A pair of spotlights at the bottom illuminated the words *The Onyx List.*

Orson savored the moment, slipping his finger under the fold and gently easing it open.

This was a golden ticket for a Hollywood hopeful like him, and so much better than entrance to a chocolate factory. This was a fast pass to the front of the line. Getting on The Onyx List would put him on the industry radar again.

If Orson made it, there wasn't anything he wouldn't do to stay there.

The year that the List first appeared, Orson was too green to know anyone who'd made it, even with *F the '90s* out and getting all of that buzz. But it awoke a new and seemingly bottomless hunger in him.

Rumors around their annual event inspired envy in everyone. The industry's biggest watering hole of potential talent. The brightest stars in tomorrow's sky all gathered in one place, for one evening, so the buyers at billion dollar studios could see those stars strutting their magical stuff.

There were no facts available. Only whispers. But there were a few truths to which the general public agreed.

The full List started at 150 hopefuls, but then that full roll call was whittled down to two dozen of the most promising stars. The bold and the beautiful. The ridiculously talented. Invited to hobnob with the faces and personalities that could bankroll a film.

Previous recipients like Harrison Turner went from nowhere to everywhere overnight. Maybe not as big as Logan White, but he was still one of the biggest stars in the world. He had his choice of roles and was in the 20M+ club, having nabbed 21.2M for his role in the *Back to the Future* reboot. Even more important to Orson, Harrison had the accolades. Immediately after wrapping the reboot, Harrison took a role in the indie gem *Alone* and delivered a performance people were still talking about a year later, in a town where a month was an eon.

Now that he was one of the most famous men in the world, Harrison did have to deal with the usual rumors of his sexuality, but that's what happened when you were beautiful and much of the planet was jealous. Orson would be thrilled to put up with such hearsay himself, if it meant being given the chance to live among the one percent of the one percent.

Orson had fantasized about the sex plenty too, because there were plenty of rumors about all that went down behind the best closed doors with the bold and the beautiful, the ridiculously talented, the faces and personalities that could bankroll a film.

He withdrew his invite from the envelope and stared, afraid to miss a moment by blinking as his heart thumped with excess decibels. The front read:

Congratulations, Orson.
You are invited.

Please visit the following URL to submit your application
theonyxlist.com/orsonbeck

THE BACK WAS naked and perfectly black.

Normally Orson was grateful for the Green Unicorn. But right now the buzz was holding him back. There was a fog around the moment, the suspicion that despite the invitation quivering in his hand, this moment couldn't be real.

He went to his laptop and laughed a little as he lifted the lid because something inside him knew that this would be the time when it finally didn't start. The thing was six years old and acting twice its age. But the LCD lit the room's shadows. Orson exhaled. Hard not to take that as a sign that his luck had finally changed.

He typed in the address on the invitation. The page

that loaded greeted him with *The invite goes to … Orson Beck!* Below, there was a video, and holy shit, Logan White stared at him from the other side of the screen, smiling.

Orson pressed play. Logan's smile exploded into a laugh that was famous on every continent.

"Orson! I'm so glad I'm getting to make this video for you! I'm here to explain what you can expect."

One of the biggest stars in the world was talking directly to him. Orson had to seriously wonder what else might have been in that Green Unicorn. It would kill him if he woke up tomorrow and discovered that he'd hallucinated all this.

"One hundred and forty-nine actors have received invitations from the Onyx List, but this is your time to shine because out of those actors, only twenty-four will make it to the Fête, which will be held at an undisclosed location, at a date and time you will only know after you pass the application round."

Another thousand watt smile, followed by that twenty million dollar laugh.

"Because you will. There's no doubt in my mind, you're going to do *great.* I watched *F the '90s* when those episodes were dropping live, and I've seen them all several times since. You *were* that show. I remember thinking, *Wow, that kid's gonna be a star.* And you are, Orson. All you have to do is fill out the application then let Fate take over."

Logan drew a breath. He looked suddenly serious.

"Answer the questions honestly, Orson. That matters more than anything else. It's not like a normal test because there is nothing normal about the Onyx List."

Then the laugh was back. "Normal is over, Mr. Beck. Get ready for the life that you've always deserved. Click *yes* and let's get started."

Orson did.

Chapter Five

Orson had been staring at the first question for five minutes, at least. He had no idea how to answer.

It wasn't that the question was hard. It was … weird.

He didn't have a problem being honest — Orson promised himself that he'd give a hundred percent before he clicked on the *Yes!* but this question felt like a trick.

How long can you sit on a volleyball?

Orson couldn't remember ever having sat on a volleyball. Not even once. He'd been racking his brain, considering the various scenarios that could see him either conquering that ball for hours like some sort of Zen master sitting atop a mountain summit, or send it sailing out from under his ass immediately.

He could easily imagine either, but which one was right? And what were they looking for — someone with grace, or humility?

It shouldn't be this hard.

Orson finally swallowed and started to type.

Because I have never been asked to sit on a volleyball and have thus never had the opportunity, I could see this being something that surprises me by being much more difficult than I might imagine. But if I am guessing, I think I could sit on a volleyball for several hours, since I am the kind of person who tends to be very patient when I know my goal.

Orson exhaled. Had he really been holding his breath through that entire question?

He clicked *Next.*

If you could eat underwater, what would you serve at your next dinner party?

What the fuck? Logan had told him that this test wasn't normal (Orson still couldn't believe his last sentence was true), but this was just … *weird.*

I don't want to overthink this, but I have so many questions about a dinner party underwater. How would we sit? Would we be using utensils? What would we be wearing? Without understanding the specifics of our party environment, I would have to say that sticking to liquids would make the most sense. Then it would be like we were invisible.

Wait. That was stupid. Or worse, it didn't make sense. Orson read it over and had no idea what he even meant.

He pressed delete, but the words wouldn't go away. Even after trying five times. On the sixth, a counter appeared at the bottom of the screen.

60 … 59 … 58 …

No. This couldn't be happening. He'd answered that last question like an idiot. Why wouldn't they let him change it?

With no other choice, he clicked *Next.*

If you could buy the ability to paint a masterpiece, how much would you pay?

The counter was still on the screen. *60 … 59 … 58 …* Shit.

If buying the ability means paying to learn from experience, then I would pay slightly more than I could afford, for slightly longer than

I could afford to. But if it was just "buying" the ability like magic, then I would not be interested.

After a moment's thought, he added, *Because then the ability to paint wouldn't* really *be mine.*

The counter showed up on the next screen too, but now he was feeling it. He blazed through the application. He couldn't delete, and the counter ticked down every second he spent without typing. So he let himself type without thinking.

OL: *For the rest of your life, would you rather produce body odor but be sweat-free? Or free of odor while producing sweat?*

OB: *I would rather be free of odor because then the problem is mine rather than the people around me.*

OL: *Does bread dough rise in gravity?*

OB: *I have no idea, but being the curious person I am, I will be Googling for that answer after this.*

OL: *Describe a time that you challenged authority.*

OB: *While I do believe that authority should be questioned when necessary, this has never been easy for me. But when it comes to the pursuit of my dreams, everything changes. Like when I quit college to come out here to California. Everyone told me that was wrong. My parents were against it, and so was my older brother. They were all authority figures in my life. But what I really—*

The question timed out and a new one appeared.

OL: *What is your philosophy toward life?*

That wasn't fair, timing out on a simple question then asking for someone's personal philosophy toward life with the next? How was he supposed to cram an answer like that into sixty seconds? Or fifty-three.

Forty-nine.

Fuck!

Orson typed as fast as he could, not sure if he was making sense but determined to get down as much of an answer as he could before the clock ran out.

OB: *No one owes you anything, but if you do all the work and you do it long enough, then good things are going to happen to you. If they don't, then it's probably your fault and there's something you could have done to fix it. You can always think of a better way to see things. Money is good but attention is better. All problems can be solved, but conflict should only come as a last resort. Rules and emotions are both good but neither should define you. There's no such thing as a—*

OL: *What do you like about yourself?*

OB: *I'm always willing to work hard. Even if I'm not the most talented, I'll get there if given the chance. I listen to people who know better than me. I'm a good student, but I need to be around teachers who care.*

OL: *What do you dream about most often?*

OB: *Red carpet. Black tie. The Oscars. Everything that comes before and after. The life. One percent of the one percent, on and off screen.*

OL: *What sacrifices have you made to achieve it?*

Orson couldn't stand to see the numbers count down but felt the question's importance like cement underfoot.

OB: *I totally pissed my parents off when I left college like five minutes after I got there. I didn't graduate high school as valedictorian or anything, but I was top ten percent and my teachers liked me. But I couldn't stay in college when the dream was all the way out here. I gave up everything to get it. And I give it up every day. My son Connor, he's the most important thing in the world to me and—*

OL: *What does suffering mean to you?*

OB: *Not being with Connor. Thinking that I'm letting him down. Knowing that I'm not living up to my potential and that my parents and brother are disappointed in me. Feeling like a failure. Looking my ex-wife in the eyes and knowing what she's thinking about me. Being able to smell the success all around me, but never actually taste—*

OL: *What's your second biggest regret?*

Second biggest? The question caught him off guard.

Why weren't they asking for the first?

Was this a trick question?

53 ... 52 ... 51 ...

OB: *I don't know how to answer this. I have a lot of regrets, but I couldn't really put them in order, and really actually none of them are even regrets because I don't know that I would have done anything different. Leaving college was hard but I don't regret it, and having my son was hard but I don't regret it, and still going to acting classes and trying to climb the ladder is hard but I—*

OL: *If the paparazzi were following you everywhere and you had to escape, where is the one place that you would go?*

Orson had no idea. He thought, but five seconds didn't help, and neither did six or seven. He would have to make something up.

OB: *If I were hiding out from the paparazzi then I would need a space where no one could find me so I would look for a space that I had never tweeted or put on social media or talked about before.*

22 ... 19 ... 18 ...

This stupid question shouldn't be hard.

8 ... 7 ... 6 ...

OB: *I would ask my friend Ellis—*

OL: *You wake up tomorrow and realize that God has taken away the most important thing in your life. What has disappeared?*

OB: *My son Connor.*

OL: *Would you have plastic surgery to land a role with Oscar-winning potential?*

OB: *Probably not. I cannot imagine a scenario where that would be truly necessary.*

OL: *What's the worst thing you've ever done and gotten away with?*

OB: *When I was fourteen I snuck into my neighbor's house while she was watching TV. She was deaf and my friends and I could all see her from the back door. I snuck in and kept making faces at her to make them laugh. I got snacks out of her fridge and started eating them right behind her. She—*

OL: *If your parents received a hidden-camera video that showed everything you have done in the last twenty-four hours, who would they think you are?*

That was a good one. Orson thought, ignored the seconds, then when there were only thirty left, after he'd thought about everything from beating off when he woke up to dealing with Alexis' bullshit at work and that bowl of Green Unicorn at the end of the day, he knew exactly what he'd say.

OB: *Human.*

OL: *Would you rather get drunk or stoned?*

OB: *Drunk.*

OL: *Why?*

OB: *Because I like drinking around people and smoking alone. I would rather be around people.*

OL: *You just discovered that the cute girl who came home with you from the party is married. She doesn't know you know. Do you sleep with her?*

OB: *No way.*

OL: *Why?*

OB: *Because I wouldn't want to be that guy.*

OL: *What did you do at your very first talent show?*

OB: *I was fourteen years old and I did the full rap to Country Grammar. It was flawless.*

OL: *Would you shoot a sex scene with the person you hate most in the world?*

OB: *Absolutely.*

The questions went on. Deeper. More personal. Raw.

But Orson didn't mind. He wanted to become a better artist, and that meant knowing his insides as well as he wanted the world to know his exterior. This was a chance to delve deeper into his psyche.

There was no progress bar, and after the second hour of answering he finally stopped caring, delighting in a runner's high of ridiculous questions. Nearly three hours later and the test was finally finished.

Congratulations, Orson. We can't wait to meet you at the Glass House for our annual Fête. Please arrive at 7:30 prompt.

Then there was an address.

Orson wanted to scream, but for the first time in years, it was with joy.

Chapter Six

Orson had been walking the Mill for a half hour or so before his phone started ringing.

He looked at the screen, saw Alexis' name, and wondered if he should ignore it. He'd promised her – and himself – that he wouldn't do that anymore. Answering the call was the right thing to do. Except that he was feeling good right now, closer to great than he probably had in years, and losing that feeling would suck.

He'd strolled the open air mall plenty of times, but this time everything felt different. His world had changed, and that changed the Mill. It was one of SoCal's most popular shopping destinations. Tons of mostly high-end retail, posh restaurants, and trendy entertainment.

Like working at Provisions, being in a place like this usually reminded Orson of all the things he didn't have and couldn't get. But not today. He'd come here specifically to soak up the possibilities of the better, brighter tomorrow that was surely on its way.

He could cheer himself up after the call by reminding himself that all this would be within reach soon.

"Hey, Alexis," he said just before it went to voicemail. He stopped in front of his final destination — the main reason he'd been willing to come all the way out to the Mill.

"Wow. You answered. I was expecting to leave another voicemail."

"I promised that I would pick up when you called. Did you not believe me?"

"You promise a lot of things."

She was already pissing him off. "Actually, Alexis, I don't. If I use the word *promise*, then—"

"It took you four rings. You only answered because you were feeling guilty."

"I'm at the Mill. I needed to find somewhere more private to take the call."

She scoffed on the other end of the line. "Somewhere private at the Mill? Good luck. And why in the hell are you there? Is there a pop-up giving out free samples or something?"

Fuck you, Alexis.

But in a voice that was much kinder than he felt, Orson said, "What do you want?"

"To be nice. I have a surprise for you."

"Oh?" Orson felt disarmed. "What is it?"

"I thought you might like to spend an afternoon with Connor. Without having to wait until the weekend."

"That would be great." He grinned. "Thank you! When?"

"Right now."

But then it crumbled. "I can't right now. Like I said, I'm at the Mill."

"So leave."

"It took me an hour to get here, and I have errands."

Alexis laughed. "Errands? Like what, getting in your steps? You can't do that in the ghetto?"

"Fuck you, Alexis."

Orson chewed on his bottom lip. He shouldn't have said that, really wished he hadn't.

He had to keep things in check. Making the List meant that he'd be in the public eye soon. He needed to learn how to play it cool, even when Alexis was challenging him, because there was no way she'd ever stop.

If I don't make the cut, it'll be Alexis' fault for making me look bad.

"Way to talk to the mother of your child," she said.

A deep breath, then calmly Orson said, "You're right. Let's make a deal. I'll be nice to you if you don't bait me."

"I'm not baiting you."

"But you are, Alexis. You're acting like you're doing me a favor by giving me time with Connor, but you're really just looking for someone to help you with a little last-minute child care, probably so that you can do something with Tyler. That's not a—"

"It *is* a favor. You're always asking for more time."

"And I'd love more time. More weekends, more weekdays, whatever. But I can't just drop everything to be at your beck and call."

"You're not working today. So if Connor is important to you, then I can't think of a single reason why you couldn't come spend the rest of the day with him. I'll be home before midnight."

"Midnight?" Again, Orson was too loud. More softly, he said, "Sorry, Alexis. I can't do it. I'm busy."

Now she was laughing. "Grab a FASTr and I'll pay. Then you don't have to be around all those things you can't have."

Alexis could have stopped there, that was mean enough. But stopping wasn't her style.

"If you leave now, then you won't have to think about all of the ways you've failed as a husband and father, an artist, and as a person in general."

"Fuck you, Alexis!"

Too many people were looking. He had to stop.

Alexis stopped laughing. His rage was thick enough to stir.

"I'm sorry. But you don't have to—"

(be such a total fucking bitch all the time)

"—say things like that."

"And you don't have to abandon your son."

"I would never abandon Connor. I have an interview."

"For a job?" She sounded suspicious. Maybe intrigued.

"For something."

"For something like what?"

Orson wasn't sure why he didn't want to tell her. He hadn't told anyone yet. He was terrified that something would happen to make it disappear.

Worse, he kept picturing the look on Jess' face when he inevitably did. He couldn't even imagine how hard that would be for her. But if he hadn't told either her or Ellis yet, then he definitely couldn't tell Alexis.

She was petty enough to mess this up for him. With Tyler's connections, maybe she could. Besides, Orson was looking forward to rubbing her perfect little nose in it, after he exploded onto the gossip blogs as an overnight success.

"It's nothing for sure. An opportunity."

"Wow. That's so super specific, Orson. I can see why the best stuff just keeps falling right into your lap. Is this a *job* job, like a real one where you can actually afford to pay me what you owe, and do better than mac and cheese when it's your turn to feed our child? Or is it an audition because you won't grow up and accept the truth that *it's never going to happen for you.*"

"It *did* happen for me."

"Right. Then you blew it."

Orson imagined himself walking the red carpet. He saw Jess on his arm. The images dumped a bucket of ice into his boiling rage. Clinging to the thin veneer of calm, and very aware of the clusters of people still watching in the aftermath of his mini-outburst, he said, "I didn't blow it. Everywair dropped the funding, and the show got canceled."

And everyone went on to do something big except you.

Then on cue she said, "And the entire cast and crew all made it anyway!"

Close enough.

Fuck you, Alexis. So a few people from F the '90s made it big. That's not the "entire cast and crew."

"I have an opportunity that I can't say no to, and I need you to support me."

"You only get to see Connor every other week. This is an opportunity. What, should Tyler have to be the father here?"

Ice wasn't going to be enough. "Don't start with me, Alexis."

"You started it. I was just asking for a favor."

"You're pushing my buttons on purpose."

"By offering you some of the time with your son that you are always begging for?"

"By bringing up Tyler. Fuck that guy. He doesn't have an artistic bone in his body."

"Just artistic enough to pull in forty-eight thousand dollars an episode."

"If he's making fifty grand a week, then why in the hell do you need my paltry bullshit child support?"

"I've told you a million times, it's not Tyler's responsibility to pay for our child."

"You don't need anything. Your father is rich, Tyler is rich, and *YOU'RE RICH!*"

"It's the principle of the thing, Orson. Hopefully one day you'll grow up enough to realize that."

She hung up.

He looked around. The crowd dispersed, including a teenage kid who had captured the exchange on his phone. He dropped it into his pocket, held up a fist and yelled, "*F the '90s!*" then hopped on his skateboard and skated away.

Orson's phone rang again.

Great. Alexis either wanted to yell at him more or apologize. He didn't have the patience for either. He'd come to the Mill on a legitimate errand, and he hadn't even started.

"Can we please not do this?" Orson answered.

But his speaker filled with a laugh. Full-bodied and warm. Familiar, not just to him but to the entire world.

No. It can't be.

"Let me guess," said the voice. "Girl trouble."

"Who is this?" Orson asked, just to be sure.

"It's Logan." After a beat of silence he added, "White."

Orson couldn't get his tongue to work, so Logan filled in the silence.

"Hey, I know you're busy. I just wanted to reach out and see if you needed anything. This weekend is about to change your life, and I'm just so excited for you. I remember how it felt," Logan laughed, like it had been some crazy shit. "Anyway, it's all been a bit impersonal so far, especially for something that's ultimately so intimate. Is there anything I can help you with?"

Orson pressed the phone harder against his ear. He looked around at all the people. None of them could have any idea that he was talking to one of the world's biggest movie stars.

And this man was asking *Orson* what he could do for *him.*

"Can you tell me what to expect? What is the Glass House? I looked up that address online and it looks like a parking lot."

Another million dollar laugh. "It is a parking lot. The location's a secret, which is why you'll be meeting in the parking lot. You'll be shuttled up to the House along with the other guests."

"What will it be like?"

There was a pause, then, "You'll see." It was so easy to see Logan smiling in his mind. "Just make sure to dress the part."

"What's the dress code?"

"Red carpet black."

Should he ask? He didn't want Logan to think he was an idiot. But he also didn't want to blow his entire future because he'd been afraid to ask.

"Do you mean—"

"Red carpet casual. Black tie attire, but don't overdo it. Use your instincts. They're already great, or you wouldn't have been invited."

Orson thanked the megastar, already feeling guilty for keeping him on the phone for the minutes he did, then looked up at the Crossroads storefront, the reason he'd come to the Mill. Red carpet black. He'd expected that, and he didn't own a single thread that was worthy of such distinction. But dressing the part meant getting the part, right?

He went inside to make his dream come true.

Chapter Seven

Orson had only dared to enter Crossroads three times before.

The first was at the tail end of *F the '90s*. He'd been enamored while with some friends for a night on the town. He'd wandered in, spent forty-five minutes trying on this and that and feeling like the rock star actor he'd always longed to be, then left without a single bag. No need. He could always come back.

The second time he went in with Davis Franks, after the show was already over. And despite what Orson had said to Alexis, it definitely felt like a loss. Davis was doing fine. He had a handful of offers before *F the '90s* was even over but had decided to work on his directorial debut instead. That night Orson hadn't tried a single thing on.

The last time, he was feeling sorry for himself. In and out in less than a minute because the idea that he would never be able to shop here made even trying on a shirt too depressing.

This time was special. It would never be like this again.

Because the next time Orson came in here, he would

be rich. The clerks would all know his name, and they'd probably scurry to help him. Or if not the next time, then maybe the time after that.

Today was going to hurt, but after that the pain would finally stop.

He had to buy something to help make his ultimate dream come true, so he might as well buy it from one of his smaller dreams.

He took a deep breath and went in.

Something, okay *everything* about the clothing in Crossroads spoke to him. He loved their tagline, *Moral Fiber*, as much as he loved the fibers themselves. And the colors. All earth tones but in shades that God might have chosen specifically for Orson. The place was very LA. There wasn't a sweatshop within miles of its stitches, and they used only top-of-the-line, eco-friendly fabrics, natural dyes, and softening techniques. Their blazers felt like lingerie, their denim almost like lace. But unlike so much of the bullshit at Provisions, this was a price difference that Orson could *feel*.

If there were such a thing as red carpet black, Orson would find it at Crossroads.

He ran his hand over a linen jacket. Not right for the Fête, but it was more toward the back, and doubt was starting to creep in, cracking the edges of his confidence.

Orson did the mental math again. He couldn't use his debit card; even a small purchase wouldn't go through. All of his credit cards were maxed except one. It had a thousand dollars left, give or take, but there were a few outstanding charges that might not have been included when he called to check the balance. Now that he was really thinking about it, Orson wasn't sure whether his recurring payments (there were a few, from Netflix to

FukIt, he was embarrassed to admit) would start dropping, and they had all been moved to that card.

What if he got the math wrong and the cashier had to hand him his card back with a frown?

It had happened before. A few times.

He shook his head and forced himself to smile. Act the part. Make his way toward the back of the store.

This was his time.

He was made for this.

The only thing that could stop Orson was Orson himself.

The clothes were incredible. He wanted to touch them all.

"Can I help you with anything?"

Orson turned from the pile of neatly folded sweaters to see a beautiful woman in her twenties, who either wanted to assist him with getting something to wear for the biggest event of his life, or was late for the runway.

He gave her his widest smile because someday soon, she was going to exclaim to one of her friends, "I helped Orson Beck buy that jacket he wore to the Onyx List party!"

"I need a jacket. Probably a shirt. Maybe some pants."

She laughed, a little like music. "Special occasion?"

He leaned forward, conspiratorial. "Do you know about the Onyx List?"

"Of course." Then, as both expected and hoped for, she ran her eyes up and down Orson's body.

He smiled because he didn't have to say it.

"Well then," she said, "let's get you all set up."

Orson enjoyed his *Pretty Woman* moment, trying on one outfit after another until he had the perfect ensemble.

He managed to talk his way out of a belt – they were all

too expensive, so he dug his heels in with the excuse that belts reminded him of his father. It was a bit of a battle. Orson argued for a French tuck, and Chelsee (*double E*, the salesgirl told him twice) insisted that while under most circumstances he could pull that off, this was LA and not New York, after all.

"*These* do not need a belt." Orson held up the perfect pair of pants. "If these fit, with this shirt," he showed her the shirt in his other hand, "then I don't need a belt."

Orson wasn't sure if Chelsee agreed because he was right or because she wanted to fuck him. Her vibe was suggestive of both. She helped him find a jet-black blazer that matched his pants perfectly. No tie or belt. And his bright white dress shirt had crimson gossamer threads running throughout it, visible only up close.

Time to do some more math, and there were a lot of unknown variables. He wasn't exactly clear on the cost of his chosen clothing. The jacket and pants were both seventy-five percent off, but the shirt was full-priced and unmarked. In a place like this it could have been 150 dollars, or four times that much. If it was over 200 dollars, or if too many pending charges affected his balance, Orson might get declined. Then he might not ever make it back into Crossroads for a fifth time, even if he had all the money in the world. The humiliation would be too much.

He lined up behind the man already at the counter, who was pulling out his wallet to pay for several small piles of clothes. Shirts and sweaters, denim and dress pants, a trio of belts. The guy was about to spend more than Orson would make in a year at Provisions. And the asshole looked bored.

It made Orson loathe him. He'd clearly lost appreciation for how lucky he was, how privileged his life had become, or maybe always was. He was spending tens of thousands of dollars on clothes, and the man couldn't even enjoy it.

But was he any better? Orson was spending a personal fortune, and rather than focusing on the magic that had entered his life, he was fretting instead, fixated on what he shouldn't be doing, letting guilt shove him under before lighting the surface on fire.

Because now he was thinking about Alexis and what he legitimately owed her.

He could hear her yelling at him and knew that he deserved every word.

He shouldn't be blowing his money on this.

This weekend is going to change your life, and I'm just so excited for you.

Orson waited for Chelsee to ring him up, trying not to sweat through his four-year-old shirt.

"You're going to look *amazing*," Chelsee assured him as she started scanning tags.

"Thanks." Orson swallowed. He'd never had to piss more in his life, even though he hadn't felt a drop in his bladder only moments before.

He wished she would hurry. While Orson appreciated the attention to detail, putting care into the folding and packaging of his purchase, every second of waiting for that total was agony.

Then there it was. She turned the tablet toward Orson and showed him the total: *$1,294.86.*

"Great!" Orson told himself he wasn't dying inside and handed over his credit card with a smile.

Chelsee smiled back, took his card, swiped it through the tablet attachment, and waited with him through the longest seconds of his life.

It felt like the Earth stopped turning, opening a window through which Orson could see every one of his life's many failures, cascading into something that looked like a stain, something he couldn't scrub out of his daily existence, and that was growing larger even now.

Because there was zero chance that the transaction would go through.

But then Chelsee said, "Would you like a printed receipt? Or would you like me to email it to you?"

Orson didn't want to say it, and the words tore at his throat as they left him, but he opened his mouth anyway. "Can any of this be returned? You know, if I decide to wear something else?"

Chelsee gave him a delightful little frown. "I'm sorry. The pants and the jacket are non-refundable." Then she brightened. "But you can return the shirt if you don't want it."

"Oh, I want it," Orson said, holding his grin.

But if he screwed up the Fête, he'd have no choice but to suffer the humiliation of bringing it back.

Because this wasn't just his second chance, it was also his last chance.

Chapter Eight

Will you hurry the fuck up oh my fucking fuck you have got to be kidding me I swear you are going to die before you finish counting all of those fucking pennies.

Orson smiled at the old woman and looked at his watch again.

Pennies should be outlawed. Most Provisions customers barely knew what they were, But this old bag had a bucket of the fuckers.

He tapped his foot, just like the people behind her would have, if she hadn't been his last customer.

She finally finished counting and looked up, both delighted with herself and somehow pleased with him.

"I'm lucky," she said, giving him a wide smile that looked odd on her shriveled face. "To have a man as handsome as you ringing me up for my groceries."

Then she gave him a nervous laugh and covered her mouth. "When you get to be my age, you're allowed to say things like that."

Orson smiled at the old woman, and this time he meant it.

He wasn't usually *this* impatient. But when you were only hours away from everything changing, even seconds felt like days. And in those terms, this old woman was costing him years.

"Thank you for saying that, it's very kind."

Orson reached out and touched her hand, making her blush harder under her heavy makeup. Then he gently finished bagging her groceries, because every bagboy in this place was a lazy hipster sack of shit, told her to have a wonderful day, and tore off his apron and got the hell out of Dodge.

He checked his FASTr app, saw that the wait for a car was fifteen minutes, cursed himself that he'd had to cancel the last one due to the old lady, then *ran* at top speed, stopping only to clutch his stomach and curse himself every other block or so. He made it all the way to the Brick, soaking through his pants and shirt as he climbed the front steps panting.

No time for mail or for Angus to ask him how he was this fine afternoon, Orson waved at the old man as he passed him, racing up all six flights as fast as he could.

Inside the house, he closed the door behind him, then went and laid out his clothes on the couch. He took a moment to admire them because this all still felt so impossible.

He cursed the broken boiler as he hurried to wash himself in tepid water dribbling from the shower head. He dried off, making eyes at himself in the mirror.

He looked good. Great even. The big white teeth that family and friends had been commenting on and complimenting him about for his entire life looked almost professionally lit. His body was toned. He watched what he ate, and though he didn't work out all the time like he did back in the *F the '90s* days, he walked for several miles each day and lifted light weights every night. He hadn't had a haircut recently, but that seemed to work for his benefit. Orson was already shaved, clipped, and everything else. He'd taken care of that before work. And now, freshly scrubbed, he was ready for his new life.

He wrapped the towel around his waist, and he was glad he had when he stepped into the living room and saw Jess sitting on his couch.

"Hey …" Orson had no idea what to say.

"Hey," she laughed. "I agreed to dinner. I didn't know I was getting dessert."

"You agreed to dinner?"

"It's an expression. I agreed to give you a ride. I didn't know I would be getting this." She eyed him up and down, still laughing. "But don't worry. I like it."

"How did you get in?"

"I knocked a bunch of times, but I guess you didn't hear me. The door was unlocked, so …"

"So you thought you'd scare the shit out of me."

"Something like that." She smiled, still eyeing him.

It was embarrassing enough, needing a ride. Not being able to afford a car was bad, but knowing that he didn't even have enough to use the FASTr app was humiliating. But somehow, getting caught almost-naked by Jess was worse than both put together.

He tightened his grip on the towel.

"I'm glad you told me," she said.

"It was you or Ellis, and I figured you would have much better odds of at least seeing where I was coming from."

"I've been thinking you were going to have your big break soon."

But she looked like she was thinking about what he'd look like with the towel off.

Orson walked over to his clothes. She whistled as he did his best to gather them in one hand, still holding his towel with the other. Dressing in the living room was clearly out of the question now.

"Fancy. I can't wait to see you all dressed up." Then she added, "Though you look great as is."

Orson hesitated. Would it be unfair of him to ask?

He decided to risk it.

"I know that you don't have any desire to be around all of this, anymore. And I get it. That's the big reason I was shy about telling you. But I wanted you to know, and I was also wondering if you have any advice for me. You're experienced here, I'm not. And you're one of my best friends. So … any words of wisdom?"

Her lips tightened. She was obviously trying hard. "It's a dangerous world. I don't know what to say."

"Do you ever miss it?"

"Never." She shook her head. "All the time."

Orson stared.

Jess stared back.

Then she said, "It was the best time of my life, and it led right into the worst. I didn't like who I had become, or what others wanted or needed or expected me to be."

"But knowing all of that, wouldn't you do it differently … if you were given a second chance?"

"Of course."

"So … can you help me? It can kind of be like your second chance."

Jess laughed. "Except that you get all the attention and money?"

He laughed back. "I'll share."

"What do you actually want to know, Orson?"

"Do's and don'ts. What should I look out for?"

"All of it." She sighed. "The entire industry is predatory. Ask Ellis, if you want your ears to start bleeding. Some people are better than others."

"Like?"

She shrugged. "I haven't heard the best stuff about the Shellys."

"I have. They're a hit factory."

"Because they're ruthless."

"Because they have to be."

"Aren't you the one who just asked me?" Now she looked irritated, and it was all his fault.

"I'm sorry. You're right. This is just bigger than big for me."

She smiled sadly at him; her nod was as knowing as her eyes. "You're imagining what everyone back home is going to be saying after they hear the news. Your family and your friends, but especially your parents and your brother. Right?"

"Right."

"I've been there. Not *exactly*. But close enough. You're going to do great, Orson." She smiled again, but different this time. She reached up and playfully tugged at his towel.

He retreated, one step then three. All of a sudden he was back at the bathroom door, turned so that Jess couldn't see the fatty that wasn't about to go away.

Orson was beyond tense, and here was Jess obviously wanting to get closer, practically begging to help him out.

"Sorry," he said, then slipped into the bathroom and closed the door behind him.

This wasn't her fault, it was his.

It wasn't that Orson didn't like her, it was that he liked her too much. He might even love her. He had sure thought about it enough times, lying awake at night, knowing that she was right next door, dreaming of a time when he had more to offer., He'd wanted to march right over and present her with everything she deserved.

But he wasn't good enough yet.

He wasn't financially stable.

It wasn't—

And goddammit!

Why did this have to happen now, when he couldn't afford to let it? Why couldn't she have tugged on his towel *tomorrow*, after everything was different?

It was fine. This was exactly what he needed to get his shit together and keep it that way. Jess wasn't the kind of girl he ever wanted to lose once he had her, because she was the kind of girl he could be with forever. The kind of girl who would be a great mother to the son he already had and to the children they might make together.

Orson stopped buttoning his shirt two from the top, then donned his blazer.

He looked in the mirror. Studied himself. He smiled then frowned. He looked serious then aloof, humble then arrogant, victorious then defeated. He tried on most of his best faces, settled on the one that felt most like himself before going back into the living room.

Jess sat on the couch, her eyes still hungry. She eyed him up and down again, looking even more wanting.

"You look ready for the red carpet."

He'd never been more ready.

Chapter Nine

Jess had thought tonight would finally be the night.

She'd wanted to send him off to the Fete the right way, remind him that she'd be waiting for him when he got home.

Because she couldn't stand the idea that he was going to forget her as soon as he had a chance to party with a new crop of starlets.

It killed her that Orson might think she was only interested because he'd made the List. She had *always* been interested. And so had he, which is what made his constant refusal so completely infuriating.

He didn't answer when she'd knocked, but Jess hadn't minded. She wanted to catch him off guard. And they all had each other's keys – she, Orson, and Ellis – in case of emergency.

So she let herself in and waited.

She was wet and ready and wanting.

But Orson had refused her like always.

Now the quiet in the car lay like a corpse in between them.

Orson looked like he wanted to talk but didn't know what to say. She knew exactly how he felt.

She wanted to break the silence with something bright and cheerful. She wanted to wish him all the luck in the world. And she wanted to mean it.

But Orson had her squirming with frustration. Everything she wanted to say would sound desperate, or needy, or downright slutty.

"So what are you doing tonight?" Awkward, but at least he was talking.

Without even meaning to, Jess told a lie. "I have a date."

"A date?" Was he actually hurt? After he'd just said no to her?

She shrugged, trying to take it kinda, sorta back. "A guy I work with. No big deal."

Orson crossed, then uncrossed his arms. Same for his ankles. He shifted in his seat. Fidgeted with the window buttons, but they were locked from her side.

"You going to surprise him while he's coming out of the shower, too?"

He definitely sounded hurt.

Her phone buzzed and she let it. Jess never texted or even talked on her phone while driving, one of her unbreakable rules. Phones were the new drunk driving, and she wasn't about to take a shot.

But even though she wouldn't feel good admitting it, Jess was grateful for the buzz. If it made Orson jealous, maybe he wouldn't reject her the next time she embarrassed herself trying to touch him.

Like tonight, when he gets home.

Because she wouldn't be able to sleep while he was gone anyway.

He'd been as hard as she was wet, before he retreated

into the bathroom like a little baby. He was an idiot if he thought she couldn't see it. So what in the hell was he waiting for? She'd promised herself that tonight was the night, even set a stupid reminder for herself.

She thought about the first — and only — time he'd kissed her. It didn't even count. Because nothing happened. It couldn't have because Orson was too much of a gentleman. Back then she had loved it, felt respected rather than rejected. But tonight, she wished he respected her a little less.

They'd been at his place, drinking way too much. Orson kept pouring the wine, refilling her glass before she emptied it, while they talked for hours. Jess had no idea how drunk she actually was until she finally stood and tried to wobble her way next door.

They'd had a delicious, unforgettable, sloppy kiss in the doorway. Remembering it now, Jess had to squeeze her legs together. She pulled Orson next door, dragged him really, desperate to get him into her bed.

But she'd locked herself out, and Orson had lost track of his copy of her key. So she took him around the corner and showed him where she stowed her spare.

Then she dragged him back to her door, gave him another sloppy kiss, and dropped to her knees, ready to give him a blow job right there in the hallway. The Brick wouldn't mind, and Jess would only be horrified in the morning.

Not that it mattered. Orson refused her. The only man to ever reject her open mouth. He said that he couldn't take advantage of a girl who wasn't exactly acting like herself. When Jess insisted with slurred words that this *was* herself, he reminded her that she had just taught him to break and enter his way into her apartment.

The words still hurt. Same for his refusal. Orson

seemed to love the Midwestern girl that she was, but Jess was terrified that he would hate the rest of her, as soon as he learned who the rest of her was. Their first almost-encounter came close enough to proving it, the second now felt like their last.

Her phone buzzed again.

At the next red light, she reached into the backseat to grab and silence her phone, then dropped it back into her purse.

"Your hot date?" This time he tried to make it sound like a joke.

"Probably."

"Want me to—"

"No."

More silence as Jess pulled into the parking lot at the given address. It was empty except for the pair of black Mercedes shuttles. At least there weren't a lot of lookie-loos.

She would have the chance to make this right.

She parked and turned to Orson. "I'm sorry I came into your place without knocking. I wasn't trying to invade your privacy."

"It's okay. I understand."

"It's just that—"

Jess jumped at the loud knock on the window behind her. Orson seemed startled as well.

She turned around. There was a man dressed like a butler, motioning for her to roll down the window.

She did. "Yes?"

The man looked past Jess and spoke directly to Orson. "Good evening, Mr. Beck. Everyone is waiting. The shuttles will be leaving in less than a minute. Please board the one on your left."

The butler didn't leave, or even withdraw his head an inch. He waited, staring at them like a stone gargoyle.

"Well then, I guess this is it." She looked at Orson, hoping that he'd disagree.

"Guess so," he said, looking like he wanted to bolt. "We'll catch up tomorrow. I'm sure we'll have lots to talk about."

"I can't wait," Jess said with a brittle smile.

Then she grabbed her phone and looked to see what the buzz had all been about.

She saw her reminder: *Tonight is the night.*

She threw it onto the passenger seat and peeled out of the parking lot.

Chapter Ten

I can't wait.

Orson didn't know what to do. Jeeves was knocking on the window and cockblocking him, even more than Orson had already cockblocked himself. Jess was mad at him; he could tell even though she'd smiled and wished him luck. He felt like such an asshole, making her mad when she was helping him reach his dream.

But his bus was leaving in less than a minute. He followed Jeeves to the Mercedes on his left.

The look on her face as he'd gotten out of the car ... Hurt, disbelieving, and maybe even a hint of jealousy.

Orson was surprised by his own ugly emotion, the one that followed his aching. A twinge of satisfaction at her wounded, wondering expression that made him feel more alive.

I am an asshole.

"After you, Mr. Beck."

Jeeves gestured toward the Mercedes' open door and stepped out of the way.

Orson heard the squeal of tires as his foot hit the bottom stair. *Total asshole.*

He climbed into the shuttle and tried not to stare at the beautiful people inside. There were eleven passengers besides him. He only recognized three.

The first guy's name was Foster Lock, and Orson had seen him around at a thousand different auditions. At least it felt that way. Foster looked like a born movie star, an action hero for sure. He was six foot three or something, a beast next to Orson's five-foot-eleven. He tried not to hate Foster and his granite jaw, but in his mind, he called Foster 'Hulk' even though he knew 'Hunk' was more fitting. The guy had always been friendly to Orson, despite their competition for roles.

Orson didn't know the second guy's name, or at least he couldn't think of it off the top of his head, but he'd seen him around and heard a few stories. The guy was Irish and drank enough to prove it. But he was young and wild and had all the makings of a shooting star. Orson wasn't surprised to see him at all.

The last guy was almost a friend, Kevin Walker.

He smiled at Orson and gestured to the seat beside him.

Orson sat next to Kevin, and before they'd finished shaking hands, the shuttle was moving.

"Can you believe this shit?" Kevin asked.

"Not even a little."

"Do you know why you're here?"

He didn't sound surprised that Orson was there at all, just curious. Like he still hadn't figured out how he'd ended up with diamonds on the soles of his shoes and hoped Orson had been filled in.

"No idea," Orson admitted. "How about you?"

"I don't know, man. I've been wondering about it ever

since I saw the invite. I've been hustling, doing some decent enough work, I thought I killed it in my audition playing this college DJ for a remake of this show called *WKRP* or something, but the pilot never got ordered."

"I figured it was probably for your music."

"Might be. I do have a song on Hrdit that's doing well, "Game Face"."

"Good shit. I bought it when you posted it on LiveLyfe."

Orson had meant the compliment, but Kevin didn't reply, distracted by a gorgeous woman in diamante giving him a sultry wave. She looked like a young Charlize Theron. The man sitting next to her could've been a fresher-faced Hugh Jackman.

Kevin must be more connected than Orson would've guessed. "You know a lot of these guys?"

"Not like I know you, but yeah, I know a few." He lowered his voice, not that anyone else was paying attention. There were six such conversations happening throughout the shuttle.

"That girl up there ..." Kevin nodded at the Charlize. "Yeah?"

"She almost got the Courtney Love role in Cobain."

"I thought that was always Margot Robbie?"

"Margot fought and won it, but from what I heard, Cassie -- that's her name up there, Cassie Lark -- she *was* Courtney Love." Kevin grimaced. "I'm such a lightweight compared to so many of these people."

"Dude, I just finished a shift at Provisions a few hours ago, and that's the most impressive thing on my resume."

Kevin laughed. "You underestimate *F the '90s.*"

"No one even saw that."

"Bullshit. It's already a legend and you know it. Don't pretend like you're not checking the views each week, seeing how many more people have watched it. That shit was classic, and you were one of the best things about it."

"You mean the one who didn't do anything with it."

"*Yet,*" Kevin said. "Of course I care if I get it, but I gotta say that I don't care if I get it, you dig? I just want to think of this as one of the best nights of my life, no matter what happens."

False modesty? Or was Kevin really that cool?

"For sure," Orson agreed, even though he *did* care if he got it. Very much. Whatever it was. "What do you think is going to happen?"

"I've heard a bunch of shit, just like you have. Who knows how much of it's true? None of it or maybe all of it, hell if I know."

"I heard that Logan White made the first list a few years ago, and that he landed his role in the *Something About Mary* remake like two days later."

"I heard that Harrison Turner made the list and had an actual bidding war on his next two pictures the week after."

"Yeah," Orson nodded. "I heard that too. Hey, did Logan White record a welcome video for you? Or give you a call?"

Kevin shook his head, awe in his eyes. "Nah. I got Denzel."

"Unbelievable."

"You said it."

They said plenty more after that, giddy and nervous, like freshman cheerleaders on their way to their first tryouts. They talked about the success stories, but they'd heard some of the nastier buzz, about losers who made the list and got nothing. Occasionally one of those losers would complain, but they always recanted.

Orson decided he would ignore the look in Jess' eyes

when she'd told him to be careful, and imagine the look when he came home holding the prize.

The shuttles had made it to the hills. Orson's was second in the procession, weaving up the winding road as the sun dropped behind the horizon. They all seemed to sit closer, even though their eyes were further away. They were close and everyone onboard could feel it.

"So this is it," Kevin said in almost a whisper.

"Looks that way."

The shuttle was a vacuum of sound with everyone's eyes out the window. Orson looked at Kevin. It was the first time he'd ever seen his smile go missing.

How could he smile in a moment like this, with both the Glass House and all of its promises lying ahead minutes away?

He studied the other passengers, aware that they were studying him too, because now things had changed. Shit was most certainly real. Legends would be made tonight, and if Orson played his cards right, his name would be among them.

Orson Beck couldn't do a single thing to change his past, but as he stared up at the Glass House, looming before him like an idol overlooking a helpless pueblo below, he knew that his future was all up to him.

Chapter Eleven

Orson was completely unprepared him for the opulence of
the Glass House.

He'd expected a mansion with many windows, but the
house itself seemed to be mostly gleaming steel beams and
polished glass walls, with a western wing covered in colored
cast-glass panels. *Blade Runner* chic.

Orson had lost the ability to breathe. Or speak.
Everyone else seemed to be equally awestruck.

The shuttle stopped. The driver didn't say a word.

Were they supposed to stay? Go? Wait for instructions?

Everything felt like a test.

Probably because it was.

Orson wasn't confident or assertive enough to be the
first person onboard to make a move, but he felt good
about being the sixth in line to stand. Everyone else
popped up behind him, all of them making their way out
of the Mercedes and onto the sprawling lawn.

"What now?" Kevin whispered.

Still gazing around the Glass House grounds in awe,
Orson said, "I have no idea."

"Do you think we're just supposed to stand here?"

"Maybe we're supposed to go inside the house?"

Both shuttles were empty. Two dozen beautiful men and women standing around, waiting for direction, eyeing each other with uncertainty, all of them surely wondering what they should do. Could they really just walk into a house like that without being led?

Probably. They had been invited after all.

Orson had already waited a lifetime for this; even another few minutes felt like eternity.

"I'm going in." He slapped Kevin playfully on his shoulder, broke from the group, and made his way to the house.

Kevin followed, then so did several other hopefuls.

Orson ignored them, stopping halfway up the drive as he detected the notes of a party, somewhere outside, probably in the back yard. If you could call the grounds of this mega-mansion a 'yard.'

He rounded the side and saw all the signs of wild, drunken revelry waiting to happen. A lush lawn like carpet with plenty of outdoor furniture scattered across it, an infinity pool overlooking the billion lights of LA, a sauna, and an outdoor theater made to resemble a miniature Hollywood Bowl, also staring out on the skyline. Each of the theater seats looked like it cost more than all of the furniture in Orson's apartment, even from here. The grounds were peppered with life-sized versions of childhood games, like Connect 4, Jenga, and Tic-Tac-Toe. He counted three full bars, and the entire area was dripping in twinkling white lights.

A hundred or so of the city's most elite citizens milled about. Valets and servers dressed in red and black — not too differently from Orson — stood ready at attention.

Shit. The last thing he wanted to do was blend in with the hired help.

A hand found his shoulder.

"Mr. Beck."

Orson turned toward the voice and saw an older man with perfect skin, bright blue eyes, and even brighter white hair. He pointed to the closest bar and winked. "Enjoy yourself."

The next hour of the best night of his life was … excruciating. Orson felt half out of his body. His fellow guests were drinking and socializing, mixing it up with the people who were already here. He'd engaged a few people, but then retreated when each of those conversations went awry. The first time, he made the perfectly logical mistake of assuming someone's gender. The second time, he found himself talking to someone who didn't know how to draw a breath between monologues. She spoke for at least five minutes about the evils of cheese without stopping. When she finally paused to let Orson respond, he had no idea what to say.

Then he got tongue-tied when Angel Whitley started a conversation with him. She was one of his favorite actresses, and one of the few to make him both laugh and cry more than once. In person she looked *tiny*. Orson could probably lift her over his head. Mesmerized, he couldn't breathe a single word. He tried, too hard even. Then she finally left, after patting him on the shoulder to make him feel better.

This sure as hell didn't feel like any sort of job interview, and it was barely a party. Nothing like he expected.

Everyone else seemed to be partying happily. What was his problem?

He could do this. He was an actor. He didn't need a

script to play the role of Hollywood hopeful about to score a big break.

He imagined himself as next year's *Entertainment Weekly* cover boy, the one name on this year's Onyx List that really, truly mattered. That was why he'd been brought here, because someone else thought he mattered too.

So he tried again.

But he kept finding himself either milling around the periphery of a conversation or standing around waiting for a place to interject that wouldn't sound like interruption. Every conversation felt forced. He'd never worked harder to sound intelligent. Never put more effort into his natural wit. His best wasn't cutting it.

In addition to the bars, there were also medicine tables, filled with the world's best smoking strains and edibles made with their oils. Of course they had Green Unicorn – if Ellis could get it, Hollywood's elite shouldn't have a problem. But weed wasn't going to help him. He needed an old-fashioned drink. Since that was the thought that brought him to the bar, that's exactly what he ordered.

"I'll have an Old Fashioned."

"You got it." The bartender — pretty enough to be a starlet herself — smiled.

He glanced at the tip jar and felt a pang. It was filled with ones and fives and tens and twenties. But he also saw one fifty and a pair of hundreds. Orson didn't even have so much as a quarter in his streamlined, pocketless pants.

She slid his Old Fashioned across the counter, and caught Orson eyeing the tip jar again. "Don't worry about it, really. It's already ridiculous."

"Thanks," he said, taking his drink.

He turned to go, but froze instead.

The most beautiful creature he'd ever seen in real life

pointed at Orson's drink and said, "I'll have what he's having, but I'd like mine with lemon please."

Another smile from the bartender, followed by another *You got it.*

The stunning woman turned to Orson.

He could barely concentrate. Her features were perfectly delicate. Her body was strong and lean, not an ounce of fat, but in no way waifish. Her hair was the color of fresh hay. Her eyes looked like they should have been bright blue, but were almost black instead.

"I'm Hadley." Her tiny mouth turned up in a smile.

"Orson."

The bartender handed the woman her drink. "One Old Fashioned with a twist of lemon instead of orange."

"Thanks." She took a sip and turned to Orson. "What made you order an Old Fashioned?"

"Trying something new." That sounded better than *I've never had one before.* "I don't even know what's in it."

"Whiskey. It's a Kentucky cocktail, developed by a bourbon aristocrat. For most people, the main difference in an Old Fashioned is whether they like their drink heavy on bitters or on the sweeter side. I couldn't give a shit. Bartender's choice is fine with me." Hadley gave the bartender a wink. "This drink's most important detail is the garnish. Everyone does orange peels and cherries, but I like it classic, the way it was invented, with a twist of lemon."

"I didn't know that." The bartender sounded appreciative, lighting up at Hadley in a way she hadn't lit up for Orson.

"Me neither."

"Of course not." Hadley looked at Orson and laughed. "You didn't even know what was in it."

Her voice was playful, but he didn't get the sense that

she meant to insult him. She took another sip, then looked out at the crowd. "Bet you expected this little soirée to suck a little less."

It could have been the Glass House, the uncertainty of it all, or Hadley's perfect, porcelain beauty, but Orson had never had a harder time finding words in his life.

"It's not like I expected at all, though you're the type of guest I had imagined I'd meet."

"Oh?" This seemed to strike her. "How so?"

He took a moment, terrified that he might get this wrong. Ruin this conversation like he ruined everything else and soil his chances for this evening.

"You're gorgeous," Orson admitted, finding those particular words easier to say than he imagined. That truth was surely obvious to everyone after all. Hadley had probably been hearing the same thing all of her life.

"Thanks," she said, not sounding entirely happy.

"Are you tired of that?" He took a chance. "Of people pointing it out?"

Hadley turned and looked at him. Really *looked* at him. Then she laughed. "You have no idea."

Orson smiled and pinched his fingers together. "Only the tiniest bit."

Then Hadley told him how hard it had been to build a career with her beauty. It was a problem that Orson had never heard of but made perfect sense once she explained it.

"Everyone knows that you have to be at least a certain level of good looking to land one of the main roles. Physically unattractive people can get supporting parts, but even then they're 'Hollywood ugly,' which isn't real-life ugly at all. But if you happen to look more natural on a runway than in a living room, that might be the end of your story."

"The world loves a beautiful woman." Orson tried not

to ogle her. They were headed away from the bar, walking off to nowhere in particular.

"Of course. But it's all context. It's more important that they *believe* her on-screen. And there aren't a lot of meaty roles for women who look like me."

Hadley must have seen the look on his face. She started laughing.

"I'm *not* complaining. Or at least not like it sounds. I know how many doors this face has opened for me. But it's kept a lot of them closed too. And that hurts because they're the doors I care about the most."

"I understand."

She blinked her beautiful black eyes.

This woman wasn't real. Her energy was incredible, immediately putting Orson at ease despite her being twenty thousand miles out of his league. She was stunning, confident, self-assured with a bit of an edge. He couldn't believe she was even talking to him, let alone … whatever this wonderful thing was.

It made what happened with Jess hurt a lot less.

"Where have I seen you before?" Orson asked.

Because Hadley seemed vaguely familiar. But she looked too incredible not to recall. If he'd seen her on a callback, then surely he would remember.

"I've been wondering the same thing. Where have I seen *you*? I'm easy to spot, just hard to remember. I'm washing my face in Skinesta commercials, and walking the runway on those Chantal ads, but even if you've seen me, you've definitely never heard me speak before tonight." Hadley took a sip of her drink and faux-whispered, "I'm not usually allowed to talk."

"I could listen to you all night." Then, "May I?"

Hadley looked at him, beaming. Then she finally got it. "You're Tony from *F the '90s!*"

Orson smiled, bashful but not really. "Guilty."

"You were the best thing about that show."

"It wasn't really a show."

"All my friends watched it."

Orson felt suddenly uncomfortable in the spotlight, especially standing next to a woman who was clearly born for it. "Have you always lived here?"

"Oh, hell no," Hadley laughed. "I moved out here three years ago. Things happened fast, before they dried up."

"Yeah," he nodded. "Ask me how well things have gone since *F the '90s*."

Seriously, Hadley said, "How well have things gone since *F the '90s?*"

"I don't like to brag, but you're looking at the assistant manager of one of the newer Provisions."

"Really, aren't they all *newer Provisions?* That chain is barely a toddler."

"A toddler who knows how to rob you."

"No shit. Every time I go in there I imagine the face of my eighth grade home economics teacher, Mrs. Kenny. I can imagine her gasping: *Shiitake mushrooms!*"

Orson smiled. "So, why do you think you made the List?"

"I didn't." She gave him a hungry look. "I was invited to this shindig."

"Oh." He wanted to ask who had invited her but worried it might be rude. "What's next? Do you have plans to get into movies? Or TV?"

It was a stupid question and both of them knew it. But at least she didn't roll her eyes.

"Of course I have *plans.* But that doesn't mean that the powers that be agree with them. I'll give it another year, then I'll probably end up in porn like everyone else. Maybe become a star that way."

This time Hadley's laugh had a broken heart. Without preamble, she pulled out her phone and started texting. Orson had no idea if she was joking about ending up in porn or not, but he couldn't help his arousal. Same for when they made their way back to the bar, this time for a pair of Moscow Mules. The way her tongue made love to the straw …

But Orson wished that she would stop texting whoever was stealing at least half of her attention. Hadley was his a hundred percent when the phone was in her purse, but he felt excluded each time she pulled it out and dropped her eyes to the screen.

And still, the night lingered. Orson kept expecting new people to show, but it was the same handful of hopefuls, the same small clusters of people who looked like they wielded the power to refashion lives, and eye candy like Hadley, though he would never dare to call her that. And after a couple hours of conversation, he had to admit she was one of the cleverest confections that he'd ever had the pleasure of conversing with.

But Orson was shocked by how few of the others he recognized. He'd thought that for sure he would have seen Bay, Bruckheimer, or Bloom; Silver, Spielberg, or either one of the Shellys, maybe both.

"So you think this is it?" Hadley asked Orson the same question that he had been pondering since his arrival.

"I guess?"

"You can't help but feel disappointed, right?"

Orson looked around. He sure as hell didn't want to be. But all the other actors were hanging out in clusters, milling about, talking to the staff, looking a little lost. The powerbrokers were talking to the eye candy. There was no loud music, no orgies, no out-of-control party. People weren't doing coke off of naked bodies or jumping into the pool with their clothes still on. But it wasn't restrained either. It felt like a gathering with nowhere to go. Orson couldn't believe that he'd been worried about having to work the next day.

"You would think so …" Orson looked at Hadley and polished off his sidecar — his fifth drink in Hadley's Cocktail Tour, this one served in a chilled coup glass with equal parts brandy, orange liqueur, and lemon juice. "But I'm having a great time with you."

"I'm having a great time with you too, Orson Beck."

The event might have been a bust, but their time together wasn't. By the time Orson had finished his classic Manhattan, he had forgotten the scooped-out area that Jess had left in his heart, and he really didn't give a shit that the Fête had been the most boring sort of nonsense.

He laughed, remembering how much he had paid for his stupid suit, and how now he didn't have a pair of dimes to rub together.

What the fuck had he been thinking?

This wasn't Orson's last chance, this was his bottom.

Tomorrow he would have to get his shit together, and rethink his life from ground zero. Being an actor would remain forever out of reach.

But tonight, getting trashed with Hadley, Orson felt like a man who could have what he wanted. So he ordered another drink then another, following this stunning creature's lead, laughing and even lying a little whenever he felt like that was what she wanted.

Hadley was smaller than Orson and apparently even drunker than he was.

He could get his shit together in the morning.

They ordered one last round, appropriately called The

Final Word, a Prohibition-era cocktail with green Chartreuse, lime juice, gin, and maraschino liqueur, shaken and served with a wedge of lime.

"Are you ready?" Hadley asked as she finished her drink.

"For what?"

She smiled like the porn star she joked she might be. Then she licked her lips.

"For the best part."

Chapter Twelve

Out of the party and into the FASTr, without a single goodbye.

Hadley attacked him the second they hit the backseat, her tongue tasting his as he struggled to close the door, then leaving his teeth and his lips with a lick. After a satisfied pant, she said, "You never know, with all the cameras."

Then she kissed him again.

She lowered his zipper then her left hand snaked inside his pants, her right at the back of his neck as she pulled his face to hers.

Up and down, stroking, and now she was nibbling his ear. *"How hard are you going to fuck me?"*

Orson didn't know, but he was dying to find out.

He pulled away, not wanting to spill in her hand, especially when he was so suddenly thinking of Jess.

"What's wrong?"

He stared at her. "Absolutely nothing."

Orson kissed her hard, pretending that their driver wasn't stealing glances when he could. He pulled away.

"Where are we going?"

"Somewhere you can do whatever you want to me," she said.

Her hand was back on his cock, back to stroking. She opened her mouth and leaned down. Orson pulled her back up. She looked at him, confused.

It felt too good. He needed to feel that good. And maybe he even *deserved* to feel that good.

But not here, not in the FASTr, not with the driver still stealing glances.

"Not here." He wondered if he looked as helpless as he felt.

"It's okay if you cum. It won't be the only time."

Orson nearly lost it right there. He throbbed in her hand. "How much longer?"

"Five minutes."

"I want to wait."

"Okay then," she said, releasing him but pulling him down for another kiss..

Hadley's place looked like a lot of the newer, fancier apartment buildings in LA, and Orson was sure it came with the same amenities, from oversized gyms and private screening rooms to pools that looked out over a star-filled city. He'd been invited to parties in places like this a few times but never dragged, and certainly not by someone so stunning that — despite the surreality of it all — he was about to have sex with.

She practically shoved him into the elevator, then hit the button for the fourteenth floor.

"You live on the top floor?"

Orson was impressed. He lived on the top floor too. But that was at the Brick, so it was like living in the top of a toilet. He laughed. Man, he was drunk.

The door opened and they drunk-walked down the hallway.

Hadley stopped at the end and put her thumbprint on a small black box beside the door. Then she turned the knob and entered.

She slammed it behind him and fell to her knees.

His cock was in her mouth before he could even exhale. All the way. Touching the back of her throat.

He groaned as she held it there.

She started to bob, sucking and slurping and swallowing all of her spit.

He was about to cum when she stopped. Stood. Pulled off her dress and showed Orson that she wasn't wearing anything else. No bra, no panties. Just a perfect body, glistening where there wasn't any hair.

"How do you want me?"

Orson didn't know. He had never been asked like that.

"I don't know …" he shook his head. "I just *want you*."

She walked over to the cream-colored sofa and bent over, touching the edge of the cushions with the tips of her fingers. She was pink and blushing, her center like a strawberry sitting in milk.

She looked back at Orson and asked him what he was waiting for.

He didn't know.

But there it was again, another thought of Jess.

It wasn't fair. They weren't even together. And this was happening now. Tomorrow Old Orson would have to become Grown-Up Orson. Tomorrow he had to let his dream die.

But tonight he planned to live it in full.

He stripped, strode over to Hadley, and made her scream with pleasure until she was all sticky and he had to stop.

Then he did it again.
And again.
And again.

Chapter Thirteen

Orson's first thought when he opened his eyes, only a few seconds after he opened his mind, was that the world smelled better than it usually did. There was something sweet in the air, and if scents could be warm, then this was definitely that. But it was also unfamiliar and …

He suddenly remembered, an impossible reality raining into his awareness. He looked around the room as his mind and his memory began to agree.

He didn't recognize the richly decorated bedroom. The LCD TV on the wall had to be sixty or seventy inches. The walls and floor were done in deep earth tones like the clothes at Crossroads, and sumptuous framed art hung on three of the walls.

"Rise and shine," Hadley said, sitting on the edge of the bed and stroking his hair. "How did you sleep?"

He wasn't sure how to answer that. It seemed like Orson had slept better than at any other time in his life. Made sense that he would crash so hard after all the alcohol and acrobatics. But then again, this might be the worst headache of his life. Soon it would be screaming.

His stomach dropped. He had to work, and whatever time it was right now, his shift had probably already started.

"What time is it?" And still looking around, "Where are we?"

Hadley laughed. "We're at your place."

My place?

That was the last place in the world they could possibly be. Orson would never take any girl back to the Brick, but he'd rather die a violent death than take a girl like Hadley there. Not only was the place an absolute dump that would horrify him to admit that he paid for each month, Jess lived right next door.

And *FUCK.*

Jess.

Something withered and died inside him. Half of Orson wanted to tell the world he'd spent the night with Hadley because it was definitely worth bragging about and still seemed so hard to believe, especially seeing as how the sex itself lived up to the fantasy. Because yes, Hadley fucked like a pro. Last night was the best he'd ever had, by far.

But the other half hoped that this would stay a secret forever, so he would never have to see the sadness in Jess' eyes, like the look on her face when he left her for the shuttles. But darker.

"What do you mean *my place?*"

Maybe she means it like *mi casa es su casa.*

"Come on." Hadley tugged at his hand. "Let's get you dressed. I want some breakfast."

Orson didn't have an appetite, and thinking that he might have fucked everything up with Jess forever, he wondered if he ever would again. He wanted to get the hell out of Hadley's apartment and back home. Get his shit together before his shift at Provisions. And goddammit, how was he even going to get back to the Brick?

But he also couldn't be rude. Regardless of what had to happen now, he and Hadley had shared a magical night. Both before and after they'd got to her place. They could share some breakfast, though Orson hoped she meant something from her kitchen because he wasn't even sure that he could manage to foot the bill for a shared cup of straight black coffee.

Hadley kissed him on the cheek, moved to get out of bed, then apparently thought better and pressed her lips to his, despite what had to be some of the world's worst morning mouth — on him, not her. Then she walked over to an overstuffed armchair in the corner, where a pair of jeans and a crisp red shirt lay neatly on the seat.

"Come on, slowpoke. Out of bed." Hadley tapped the top of the chair. "These are for you."

Orson eyed the unfamiliar clothes, thinking this was all a little weird. How often did Hadley sleep with strange men that she had extra clothes to lay out like she was their mother?

"Thanks," he said.

He might have thought of something else, if thinking wasn't so extra hard this morning. He imagined his pile of clothes in the front room where he had stripped them off of his body. He'd sweated through his shirt, and the pants and jacket were rumpled. He'd never be able to return the clothing to Crossroads now. They'd become an uber-expensive memory of the night that could have been, before it all went bust.

Except for his time with Hadley.

Orson got dressed — both the jeans and tee were impossibly soft — then followed Hadley out of her bedroom, thinking that the decor seemed too masculine for a girl like her, and wondering if it was an extra she kept for stray men.

The apartment itself was even more gorgeous than he'd realized last night. A two-minute tour was enough to make Orson feel even sicker to his stomach, serving as a heavy reminder of all that he would never have, no matter how hard he was willing to work or how much he was willing to sacrifice. Her place had a stunning sundeck with a grilling pavilion, stainless steel appliances — oversized like everything else, from the sofa to the ceiling fans — quartz countertops, tile backsplashes, polished hardwood floors, high ceilings, and an oval soaking tub that looked sturdy enough to cross the Atlantic. The building had a state-of-the-art fitness center, on-site restaurant, a matching set of swimming pools, plus a clubhouse with lounge seating and a movie theater screen.

"Why are you telling me this?" Orson asked.

"Because you should get comfortable with it," Hadley answered.

Mi casa es su casa.

But despite the giant refrigerator and the surely stocked pantry, they didn't stay at Hadley's for breakfast. And despite their taking a FASTr home the night before — *her hand on his cock, stroking, opening her mouth, and leaning down* — she had a car waiting in the underground garage.

Orson was sweating during the drive because no matter where they went, he would feel an obligation to pay, or at the very least offer to cover his share.

But with what?

"Where are we going?" he finally asked.

If they were just going to grab a bite, they were passing plenty of places, and he did have to get back in his right mind. Not to mention, ready beg Lester to forgive him for missing part of his shift.

"Breakfast," Hadley laughed. "Like I said."

"But *where* are we going to breakfast?"

"To the place with the best homemade syrup in the city." Hadley laughed louder.

So Orson joined her because that's exactly what any actor worth his salt in this situation would do.

They pulled up to a sprawling mansion and stopped at the gate. Hadley rolled down the window and pressed her thumb onto some sort of digital pad, just like the one that he had seen outside her apartment. The gate swung slowly open and she drove inside.

"Where are we?"

This was getting weirder. Orson was really starting to wonder if Hadley was nuts. Or what she knew that he didn't. Plenty, obviously, and every time he asked her a question, she met it with either silence or a laugh. He couldn't help but feel like she was dragging him into some sort of trouble. Here they were on a Sunday morning, dropping in unannounced on … someone very, very rich.

They got out of the car, but Orson reached out to stop her as she reached for the doorknob of the Hollywood mansion before them.

"Are you going to tell me where we are? I don't want to just barge into someone's house." Then, to make a joke, "Even if their syrup is the best."

But Hadley just shushed him as she opened the unlocked door and strolled inside like she owned the place. He had no choice but to follow.

Orson was gobsmacked. Wonderstruck. He practically wanted to genuflect. He hadn't been allowed into the Glass House, so maybe that was more extravagant, but this was definitely the most lavish home he had ever been inside.

Hadley had clearly seen it all before. She led him through the massive foyer, toward the back of the house, then out onto a patio overlooking an infinity pool that appeared to spill right into the city below. Twin Pomeranians snuggled in a basket beneath a nearby table laid out with a feast and already occupied by a couple he immediately recognized, because how could you have a red carpet dream in this town and not?

Dominic and Melinda Shelly of Shellter Productions.

They seemed to be waiting for him.

Chapter Fourteen

Orson could barely breathe. Hadley took his hand, squeezed, then let it go.

She let him go, too. He watched, confused but maybe relieved, as Hadley skipped over to the table and greeted Dominic with an open-mouthed kiss, while his stunning wife Melinda watched them with a smile, petting one of the two cinnamon-colored Pomeranians at her feet.

Dominic stood. "This is him?"

Her eyes drifted over to Orson in appraisal.

Dominic examined Orson as though he were shopping for a thoroughbred. His laugh was deep and hearty, pleased with itself. Dominic looked back at his wife. They traded a knowing glance.

"Congratulations on making it through the first round of interviews." Dominic clapped him on the shoulder. "Hadley speaks very highly of you. At least until she stopped texting."

Dominic gave Hadley an admonishing look, then laughed again before turning back to Orson.

"So what did I miss?" he finished.

"A Plus, all the way," Hadley said. "From drinks to dessert, he's your next star."

"How did he hold his liquor?" Dominic asked.

"Like a pro. He drank a lot, but he was never belligerent and he refused to drive drunk.

"What about his dick?" Melinda asked, as though Orson wasn't even there.

Hadley looked like an angel, borrowing the devil's smile. "*Perfect.* And he knows how to use it."

The Shellys traded another glance. What in the hell was happening?

He knew what he hoped it was. The opportunity he had been waiting a lifetime for. He'd squandered every last cent of his available credit on clothing that he couldn't afford, just so he could maybe get an audience with someone like Dominic and Melinda. So he would listen and learn and smile as much as he needed to.

He surreptitiously checked his watch, praying this meeting would make the hour irrelevant. Lester was always looking for any reason to penalize him. Docked pay, lost shifts, a ding sent to corporate. The guy was a cock, and Orson couldn't afford to lose this job.

"Are we keeping you from something?" Melinda asked.

He had no idea how she had seen him checking, at least not that time.

Embarrassed, he said, "I work at Provisions. And I've been working every other Sunday because everyone hates that shift, but if I work it then my boss Lester lets me get every other weekend off in full, and I need it because that's when I have my son Connor."

"Oh, that," Melinda laughed, now petting her other Pom. "Your job is taken care of."

Taken care of?

"I'm sorry ..." He felt uncertain, and maybe even a

little stupid, definitely out of his skin. "What do you mean *it's taken care of?*"

"Your job, Orson," she said, as though stating the painfully obvious. "You can't work for us *and* someone else. That shitty job was beneath you. Didn't you feel that every time you punched in and out? Couldn't you feel your life draining away, one second at a time? We'll need to expunge that line of work from your record. It's too depressing, and you worked there too long."

He couldn't help but feel offended. "Lots of actors work in places like that. Or they're waiters or—"

"Not you," Dominic cut him off. "What don't you get? You quit this morning. You work for us now."

Orson didn't know what to say or think. This was all happening so fast and without any script. He couldn't afford to fumble his lines and lose the role of a lifetime.

But this felt wrong. Sure, his gig at Provisions was shit. But it covered his baseline needs, savings for Connor, and basic insurance. Like it or not, he needed that job. He'd been around Hollywood long enough to know how things worked. If there wasn't a movie or show in the works, then the actor wasn't getting paid. What was he supposed to do in the meantime? He had to take care of Connor and keep Alexis off his back. He would work hard and do whatever needed to be done, but he had to keep that job until he could buy himself some breathing room.

"I'm sorry," Orson said, his heart beating like a punch to his throat, "but I have to keep my job. At least for now." Then, so it would seem responsible rather than unappreciative, and exactly like the team player they were probably looking for, he added, "I made a commitment. So I can't just not show up, you know?"

"It's taken care of," Melinda assured him.

Hadley stood off to the side, slightly shaking her head.

But Orson could only think of Connor and how much he might be letting him down. How much he already had. He couldn't stop himself. "Can we talk about the pay? Or the benefits? When that all might be coming … for whatever this is?"

Everyone stared at him.

He cleared his throat. "I've got a kid. I'm just trying to—"

"Is that what you *really* want?" Dominic's brows were drawn together, red spots warming his tanned cheeks. His eyes darkened as spittle flew from his lips. "Do you want the complacency of your day job or the pursuit of your dreams? Are you going to stand there like a pauper talking to me about pennies when you could be talking about the millions that come from being a prince in this town?"

Orson had spent his whole life wanting that exact thing to happen. To be discovered and handed everything — fame, money, luxury — on a silver platter. But now that someone was actually offering it, he couldn't believe it was true.

"Why would you—"

"Do you know what all of this costs?" Dominic waved his arms theatrically about. "That salt shaker, right there, Orson." Dominic pointed to the chunky ceramic on the table. "How much did that cost?"

"I have no idea." Every one of his four words felt wrong.

"Guess."

"A … a hundred dollars."

"Four hundred and nineteen. Count the pepper and it's 836. That's what we paid for the set, Orson. Nearly a grand so I can add to my cholesterol a dash at a time. And if a groundskeeper dropped that in their pocket on the way out, I'd have to shrug and figure that whoever stole it must have needed it more than I did, then I'd buy another one and probably spend twice as much the second time. Money doesn't matter once you know how to make it, my friend. And that's what we do. My wife and I just gave you a chance to do some of that with us, and you responded to our offer by telling us that you would prefer to stock shelves and be broke for the rest of your life. Fuck you, Orson Beck."

What the hell was this? They expected to play God with his life — no contract, not even a verbal offer on the table — and he was supposed to go along with it? No questions asked?

They expected him to trust his son's future to strangers? Powerful, famous strangers who could make or break an actor's career, but still, he'd known them for about five minutes.

"I just want to—"

"We know all about you, Orson. We know exactly how hungry you are to achieve your dreams. The results of your Onyx application are public to those of us who can afford to buy them." He glanced down at the salt and pepper with a laugh. "Three hundred and eleven. That's how many questions you answered. I bet you lost count."

He had. But ... what did that have to do with anything?

Dominic smiled at Orson, enjoying his confusion. "AI these days is incredible. Again, if you can afford it. Between your answers, your online profiles and postings — and thank the AI again for all that — and what we could scrape off of your sad little IMDB page, we know all that matters about you. And until a few moments ago, my wife and I liked what we saw." He peered at Orson. "Do you have anything to say?"

"I wasn't sure that—"

"You're twenty-seven," Dominic interrupted. "Grew up in a Tampa suburb. Shit place unless you regularly ate at Bern's, which you didn't, since middle class won't get you upstairs to the dessert room often. You were a decent kid and a diligent student. You had plenty of extracurriculars, thanks to your parents Carol and Douglas. You were never a genius like your brother Samuel, who set the precedent early. You looked up to him, but you knew from the start that you'd probably never measure up, and that stirred something inside you."

Dominic stopped. Took a sip of his coffee. Wiped his mouth as he glared, as if daring Orson to utter a word.

But what could he say that wouldn't make this ten times worse?

What if his only chance at fixing this was to let Dominic's anger burn itself out?

What if his only chance at fixing this was to stop Dominic before his rant ended with Orson's dream offer being snatched back?

Or was it already off the table? He had no clue what Dominic wanted from him.

Not to speak, apparently. The man interrupted him every time Orson opened his mouth.

"Your parents always impressed upon you the importance of working hard to get what you want. You weren't valedictorian, but you were top ten percent, and that was good enough. From soccer to drama, people liked you well enough, and even those who didn't want to. You learned early that that's the way it is for the beautiful. Proving early that you have no problem with cliché, you landed the role of prom king, which was probably much better than your performance as Harold Hill in your high school version of *The Music Man*, but not nearly as good as when you played

Tony, a similar character on *F the '90s* just a few years later."

Orson felt invaded, flattered, and deeply, deeply curious. "Wha—"

"I wonder what would have happened if Marisa hadn't gone east."

Orson blanched.

It hurt, hearing about when two horizons yawned further apart.

"Oh, we know about her too. She played Marian and gave you your first taste of love. You lost your virginity to her, before she broke your heart. You always figured that the two of you would get together because back then everything always came up Orson Beck. But she went off to Bryn Mawr and never thought about you again. You doubled down on the drama, first with a full scholarship, then later by taking a shit right on top of it. Your parents wanted you to be a doctor, but you begged them for a different path then betrayed their generosity. You thought you knew best, and for a minute and a half maybe you did. But *F the '90s* was over four years ago, Orson, and you've been working at your dead-end job ever since. You can't even cover Connor's child support. We give you an apartment and a car and the chance of a lifetime, and you're asking about your benefits …"

Dominic let it hang.

Nausea coursed through Orson as he tried to process the possibility that someone had just tried to make his wildest dreams come true, and he'd turned it down without even realizing that's what they were offering.

The nicest apartment he'd ever seen. The most expensive car he'd ever touched. The only career he'd ever wanted.

But his brain had taken too long to catch up with his mouth, and now he was about to lose it.

Such. An. Asshole.

Hadley looked at him, broken-hearted, mouthing the words *I'm sorry* with her sensuous lips.

But how could he fix such a horrendous mistake with two words?

Melinda shook her head, the few lines on her face all sloped in disappointment.

"Open your hands," Dominic said.

"I'm sorry?"

Orson's heart pounded harder than it ever had before. He thought he might pass out. When was this going to stop? When would he have a chance to speak?

"Open your hands," he repeated.

Orson presented his open palms.

Dominic reached over, grabbed the salt and pepper shakers, then placed one in each of Orson's hands before gently closing his fingers around them.

"I'm sorry we made you late, Orson. I hope this covers it. You may see yourself out."

Chapter Fifteen

"What is it?" Lester sniveled into the phone.

Orson staved off his hate long enough to finish the exchange. "I'm going to be late, but I'll get there as fast as I can."

"Late for what, Orson?"

What an asshole, making me say it.

"For work."

"You don't work here anymore. So if you're reporting about the punctuality of your new job, I don't care, but tell them congratulations. I'm glad they're getting a new and improved Orson Beck."

What the hell?

Dominic had been serious. He really had *taken care of it.* And Orson had spit in his face without realizing it.

Now Orson didn't have his job at Provisions to fall back on.

Given his bank balance, he'd be homeless by next month.

SHIT.

"We'll send you your final paycheck. Or you can just come in and get it."

SHIT. SHIT. SHIT.

"Orson?"

"Yeah … okay. Paycheck. Thanks."

He hung up.

He looked back at the Shellys' house and wondered what he should do.

He had no idea how to convince Dominic and Melinda to give him a third chance. Not after he'd refused their second one.

He retrieved the salt and pepper shaker from his pockets where he'd shoved them as he staggered out of the mansion. Squat, misshapen in a way that could be amateurish or avant garde. Hand-painted in a cheery shade of yellow that made him hate himself even more.

It felt wrong to sell them, even though Dominic had suggested he do exactly that.

Getting home was a more immediate problem. His cards were all maxed, so he couldn't even pay for a FASTr.

Could he stand the humiliation of that long walk through the open gate, up the drive and back inside, to beg for cab fare from the couple who'd just offered him a chance to make millions?

No. He'd had all the humiliation he could take for one day. The impending headache was threatening to become a migraine-level head-splitter, thanks to the adrenaline rush that would probably wear off halfway home to leave him hollow and exhausted.

He was desperate to get home and crawl into his own bed, but how was he going to get there?

He got an idea.

He took out his phone and called an old-fashioned cab. Twenty-three minutes later, he was sitting in the back of a bright yellow Prius. Five minutes after that he was already halfway into his hustle.

"I've heard of Green Unicorn," the cabbie admitted with something like lust in his eyes.

Orson had really lucked out. He wasn't sure what he would have done if he got someone who didn't fit the profile. But this driver was everything he'd been hoping for -- late twenties and a slow talker. Because everything else in his life was a shit show, the good Lord smiled when the cabbie pulled away from the gate and turned back to ask Orson if it was "chill if we listen to Sublime?"

"But have you ever smoked it?" Orson asked.

"Nah. Of course not."

"It's the best smoke there is."

"So I've heard."

Orson leaned back in his seat. Took a moment. Then he leaned forward. "I have a tiny bit at home."

"Oh yeah?" The cabbie raised his eyebrows, probably wondering what this was.

"Yeah. And it's the fucking *best*. But I also have a confession."

"Oh yeah?"

Orson could hear the cabbie's suspicion deepening. Time to play the last card.

"Look, I'll level with you. I've had a really crazy night and an even crazier morning. I just got handed the opportunity of a lifetime, then I took a shit on it." Orson made himself laugh, even though it made his head hurt worse. "I have a wallet, but there's nothing in it. I don't have any cash, and all my credit cards are maxed."

The man's expression darkened. Orson kept talking.

"You can let me out here and I'll figure something else out, or you can take me another couple of miles and I'll give you the best bud on Earth."

With legalization, it was all about the strain. And since Green Unicorn wasn't sold in dispensaries, it might as well have been illegal.

"How do I know it's really Unicorn?"

"You'll know it the second you smoke it, then you'll never doubt it again."

Orson was really selling it, promising nirvana.

"Okay," the cabbie agreed. "But don't fuck me."

"I'm just looking for the win-win."

After they pulled up to the Brick, he ran past the mailboxes and Angus yelling, "How are you this fine afternoon?" Then up six flights and right into his open but empty apartment.

Empty. Every stick of furniture was missing.

His *what the fucks* were adding up.

Orson went into his bedroom and his bathroom. Both were as empty as the kitchen and living room.

He shook his head, trying to clear it.

This was absolute batshit crazy. What in the—

"Excuse me," said a voice.

Orson turned around and saw two teenaged kids, each of them holding the end of a sofa that might have cost a cool twenty at a yard sale, if they overpaid.

Dumbfounded, Orson said, "Sure," and fell a step back.

The building manager, Benson, stepped through the still-open door. He marched right up to Orson and held out his hand. "Your key."

"I'm sorry?"

"Your key. You did break your lease last night, right? With an *emergency* email?"

Orson looked at Benson with his mouth open, slowly shaking his head. "Um … no?"

Benson grunted and irritably got out his phone. His

thumb did the mambo, then he turned the screen to Orson.

"See," he said, showing him an email.

Orson did see, but that didn't mean he understood it. At all.

Then he did. Dominic and Melinda. Those devious fucks. They dismantled his life while Hadley distracted him, then they made him an offer. If he said yes without question, they were *taking care of everything,* which meant burning all his bridges, so he had to sign whatever contract they offered.

And if he said no? Well, this was his punishment. No job, no apartment, no prospects.

This wasn't fair.

It might not even be legal.

"Sorry if you're having second thoughts. But rent is cheap, kid. This place went in hours. Now can I please have your key?"

Benson held out his hand again. Numbly, Orson removed his key from its chain and placed it into the man's open palm. Then watched as he walked right over and handed it to the older teen.

Orson turned toward the door, but — wait. "Where are all my things?"

Benson looked at Orson like he was crazy. Crazier. "The movers were here early this morning. *Too early.* Like before six, which is bullshit if you ask me. But it did open the place up, so *ce la vie.*" He looked Orson over. "Maybe you shouldn't party quite so hard, huh?"

Then he left.

One of the teens cleared his throat and gave Orson an expectant look.

Oh, right. I'm in his apartment.

Orson stepped into the hallway and knocked on Ellis' door.

"Dude …" Ellis said after opening the door. He looked somehow bothered, but it wasn't that early, even for a Sunday morning.

"I need a favor."

Ellis looked past Orson, then back at his friend with a puzzled expression. "Is Connor here?"

"Not that kind of favor. I just need a fat nug of Unicorn."

"Is that why you look so stressed?" Ellis smiled, tugging on his big red beard. "This is a weed emergency?"

"I needed a ride home and I didn't have any money. I talked the driver into trading for some Unicorn, but then I got home and all my stuff was gone."

"That's happened to me before. It's hard to keep track of how much you smoke."

"No," Orson clarified. "It's *all* gone. Everything I own."

"You were robbed?"

"Not exactly. I'll explain in a bit. But I need to hurry, so can you please—"

"Say no more."

Bothered or not, Ellis was the kind of friend who would not only happily share his weed, he was also the kind of friend who didn't need to be asked more than once. He was back at the door in seconds with an impressive wedge of red-threaded weed. The little thing was twisted into a small baggie and practically looked gift-wrapped.

"Here ya' go, my friend."

The cabbie was still waiting downstairs and looking like he was ready to explode. His mouth was open and he seemed about to yell, but he relaxed the second that Orson opened his palm and delivered on his promise.

Then back inside, no Angus this time, and up all six flights.

Ellis and Jess were both waiting in front of his open door.

Neither looked happy.

"Dude," Ellis said. "You weren't kidding. All your shit's gone."

"What happened?" Jess asked, looking more than concerned.

Orson shook his head. "I have no idea. Apparently I broke my lease early this morning."

"What?" Jess said, "How did you apparently break your lease?"

Orson was still shaking his head. "I have no idea. But the manager showed me the email."

Ellis shrugged. "Maybe it had to do with your nocturnal activities.

And there it was, that look on his face. He knew about the List.

"You know where I was?"

"Of course," Ellis said. "You know what I do for a living. Why wouldn't you tell me?"

"I don't know," Orson admitted because he didn't. "I didn't want anyone to know."

"Jess knew. And you told her not to tell me."

Orson glanced at Jess, disappointed but also a little pleased that she had the decency to look ashamed at betraying him.

"Ellis, it's not because I didn't want you to know, it's because I wanted to be the one to tell you."

"Then you probably should have done that before pictures of you from last night were plastered all over the

Internet. Seriously dude, we used to talk shit on Hollywood and you looked like one of the pod people last night. You're one of the few people who know about the Hollywood Hunt. Why wouldn't you tip me off?" He shook his head. "I thought we were friends."

"We are." But Orson could see why it didn't look that way right now. And he couldn't stand the way that Jess was staring at him. But he also couldn't help asking, "What was online?"

Jess spoke up, her voice thin as a spider's leg. "Pictures of you with Hadley Witt, walking really close and getting stupid-drunk at a bar. Everyone's asking, *Who is Hadley's Mystery Man?* They're all framing it like you two were on some super romantic date."

"We weren't," Orson said, hating that he was such a liar, thinking about the night, the ride home, and Hadley falling to her knees behind the closed door. "You know who she is?"

"Of course we know who she is," Jess said, casting a glance at Ellis. "She's an up-and-coming model who thinks she's an actress."

The pair of them were standing there, looking at him with wide and disappointed eyes. Orson still didn't know what to say, but now he wasn't even sure that he wanted to. Even if he could remember everything that happened last night, both of them looked like they'd already made up their minds.

His phone rang. *Fuck.*

Orson sighed and checked the screen. Alexis. Great. Like things could be any more fucked up. He wanted to cry or scream or leap over the railing to fall six flights to the asphalt. He couldn't believe where his life might have gone just an hour ago, compared to where it was now.

"It's Alexis. I have to take this." Then into the phone, "Hey, Alexis."

Orson expected her to start yelling because that was how she usually started her calls. This call started with a scream too, but it was a sort of joyous scream he hadn't heard in a while.

"Thank you so much!" Alexis squealed.

"Sure thing." Then, "For what?"

She laughed. "For all the child support."

What.

The.

Fuck.

Was he so shitfaced that he'd robbed a bank last night and wired her money? Obviously not. This was more of Dominic and Melinda maneuvering him into a corner.

Well, he wasn't telling Alexis to send it back. They'd intervened in his life without his consent. He couldn't be held accountable to any claims of obligation if he hadn't agreed to them, could he?

"Are you still there, Orson?"

"Uh. Yeah. You're welcome."

"I'm sorry I've been such a bitch, but this is what I've been waiting to see from you. Thanks for showing me that you could do it! I was thinking, how would you like to have Connor next weekend *and* the weekend after next?"

Orson brightened. Alexis had never given him two weekends in a row. "That would be great."

Ellis and Jess were still eyeing him, but both still looked disappointed with him. Not just disappointed. Also, angry. And maybe betrayed.

"You deserve it," Alexis gushed. "Besides, Tyler and I really need some more alone time. Things are getting serious, you know?"

"Yeah."

"I mean, really serious. I think this is it."

"I'm glad to hear that. I'm happy for you. Really."

He might even have meant that. It was hard to tell when he was still in shock.

"Well, I just wanted to say thank you for the money. It was a real surprise, waking up to that."

Orson gave her another *sure thing* then said his goodbye. He had no idea what was happening, or how he could fix it. But he knew where he had to start.

"I've gotta go," he said to Ellis and Jess, dropping the phone in his pocket.

"Okay, dude. Whatever." Ellis turned back toward his apartment. Jess followed. No protest. No *aren't you going to tell us what's going on?*

It was like they'd already given up on him.

Orson stood there for a moment alone, then stomped toward the stairs.

Fuck you, Ellis! All you do is shit on the industry that I'd give my left nut to be in.

Fuck you, Jess! My dick and where it goes is MY business. Weren't you the one with a hot date last night?

And fuck you, Alexis! Using my child like a bargaining chip to squeeze me!

But he would have to fix shit with them later. Right now he had to fix his entire life.

Orson walked to the closest bus stop and waited for a ride to the only place he could go.

Chapter Sixteen

Hadley stood in the Catalyst lobby, waiting for Orson.

"He'll show," Dominic had assured her.

And whatever Dominic said, Hadley went with. She wanted this more than she had ever wanted anything, and she was willing to twist herself into a physical, emotional, and spiritual pretzel to get it.

She refused to let Dominic and Melinda down. She would continue to prove herself indispensable. The plan didn't have to make sense. She was smart, but they were brilliant. And she had faith in them. Or at least she had faith in what they wanted to do with her career.

So in the meantime, Hadley followed every order with her cover-girl smile.

Sleep with a director? *Fine.*

Do a line of blow off the bathroom floor? *Cool.*

Fuck Dominic while his wife watches? *Not a problem.*

Make a relationship with this guy Orson work out? *Easiest thing I've done all week.*

Hadley had been waiting a long time for things to take off. She'd made the Onyx List two years ago. Paid her dues and waited for her turn. Her turn was behind schedule, but she wasn't willing to let it expire.

She wasn't bitter, not at all, but Hadley often had to wonder why Dominic and Melinda chose her, if they were planning to keep her on the bench for so long.

You're too pretty.

We need to roughen you up a bit.

Build your reputation. Break you in.

Starting out on the modeling circuit had been demoralizing in too many ways for Hadley to count. She'd come to LA to walk the red carpet, not splash water on her face in some dumb commercial.

But how could she complain? They gave her everything she needed. Her apartment was covered at five grand a month, same for her car and insurance and all that other shit she didn't want to think about. Shellter had paid off all of her old debt, same as they were doing for Orson, and cut her a nice check each week that went straight into savings, since her daily allowance for being their O-Lister, as they liked to call her, was a zip code or two beyond generous.

Dominic and Melinda had done more for Hadley than anyone back home ever had.

She walked over to the table centered in the lobby. It held an oversized pot stuffed with enough bright white orchids to impress an emperor and several carafes filled with ice water. Hadley poured herself a glass and sipped as she waited.

Dominic conducted the city like a symphony. He was the maestro, and Hadley was a slave to his music. So when he and Melinda told her that she got to recruit this year's recipient, that sounded like a golden opportunity.

Whoever Hadley chose would *almost for sure* be co-starring with her in one of Shellter's upcoming Oscar-bait flicks. As long as the chemistry with her chosen one was right, the role would make her two-year wait worth it, then some. Assuming he showed.

She liked him, a lot. Orson was the type of guy she could see this playing out with long-term. She was also thrilled that Orson could fuck. He nailed her like she needed it, all three times. That was a shot in the dark because you never knew until the door was closed, but Orson Beck had delivered, and she was looking forward to him giving it to her again.

She wondered if that was just luck, or if Dominic and Melinda had chosen him because he was a good match for her.

Of course she felt a twinge of sympathy at his confusion, and empathy for what he still had to go through. It had been the same for her.

Hadley would keep up her half of the deal regardless, but she was grateful for the spark between them. It would make this so much easier.

She also liked that he was loyal, and that Orson's first thought was about his kid, rather than kissing Dominic's ass. But he also seemed scared when the boss was putting on that fireworks show, and there was a part of Hadley — barely there, just a seed that had yet to see sunlight — that was starting to think that maybe Orson wouldn't show.

But then he did, almost as if Dominic had written the script for this afternoon, which she supposed he kinda, sorta had.

He was clearly unhappy, so Hadley had some work to do.

"Orson!" She threw her arms around him and planted a kiss on his cheek.

"Why are you here?"

Disappointing that he didn't sound happy to see her.

"Waiting for you, of course, because I knew you would come here."

He looked at her suspiciously. He was breathing hard, genuinely upset. "How did you know that?"

"Where else would you go?" She smiled and gently took his arm. "Come on, Orson. Everything will get better from here. Trust me."

And even though he said nothing, Orson's body seemed to relax. He followed Hadley into the elevator.

She pressed the button for the fourteenth floor then sank into his silence. Let him be the first to talk. He had to have a million questions, and he'd be more receptive to the answers if he couldn't stop himself from asking.

The elevator dinged and they walked the posh hallway, so much steadier than the last time. When they got to his door, Hadley pointed to the small black box with the digital pad above the doorknob.

"Your turn."

Finally, a smile tickled the corner of his mouth. He pressed his thumb on the box and turned the light green. Then he opened the door with awe on his face.

Tonight would be easy. Her only orders were to *get closer to him*. That was already happening.

Orson walked directly to the sofa, impressively so, almost as if he owned the place. Maybe because he was thinking about how he'd fucked her on it.

He sat and said, "So, will you tell me what's going on?"

Hadley sat beside him. She put her hand on his knee. The tension in his muscles betrayed the façade of calm he was working so hard to project.

Beneath that serenity there was a growl of frustration. He was still pissed.

And something about that rankled her because that meant he still wasn't getting how great the offer was. Part of her job was to make him see, to make sure that he understood.

"What do you think has happened in the last twenty-four hours?" she asked.

"I'm not exactly sure. But it's a lot of shit that I didn't have any control over and should have. Major life-changing decisions were made without my consent or even my input."

"Has anything *bad* happened in the last day?"

He took his time thinking about that one. Hadley practically expected him to start stroking his chin. Finally, almost begrudgingly it seemed, Orson said, "No."

"And have your circumstances improved?"

This one was immediate. "Yes. Definitely."

"I understand what you're going through. I went through it, too. You don't know anything because being kept in the dark is part of the process. That was a test, to see how you respond."

"Oh. So how did I do?"

"You're here, aren't you?" Hadley gestured around the room. "Play ball and this is all yours. The Shellys are taking care of everything. Your rent, Connor's child support, your publicity. There's plenty more where that came from. But you have to trust them. Look at the stars who have come through Shellter. They have a way of doing things."

"What do I have to do?"

"Nothing for now. Say yes. Dominic and Melinda are preparing your contract right now. Sign it and your new life starts right away."

Disbelief was etched in his face. He shook his head, slowly absorbing the surreality of it all. "Who are you … to them I mean?"

"I work for them. I was on the List two years ago." She

took his hand. "My success is sort of dependent on you. We're in this together."

"Together?"

He made it sound like a four-letter word.

"Yes," she said. "Together, in art and life, at least for now."

That anger she'd sensed under the surface peeked out. "What about you and Dominic ... you two looked ... I don't know ..."

"Together?" She laughed. There was a lot of *together* in this conversation.

"Something like that."

"Exactly," Hadley agreed. "*Something like that.* No, we're not together. But the Shellys are open-minded, and they like to have fun."

"Okay." He didn't look as angry, but he also didn't look happy.

Fortunately, this was the easy part.

Hadley let go of his hand and reached into his lap.

Orson looked up at her as she fumbled with his zipper, but then he pulled away.

"Not right now." He shook his head. It looked almost against his will. "Do you mind if I spend some time here alone?"

Now she was getting pissed. Because he wasn't getting it. His denial wasn't in the script.

She reached over again. But he put out a hand to stop her.

"Hadley ..."

She was committed to the role. But maybe she'd misread this page of the script.

It was one of the hardest things she'd ever done, when her instincts were screaming for her to stay until she'd locked him in, securing her own future. But Hadley flashed a smile. "Of course. I understand. Been there myself."

She stood, then leaned down to kiss Orson on his cheek. "Call or text or whatever when you want me." Then she gave him her most sensual smile. "I'll be back."

Hadley was in her Lexus and two lights away from his place by the time she finally allowed herself to feel pissed.

How dare he turn her down. How dare he tell her that he'd rather be alone. How dare he refuse the most beautiful girl he had ever been in a room with, especially after last night's acrobatics.

Hadley drove faster.

How dare he, indeed.

Chapter Seventeen

Ellis walked up to the bar, feeling better than he'd expected to.

"I'll have another two of whatever I had the last time."

The bartender nodded, then returned with a pair of frothy somethings. Orson had ordered the first round, though Ellis paid twice. He walked over to where Orson waited for his turn at the darts and handed him the beer.

"You're gonna buy *all* the alcohol when you're rich and famous."

"Gladly," Orson said.

Yes, things had gone much better with Orson than Ellis expected. He hadn't known what to expect. Orson's move to a new place had been sudden. And a little too Hollywood for his taste.

But then again, Ellis might have been jaded. His job was to dig, and he rarely liked what he found. Hollywood was full of rotting bones, graveyard of depravity that it was. He feared for his friend and didn't want to see him get sucked into it. Unfortunately, that seemed to be his only dream. Ellis had been hoping that the last few years had convinced Orson to embrace a better life, but apparently he wanted it more than ever.

Ellis had been working on something big for more than a year. If he was right, then his upcoming series would explode the lid off of Hollywood's toilet, and expose all of the shit he could find that they couldn't flush. And Orson was going to help.

But for now, darts.

"I'm glad you could make it," Jess said to Orson. "I wasn't sure that you would."

"I've only missed four so far. Two per year's not bad."

"Admirable." Jess let her dart fly and nearly nailed a bulls-eye.

The Litter Box was two blocks from the Brick, and at least two out of the three had met each Wednesday night for more than two years. Orson had the best track record of them all.

Jess was working hard to be positive, but she'd been a wreck all morning. She didn't want to admit that she was hurt by the pictures of Orson with Hadley, by his moving away without any warning, and by his seeming indifference to their feelings about his sudden metamorphosis.

She wasn't overly emotional and often kept things to herself. But Ellis had known her since Skokie, and he knew what her mouth looked like when she wanted to vomit, and what her eyes looked like when she tried not to cry. Jess wouldn't want to give Orson the ego stroke of knowing that he'd caused her pain. Ellis would do whatever he could to support her in that.

She finished her turn and turned around. "So, you're not hacking us? You really have some fancy pants place?"

Orson looked embarrassed. And enchanted. "Yep. For real. At the Catalyst. Totally paid for."

"Shit." Ellis shook his head. He didn't mean *shit*, like he was sure that Orson had heard it.

"Shit." Jess echoed the sentiment, and Orson seemed to like it even less from her.

"Yeah. It's crazy. I'm sorry it's all happening so fast. I had nothing to do with that. They sent the email to the management company and paid off my lease, called Lester, and even wired money to Alexis."

"We heard," Jess said.

Orson kept going.

"It looks like everything is taken care of, so now I can concentrate on my career."

My career.

Ellis had heard those words twenty times in the last hour. He would have to get used to it.

"So do you have any specifics? Other than *everything is great?*" Ellis asked. "As in, what does 'concentrating on your career' mean? Do the Shellys have a project lined up for you?"

"I'm not exactly sure. I wish I had more to tell you. I'm supposed to get a contract any day now. They said it would be coming soon, but that was on Sunday."

"Who's *they*?" Ellis asked. "Dominic? Melinda?"

A beat, then, "Yeah."

Jess pressed this time. "Which one?"

Another beat. "Both of them."

There was something on Jess' face, and Ellis felt sure that he knew what it was. She wanted to ask about Hadley because even if she had never admitted it to him, Jess had serious feelings for Orson, and that made Ellis feel protective of her. He also knew that Orson felt the same way about Jess, even though he would never admit it. Still, he could practically smell their attraction.

But Orson was becoming more Hollywood by the

second, and that was a danger he didn't want to be around his oldest friend.

"This is going to be so great for Connor."

"Which part?" Ellis said.

"Are you serious?" Orson looked offended. "All of it."

"All of it won't be good for him." Ellis shook his head. That was all he could say about that, at least for now, and still keep his friend.

"Oh, I don't know, the money, the security, the time I'll have to spend with him, less time that he'll be growing up around Alexis and her bitching. And fucking Tyler."

Framing his new situation in terms of Connor didn't make it any less about him.

"I'll finally have the chance to be the dad I've always wanted to be. The dad I *can* be. Once the courts and Alexis see that I'm more financially stable, they'll have to give me more time with Connor."

"Probably true," Ellis said.

"I saw another picture of you and Hadley," Jess said, her face showing little of the strain Ellis was sure lived inside her. "You guys were eating at a Reggie's."

"Oh. That was yesterday."

"You looked close," she added.

"Not really. But she works for the Shellys. She was on the List two years ago. She's helping me get settled." Orson tried to change the subject. "Are you guys feeling brave enough to order the nachos?"

"Her career has really exploded … two years later. I think about her at least one out of ten times that I wash my face."

"Jess," Ellis said.

"I'm sorry. That wasn't nice."

"It's fine," Orson said, though his face disagreed. But

before Ellis could say anything else, Orson's phone buzzed. He checked the screen.

"Is it from Hadley?" Jess asked.

Ellis gave her a look, but she pretended not to notice.

Orson said, "It is. There's some black tie thing I need to show up for. I have half an hour to get there. Fortunately, I had something in the car just in case. I'm sorry, I've got to go."

"Of course, man." Ellis clapped him on the shoulder. "Just promise you'll read the fine print before you sign anything."

Orson laughed. "I'm not an idiot."

Debatable. But this wasn't the time for Ellis to have that discussion with him.

Jess said, "I'm sorry."

Orson replied, "Me too. This is all happening fast. But just because my luck has changed, that doesn't mean that I want things to change between us. Let's get together soon. Just the two of us. Ellis can stay home and beat off."

Ellis laughed. "Sounds good to me."

"Me too," Jess said, "except the part about Ellis beating off."

Orson thanked Ellis again for the beers, then gave them both hugs and headed out the door.

"You know, *soon* is what people say when it's not gonna happen for a while, right?" Jess said.

"Indeed I do." Then, "Do you think it's funny that he didn't have enough cash or credit to pay for drinks, but he's leaving here in an eighty thousand dollar Lexus?"

"It can't be that much."

"He said it twice. Lexus GS F. I looked it up."

"Shit."

"Yep," Ellis said. "Exactly."

Something wasn't right with Orson's new life, and Ellis was going to figure it out.

Hopefully, while they were still friends.

Chapter Eighteen

Dominic finished with a smile.

Reading the news was for the common folk. Reporting it was slightly better. Being a part of it bested them both. But nothing was better than *making* it.

Except for designing it ages ahead of time and always seeing it through.

In a culture that had been folding ever more to fake news, Shellter (or at least her shell companies) had been playing origami with the truth for years.

Amateurs made movies with their stories, but the Shellys made stories with their films. There was an art to what they did, and together, he and Melinda were better than Picasso.

There were only two blogs that mattered in this town. That gossip rag with a monocle, Hollywood Hunted, and the one that moved the mightiest mountain of traffic, You Didn't Hear It From Me.

Three people knew that the Shellys owned You Didn't Hear It From Me, and the Shellys were two of them. That was the mothership. They also owned an additional forty-one blogs and their associated social media profiles. Shellter ran this through a satellite company called Brilliance Media. Each of the forty-one blogs believed they were exclusive, but the whole thing was designed in a writer's room, with assignments constantly being distributed to the unwitting participants to tell a global, sprawling story that the Shellys wrote as they went.

Dominic and Melinda had built an unstoppable publicity machine. They had the formula for making a star.

Hadley plus Orson would equal an impossible fortune, if they worked all the variables.

This latest engineered rumor was Orson's consideration for a coveted role in Shellter's upcoming indie film *Bottleneck*. The timing was perfect. Hadley invited her new beau to a black tie gala that he didn't know about. If he dropped his friends and their usual Wednesday in squalor to attend, then Dominic could feel bullish on Orson Beck.

Melinda came up from behind and kissed him on his neck.

"I like him," she said.

"I know you do." Dominic wasn't quite as sure on this one, but he was willing to play and agreed that the kid was the best of this year's bunch.

"What is it that makes you unsure?"

"I'm not unsure," Dominic said. "He wouldn't be here if I was. But he's not as compliant as I like them."

"There's nothing wrong with that. Not for this."

"We've never had as much at stake."

Melinda didn't say anything. She didn't need to.

They watched from their table as Orson and Hadley hit the red carpet, arms linked.

"This looks promising," Dominic said.

"It does." Melinda couldn't have smiled wider.

Red carpet.

Black ties.

Beautiful gowns.

Limos, crowds, and cameras. People screaming.

"The screams are louder than usual." Melinda pointed to a group of girls in their late teens or so. "They all want to fuck him."

"Agreed," Dominic said.

She pointed to the pile of photographers. "It looks like they love him even more than the fans. Jesus. Why is that?"

Dominic felt a lot more satisfied than he showed with a shrug. "Just the way it is sometimes. I'd say that you can't really predict it, except that it looks like we've figured that out."

Melinda laughed, then nodded to the photographers grabbing endless shots of Hadley and Orson, who looked like a couple already. "How do you think that's going to go over with Little Miss Skokie?"

Dominic shook his head and pursed his lips. "Oh, I don't think that will go over well at all."

"He's so green."

"Like Oscar the Grouch on St. Patrick's Day," Dominic agreed.

They watched Orson as he mugged for the camera, lapping it up because it was all so beautiful and new.

Except that it wasn't. He'd tasted it before, and that made him want it even more now. Good. Tonight, they needed him in heat.

"They're shouting his name. That's an excellent sign. Did you notice that the Hunter didn't run anything on him?"

"I did," Dominic said.

"Any thoughts?"

A reporter yelled at Orson, and asked him how he felt about being considered for *Bottleneck*.

"Not so far." Then Dominic laughed. "Do you think that's the first time he's heard the rumor?"

"I'm sure," Melinda said. "I do think he'll fare better than Harrison ever did. Over time. They don't get more earnest, at least without losing their edge."

"Exactly. Everyone loves the biggest blues eyes in Hollywood, especially if they came from somewhere else. This kid is genuine. Endearing. It really looks like he means it."

"That's because you picked him," Melinda winked. "You're so fantastic at everything you do."

Damn, his wife was sexy. All legs and tits in that gown. He couldn't wait to spread the former, then cum on the latter. Maybe even take Hadley home, if Orson didn't want her tonight, though he probably would.

Beautiful as his wife was, hot as Melinda still made him, it was nothing compared to what he felt for this thing they were building together. The same was true for her. Dominic was her first and only love, but he paled to what she felt for Shellter, and all it would usher into the world.

Dominic and Melinda were building something that the world wasn't ready to understand. He admired all that Walt Disney had built before his death and the legacy he left behind him, but the planet was a different place today, and it was ready for the funhouse version. Or it would be soon. And Shellter wanted to build that before anyone else got the idea.

Vice was a bottomless market. The chasm between mainstream and porn was growing ever more narrow. Someone was going to figure out the sweet intersection, and they would be an unstoppable baron in a brand new world. It would either come from massive budgets and pools of talent, with sex scenes that went further than any before them, or some porn would elevate itself and morph into a new form of entertainment with writing and acting that was undeniably worthy of consideration on its own merit. Remakes of classics with full penetration. *Ocean's Eleven* with orgies. It would happen, and Shellter wanted to be bending the curve when it did.

And, because the world deserves a happily ever after, the planet would also be a better place because the normalization of sex was healthy. The shame that America inflicted on its citizens through their pox of shame was a cancer.

The Internet had already begun to end an antiquity of thought that the next generation of entertainment would vanquish forever. Dominic and Melinda would be two of its fiercest crusaders.

"They're coming," Melinda said, giddy and grabbing Dominic's arm.

Hadley led Orson to their private table.

The Shellys stood, then traded kisses with Hadley and handshakes with Orson.

"Thank you for making it on such short notice," Dominic said, clapping Orson on the shoulder and gesturing for him to sit. "Your first red carpet. How did you like it?"

The kid was a thousand watts bright.

"I loved it."

"Was it just like you fantasized?" Melinda asked, more salaciously than she needed to.

"For sure. I mean, you always imagine, of course, and I had a few red carpets when I was a guest during the *F the '90s* days. Well, okay, there were two, but neither one of them was like that because no one said my name or anything, and they didn't care who I was with, and I just walked right into the theater without anyone stopping me."

"People are talking about you now," Melinda said.

Orson blushed, like the perfect specimen he was.

Dominic and Melinda were long-term thinkers. Eventually, they wanted to own a little of everything. But they had to grow it, piece by tiny piece. A production house here, a graphics department there. Two directors. More actors than they could count. A distribution company. A porn studio. A warehouse with empty rooms and modern furniture. Two bars. A lot of empty office space.

Their company was constantly growing, and no one saw the whole picture but them. Whenever the Shellys made money, they spent it on smart ways to make more in the future. They had the house and the cars and the clothes and the dinners because that's what everyone expected. But never more than they needed to play the part. What they really wanted was more of the media pie because one day Shellter would be like Disney, if the House of Mouse were turned upside down.

This kid, Orson Beck, was the next step in the game plan.

And right now it was Melinda's time to shine.

"You looked fantastic out there." She touched Orson on his arm. "But you know that, don't you?"

The kid couldn't stop blushing.

She looked from Hadley to Orson. "The two of you look good together. The cameras love you. Don't forget that. It works for you both."

Hadley beamed, and again the kid blushed.

"You know why you're here, right?" Melinda asked Orson.

He nodded, but he looked unsure, just like she wanted him to.

Dammit, she was great. Again Dominic felt that twitch in his pants.

She put her hand on the kid's. "We need your help, Orson. Will you help us?"

He swallowed. "What do you need?"

"You're going to be a big star. And your star is going to shine its light on all of Shellter Productions. We want you to have it all, Orson Beck. The money, the fame, the life. Everything you've ever dreamed of. Do you want that, Orson?"

He looked her dead in the eye. "I do."

"And are you willing to work hard to get it?"

"I am."

"No matter the cost?"

He nodded, emphatic. "No matter the cost."

"Excellent," Melinda said, beaming. "We believe in win-win relationships, so before you get to the contract and see how the lawyers ruin everything like they always do, with all of their bullshit language, I want to make this simple. Your expectations of us are that we will make you both rich and famous, providing the Hollywood life that you've always dreamed of. And in exchange, you'll follow a few simple rules. Our Ten Commandments, if you will."

"Okay," Orson said.

Melinda slid the card stock across the table. The rules were typed in Courier.

1. *Never miss work under any circumstances without approval.*
2. *Shellter Productions shall have all rights of first refusal.*
3. *All NDAs must be honored.*
4. *Weekly grooming sessions are mandatory.*
5. *Career counseling is a must.*

6. *One-third of all consumed meals must be from Shellter's Nutrition Program.*
7. *All sexual partners must be approved if photographed in your company.*
8. *Any unauthorized sex tapes will become the sole property of Shellter productions.*
9. *All medication must come from authorized doctors.*
10. *No unauthorized interviews.*

ORSON LOOKED up from the rules. His eyes said that they seemed reasonable enough.

Melinda smiled. He smiled back.

So Dominic slid the contract toward him.

Orson signed it without reading a word.

Chapter Nineteen

Life had never been better, but this scene was tripping him out.

"You okay?" the director called out.

Orson nodded at Adrian. "Mind if we take five?"

Adrian nodded and yelled to his cast and crew, "We're taking five!"

A lot softer than Adrian had asked, Hadley said, "You sure you're okay?"

"Yeah." The smile felt uncertain and crooked on Orson's face. "It's just a little weird."

He laughed. It sounded even less certain than he was sure his smile looked.

"Yep." Hadley laughed back, though hers sounded perfectly moored. "Sex scenes are weird."

She playfully swatted at his taped down cock and he pulled away.

"Stop it. People are watching."

"Okay. Whatever, prude. Take your minute. I'm grabbing some coconut water." Then Hadley laughed harder and walked off to the craft service table.

Orson looked around the set, still in disbelief.

It wasn't that his dreams were all coming true, it was more that they now had a schedule.

The Shellys had made him many promises, in exchange for a few vows on his end, and things had been coming up Orson ever since.

The last few months had been a whirlwind of triumph and change. He went home for both Thanksgiving and Christmas, something he'd not done in a while, and never with Connor. It was already one of Orson's favorite memories, watching his boy unwrapping presents from Santa in the home where he'd done the same thing at the same age and with the same ecstatic smile.

His parents had beamed with pleasure and pride. All was forgiven, even with Samuel. Everyone cooed over Connor.

His entire life was now different and new. He lived in the Catalyst overlooking the city. He had no credit card debt, but did have a credit card and a monthly allowance to pay it, in addition to his salary. His savings account was quickly growing. Connor's was exploding. Shellter had a few rules, but they weren't all reasonable or in his interests, he was realizing.

The Shellys had ensured Orson a nice little run-up of small wins leading to their ultimate conquest, which wasn't really much of a conquest at all, since it was almost Calvinistic in its pre-determination.

The role he was rumored to have been up for back in November when he walked that first red carpet with Hadley, then made his dreams come true at a private table upstairs, was his. But it always had been. At least once Orson made the list. He wasn't sure exactly how long that had been in play, since it wasn't like the movie itself could have possibly been written for him, yet the Shellys had clearly been moving pieces around on their board for a while. By the time there was a rumor, it was only reporting on things that were days away from a signature.

The whispers were confirmed, Orson was cast, and that casting triggered an immediate trio of appearances. The first was as a walk-on opposite Angelo Swart in *Nowhere Man*, a serious role. The perfect few minutes to show his serious side before displaying his comedic chops in back-to-back single episode stints on *Is Anyone Out There?* and, ironically, *Greens*. The rumors of his playing Jack Tripper in the upcoming *Three's Company* reboot were ridiculous — they never had a chance because that was never part of the plan — but they kept fans excited about him.

Now it was already February, and they were into the second week of shooting *Bottleneck*, with he and Hadley sharing the spotlight as promised.

He loved the character almost as much as Orson loved his life. Eddie was just enough like him to make the guy easy to sink into, but different enough from Orson that he wasn't playing himself, a Midwestern kid who had spent a few too many of his years, who'd only found direction in his late twenties. In the movie, that direction came from Cassidy, the girl played by Hadley. Cass was an addict who took the worst stuff. Orson had to save her from meth to save himself. Cliché for sure, but the formula worked.

Bottleneck was written and directed by Adrian Frank. He made exactly one movie a year, and they were always gold. Critics loved him and movie buffs opened their wallets. Orson had heard Dominic and Melinda refer to him as 5X because no matter what he spent on a movie, it made at least five times their spend. That had been true now five times in a row.

He was the first director they had "made", and this was

his sixth film, with the biggest budget so far. At 39M, it could hardly be called an indie flick. Orson had some serious doubts that a movie about a meth addict and her loser boyfriend could possibly end up earning nearly 200 million dollars. Orson also didn't understand where all the money was going. The movie was beautifully shot, and the Shellys were paying through the nose for rights to certain music and a few very expensive cameos, but from what he understood about the business, the math wasn't adding up.

But the longer he spent with the Shellys, the less Orson realized he knew.

Dominic told him that most of this movie's budget would be in the marketing, rather than in "idiot advertising." They would be doing it the Shelly Way. It was never made clear exactly what that meant, but the Shellys were proud of their method, and there was zero doubt that it had been working as though crafted by Swiss engineers. When Orson asked Dominic how much of the movie's total budget was earmarked for marketing, the mogul didn't answer. Instead he told Orson a story about how the big cereal companies spent twice as much on getting you to buy the box than they did on the ingredients inside it.

Orson was still in awe of what the makeup, production, and costume artists on this film had done to Hadley. She had to spend several hours in the chair each day to become unrecognizable as her character Cassidy Dawn, a soul-lost junkie in need of redemption. She was a hell of an actress. The girl was wicked smart and driven to kill it.

But today was the second day of something entirely different. Adrian was waiting for the perfect shot, with the sun setting behind them, for a scene that would come somewhere in the middle of the movie, but that he had wanted to shoot last. It was Orson's first sex scene with

Hadley, his first sex scene ever: a drug-crazed orgy that wasn't really an orgy, or drug-crazed, in front of an audience, under far too many lights.

He'd thought he was ready, but it all felt so weird. They'd tried and failed to get the shots the day before.

Someone dropped a robe on his shoulders and Orson was suddenly warm. "Thank you," he said, to no one in particular.

He took a step and suddenly Adrian was walking by his side. His hand found Orson's shoulder and squeezed.

"You did great out there, Orson. You are a seriously talented actor."

"Thank you. Like I've said, I'm a huge fan of your—"

"I appreciate that, Orson. But you don't have to tell me that every time it's just the two of us." Adrian laughed, a light little chuckle. "It's been a month now."

"Of course. Sorry." This still felt so new.

"I just wanted to tell you how impressed I am so far. I don't just believe in this film, I believe in you. And Hadley. The two of you are crackling, and today ..." He whistled.

"Thanks for saying that. Because it felt ..."

"Weird, I know. Sex scenes are weird, and this is your first one. But I've gotta tell you, it doesn't ever look or feel more natural than that. You guys were great. Everyone on set could feel you two. The final shot will be great, then we can call it a wrap."

"That's because it's real," Hadley said, suddenly appearing beside them. She looked at Orson with her adoring eyes. "What we have is really special."

Adrian smiled. "You can tell."

He wondered if Hadley really meant that. Hadley seemed infatuated with him, but like Orson reminded himself every day, Hadley was a hell of an actress.

Orson liked Hadley a lot, but he definitely didn't love her, and he wouldn't let her move into his place, even though she kept hinting and hinting and hinting and hinting, until she finally flat-out asked him last week as they were easing into their final week of shooting, and he had to calmly deny her, even though Orson was feeling agitated at having been put in that position.

Part of him felt so indebted to have the apartment that he was almost willing to agree. But that didn't feel right. If it was supposed to be his space, then it should be *his* space, and if Hadley wanted to come over and fuck him every night, then that was her choice. He offered to come over to her place all the time, and she always refused him. If she was hoping that he'd eventually give in and just tell her to go ahead and bring all her shit over, then she would be waiting forever.

He didn't want to think about Jess, but there she was pushing her way to the front of his mind. Something so simple as the sound of her laugh. Or with the depth of a well like their shared drunken kiss.

He'd been so disappointed that their post-List relationship had been reduced to a few broken phone calls and awkward Wednesday get-togethers that Orson now missed more than he made. He'd thought that once he had something to offer, it would be easier to ask her out on a real date, but now that he was successful, she seemed to like him less and less. When he'd finally invited her to a friendly dinner, to catch up, she'd hesitated so long that he'd been sure she was going to say no.

But she hadn't. Dinner was tomorrow night, and Orson could hardly wait.

Hadley took his face in her hands, and said, "There's nothing I wouldn't do for this man."

Then she kissed him long and full on the mouth.

And Orson kissed her back because people were watching, and in public he had to mean it.

Whether he wanted to or not.

Chapter Twenty

"This is the most fun we've ever had before, isn't it, Daddy?"

Connor beamed up at his father.

"It sure is." Orson beamed back. The best part of his new life meant that he could give Connor all the things he'd never been able to afford before. Whenever he and Connor got to spend any time together, which happened a lot more now than it ever had before, Orson wanted to try and make it *their best time yet.* That was the promise he had made to his son, and he hadn't dropped the ball yet.

He was stacking the adventures in his favor, each one a little bit cooler than the last. Soon they'd have to hit Disneyland, but that was still a ways away. And besides, Connor had already done Disney with Alexis and Tyler, so Orson didn't want to do it until they could stay in one of the hotels and make it a bigger, better memory.

Last week, it had been the Santa Ana Zoo, which was barely a zoo — Orson had gone to a party at Wesley Arlington's house, and that guy probably had a bigger and better collection of animals. But Connor had loved the tiger and the snakes.

The Los Angeles Zoo was that and ten times better. He'd let Connor eat all the hot dogs and ice cream he'd wanted, and they'd spent nearly an hour watching the spider monkeys chase each other and swing from branch to branch.

"What was your favorite thing?" Orson asked Connor in the gift shop — he'd promised his son any toy he wanted. He'd have bought the whole shop for him, except then Alexis would start yelling about how he was spoiling their kid.

"I don't know yet." Connor picked up a stuffed giraffe, examined it like a connoisseur, and carefully put it back on the shelf.

"I don't mean in here. I mean out there." Orson nodded toward the exit.

"Oh. The petting zoo."

That had been Orson's least favorite. Because animals smelled like shit, and except for dogs, he didn't really like to touch them.

"What did you like about it most?"

"Petting the animals."

"Did you know that if you pet them hard enough, you'll turn into a goat?"

Connor laughed. "That's not true."

Until recently, the kid had believed around ninety percent of even Orson's tallest tales. It made Orson both happy to see his son getting smarter and a little sad that he wouldn't be able to play that game much longer.

"Okay, then I guess you'll never get to know what it feels like to be a goat." He picked up a rather friendly looking stuffed gorilla. "How about this guy?"

"I want a shark."

"I don't think they have sharks here."

"Oh," Connor said, looking sad.

"Just pick two. Two is better than a shark."

Connor hung his head, as if remembering a tragic event. "Mom said that I could only bring one home 'cause I've got too many stuffies."

Alexis sure as hell didn't feel that way when she or Tyler were the ones buying them. Connor had a fucking zoo in his bedroom.

"I'll explain to her that you needed two." He handed Connor the gorilla, then grabbed a proud-looking lion, larger than most of the other stuffed animals, from the highest shelf. "This one is for me, but I'd really like to keep him in your bedroom. His name is Leonardo and he likes to watch over all the other stuffed animals. That's why they keep him all the way up here. He can do the same thing in your bedroom, okay?"

Connor looked up at him, his little grin making his face appear larger than usual.

After years of disappointing his son, nothing made Orson happier than seeing Connor's smile and knowing *he* had helped to put it there.

Orson paid for the animals, then they walked hand-in-hand to the new Lexus that he could still barely believe was his, despite the more than 7,000 miles he'd already put on it, making up for all of his time in LA without a car.

"How are you doing back there?" Orson looked in his rearview, delighted to see Connor playing with his stuffed animals. The lion and gorilla were already the best of friends, and seemed to be getting along famously in an exchange of high-pitched gibberish.

"Leonardo is mad at Gabriel because he told him that he couldn't meet his brother."

Connor was starting to not like being an only child,

and had asked Orson more than a few times if he and Mommy were going to give him a brother or a sister. Orson told him no every time. Once Connor had asked, *Is Tyler supposed to do that now?*

That felt like being stabbed in the ribs.

Orson took a breath. "Why doesn't Leonardo want Gabriel to meet his brother?"

"Because his room isn't clean."

"Oh," Orson nodded. "That makes sense."

By the time they made it back to Orson's apartment, he was nervous again. It would be his ex-wife's first visit to his place. She'd hated the Brick, but she'd probably find something wrong with this place too.

The doorbell rang with the discordant notes from *Jaws*. He smiled. Still did every time.

Orson opened the door. Connor rushed past him. "Mommy!"

Alexis smiled at him then reached down to scoop Connor into her arms. "Hello, you little Gobstopper!" She covered him with kisses, then set him back on the floor and took a look around. Connor ran back to his stuffed toys the second his feet hit the floor.

"Impressive," Alexis said to Orson. "You haven't had to blow anyone yet, have you?"

This wasn't her usual bitchiness. She was actually playing with him.

"Not yet. So ... impressed?" It hurt to ask. It would hurt more if she answered wrong.

But she said, "Great job, Orson."

It was remarkable, how much those three words meant to him. His parents had said the same thing, and Samuel, and it nearly sent him to his knees every time. He wasn't the fuck-up that everyone had decided he was after *F the '90s* was cancelled.

"Thanks," was all he managed, before they fell into an awkward silence.

"So," Alexis said, looking at him a little more like she used to. "Connor's party is in a few days."

"Yeah?"

"We're having it at my place. Everyone from his class will be there. Next Saturday 12-4. I'd love it if you could make it … and I know it's short notice. I'm sorry I didn't invite you sooner."

Surprisingly, perhaps even shockingly, it suddenly looked like Alexis might cry.

"Are you okay?" he asked.

"Yeah, I'm fine." She tried to smile, wiping her definitely leaking eyes.

She'd smeared her makeup a little, revealing a small bruise under her right eye. Orson wasn't about to ask; that had never gone over well before. She always shut him down, told Orson to mind his own business. But today, it felt right pulling Alexis into a hug.

She let him, and there she was with her head on his chest, quietly crying.

"I don't want him to see me," she said, turning away so that Orson was obscuring Connor's view.

He held her. There was nothing romantic about it. Certainly not what he felt for Jess, or even for Hadley, but Alexis was the mother of his child, and always would be. He wondered if she felt the same longing for the possibility of what might have been yet could never be again.

Orson's success had come too late for Alexis. And that was probably better for him because he knew in his heart that he could never love Alexis the same way that he could love a woman like Jess. The way she made him laugh and think and feel about himself, she was the heads to Alexis' tails.

But he would always love her as Connor's mother and want to take care of her. At least more than her asshole parents, who hadn't seemed to give a single shit about Alexis through her entire childhood.

Alexis broke away. "Thanks, Orson. It's great to see you doing so well, really. I'm just feeling emotional."

"Because of Connor's birthday?"

"That, and all the shit that comes with it. But …"

Orson couldn't tell if Alexis wanted him to draw it out of her or whether she genuinely didn't want to say.

"You can tell me." Then he added, "I want to hear."

She took a deep breath. "Life is actually going well. Most of it anyway. But honestly, things aren't so great with Tyler, at least not consistently, but personally, I feel like I'm better than ever. I've been reading a lot and working on myself. And obviously things are going great for you. Our son has both of his parents finally figuring things out …" Her voice broke. She choked, swallowed, continued. "It's just too bad that they can't do it *together*."

Orson didn't know what to say. "Alexis …"

"I know, I know," she said, wiping her eyes. "Believe me, I don't think we should be getting back together. I just …"

"I understand."

They shared a moment, the nicest they'd had in years. But before either of them could see where it would go, the door swung open and Hadley entered.

"Knock, knock," she said.

It irritated him that, while he had been able to add his and Connor's thumbprints to the box, Hadley had to help him with both and hadn't deleted hers, or taken the hint. She came and went as she pleased, and Orson hadn't had the balls yet to stop it.

Alexis seemed flustered. "Hi," she said, holding out her hand for Hadley. "I'm Alexis."

"Good to meet you." Hadley gave her a hug instead. "I *love* your son. He is literally the sweetest kid I have ever met."

"Thank you," Alexis said, seeming both pleased and ruffled. "I really should go. I don't want to be in the way." Then, in a louder voice, "Connor!"

Connor came running over with Gabriel and Leo, one in each hand. The lion looked almost big enough to eat him.

"Bye, Daddy!"

"Bye, kiddo." Orson squatted, gave his son a supersized hug, then stood and smiled at Alexis. "I'll see you on Saturday."

She smiled back. "See you on Saturday."

After she left, Hadley said, "What's on Saturday? You getting two weekends in a row again?"

"Connor's birthday party. I was invited."

"Oh, fancy. Do Dominic and Melinda know?" Hadley laughed. "Does Connor's party make the approved list?"

"I hope not," he joked. "I'd like to go off book for once."

But Hadley didn't laugh.

That was the problem with their relationship. Orson was fine following a script when that was part of the job, but he wasn't fine with a *life* full of lines. And that's what his relationship with Hadley felt like far too often.

If only he could make a connection with her that hadn't been orchestrated as part of a publicity campaign, maybe something real could develop between them. But as long she was part of a business arrangement, Orson wasn't all that interested in playing house.

Maybe it was for the best that Hadley couldn't stop

acting, even when they were alone. Because every time they were photographed in public, Orson couldn't help but wonder what Jess was thinking when she saw the photos.

Then he wondered if she even did because Ellis never posted anything about Orson or Hadley. He wasn't sure if Ellis did that out of disgust or respect, and the few times when he'd still show up for their Wednesday date at the Litter Box, Orson hadn't had the balls to ask.

But maybe he'd find out tonight at dinner. He was supposed to pick Jess up in less than two hours.

"So what do you want to do tonight?" Hadley asked, walking toward the kitchen to riffle through his refrigerator like she always did, as though she didn't drink three times more than she ate.

"I told you. I'm having dinner with my friend tonight."

"Oh right," Hadley said, as though she genuinely hadn't remembered. "Your friend Jess."

And here it comes.

Her face looked serious. "Have you told Dominic and Melinda?"

"Like I said, there's no reason to tell them anything. Jess is only a friend."

"They'll want to know."

"Then I'll tell them afterward."

Hadley walked back over from the kitchen and looked Orson in his eyes. "I'm worried about you."

"Why would you be worried about me?"

"I just don't want you to do anything that would jeopardize all of this." She looked around Orson's giant apartment. "Or us. I know we've never said we're exclusive or anything, but I'm really not sure that you should be going on a date."

"It's not a date. But I do need to get ready."

Orson had become an expert at choosing his battles

with Hadley, and this wasn't one he was willing to fight right now. He couldn't let Hadley ruin his evening.

"Are you asking me to go?"

"I can't imagine it's very much fun watching me get ready."

"Want me to come over after?"

Not really.

"If you want."

"You'll probably want to fuck, especially if this really isn't a date and you can't fuck your friend. We can do whatever you want."

His dick twitched. Fucking Hadley. She knew exactly what he was doing.

"I'm not sure when I'll be home."

"Just text me. I'll wait."

"Okay," he said, knowing he wouldn't because he'd rather masturbate and think about Jess than fuck Hadley.

Hadley liked him for what he could do for her career, but Jess had liked him when he had nothing to offer.

He wished he'd realized how much better that was *before* he'd made the Onyx List.

Chapter Twenty-One

Jess showed up early for her dinner with Orson because sitting and waiting at La Boca was infinitely better than doing the same thing on her couch inside her shitty little apartment, which felt even littler and shittier since Orson had moved out. Jess had spent at least a bit of every day since wishing that she could do the same thing herself.

She was surprised when he finally texted her with the invite:

It's been too long. Can I take you to La Boca so we could catch up?

Jess would have preferred something more casual. Hell, she would have been fine if the two of them got together at a stupid Hill of Beans. But if he wanted to show off by dropping a hundred dollars on dinner, she would be grateful for the time and enjoy the unforgettable meal.

But as Ellis kept reminding her, she had to manage her expectations – half the time when Orson made plans to hang out with them, he blew them off. She'd come to La Boca prepared for Orson to let her down. It didn't feel great, but heading into the evening without any armor would be profoundly dangerous.

The whole thing with Hadley hurt Jess a lot more than she wanted to admit. It was like being slapped in the face over and over, every time a picture of Orson and Hadley appeared on *You Didn't Hear It From Me* and a dozen other blogs that she really shouldn't be reading. Every time Orson missed their Wednesday get-together, she couldn't help wondering if he'd stayed home to fuck Hadley.

"Miss Lindley," said a deep, confident voice.

She looked up, surprised to see none other than Dominic Shelly, the man who had taken her Orson away, though Jess would never admit that she had assigned that description to him.

"Yes," she said, lowering her menu.

"It looks like you're waiting for someone. Would you mind terribly if I shared your table in the meantime?"

Jess wondered if this was a coincidence or something else. Orson hadn't said a thing about his boss joining them. If this was a business meeting then she was probably going to throw up in her mouth.

"Okay," she agreed, a little unsure.

Dominic sat, then raised his hand for a waiter. The man appeared as if summoned by magic, making a little bow at the edge of their table.

"Yes, Mr. Shelly?"

"Red or white?" Dominic asked her.

"Red," Jess said, not exactly sure what she was agreeing to because with a Shelly it was surely more than the wine.

"Can we please get a bottle of Bannockburn Serre Pinot Noir for the table please?" He held up his fingers: *Three glasses.*

"Of course, Mr. Shelly," the waiter said before disappearing.

Dominic looked at his watch. "Orson should be joining us in just a few minutes."

"I'm sorry," Jess said. "But will you be eating with us? I really don't mind, it's just that I didn't know. Orson didn't tell me."

Dominic gave her a long, hardy laugh. "No, of course not. I would never want to intrude. I was just hoping for a few minutes with you before he got here."

"With me?" Jess said, surprised. "What could you possibly want with me?"

"I know how important you are to Orson, and that makes you important to me."

He smiled and Jess was surprised to realize that she felt safe next to this man, which was the very opposite of the emotion she had expected to feel. She'd heard some stories, but this man's energy didn't match that narrative at all.

"We're actually not all that close these days," Jess admitted. It was a little like stabbing herself.

Dominic looked pained. He leaned back a little in his seat and shook his head apologetically. "I'm afraid that's at least a little my fault, and why I wanted to talk to you two for a few minutes. I'm glad that you're an early bird." Another smile. "This is a small town, Miss Lindley, and I am a well-connected man. I'm sure it comes as no surprise to you that I've heard a few stories of your escapades."

Jess worked to hold her head high, though every part of her wanted to start inspecting the tablecloth.

Thankfully, the waiter appeared with the bottle of Bannockburn. Following the ritual of presenting, opening, tasting and pouring, and the required sip, the waiter finally left and Dominic got to the point.

"I want to help you."

"Help me? How can you do that?"

"First, I wanted to tell you that I understand. The

stories I've heard … I understand how the media works, especially in this town, and I'm sure that much of what I have heard was surely blown out of proportion. How Orson feels about you is much more important to me."

Dominic was obviously building up to something. He seemed to be carefully choosing his next words.

"I feel like I owe you an explanation."

"Okay," Jess said, now dying of curiosity.

"Hadley …"

He let her name hang.

"Yes?"

"She's …" Dominic leaned across the table. "Just a farce for the press. I don't mean Hadley herself. She's actually a wonderful girl. I mean her relationship with your Orson."

"I don't know that he's my—"

"It's engineered. Probably a lot like those stories about you. I'm sure you've been seeing pictures and reading stories for a couple of months now, and that's likely given you a lot of doubt around your relationship with Orson. How are you supposed to feel about him now, or all the things that are happening? You're a good friend, so you want to feel happy, but you can't ignore the hurt that you feel whenever you see a picture of Hadley. Am I right?"

This was creepy. How did one of the most powerful men in Hollywood know so much about her personal life?

"I feel responsible for a lot of that. So that's why I'm here, Miss Lindley. To give you and Orson my blessing."

"I don't know that …"

But now Jess couldn't finish because Orson was approaching their table. He slowed when he saw her, and by the look on his face, Dominic's presence at their table was just as big of a surprise to him.

So Orson hadn't been involved in the orchestration of this conversation. That made her feel better.

Dominic stood. Slapped Orson on the shoulder with one palm and vigorously shook his hand with the other. "So glad to see you. Sit."

Dominic gestured at the empty seat. Orson obeyed.

Then he said, "I'm sorry, Mr. Shelly, but I'm on a date with Jess."

Dominic's eyebrows went up, and fear flashed across Orson's face.

"I mean, I'm not sorry that I'm on a date with Jess, I mean that we're not really going to be able to share this time with you, and I'm sorry that I know I broke one of the rules by being here and not telling you. But Jess is important to me. I'm done playing house with Hadley. I hate it, and this dinner tonight is long overdue."

Orson wanted this to be a *date* date? Not a casual friends-catching-up date? Jess had to hide a grin. She'd been so afraid to hope.

Orson looked at her and smiled, seeming a little more certain by the word.

"This is the one rule I have to break, no matter the cost. But I'd prefer that we don't look at it that way. I'm confident that we can make this work. There must be other ways that Hadley and I can boost each other's careers."

Silence was like thunder in the desert, but then Dominic's laugh was the lightning.

"I'm proud of you," Dominic said. "And I agree. It's excellent to see your instincts so sharp on this one. The difference between the good and the great in this game is that the great know when to follow their gut. That's what you did here tonight, first by making this date with Jess, then by telling me your feelings in no uncertain terms. You didn't break any of the rules, my boy. You helped to define them. That's what you're supposed to do."

He poured Orson a glass, then added, "Lao Tzu said, 'Being deeply loved by someone gives you strength, while loving someone deeply gives you courage.' I don't know if this is love—" He looked from Orson to Jess. "—But it deserves a chance."

He raised his glass, looked Orson in his eyes, and said, "I'm nothing without my Melinda, and Hadley can never be that for you."

"Thank you," Orson said, looking relieved. "Tomorrow I'll—"

"Don't worry about Hadley. I'll handle her." Dominic stood. "Enjoy the bottle, and please order another. They have my card and dinner's on me. Thanks for indulging me."

Then he was gone.

"Well," Jess said. "Now that we have permission …"

Chapter Twenty-Two

Orson hugged Jess closer.

The feel of her bare skin against his waking him with a jolt. Last night had been …amazing. They'd drunk the whole bottle of ridiculously expensive wine and another one after that. By the time dinner was over, Jess was looking at him the way she used to. Like Orson was the most important person in her world, and she wanted to make him happy.

Ironic, because all he wanted was to make her happy.

They'd spent the rest of the night making each other happy then happier.

Jess woke up and made a little humming in the back of her throat, then whispered, "Good morning."

"Good morning. Or great. Can I say, 'Great morning'? Is that a thing?"

"We could make it one."

"Great morning then."

She finally sat up with her shoulders resting on the backboard. "I have the *worst* headache. I wish I didn't feel so hung over."

"I know what'll help." Orson led Jess toward the balcony.

She balked on the threshold. "I'm naked."

"I'll fix that." He packed her a bowl of Green Unicorn, handed her the pipe, then retrieved one of his button-downs from Crossroads.

She put it on, while he shimmied into last night's pants, then offered her a lighter.

She took a deep drag from the pipe, then handed it to Orson. It was Italian glass and embarrassingly expensive. The thing had cost enough that he felt compelled to give it a name: *Pipette*, since it was Italian.

As soon as the buzz rolled through him, he wanted to make love to her again.

But it looked like he wasn't going to get the chance because his phone buzzed, and Dominic's name was on the screen.

"I have to go," he said. "But you can totally stay here if you want to."

"Will Hadley drop by? Because if so, no thanks."

"Good point. I'm sure she's super pissed. I didn't even text her back last night."

"Good luck with that."

"Ugh."

"Yeah, sorry you've had to fuck a model for the last couple of months. That must have been rough on your dick."

"Only on my heart," Orson was surprised to hear himself say.

Jess looked surprised, too. She stood to kiss him. Then she pulled away and said, "What did it say? The text, I mean."

"Just that Dominic wants to talk about some movie."

"*Bottleneck?*"

"No." He shook his head. "Something else. A Grady Blum project, and the Shellys want me to audition. So I'm sure there's been something there, and they always like to talk in person. They're not big on texts or phone calls except to tell me to get the hell down there."

Jess glanced back into his apartment. "Seems fair. And wow, Grady Blum."

"I know, right?" Orson laughed. "So, we'll continue this later?"

"I can't wait."

Another kiss and a reminder that all she had to do was leave and the door would auto-lock, but that she wouldn't be able to get back in, so she would need to make sure she grabbed everything before it shut behind her.

Then one last kiss after that.

Twenty minutes later, Orson sat on the other side of Dominic's Texas-sized desk, listening to Dominic's update on the newest Grady Blum, a movie called *Farewell, Atlantis.*

"It's already been decided that the Abraham role will be going to either you or one other actor."

He couldn't believe this. Grady Blum wasn't just one of the most well-respected directors in the world, he was one of Orson's favorites. The Shellys clearly weren't just worried about his box office potential, they wanted him to garner a bit of critical acclaim.

Orson tried to sound casual, like he wasn't practically peeing his pants at the chance to work with Blum. "Who's the other actor?"

"Tyler Crane. As in, your ex's present beau."

Of all the answers he'd been expecting … How was he supposed to handle this? Was he supposed to declare war on his enemy? Or did Dominic expect him to be happy no matter who got the part?

"How important is this for me to get?"

Dominic laughed. "If I were you I'd want to stick it to the guy who's giving it to my ex. But forget about that. This is the movie that changes everything for you. And I mean *everything.* You know Blum. His movies make money, but that's not the point. They're big for everyone involved because he only makes the kind of movies that people like to talk about."

"Do I really have a chance?" Orson asked, hating that he was doubting himself and knowing that Dominic would likely hate it too. "I mean, I'll do whatever you tell me to, but I'm just wondering because the media really seems to love him and—"

"Crane's a pretty boy pile of shit. Believe me, people would much rather see someone like you land this role. You just need to give them a reason to pick you over him, then prove that you were the right choice. Have you been studying the script?"

"I know it by heart."

"Good boy."

"Anything else I can do before the audition?"

"One thing." Dominic's face changed. Still friendly, but more serious. Almost concerned. He picked up his tablet, turned it on, showed the screen to Orson.

His heart fell on top of his toes. He could barely breathe.

"Holy. Shit."

"Exactly," Dominic agreed.

It was the gossip site *You Didn't Hear It From Me.* Above the picture of a very naked Jess holding *Pipette* in one hand and Orson's shirt in the other, her most sensitive areas sanitized with neat black bars across them, read the headline: *Hollywood's Newest Brightest Star Meets an Old Bad Seed!*

Jess was going to be devastated. And it was all Orson's fault.

"Do you want to explain this?" Dominic asked.

Orson didn't even know where to start. "How did they—"

"What is your new girlfriend doing out there on the balcony, naked as jailbait on Chat Roulette?"

She wasn't on the balcony, Orson wanted to protest, but what difference did that make?

He was so stupid, not realizing that an asshole with a telephoto lens could take a picture from who knows how far away? Whoever it was could've been hiding on the roof of the next building or peeking out through a window across the street.

"Your new girlfriend that I approved not even twenty-four hours before this picture was taken, I should add."

Dominic looked expectantly at Orson.

"I'm sorry. I don't know what to say. Jess doesn't deserve this. She's the nicest girl I know."

"That doesn't matter." He turned the tablet around, swiped, then spun it back to Orson, showing him the many ways that Jess was getting dragged through the mud in the gossip rags. "The truth doesn't matter. That's always been true, but never more so than now. Perception is everything, and the perception here sucks. You see her as a sweet Midwestern girl, but as of this morning, everyone else sees her as a temptress corrupting the new kid that everyone is ready to love. The world loves a villain, and it looks like she's stepped into that role in your story."

Horrified, Orson kept swiping. Dominic had prepared quite the queue. Headlines came in three varieties. *Bad seed ruins golden boy, home wrecker works to destroy Orson and Hadley,* and *Jess Lindley is at it again.*

The sites decayed in quality by the swipe. Soon Orson hit the ones where there were no black bars around their privates. He didn't mind that he was there in all of his glory, but Jess? When she saw these …

He'd dragged her right back into the worst part of this industry, the part that had driven her right to addiction. How he could ever possibly make any of this right?

And what about Hadley? Not that Orson was overly concerned about their artificial relationship, but even if it was all just a farce, seeing this would still hurt her for sure.

Orson looked up from the tablet.

Dominic said, "You promised that you could handle this. Do you still feel confident?"

His heart wanted to pound right out of his chest. "Yes. I'll land the role in *Atlantis* and get this stuff with Jess under control."

"Great. You can see her later. Right now you have something more urgent to take care of."

"Just tell me what to do."

Dominic pointed to the tablet, one of the fully exposed pictures of Orson. "We'll work to get these taken down, at least the ones that aren't redacted. There's nothing we can do about the other ones. But in the meantime, that's just embarrassing. You have some grooming to do."

He handed Orson a card. "You'll need to hurry. Your appointment is in less than half an hour."

Orson would rather face down a hundred Hadleys.

Chapter Twenty-Three

Jess was on the verge of a panic attack.

She hadn't been paying attention to her phone, so when she finally grabbed it — after a long, hot, and delicious shower, where she gave herself the seconds she was hoping to get from Orson that morning — and saw all of her texts from Ellis, along with a trio of missed calls, she had to pick her racing heart up right off the floor.

She should've known there'd be paparazzi stalking Orson. She should've remembered what it was like to be hounded by the pack of coyotes that were the mainstream news and the vultures who wrote for the tabloids, looking for a scrap of flesh they could turn into profit.

She should've been the one teaching Orson how to protect himself against the clicking cameras and the barrage of questions that no human had the right to ask another one.

But instead, she'd acted like the most naïve of starlets, so intoxicated with Orson after wanting him for so long.

She didn't even have an agent to help her counteract the tidal wave of shit about to roll through her life.

The tabloids painted her as a party girl, but really, the coke and oxy had been the only thing that buffered the constant, crushing pressure of knowing every moment belonged to the world, that every comment could be a career-ender, and that every smile deepened the lines in her face that would make her *too old* for leading roles by the time she turned thirty.

The Hades of addiction wasn't her fault. It had been theirs. Everyone who'd speculated on whether or not she'd had a nose job, would have a nose job, should have a nose job but was stubbornly sabotaging her own career by not getting one.

Everyone who'd whispered that she hadn't earned her big break, that she'd blown a director, a producer, an orgy of producers.

Everyone who complimented Jess' performances to her face and wrote scathing reviews online afterward.

She wanted to scream, but she couldn't breathe.

Orson's text: *r u ok?*

How could he even ask that? Knowing what she'd been through before?

Back when she'd been in recovery, her therapist had told her over and over that it didn't help to blame others, that she needed to take responsibility for her choices if she wanted to make better ones in the future.

And that future was finally here.

It was her fault for not warning Orson that even when he thought he was alone, he might not be.

It was her fault for letting Orson lead her toward the open balcony before she'd dressed.

It was her fault, for not acknowledging to herself what a big deal Orson was now. She'd gotten so used to thinking of them in the same place, former actors who'd moved on to real life.

She wasn't going to blame him or anyone else. She was going to take responsibility for this mess and make sure it didn't happen again.

So she texted back: *Fine. Sorta. When can I see you?*

Not sure. Soon. Have an errand first.

He'd been naked in that photo too. Did he not care? What could possibly be more important than coming up with a plan for damage control?

Maybe he had a plan and the errand was step one.

What kind of errand?

I don't want to say, lol.

???

I have to go in for a grooming session. They're going to manscape me.

Seriously? That was his idea of damage control? Make sure that the next naked photo was more stylish?

Jess was starting to wonder if maybe she didn't know Orson as well as she thought. *That sounds miserable.*

I'm sure it will be. The place is called Pretty Pretty Pussycat, so I'm sure I'll be the only dude for miles. It's across the street from the Shellter offices.

Okay, so it probably wasn't his idea. That made her feel better, although she still wished that Orson demonstrated some sense that he understood how awful this felt for her. But that was a conversation she'd rather have in person. So she tried to turn it into a joke.

Makes sense. That area has a lot of hairy pussies in desperate need of waxing.

Can't wait to see you. Maybe lunch after?

I'm still at your place. I'll get dressed and head over.

Great, Orson texted. *I can't wait to see you.*

Jess called a FASTr and waited outside.

Twenty minutes later she was at Market Plaza, the elegant strip mall (if that wasn't an oxymoron) across the street from Shellter Productions. It had all the usual suspects: a Provisions, a Hill of Beans, an Inside Scoop, and a Pretty Pretty Pussycat.

Jess was looking around at the selection of fast casual restaurants when she saw Dominic across the way.

Their eyes met. He looked surprised, then … *sorry?*

He walked briskly over and gently took her hands, shaking his head.

"I'm so sorry. I wish I could say that I can't believe it, but I'm used to the press in this town. Fucking parasites, all of them."

The way he stood over Jess, holding her hands and offering words of comfort reminded Jess of the dad she'd left behind in Skokie.

Dominic glanced at the pink-and-black sign hanging over Pretty Pretty Pussycat and gave Jess a hearty chuckle. "You'll love it, I'm sure. Melinda definitely does. But you're going to have a helluva wait. This process isn't fast, especially the first time. They did a little trimming for *Bottleneck*, but it was nothing like this. Have you eaten?"

"Orson and I were going to eat, after he's finished."

"Come on," Dominic said, again taking her by the hand. "We're going to lunch."

It was the last thing she expected — he'd been so kind to her, despite his reputation as a ball-buster, but that was probably one more thing the press manufactured to sell ads.

Was it possible that Dominic could help her weather this with the grace that she'd so sorely lacked the last time she'd been at the center of a scandal?

He took her arm and began to question her as they walked, starting with how she was feeling and transitioning into what she saw as her next best move and what did she want to do with the rest of her life? Before she knew it they were across the street and walking through the lobby of Shellter Productions.

"I thought we were going to lunch."

Dominic laughed. "You deserve the best, and that's what you're going to get."

Minutes later they passed through his office, then through another door.

Dominic opened it and gestured for Jess to step inside. When she did, she understood.

Of course the man would have his own private dining suite. He walked to the small table, with a small intercom box and a setting for one, and pulled out a chair for Jess. She sat and he followed, but before Dominic's ass had kissed the seat, another door on the opposite side of the suite swung open and a chef sauntered into the room, dressed in his whites.

"Good afternoon, Warren. My apologies for the lack of notice, but we have an extra guest for lunch today. This is Miss Jessica Lindley."

"Good to meet you, Miss Lindley," Warren bowed. "Is there anything I can start you off with to drink?"

"No, thank you." Jess shook her head, feeling embarrassed.

"Any dietary concerns I should be aware of?"

This was kind of amazing. "Um … no. But thank you for asking."

A smile. "Of course, Miss Lindley."

Warren left and Dominic smiled like he was juggling an armload of secrets.

"What?" Jess asked.

"You just have no idea what you're in for. Warren is really something else."

"I can't wait," she said, surprised to find her mouth filling with saliva. A few minutes ago she'd thought she might never be hungry again.

There were three promised courses, all of them small, and all of them amazing. The first was some sort of shrimp dish, but it wasn't prepared like anything Jess had ever eaten before, and she didn't really know how to describe it other than something where the seafood melted in her mouth and the breading simply dissolved.

They were on the second course now with a second pairing of wine. This was a Cornish game hen roasted in a truffle sauce.

She was enjoying the food so much that she'd forgotten who she was talking to, so she was blindsided by Dominic's question.

"After all the success you had, I've gotta ask, *Why did you give it up?*"

"I didn't give it up. I was spit out. I didn't have a choice."

"You should have stuck it out, if you'll forgive my saying so. I know this business, and you could have been very, very successful. You have a terrific look. Classic. And you're a writer first, I can find you twice as many opportunities as I could for an actress like Hadley."

Jess laughed. Loud and long and bitter. "Any chance I had was shot to hell with those photos this morning. They make me look like a whore."

"They don't make you look like a whore."

"Well, that's what everyone is saying anyway."

"That's what they do. This will all go away." He put his hand on hers, but it was kind, fatherly. Jess didn't feel threatened at all. Only comforted. "In the meantime, I really should apologize."

"Apologize?"

"Of course. I can't help but feel that some of this is my fault. You were thrust into this all so quickly, and we didn't really have a plan for what might happen after dinner. I should have taken care of that." He gave himself an admonishing laugh. "I sure as hell know better."

"None of this is your fault. You were trying to help us!"

"Fat lot of good I did. Now I have Hadley mad at me, my rising star in the wrong kind of spotlight, and a sweet innocent like you getting tarred and feathered." He waited a beat, then said, "Let me make it up to you."

"What do you mean?"

"I can look into some potential auditions, see what strings I can pull, because again, I think you have genuine potential. It's not just that you could make it, it's that you're the kind of girl who could make it *big*. You came close once, and with the right help you could do it again."

"I don't know …"

"I insist. Not that you do it, but that you at least *think* about it. Show up for one audition and see how you feel. Believe me, this is the best way to fight the press. You can forget it entirely because in a day they'll be talking about something else. But you're on their radar right now, so if you want to leverage some of that attention and get a little love from Shellter to help you on your way, you might be looking at that big second chance that you rarely ever even allow yourself to believe you deserve."

It all sounded so wonderful and terrible and scary, because even though she'd been telling herself for years that she was happier living a humble life, staying clean, making a decent living, there was a part of her that desperately wanted what Orson had lucked into.

And she'd learned her lesson, hadn't she?

With the help of an agency like Shellter and with Orson at her side, she could be one of those stars who managed to stay grounded even as their career took off like a rocket.

"I promise," Dominic said, "this is the one thing in the world that will make you forget that mess."

Was this her second chance? Or her biggest temptation yet?

"Just say yes, Jessica. Then everything changes."

She thought about her shitty apartment and Dominic's elegant one.

She thought about how hard it would be to afford the kind of clothes she'd be expected to wear if she was going to be seen on Orson's arm at events.

She thought about how exhausted she was of pretending she didn't care about everything she'd lost.

Her answer came out as a squeak. *"Yes."*

"Good. Now let's celebrate."

Jess was expecting dessert, maybe champagne to go with it. But what Dominic pulled out of his jacket pocket, she should have seen coming.

"I've got a new guy." His smile was proud, like he had manufactured the snow himself. "This is the best bump you'll ever have." He laughed. "It's the best I've ever had, *and I've had a lot.*"

Dominic set his vial to the side, laid out a pair of lines on the mirror, snorted one down to nothing, then looked up at Jess.

Maybe he saw the look on her face, or smelled her sweat. The way she was shifting in her seat and clenching her fists, he had to know how uncomfortable she was.

He stopped, seeming horrified.

"I am so sorry." Dominic looked down at the mirror,

embarrassed. "I don't know what I was thinking, when you've worked so hard to quit. This stuff is the best, and I suppose I got carried away. Please forgive me."

Jess flushed. Even being *around* cocaine was difficult, especially since she had been slacking so often on her meetings. Life got hard, and she kept promising herself that she'd go tomorrow.

"It's okay," she said, even though her heart was punching holes right through her.

She remembered the rush, the smell, the nirvana massaging her cells.

"It's not." He picked up the mirror and dropped it in the trash.

His intercom buzzed. Dominic gave her a look — *Sorry* — then answered.

"Yes?"

"Harrison is here to see you."

"Shit." Then to the intercom. "Tell him I'll be right out."

Jess had to stop staring the vial. Her palms were sweating, and it was everything she could do not to grab it. She forced herself to look at Dominic as he stood.

"I'm so sorry, but I can't cancel this meeting. Orson will tell you, I never want to keep my actors waiting. Please, enjoy dessert. And don't worry about a thing. I'll make some calls and we'll get everything back on track for you. Don't give those pictures a second thought. In another week, no one else will either."

Then Dominic left, but Jess still had plenty of company. Not only was she stuck in her chair with all the regrets and doubt and every one of her insecurities, not only was she a slave to the relentless thoughts that kept stomping through her mind, she was also in arm's reach of the one thing that would dissolve her panic and fill her with confidence. Enough to make it through the next few days, until the world forgot what she looked like naked.

All she had to do was reach out and grab it.

So she did.

Chapter Twenty-Four

Orson had never seen Jess with so much energy. She seemed so happy, and she'd barely stopped talking since he'd picked her and Ellis up. Maybe she was as excited as he was for Connor's birthday party. He had a crazy amazing present for his son... And he was so grateful to Alexis for including him.

"There's no way that Connor's gonna be the only kid at this party, right?" Ellis asked.

Jess laughed. "I thought you liked kids! You're always talking about how much fun you have with Connor."

"That's because Connor is awesome. But most kids suck. Practically all of them."

"I can guarantee other children," Orson said. "Many of them. But seriously, thanks for coming."

"Of course," Jess said, then launched into yet another story. Once again, she seemed to be answering a question that no one had been asking. "The best birthday party I ever went to was when my friend Stephanie turned thirteen. Her mom was kind of cool but also kind of not, and she was always trying to teach people things. So she had

Stephanie's birthday party at Target. She gave us each a $25 gift card, and so for a while it was like totally awesome because we could pick out anything we wanted, and I already had a ten dollar bill from my grandpa because he knew I was going to Target and he always liked to spoil me. So we picked out all of our stuff and I had three graphic tees, and I even remember that one of them said, *Dinosaurs didn't read and look what happened to them.* I also had a single for that song *Smooth* and other stuff I don't remember. But then once we had all of our stuff at the counter, Stephanie's mom made us put everything back, then she showed us all the 'proper way to shop,' which basically amounted to buying a bunch of shit that no one wanted. And none of us were allowed to get anything from the dollar bins because it was 'all totally junk, and a terrible deal even at a dollar.' When Stephanie sent out her thank you cards, they were actually apology letters."

"What kind of shit?" Ellis asked.

Orson wished he hadn't. Jess had barely taken a breath through the last unfurling of words.

But her answer was mercifully short. "Bullshit."

Orson pulled up in front of the house, feeling pride, not just that he was bringing his friends in a Lexus, and not just because of the box he had for Connor waiting in the trunk, but because he had always been envious of this place, felt like a shit-heel every time he'd compared it to his apartment at the Brick. But now, his pad at the Catalyst was nicer, and Shellter surely paid more for it each month than Alexis did for her mortgage.

Outside of the car Ellis, glanced at the trunk. "Need any help carrying that beast of a present?"

"It's not that big." Orson glanced at the house. "I hope her parents are here."

Jess raised her eyebrows. "I thought you hated her parents."

"I do. They're terrible people who've shit on me since the second we met. I can't wait for them to see how well I'm doing."

"The miniature Tesla will definitely do that," Ellis said, "among other things."

Jess started another story. "Did I ever tell you about the time I wanted to see a movie on Valentine's Day, but the guy I was with was totally not into anything other than being a creep, and washing and waxing his bright yellow Nissan XTerra ..."

Orson fell back a few steps and whispered to Ellis, "She seem a little off to you?"

"She's been like this for a couple of days. It's a lot." He looked concerned. "But shit, man, the last few months were rough. Mostly because of you. No offense."

None taken, but shit.

"Maybe it's how she's coping with the photo? She hasn't wanted to talk about it at all, even though she has wanted to talk about everything else on Wikipedia."

"... So like, literally, anyone could come out and see us at any time, but at that point I didn't even care because I'd gone from being bored to really, really horny."

She stabbed the doorbell. "You've been there, right?"

Tyler opened the door.

Of course.

Orson had been trying not to think about Tyler. He had to know by now that they were both vying for the same role. Would he acknowledge it? Or would the two of them play chicken throughout the party?

"Hey guys!" Tyler said, happy as always. Fucking actor. Then to Orson, "You brought guests."

"It's a party. Alexis always tells me to bring my friends."

"Yeah, of course. Hey Ellis, hey Jess." He nodded at Orson's box. "Want me to take that?"

Orson handed it over, imagining Connor ripping it open, then the look on Tyler's face.

"Party's out back. Make yourselves at home."

Then Tyler disappeared into the kitchen, and the three of them went out back.

But it wasn't much of a party. Alexis had said that Connor's class would be there, but he only saw a handful of kids and parents, the kids blowing bubbles and the adults in clusters, having subdued conversations. Suddenly Orson felt like an idiot for inviting Jess and Ellis.

"This rocks," Jess giggled.

Ellis shushed her, but couldn't help laughing a little as well. To Orson he whispered, "Do you think her parents are still coming? They wouldn't want to miss this, would they?"

"Fuck you," Orson muttered, casting his eyes around for Alexis. Then, "I'll be back."

He wanted to find his ex-wife, but he also wanted to look around her place. She was always *on him* every time he had been over before. He'd never had carte blanche to wander the hallways. That had always been fine with Orson before. But now that he had something to compare it all to and no longer felt like a nothing, he was eager to measure his worth against hers.

It was beautiful. Not Hollywood mansion amazing, but a lot of thought and money had gone into making it feel like a home. Alexis' thought and Tyler's money.

On the way back through the sunken living room on his way to the kitchen, he heard a commotion through a closed door behind him. It was Alexis for sure, in her highest pitched voice, the one she used when yelling at him.

He crept closer to the door, then put his ear against it.

"Let me go!" he heard Alexis say.

Then, a male grumble that he couldn't untangle. That had to be Tyler. What was the golden boy doing now?

Orson thought of the bruises, the one he'd asked about and all the others that he'd pretended not to see.

"I said let me go!"

Orson burst into the room. Tyler had Alexis roughly by her arm, and his expression was nothing that the cameras had captured before. His skin was red and his eyes three shades darker. His shoulders were hunched forward like a predator. He turned toward Orson, eyeing him like prey.

"Let her go," Orson said.

"Get the fuck out of here, Beck."

"Let. Her. Go."

Tyler gave Alexis a shake. "What are you going to do?"

Orson marched over and gave Tyler a shove, just enough that he had to let go of Alexis to keep his balance.

Alexis retreated, falling back several steps away from Tyler and Orson.

"You're out of line," Tyler said.

"If protecting a woman when she's being abused makes me out of line, then I'd like to stay right where I am and maybe buy a timeshare."

"You? Or the Shellys?"

But Orson just laughed. "You're an asshole, Tyler."

Alexis finally spoke. "I want you to go."

"You heard her," Tyler said.

"I was talking to *you.*"

Tyler looked slapped. He gave Alexis an *I'll take care of you later* look, mumbled, "I don't need this bullshit," then left, slamming the door behind him.

"Are you okay?" Orson asked.

Alexis looked shaken, and slightly surprised, though that seemed like it had more to do with Orson's interference than with Tyler's aggression. For the second time in a week, he found Alexis looking at him like she used to.

His shoulders suddenly felt tight. It wasn't that he wanted anything romantic with Alexis, but her look was a reminder of what they once had, what Tyler could have now, if he weren't so selfish. It struck him as so deeply, righteously unfair. Orson was a good guy who always tried his hardest, intent on doing the right thing. But the big opportunities always went to guys like Tyler. Self-centered assholes with at least two personalities.

Tyler didn't deserve the roll in *Farewell, Atlantis*. Orson had never felt more driven to take it from him. Tyler had everything: his gig on one of TV's biggest sitcoms, the steady paycheck that came with it, and a life with Orson's ex-wife and child. Worst of all, the media loved him.

Maybe that was the takeaway.

Maybe the media didn't love him because he got what he wanted. Maybe Tyler got what he wanted because the media loved him.

"Thank you," Alexis said, looking a few words from tears.

"Of course." Orson didn't want to pry, but it felt worse not to ask. "How often does that kind of thing happen?"

"Not that often," she said.

"How often really?"

Then she started to cry. "All the time."

"I'm so sorry."

Orson pulled Alexis into a hug and held her. In the silence of their embrace, he could hear another unsettling sound from somewhere in the house, what sounded like arguing.

They pulled apart and he said, "Do you hear that?"

She nodded then walked toward the door.

Orson followed Alexis to the kitchen, where he was shocked to see Hadley and Jess standing toe-to-toe, with Ellis slightly off to the side, eyeing the exchange with obvious concern.

"What are you doing here?" Orson said to Hadley.

She spun around, turning her attention from Jess to Orson. "I'm here because it's my boyfriend's son's fifth birthday party, and that seemed like something I should be a part of. But you've been avoiding me all week. You haven't answered a single one of my calls since all of those pictures of you with this slut last weekend!"

Jess screamed, "I'm not a slut!"

What the fuck?

Was Hadley seriously this nuts? They weren't together; they'd never been. Maybe this was his fault for not just calling her and being straight, but after his conversation with Dominic, he'd figured that any sort of breakup would be automatically taken care of for him. Why should Orson have to manage a breakup when the relationship wasn't even real and had never been his idea?

Jess and Hadley snarled at each other, their faces just inches apart.

"That's really interesting because you sure look like a slut in all of your pictures, hanging out on my boyfriend's balcony with your tits—"

Jess screamed, "*He's not your boyfriend!*"

She launched herself at Hadley.

"Stop it!" Alexis yelled.

Ellis grabbed Jess, and Orson caught Hadley around the waist. But the cats were clawing and it wasn't easy to tear them apart.

The sliding glass door screeched open on its rollers, and curious spectators started spilling in from outside.

Hadley was holding her own, but Orson was surprised by Jess.

He'd never seen her like this. His dream girl was practically foaming at the mouth.

Jess lurched out of Ellis' arms and was back on Hadley, grabbing her away from Orson and toppling her to the ground. He pulled at Hadley, but Jess was too strong.

Now Ellis was in the thick of it, pulling at Jess along with Orson.

But she was too strong for them both.

Too out of control.

As Jess pushed her knee down into Hadley's chest and punched her, Orson was horribly aware of all the phones, streaming the fight to the world.

And now Orson would have to explain this to Dominic.

Chapter Twenty-Five

Orson couldn't help but remember the time that Daniel Bellinger came up behind him with a handful of open ketchup packets at lunch, pretended to punch him, and got ketchup all over his face and clothes. Mrs. Henderson thought they were fighting and — thanks to the school's zero tolerance policy — sent both boys to the principal's office. Orson hadn't even done anything, and he'd gotten a week of detention anyway.

He may as well have been sitting in front of the principal now, here in Dominic's office, waiting for the man to scold him. Orson had let him down again. It just kept happening, and he didn't know how to stop it. He sure as hell wasn't trying to end up in another shitty headline, but he could already hear Dominic's response to the excuse that Orson wouldn't even dare to make:

Well, you're sure as hell not trying hard enough to avoid it!

And maybe he was right. The paparazzi were a lot harder to manage than Orson had anticipated.

Not even the paparazzi. This time it was a bunch of

soccer moms posting the fight to LiveLyfe because how could they resist? Video of three celebrities kicking and scratching on a kitchen floor. That shit would go viral for sure and elevate Molly's profile for years.

Images of the two girls throwing blows, or at least of Hadley taking it from his girlfriend, were now all over the net. There were a *lot* of stories, and none of them were favorable to Jess. Two scandals in one week, after Orson had promised that he would have all of this under control.

To Orson's shock, Dominic smiled.

Then he started to laugh.

"You don't get it, do you?" he asked.

No, Orson didn't. They were watching the video together, though Orson had already seen it plenty and would be perfectly happy if he never saw it again. It felt a few hundred times more fucked than funny.

"I guess not," Orson said.

Jess was a wreck after they'd left Connor's party, and she'd sobbed and ranted for the rest of the night. Now she was getting crucified online. The blogs were all making her out to be some sort of monster. To be fair, Hadley might not have been Orson's favorite person, but she didn't deserve this. If he hadn't already been in love with Jess, he might have fallen for Hadley. Under normal circumstances.

She never would have looked your way under normal circumstances.

"Two beautiful women are fighting over you, Orson. Can you really not see how good that is for you? How much attention you're getting because of it?"

"It doesn't feel positive," Orson admitted. "I mean, we're all in the news, yeah, but I don't see how that's good for any of us. This is bad publicity."

"You've never heard the saying, *there's no such thing as bad publicity?*"

"Sure, I've heard it. But--"

Dominic laughed as though Orson had delivered a punch line. "You ever hear of the Sleeper Effect?"

"No." And now he felt dumb.

"Take a well-known author, say Stephen King, Nora Roberts, whoever. They get a positive review on their new book. It's gonna boost their sales by like thirty to forty percent. Makes sense. But an unknown author with an absolute shit review is going to get that same boost because until that bad review, nobody knew who in the fuck they were. Remember Borat and all his bullshit about Kazakhstan? All of a sudden, tourist trade spikes. Or what about when Michael Jackson had his fingers in all those little boys' buttholes while sales were going through the roof?"

Orson stared at Dominic, hoping his horror didn't show on his face.

"You'll get used to all of this. But believe me when I say that your star is on the rise and that Shellter is very, very happy. We know exactly how to leverage this."

"I still don't know what that means."

"Over time, people are aware of a name, like say *Orson Beck* or *Hadley Witt*. But then they forget where they heard that name, and they only know that it means something for some reason. But they're primed to give it attention when that attention actually matters. Are you getting this?"

"What about names like *Jessica Lindley?*"

"It'll all blow over. Or not, if she doesn't want it to. I'm sure she's told you that I offered to make a few calls?"

She had. And Orson wasn't sure how he felt about that at all. Not because he didn't want Jess to be successful, if she wanted that, but she'd spent so much time since he'd met her insisting that she didn't.

It almost felt like she wasn't his Jess anymore, if she

could change her mind about something that big without warning.

"So she can wait for this to all go away so she can disappear, or she can use it to get the kind of roles that fit with how people see her. She has opportunities now that she didn't last week."

Orson shook his head. "This isn't what she wanted. Hadley, either."

"Don't worry about Hadley. She understands the game. She won't press charges, so Jess has nothing to worry about, and I'll make sure she's taken care of."

I thought you'd already done that.

But Orson didn't dare voice that thought.

Dominic continued. "Your job right now is to focus on your audition tomorrow. We're batting a thousand, so long as that part doesn't go to Crane. Where was he during all of this, anyway?"

"He wasn't there."

"Oh?"

"Yeah. He had to run out."

Dominic looked curious, but apparently wasn't going to press it. He stood.

Meeting over.

"Have some perspective. You've seen enough movies to know how this works. Even if things work out for the hero, nothing can be handed to him. Our protagonists must be tested, punished so that they can grow. And really, if your *punishment* is only having two beautiful women publicly fighting for your affections, then you should count yourself among the lucky ones."

"I do," Orson said. Dominic had a way of making him feel ungrateful, even when he wasn't.

"Go home and do another read-through of the *Atlantis* script."

But Orson wasn't ready to go home. He had another stop to make first.

Chapter Twenty-Six

Orson had to apologize.

The bullshit between Hadley and Jess would have been unfortunate regardless of where it happened, but the brawl had gone down at his son's birthday party. He never should have brought Jess there. Terrible judgment. Bringing his girlfriend over to his ex-wife's house? What had he been thinking, trying to show off like that?

No wonder Jess had seemed so unseated. How thoughtless had he been, more concerned about pulling up in his Lexus with a little Tesla in the trunk than he was in being the best boyfriend and father he could possibly be.

Alexis deserved his apology, and Orson wasn't going to say *sorry* by text.

He swung a right, now just three blocks from her house. Orson was finished with the blame game. The thirty-seven-minute drive had given him plenty of time to rehearse a full apology. She was obviously having a hard enough time with Tyler — he'd seen the signs earlier and chosen to ignore them — and he'd unnecessarily added to the drama.

Connor's party had been ruined, and his son had seen it all. What would he think of Jess now? Had Orson poisoned Connor's feelings toward her? Or worse, traumatized his son?

It was *all* his fault.

He turned onto Alexis' street. His heart stopped beating.

He'd heard the sirens a block away, but it never registered as something that might be his problem. Now he saw the ambulance in her driveway, the fire truck parked out front, and the police cruiser approaching from the opposite direction.

Orson tore out of the car and ran up the driveway, right into the house.

Alexis was on the floor, sobbing. He knelt beside her, not sure what to do.

She sobbed harder.

"Where's Connor?" Orson asked, trying to stay calm, even though the words were burning his throat and he wanted to scream them.

Alexis was too choked up to say anything. Still sobbing and heaving, sucking air through her teeth, she pointed toward his bedroom.

"I'll be right back." Orson stood, but Alexis pulled him back down.

After a long gasp, she finally managed words. "Not yet." Another heave. "I told him to stay in his room."

Relief flooded his body, followed by concern.

If Connor was okay, then this was probably about Tyler. Had he hit her again? Had Alexis called the police? If so, then why was she sobbing on the floor instead of—

Then he saw it, the stretcher being rolled down the hallway and into the living room, paramedics and a policeman beside the bodybag. One of them mumbled as he passed, "Definitely looks like an OD."

"Is that …"

Orson couldn't finish. Nor did he need to.

Alexis nodded, now calm enough to talk. "I came home from the store with Connor and he wasn't moving or saying anything. He was just lying on our bed in a puddle of drool."

Tyler was dead, and Orson was reeling.

"What does Connor know?"

"Nothing, really. I went in there alone, so he hasn't seen the body. And I yelled at him to go in his room and stay there, so he probably thinks that I'm mad at him."

"Do you want me to tell him?"

She looked up at him with haunted but appreciative eyes.

He left her with an officer and headed toward Connor's room, wondering what he was going to say. Hating himself, of course, because while Alexis had lost a boyfriend and Connor had lost a stepfather, Orson couldn't help but feel a jolt of glee as he realized that the part in *Farewell, Atlantis* was probably his.

He shoved the spark of joy aside as he entered his son's bedroom and tried to look calm.

"Hey, buddy," Orson said, closing Connor's door behind him.

"Hi, Daddy," his son said, slightly sullen.

And that was all he got to say before they heard Alexis screaming from the living room, wailing like a trapped animal tangled in a barbed wire fence.

Orson swallowed and said, "I'll be right back."

Then he ran into the living room, just in time to see the paramedics dragging Alexis away.

Chapter Twenty-Seven

Jess was shopping, but even that did nothing to improve her terrible mood.

She never should have taken the coke.

It had been as good as Dominic had promised, and until Hadley showed up at the party, Jess had been flying high on a wave of confidence and optimism. The more she'd thought about it, the more she wanted that second chance Dominic promised her.

But since the video of her fight with Hadley had gone viral … it wouldn't matter how many auditions Dominic lined up for her, no one would want to hire her now.

Fuck the coke. Her mistake had been accepting Orson's invitation to go with him to his ex-wife's house. What had he been thinking?

She thought again about the vial in her purse.

She should have thrown it away. But after the party, she'd wanted to prove to herself that she was in control. That she wasn't the person she used to be.

And she'd been good. She hadn't touched it since that awful day.

But she hadn't been able to throw it away, because as bad as things were now, what if they got worse?

What if they got so bad, she couldn't live without it?

It was like she was outside of herself, watching every awful decision, powerless to take control.

Jess was on her way to the checkout line, but she wasn't going to make it out of the store unscathed. She picked up the box of whole grain cereal that she didn't even want and traded it for a jumbo box of Lucky Charms. The she added a second box of Cinnamon Toast Crunch for good measure.

She hated what coke did to her brain but couldn't deny the damage. Her cravings were like blunt force trauma, and sugar helped her forget. She had been either binging or starving since that lunch with Dominic.

Jess stood in line, tapping her foot, wanting to get the hell out of there. She was imagining ripping open the box of Cinnamon Toast Crunch and shoving a handful into her mouth. She wondered if she should go back and grab a box of Trix.

Probably not. She really didn't need the sugar, and neither did her ass, especially if it was going to get photographed naked, which apparently was now par for the course. But then again, fuck it, she hadn't had any Cookie Crisp for years. Of course, getting the extra box would put her over the fifteen-items-or-less limit.

Not that the rule was stopping the frizzy-haired woman in front of her, who was loading a thousand items or so onto the conveyer. Next to her, a pair of misbehaving brats who kept whispering to one another and looking at Jess. One of them even pointed.

Fuck that kid and his fidget spinner.

"That's a double coupon." The woman ran a meaty

paw through her frizzy hair and leaned closer to the checker. "What do you mean it's no good?"

"It's expired," the checker explained for the second time.

"Mom." The little girl tugged on her mom's shirt.

"Not now, Lyla."

"Mom."

"Please Lyla, let me finish up here then we can go home."

"Mom!" She yanked so hard on her mother's shirt that the left side of her bra was completely exposed.

The woman was horrified. She adjusted herself and looked ready to wallop her child, but stopped to see where her daughter was pointing.

She followed the little girl's finger.

So did Jess.

Right to her face on the cover of a tabloid.

Correction: *tabloids.*

"Is she famous?" Lyla asked.

Jess ripped the closest one from the rack. The headline read, *Is Jess Desperate For a Comeback?*

She thought of the vial as she tore through the tabloid until she found the page with her story.

But she saw the picture first. Probably the worst one ever taken of her. A terrifying shot of Jess in a rage, swinging a fist down at Hadley. It was a semi-blurry screen grab from the already viral video that would for sure be feeding Jess' nightmares for the rest of her life.

She dropped the tabloid onto the floor. Then she was walking without control of her feet.

Jess wasn't moving so much as being moved, her body on autopilot, taking her out to the car. She got in, and started to cry. Softly at first, but then in a torrent.

I'll get you through this.

The vial had the sweetest voice and made all the best promises.

Fuck those people, you're better than them. You shouldn't let them get to you.

Jess unzipped her purse and reached inside.

You're going to feel better soon.

Her hand closed around the vial.

God, grant me the serenity to accept the things I cannot change and the grace to get lost in nirvana.

Chapter Twenty-Eight

"Why do I have to eat?" Connor asked.

Orson had been answering an endless battery of questions all morning. Just like he had every day for the last three weeks, since Alexis had a total breakdown and had to be hospitalized.

"Because we need food to give us energy."

"Why does it give us energy?"

"A car can't go without gas, right? Same for us. Except that our gas is food, and the stuff we eat gives us the nutrients we need."

"What about Teslas? You said they don't need gas."

"They still need energy. Gas gives most cars their energy, but it can come from electricity—"

"What are nutrients?"

"Vitamins, minerals, proteins … stuff."

This was exhausting.

Normally, Orson loved it when Connor asked him questions. It made him feel like he was being a good father to answer them.

But right now, he had so much on his mind. His work

performance had taken a hit, and he knew he wasn't giving one hundred percent to his auditions. He'd been missing appointments. And he missed the hell out of Jess, wondering where she was, how she was doing, and if there was anything he could do to make things better.

He hadn't even been able to tell her about what happened with Alexis or to apologize for putting her in Hadley's path in the first place. He'd called her right after the paramedics left, but she hadn't answered then, or since.

Connor was finally silent. Orson enjoyed the reprieve.

It didn't last long.

"Why do I need two eyes even when I am only looking at one thing?"

He looked at his son and laughed. That one was funny. Like so many of the other questions that had caught Orson off guard, he felt instantly desperate to share it with Jess.

She was clearly avoiding him, and this was obviously his fault. The whole thing with Hadley and the press and Connor's party. The tabloids after that one were brutal and worse. There hadn't been a single kind word publicly said about Jess since Orson's invitation. It had changed his life and maybe ruined hers.

So now she wanted nothing to do with him, and he was helpless to do anything about it.

Same for all the waiting. His audition was three weeks ago, and Orson still had no idea whether he'd landed the roll in *Farewell, Atlantis.*

"Why do we have to eat three times a day?"

"Because that's how much our bodies need to live."

"Can we eat all of our meals at once."

"Some people do, I guess."

His phone buzzed and he looked at the screen. Hadley. *Just checking on U. Everything good?*

Hadley had been a sweetheart since this whole thing

started, trying hard to make everything better between them. Orson appreciated it, but that's not what he wanted.

His phone buzzed again. This time it was Dominic.

I'm coming up.

At least that was something. For better or worse, Orson was about to find out if he'd got the gig.

"Hey, buddy, Mr. Dominic is going to be here in a minute, and we're going to talk, so why don't you go and play in your room for just a few minutes, okay?"

"Are we still going to watch all the *Star Wars* starting at the one?"

"Of course." It killed him that his son didn't see *Episode IV* as *the one*. Surely he'd grow out of that.

"Okay, Daddy," Connor said, grabbing his tablet off the couch and walking back to his room.

The text was Dominic's version of knocking. It was his place, after all. Just as Connor made it to his bedroom, Orson's door swung open and Dominic sauntered inside.

His smile was total, swallowing his entire face. The man was practically skipping as he crossed the living room, walking from the door to the small rolling bar on the other side. He studied the bottles, then looked over at Orson.

"Preference?"

"Honestly, I'm not sure that I even want a drink right now."

"You have to drink. We need to celebrate."

Orson wasn't quite sure how to feel. He was thinking about Connor, Jess, Alexis, Tyler, and *Atlantis*, in that order. Dominic had yet to say it, but he was obviously about to deliver some great news. This was what Orson had been waiting for, not just for the last three weeks, but for the last four years.

There was silence, except for the clinking of glass as Dominic finished preparing their matching drinks. He handed one to Orson. It might have been an Old Fashioned. If so, the man was observant.

He took a sip. "So, does this mean we got it?"

Yep, definitely an Old Fashioned.

"Yes," Dominic said after a giant swallow. "We definitely did. And that's not all."

It was awful, not being able to enjoy this as much as he wanted, but still wondering what in the hell it could be.

"There's a party tonight. A big one. And you're going."

Shit. What was he going to do with Connor?

"You don't look excited," Dominic said.

Orson smiled, but it felt strained on his face. "I'm just processing."

"Well, process this. The party is at Logan White's place. And like I said, you're going to want to be there."

His smile went from strained to natural. "What's the party for?"

"Logan is throwing it just because, but he reached out to me and asked if I would extend an invitation."

"Really?" Even though Logan had been the one to record his welcome video, and that first phone call just before he went into Crossroads to blow his every last dollar on something to wear, Orson hadn't heard from him since. He figured the whole thing was just part of the process, using big stars to entice the hopefuls.

"Really. He heard that you landed the *Atlantis* role and wanted to send his congratulations and give you an invite to his little fiesta, seeing as how you had something to celebrate. And that's not the only applause I've heard on your behalf today, Orson. So yes," Dominic raised his glass and took another swallow. "Let's make this an evening to remember."

This should be one of the happiest moments of his life, but Orson felt sick to his stomach.

It was just a little fucked up, celebrating his landing the part when Tyler's death hung over it.

Toxicology reports showed that the guy had died from an overdose. Orson couldn't stop thinking about it. He couldn't stop the images of Tyler getting rolled out of the living room in a bodybag, as though Fate wished his biggest competition out of the way. He couldn't forget Alexis sobbing, broken on the floor while their son played in his room, pretending that he wasn't scared out of his mind.

Of course he wanted to celebrate, but the guilt was too much. And even being excited to meet Logan White in the flesh, it was easy to imagine the miles of vices that would be waiting. Orson was sick of the drugs in this town.

Dominic seemed to be reading his thoughts. "You're thinking about Crane?"

"I can't help it," Orson admitted.

"That's because you're a good kid, but you need to stop. It's not like you killed the guy to get the role. He did it to himself. You can't help that the guy was a jackass with a drug problem. *You* earned that role. Regardless of what happened to him, the part was down to the two of *you.* That's your accomplishment, so why are you letting him take it away?"

"I'm not letting him take it away," Orson said, feeling a sudden need to defend himself. "But I can't help but feel like I only got the role because he's dead, and that's not really something to celebrate."

Dominic finished his drink and set it on the counter. "Bullshit. You're right, if that asshole had lived, then it probably would have gone to him. He has more cachet at this point, and the press always loved him to pieces. But you earned this role, even if the universe helped you to land it, and history will prove that Fate got it right."

"I still—"

"Can you imagine Tom Selleck as Indiana Jones? Jack Nicholson as Michael Corleone? Or Eric Stoltz as Marty McFly? Me neither. All of them would have worked well enough, and sure as hell made sense at the time, when you're using bullshit metrics like present-day box office appeal. But Atlantis has all the makings of a classic if they get the casting right. And thanks to an unfortunate tragedy, they finally did."

It all felt so great to hear. But what about Connor?

"Alexis is still in the hospital." *Hospital* sounded a lot less awful than *psych ward*. And Orson didn't want his son to think his mother was crazy. "I have to stay with Connor."

Dominic laughed. "Are you kidding? We have a service. You'll love it."

"What do you mean 'a service'?"

"A service. Natural Nurture. We don't own the place or anything, but Shellter has them on retainer. They bill us double, and in return they make sure that all of their other clients are a footnote to us. Same as Pussycat. It's the deal we make with everyone. Win-win."

Dominic looked at Orson's still-full glass. "You haven't touched your drink."

"This is all so great." This was terrible. He felt like such a pile of shit. "Thank you so much for everything. I can't believe I'm actually going to be in *Atlantis!*"

"Why do I still hear a 'but'?"

"Connor's been through a lot, and I'm not really comfortable leaving him with someone I don't know, at least not without preparing him first. We had plans tonight, and I don't want to break my promise."

"Did you really promise him, Orson? Did you use those words?"

Orson thought. No, he hadn't.

"Look, I don't want to push this, but my job is to make you one of the biggest stars on the planet. And right now you're not letting me do my job. This is a big night for you. Huge. The kind where everything changes. The last time you got an opportunity like this was when you got a little black card in the mail. Now you've landed a role that everyone is talking about. Believe me, you *want* to be at Logan's tonight. The hotter half of Hollywood will be there and ready to stroke you. So you decide, stay here and regret it, starting around nine tonight or so when Connor's in bed, and you're imagining everything that's happening without you, then for the rest of your life. Or you can go to the party, get all the stroking, and leave the evidence of your glory in Hollywood's palm."

"That was colorful."

Dominic took Orson's drink from his hand and threw back a swallow. "Your life. But it kills me to see one of my investments not even trying."

"What do you want me to do?"

"This isn't difficult, Orson. You must know *someone* who can watch your kid for an evening."

Orson thought.

Of course he did.

Chapter Twenty-Nine

"Dude, thank you *so* much."

"Of course," Ellis said, opening his door wider to let them in.

Connor ran inside, then twirled around the living room. "Mr. Ellis!"

"Just Ellis."

He reminded Connor every time, but his son insisted on calling people by their Mr. or Mrs. because that's what people with manners did, according to Alexis.

"So Logan White, huh?"

Orson nodded. "Yeah, it's last-minute. Dominic really wanted me to go."

Ellis said nothing, as usual when Dominic's name came up.

When he couldn't stand the silence a single second longer, Orson said, "Still nothing from Jess?"

Ellis shook his head. "Nada. Negative. No siree. At least not much more than a wave. Same for her emails. I'm lucky to get a sentence, even when I send her a page."

"At least she's emailing you back. Texts, calls, emails. She's totally ignoring me. I think she hates me."

"She doesn't hate you. But this whole thing really hurt her. I don't know if you've been following the blogs, and man, I sorta hope you haven't because as much as I think you should be more aware than you are, fuck, is it a brutal place. They're ripping her apart. One asshole on Twitter mouthed off that Jess was probably the one who supplied Tyler with the drugs — based on absolutely nothing at all — and that she was therefore responsible for his death. That's messed up enough, but because people on the Internet are total idiots."

Orson could barely breathe. He didn't want to hear this at all. Connor was on the couch, looking up at them every few seconds before casting his eyes back down on the tablet.

"It's not just that the coverage and the rumors are all fu … messed up, even though they totally are. It's that they're relentless. Jess didn't ask for any of this, and she sure as hell doesn't want it."

"How long has she been ignoring you?"

"She hasn't been ignoring me, exactly. It was a slow creep. Her schedule is all over the place. After that first week, she got paranoid about the paparazzi fast. She wouldn't even come out of her apartment. They were painting her as some sort of femme fatale, and she just couldn't take it. I think she's going out late at night. I hear her coming home at odd hours, but she doesn't want to talk and won't answer her door. This last week she's been a ghost."

Orson shook his head, feeling like shit. "This is the worst."

"Thoroughly."

"Maybe we can talk her into Wednesday at the Litter Box. It's been a while."

"You know I'd love that, but I also get that you're busy, and now you have Connor."

"Maybe we can do it here?"

"I'll ask, but I'm not sure that she's going to be receptive to that."

"Maybe she just needs to be asked. I'll do it too. Voice-mail, email, and text. Let's make this happen."

Ellis smiled. His best one since he'd opened the door. It filled Orson with a surprising sense of relief.

"Congratulations again. I'm really happy for you."

"Thanks, man." Orson gave Ellis a hug. "And we still have a deal. I will return with at least one juicy story."

"Please, *please* make it about Dominic and Melinda. I seriously can't believe you've been with them for months now and still haven't given me anything juicy."

Orson shrugged. "There really isn't anything to say. They're smart business people, and very direct. I could see how they might rub people the wrong way, especially if things didn't work out. But they've been great to me, and they really seem to care about the actors in their stable."

Then Ellis went silent again. Until, after a clear hesitation, he said, "Just be careful."

"I will be," Orson said. "Bye, little buddy!"

"Bye, Daddy!" Connor called from the couch.

Outside, Orson looked at his old apartment, shaking his head as he imagined his palatial loft. Then his eyes found the next door, and he felt awful again.

Maybe she was there, and maybe he could take her with him.

Maybe they could have a red carpet evening themselves.

They both deserved it. And what if that was the best

way to restore her reputation? To be photographed at a party at Logan White's house?

He pressed his ear against the door instead.

There was definitely someone in there. Jess was home.

He knocked, but no one answered.

Orson knocked again, for three straight minutes, counting to ten in between each series.

Finally, he growled against the door, hopefully enough for her to hear, but not Ellis two doors down. "Jess, I know you're in there. Let me in."

Still, nothing.

He walked toward the back stairwell, frustrated, wanting to exit through the rear so he could avoid Angus downstairs and another one of his useless *How are you doing this fine afternoon?s* that he wouldn't know how to answer.

But with one foot on the top stair, Orson paused.

Then he turned around.

Because now Orson had an idea.

Chapter Thirty

If that was Ellis knocking on Jess' door, then he could come back later.

If it was Orson, and Jess thought that it probably was, *fuck him.*

She had a dick in her mouth right now, thanks to him.

Jess purred, licking up one side of Harrison's shaft, then circling her tongue around his tip.

What in the fuck is taking so long?

She was coked the fuck up. Harrison's dick must be suffering from the same affliction.

"Jess, I know you're in there. Let me in."

"Do you need to get that?"

Jess answered him by pursing her lips at the tip of his cock and sliding all the way down his staff. It wasn't as hard as it should have been, both the deep-throating and the dick itself.

Maybe that's because it was all so transactional.

Plucked fresh from last year's Onyx List, the Shellys had since sent Harrison Turner into the stratosphere.

Harrison was Orson nine months from now, only without all the baggage and a lot more gay.

His first film had screened to some early and rather stunning reviews. *Life is a Loop* was nominated for the Palme d'Or, though it didn't win, and Harrison had needed a date for the movie's red carpet premiere.

Jess didn't want to think of the awful audition that had led her to this. She just wanted to get through it.

Dominic had delivered on his promise, but the first few auditions were scheduled while all that awful press was happening, so none of them went anywhere beyond making Jess feel more terrible about herself than she ever had before. Until the last audition. That one was so terrible that she marched straight into Dominic's office. She wanted to thank him for the opportunity, it had been awfully kind of him to help her, but she was done. Finished for the second and final time.

But Dominic wasn't in his office. Melinda was, and being a woman, she understood exactly what Jess was going through. After listening to her blubber for almost an hour, and totally putting her back together, she made an offer that both surprised and intrigued Jess at the time.

"Maybe you're thinking about this all wrong," Melinda had said. "The press only cares about tearing actresses apart when they're competing for roles and a part of the game. Let's be honest with each other. What are the things you *really* want out of all this?"

"I'd just like a decent part in a small-budget film, a chance to restart my career and make people forget all the bad stuff."

"Think bigger. You could be going to some of the most gorgeous places in the world, eating the best food, having the greatest time, never worrying about money again, spending time with some of the world's biggest stars?"

Melinda gave Jess a smile — *just between us girls* — and added, "Unlimited coke and the best sex of your life."

She had been right about the first one, but definitely not the second.

According to Melinda, escorting was huge in Holly-wood. Actresses on their way down had a lucrative window that they could exploit if they had the right contacts. And Melinda definitely did. The money was great, up to five grand a night, and the clients were both famous and discreet.

And if Jess was genuinely interested, she had the perfect client.

Because Melinda was a woman, Jess didn't see it as an asshole's suggestion.

"Harrison Turner," Melinda whispered. "He's one of our stars that we've invested quite a lot in. But the press is reporting that he's gay."

Of course they were. He'd gotten caught proposi-tioning a male masseuse.

"I'm bi," Harrison had clarified, just minutes after they first shook hands. "But I definitely *prefer* women."

Then he gave Jess a smile suggesting that maybe he didn't.

They got along well enough, once they were past the awkwardness. It was Harrison's first time hiring an escort and her first time selling her body for money. Selling her *time*, as Melinda insisted on calling it, though Jess knew exactly what she was selling access to.

Harrison had been hot enough when they first got to her place. He insisted that they go there because there would be "a fuckton of cameras" at his.

Marched her right over to her tiny kitchen table, bent her over it, doffed his jacket and dropped it on the floor, looked around the room and said, "Nice place," then emptied himself inside her in less than sixty seconds.

Apparently, that was all he had.

A bump of coke to blunt their clumsy nerves, then another to loosen up before they walked the red carpet together. Then another several just for the hell of it. That had to be what was wrong with his dick. If he really did prefer girls, then she hated to think it was her. She was a professional, after all.

That made her laugh. Enough that she had to take Harrison's cock out of her mouth. A glob of spit trailed from his dick to her glistening lips.

"What's funny?" Harrison asked, sounding defensive as he stuffed his semi back into his pants. He didn't wait for her to answer. Instead he pointed to the coke on the table. "More?"

"Don't mind if I do," she winked, "but don't put that thing away just yet." His ego was the most important thing to stroke, and besides, Jess wasn't ready to surrender. Maybe he just needed a little encouragement.

"Why don't you start stroking your cock while I take my turn, then we can trade."

He already had it in his hand, and Jess was leaning over the table.

She heard the key in the door, instantly knew what was happening, and bolted upright as her door flew open.

Jess bounded up from the couch, glancing back at Harrison, putting his pecker back in his pants, this time for good.

"Hey, Orson!" She was at the door and giving him a hug.

He hugged her back, but then gently pushed her away and looked her up and down.

His gazed moved to Harrison, then around her apartment.

Coke on the table. Black panties on the floor. Harrison's flagging cock.

His heart looked like it was stuck in his stomach.

He still hadn't spoken a word.

Jess started talking. "Hey, Orson. This is Harrison. Harrison, this is Orson. Oh my god, what am I thinking, of course you guys know each other. You both work for Dominic and Melinda, right?"

A little laugh, no one answered, she kept on going.

"Harrison and I just went to the premiere of *Life is a Loop*. It was a lot of fun. My first red carpet."

Then she added, "My first for a lot of things," before she started laughing uncontrollably, hating every that second she couldn't get herself to stop.

"Is she okay?" Orson asked Harrison.

Harrison nodded. "I didn't see you at the premiere."

"Sorry. I was with my son." Then to Jess, "When did you get into this stuff?"

"It's not a big deal, Orson. Everyone does a little here and there." She looked at the table. No point in denying the truth. "And this stuff is *choice*."

Orson shook his head at her, clearly disgusted.

"Fuck you!" Jess yelled at him. "You're so fucking judgmental! What am I supposed to do? I need something every now then to take the edge off. You have seen the papers, right? I'm sure you can understand at least some of what I'm going through, especially since you're the one who started all of this."

He stared at her, stewing, probably thinking about what to say next. He seemed to be oscillating between heartbreak and disbelief, or perhaps anger and sorrow.

Harrison broke the silence. "Hey man, you going to the party at Logan's tonight?"

Staring at Jess, Orson finally said, "Sure, I'll go to the party. Alone. I'll stick around long enough to get my picture taken. I imagine the two of you are going, so I hope you have fun."

He shook his head, looking like a lost dog.

Then he left.

Jess couldn't stand how heartbroken she felt, going to the party with Harrison instead of Orson, so she turned to the mirror and its white lines for help.

Chapter Thirty-One

Orson felt like the rotting rind of a month-old melon inside.

He couldn't believe what he'd just walked into. Not what he had expected at all.

Jess was better than this, or at least that's what Orson had always wanted to believe. Of course the tabloids were lying, or at least they were taking things out of context and control, like Jess had always insisted.

He had seen the same thing for himself, first on his balcony, then later at Connor's party.

But there was no misinterpreting what he had seen with his own eyes. He'd like to think that it was Jess at her worst, but was it? How well did he really know her? Because as well as he *thought* he did, Orson had never imagined walking in on a display of the drug that had ruined her life, or Harrison Turner's dick. Seeing both made him sick to his stomach.

His illusion of what could have been shattered.

Because Connor was everything, and an addict was a

danger to his son. He couldn't have her around him now, knowing what he did.

That knowledge was felt like a knife driven deep into his belly.

But the choice was clear. There was nothing in the world more important to Orson than Connor, and so that's what he would focus on. He kept telling himself the same thing over and over — even saying the words out loud rather than simply thinking them, as though that might lend them more power — all the way to the party.

He handed his fob to the valet with a smile, thinking how recently he might have been the one receiving keys.

One hour, then I'm out of here.

Orson ascended the long staircase in front of Logan's house, then entered through the massive foyer and into a party that was already rocking the walls.

He remembered his evening at the Glass House and how out of his skin he felt as he made his way through the house, got his first drink, and ambled outside onto yet another sprawling lawn. But even though this one was populated by some of the biggest names in the world, all just standing there without any fear of paparazzi, Orson didn't feel insignificant. He had been getting deeper and deeper into the life of a legitimate actor, and he was now on his way to being a bonafide movie star. These people were no longer untouchable. At some level, the people at this party were his peers.

"Orson Beck!" A booming laugh followed the familiar voice.

Orson turned around. Even feeling like these people were now his colleagues couldn't change the awe he felt standing a few feet from Logan White.

Then Logan hugged him. "It's good to see you in person. So … how has it been?"

Significant.

Surreal.

Transformative.

"Amazing."

"For sure. Sorry I never called you again after that first time. I'm sure you understand."

Orson laughed. Talking to Logan was like taking truth serum. "I still can't believe you called even once."

Another thunderous million dollar laugh. "That's probably the biggest thing standing in your way. You need to *believe* that you *deserve* to be here. It makes all the difference. Look around you, Orson."

Orson did. It was impressive. Logan's pool was practically a lake. His guesthouse was bigger than any home Orson had been in before receiving his invitation.

"It's amazing."

"No." Still laughing, "I don't mean the place, I mean the people. What do you see?"

"Money. Fame. Power."

"True, true, and true. But what I want you to see is *confidence.* Everyone out there believes they belong here, that they deserve the unfair share of life they've been given. That's the one thing you're still missing, and you need it to reach the top."

"I'm sure I'll get there over time," Orson said, even though that might not be true. There was a part of him, maybe even a large part, that still expected this very bright bulb to abruptly burn out.

"No, Orson. It's *all* up here." Logan tapped his temple. "We're talking headspace. I want you to walk around and have a great time tonight. I'm thrilled to see you here, but I want you to get something out of tonight. You know, something more than wasted." He laughed. "I want tonight to be another big step forward in your career. You want people to see you as not just an up-and-comer, but as an inevitable force that will be impacting this industry. Then, everything will go your way."

Orson looked at Logan, not really knowing what to say. It all made sense, but he'd never had an easy time just *believing things* when people told him to. That was usually bullshit. Advice offered when someone wanted to make something difficult sound easy.

"So have a great time tonight," Logan finished. "But remember that you belong here."

"Logan?" Orson had to force himself to say the name out loud. It felt like blasphemy. And to Logan's point, that was probably part of the problem.

"Orson?" Damn, his smile was huge.

"Why are you doing this? Helping me like this, I mean?"

"Good question. Why do you think I'm helping you?"

He really wasn't sure. Logan had always seemed like a genuinely nice guy. It was just one of the reasons he was such a big box office draw. But there definitely had to be more than that going on here.

"I don't know," Orson admitted.

Logan shook his head. "That's not good enough. You want the answer and I want you to have it, but I'll need you to work a little harder than that. If you don't *know*, then *guess*. Why do you *think* I'm helping you?"

Again, Orson considered. What did someone like Logan need? "Because helping me will help you."

Logan beamed. "Exactly. Most of the Hollywood game amounts to staying on top. Everything is always in flux. It might not be true that you're only as good as your last film, but you are only as good as your last string of them. And this is a relationship business. For those of us at the top who can clearly communicate our insights around what it took to get here, not only are we clarifying that for ourselves, but we're inspiring others. You said it perfectly: *Helping you will help me.* If this business is all about relationships, then it's in my best interests to develop the best ones I can, and the way I see it, helping out those people who are next in line for red carpet royalty is the best way to gain a personal loyalist."

Despite the warmth of his voice, something about that sounded cold. Still, Orson was glowing.

"Thank you. So much."

"Of course. Drinks or whatever you want. It's time to get your party on. Make connections, get attention, have fun."

For the next hour, Orson followed his orders, with his acting at its peak.

He remained hyper-aware of his body language, understanding what he was quietly broadcasting as he mingled. There was always a drink in his hand to make sure that he never crossed his arms, and he made sure to check out the moon every few minutes to keep his shoulders from hunching. He embraced casual touching, despite the fact that every guest at this party was usually surrounded by handlers to keep the hoi polloi away. He stayed mostly silent, asking everyone else about themselves, knowing that the best way to get people to remember him, was to convince them that he would remember the things that were most important to them.

He listened to Ashley Mansfield talk about working with Adrian Frank, Thomas Girard pontificating about priceless art, and Ella Hurt saying that she wished she hadn't become an actress so young because it had defined her before she was ready.

Two hours into the party and a full hour after Orson promised himself that he would be out of there, he found himself a lot more inebriated than he had expected to be and having to kill some more time before he could get behind the wheel.

Orson stopped drinking but still carried around an Old Fashioned, which had apparently become his drink, and waited to sober up.

But sober wasn't the best feeling, because the alcohol was helping him to forget, or at least to care less about all of that shit with Jess. The coke and the—

No. He didn't want to think about that.

"Wanna bump?"

He looked over. Britta Sharpe was offering him coke.

Orson shook his head for what felt like the millionth time. "No thanks. I'm trying to clear my head."

He was sick of saying the same thing and sick of the offers.

Maybe that would make him feel better.

It wasn't the first time he'd had that thought. In fact, it wouldn't leave his mind.

But he knew where that road would lead. He'd seen it plenty. Most recently with the woman he thought he loved and now couldn't stop thinking about, wondering if he should have stuck around and helped her out of the hole she seemed to have fallen in, rather than getting disgusted and galloping away on his high horse.

Orson looked around, knowing it was time to go. He had accomplished his to-do, getting photographed at the party while hobnobbing with all the right people. It was only three and a half hours or so into the night, but that was already a couple past what he had promised himself.

But Orson couldn't stop thinking about Jess and Connor. He wanted to check in on her, make sure that she was okay, then take his son home. He figured he might see her with Harrison, but he hadn't run into either of them, and her absence filled him with worry.

Orson looked around the party for Logan, wanting to bid farewell to his host, but after finding him nowhere, he finally just left, still slightly buzzed but fine to drive.

As long as he didn't get pulled over.

Chapter Thirty-Two

Orson's stomach was killing him as he parked his Lexus in front of the Brick. He wasn't sure what upset him more: the broken promise to Connor, the nightmare he walked into behind Jess' door, or the evening of opulence that cast his old building — and even his new apartment — into the shadows of a life best forgotten.

"Ain't no reason that beets can't be used instead of sugarcane," Angus said, waiting for Orson as he opened the front door. "The sugar is always just as sweet!"

"True that," Orson agreed, then walked up the stairs, knowing what he would do next because he'd been picturing it the entire trip home.

He passed Ellis' apartment, then his old place, and stopped two doors down at Jess'.

Orson knocked, waited the three beats that he promised himself he would, then turned the knob.

As expected, the door swung open. But the inside was a surprise.

Her place was vacant. Orson went into every room, but there was nothing left. He remembered his own exodus, and the fact that he'd nothing to do with it, and wondered if Dominic and Melinda were behind her disappearance too.

Probably. Almost for sure. But why?

The furniture was all gone. There were no clothes in the closets, boxes in the cabinets, or food in the fridge.

The place looked as empty as he felt.

His heart was now stewing in the acid on the floor of his stomach. This was worse than a thousand bee stings all over his body. It was awful, what he had walked in on a few hours ago, but even that end hadn't felt like the end because Orson kept telling himself stories about how he would fix this, how he was going to make everything better, and how — especially as the night moved on — he could turn everything around so that his life was looking forward rather than backward.

With a heart that felt a hundred pounds heavier, Orson left the empty apartment and rapped his knuckles two doors down.

Ellis answered, almost surprised to see Orson. "It's early. I didn't know that they let you out of Sodom and Gomorrah before midnight. I thought you were coming to pick Connor up in the morning."

Orson smiled, not really feeling it, and stepped inside.

"Hi, Daddy!" Connor was on the carpet in front of the coffee table, setting up a game of Hungry Hungry Hippos. "Are you going to play with us?"

Ellis said, "We had three more games, then it was bedtime."

Orson walked over, kneeled down, and gave his son a hug. "We can play in the morning. We're going to go now."

Connor crossed his arms. "I don't want to go."

Great, this was going to be a battle.

Ellis came over and set a gentle hand on Connor. "It's

cool, man. We'll play next time, and I promise to give you a head start."

The boy shook his head, and now he sounded petulant. "You said we would play three more games."

Orson uncrossed his son's arms and took him by the hand. "Come on, Connor. We can play ten games tomorrow. But it's late. We need to go."

"No." Connor yanked his hand away from Orson, then crossed his arms harder and shook his head faster. "I want to play three more games. Then I want to sleep with my Batman blanket like Mr. Ellis said I could!"

"We can take the Batman blanket home. We have Hungry Hungry Hippos there. We can play in the morning." Then, seeing the look in his son's eyes and feeling desperate to make this go away, he added, "We can play the three games at home before you go to bed."

Though really, there was a fat chance of that. Connor would be sleeping before they hit the second red light.

"Why can't we play them now?"

"Seriously man, the games take like a minute," Ellis chimed in. "We could've already played them out."

Orson turned around and glared at him.

What the fuck, man? Just wait until you have kids.

Orson took Connor's hand again, but this time it was more of a grab. Then he stood, ready to drag the boy behind him.

But Connor wasn't having it. He snatched his hand back, spun around, and climbed up onto the couch. Then he scrambled up to his knees and yelled, "I DON'T WANT TO GO AND I HATE YOU!"

Even a standard kindergartner's tantrum could still feel like a punch to the gut, and after what Orson had seen next door, this one felt like it had been delivered by the Rock.

"Sorry, man," Ellis said. "What can I do?"

"I've got it," Orson said, going over to scoop Connor into his arms.

This wasn't how the pickup was supposed to go at all. But in a way, maybe Orson was glad. Because now he had to leave in a hurry, and he wouldn't be tempted to tell Ellis what had happened with Jess. Obviously he didn't know she was gone or that would have been the first thing out of his mouth. And he didn't need to know about how far she had fallen.

Orson wasn't thrilled with her right now, but that didn't mean he wanted to hurt her, and she had been dragged through the mud more than enough.

"Text me when you get home and just let me know that everything is all right."

"Of course. And thanks for everything." Orson smiled at his friend, carrying Connor kicking and screaming all the way to the door, then down six flights, surely waking neighbors and making strangers hate him.

Mercifully, Angus wasn't in the lobby.

Orson packed his son into the back and buckled him up. The tantrum was losing steam.

He drove home, knowing that he had to do a better job as a father.

Connor was lost in a world of confusion with Alexis away. It had been hard on them both, with Orson handling both pickup and drop-off at school, which was nowhere near his place. Connor missed his mom a lot. Maybe more than Orson had realized. He had to do a better job of being present, of *staying* present.

He couldn't let Dominic tell him what to do again.

And as Orson turned into the Catalyst's underground parking garage, he promised himself that he wouldn't.

Chapter Thirty-Three

"This is *amazing*."

Melinda licked her lips and swallowed.

"And yet another example of why you should have lunch with me more often," Dominic said. "I miss you when we're not together."

"I miss you when we're not together too. But managing these actors isn't easy. They're all so fucking dramatic. How much longer do you think I'll need to stay in this agent role? It doesn't suit me."

"You're a genius at it. But I understand why you want out, and like I keep promising, we'll get there as soon as we can."

"Ugh." A swallow of wine. "It's just that they're all such babies."

"I know, honey."

"And I'd rather spend all my time in strategy."

"I know." Dominic put another bite of slow-roasted lamb in his mouth. "It's almost over. We're almost where we need to be."

"You've been saying that forever."

"Ten years isn't forever, my dear. You don't build a billion dollar company any faster than that."

Melinda rolled her eyes. "They do it up north all the time."

"Fuck Silicone Valley. They're not creating assets. Any one of them can get wiped out overnight."

She finished her last bite and dropped the fork onto her plate. "You're oversimplifying things again."

Dominic shook his head. "Maybe you're making them more complicated."

They stared at each other across the table. Goddammit she was sexy.

Melinda picked her fork back up, stabbed some of Dominic's lamb, popped it into her mouth, then tilted her head back with a squeal. She was no doubt curling her toes. "That was my last bite. I promise."

"Take all you want. I've always loved your appetites."

Melinda smiled. Blew him a kiss. "So, how do you think he's doing?"

"Like I said, *close*. Everything with Orson is going as it should be."

"Are you sure? Because it seems like he's doing his own thing and playing Daddy Day Care these days. Not exactly what we need in our newest star. And what about Skokie? Have you heard anything from Harrison?"

Dominic looked at his wife. She really was burning out. Her questions were usually better than this. "Orson is doing what he needs to do, so that we can do what we're supposed to later. Everything has its time. You know this. And do you really think that Harrison Turner is going to call me up and tell me how things are going with the paid pussy you set him up with? That's not exactly a reasonable expectation."

"I just figured you might have heard something."

"Lindley is lagniappe. It's hedging our bet, not the wager itself. You need to let this play out. It's going exactly like we designed it. We wanted *Bottleneck* to nab *Atlantis*, and *Atlantis* to nab our boy the lead in *The Story of Life*. It's a stretch, and for him to even get considered for a movie like that so soon is ridiculous. No one knew who this guy was a year ago, outside of fans of his stupid Internet show and the cast and crew. The fact that he's being considered means that other parts are rolling in. We're going to have our pick of offers, just like I promised.

And—"

"*—Soon, it's going to change the way we do business forever. And maybe even the way business is done.* I know, Dominic. I've been hearing it for years."

"You don't believe it?"

"I've always believed it. But I'm tired. I need a big win."

"We have wins every day."

"When was the last time you spoke to Orson?"

"We're talking today."

"When?" Melinda asked.

The intercom buzzed. He couldn't pay the best scriptwriter in Hollywood to pen this shit.

"Orson is here."

"Send him in," Dominic said.

Melinda stood, then leaned over and gave him a kiss.

Dominic reached out and grabbed her gently by the wrist. "I just want to see you happy."

"I *am* happy. I just need a nap."

"I thought that actors were the babies."

"Naps are good for you. We should take them together more often."

Dominic gave it a moment, then left the private dining

area for his office, where he found Orson sitting on his side of the desk, waiting with his hands in his lap.

"You're a hard man to get a hold of," Dominic said as he sat.

Orson looked confused. "I'm sorry … have you been trying to call?"

Dominic laughed. He wanted to unseat the kid, but not too much. "It's an expression. I just mean that we haven't seen you around, or really heard much at all. In the beginning you were using our facilities. Eating our food. Taking smart advantage of all the resources available to you, the resources that we pay for so that you can meet your potential. You haven't been to the Pussycat in weeks. Everything okay down there?"

He eyed Orson's crotch. The kid shifted uncomfortably in his seat.

"It's great," he said, obviously not knowing what else to say.

"Are we starting to bore you?"

"Not at all." Now he sounded worried. "Life has just sort of … collapsed."

"Do you want to talk about it?" Dominic asked, knowing that Orson didn't, and that he would.

"I don't know what to say. I feel really grateful, and I don't want to complain about anything."

Dominic waved a hand as if swatting a fly. "No reason to keep the poison inside. We're here to help you. What's on your mind? Hadley giving you trouble?"

"I haven't even heard from her in the last few days. I think she's pissed at me."

Another wave. "Hadley is fine. I wouldn't worry about her at all."

Quietly, Orson said, "I wasn't."

A lie. Dominic leaned back, waiting. The truth would come.

"It's everything. Tyler is dead, and Alexis is up in Gateways. I'm trying to do my best with Connor and I just know that I'm failing you guys."

"The only time you're failing me is when you are worrying about failing me. I need you to keep your head in the game. What is your biggest pain point, Orson? Show me where the splinter is so we can pull it out."

He looked like he was going to cry. Shook his head to delay the inevitable.

Dominic waited.

"I just feel like a failure …" The first tear fell. "… Like no matter what I do, I'm going to let someone down. I've waited forever for this opportunity, it's my dream job. But I feel like I've always sabotaged things before, and even though I'm trying really hard not to do that this time, I'm—"

"What makes you feel that way, Orson?"

"I've always wanted more time with Connor, but now that I have it I'm just … I don't know, maybe I'm not meant to do this. It's a lot. And I'm dropping balls with you. I thought I could manage it all, but now I'm just really wondering if I'm right for Shellter Productions at all."

Dominic leaned forward. *No, no, no.* This wasn't the way he was supposed to be reacting at all. Overwhelmed, sure. But the last thing the Shellys needed was this kid running away when they were trying to build this next continent of their world around him.

"This is all fixable."

Orson looked desperate, and that was good in theory. But in practice Dominic needed him just a little bit less so. Melinda was right — actors were way too fucking dramatic.

"Then tell me how to fix it."

"I suggest you focus on one thing at a time. The first is Alexis. Let's make sure she's in a happy place. Then, we worry about care for Connor, and getting you back on track." He pressed the intercom. "Have Rainbows & Roses send something to Alexis Belle at Gateways. Make it obnoxious. The card needs to read, *We're going to get through this together. I'm there for you. See you tomorrow. Orson.* No X's or O's or anything, it isn't that kind of arrangement. And make sure that the roses are white, not red."

Dominic let go of the button and turned to Orson.

"That's not going to do it, but it's a start. Talk to Alexis, give it your all, and know when to surrender. We're offering you a lot of solutions that you're choosing not to take. That can only last for so long. That offer to set Connor up with one of our teachers at Natural Nurturing is still good, and you should still take us up on it."

Maybe he would, but probably he wouldn't. Because right now, Orson wanted every moment with Connor he could get.

Dominic was sure he could fix that too.

Chapter Thirty-Four

"When are we going to the park?"

Orson had lost count of the number of times that Connor had asked him that question, but it was somewhere between ten and a million.

"Like I told you, buddy, as soon as I'm done reading this."

He dropped his script on the coffee table and tried to reset. This wasn't easy. He just needed to finish, then they could go to the park. Except that's not really where they were going. Orson was planning on taking Connor to visit his mom. Two birds, since he needed to talk to her anyway. But the script wasn't going to memorize itself, and Orson wanted to know every part, not just his own lines.

Connor was talking *so much*. He wouldn't shut the fuck up. Orson was trying not to be agitated, and he felt bad thinking in terms of his son even having to *shut the fuck up*, but he wanted to rip the overpriced haircut right out of his head. He remembered those first few months of Connor's life, when he'd encouraged that first word, desperate to hear him communicate with language for the very first time.

Now, the kid wouldn't stop.

Orson wanted to be a good dad, listen to everything Connor wanted to tell him or ask him. He wanted to hear all of his stories and everything that was brewing in his imagination. But sometimes he needed a break. And he definitely needed to do his job if he expected to keep it.

"Why can't we go now?"

"Because I have to finish reading this, and the longer it takes me, the longer it's going to take for us to get to the park. If you just give me another half an hour, then I promise we can go after that."

"How long is half an hour?"

Orson looked at the pile of pillows that Connor had pulled off of the couch to make the walls of his fort, wanting to punch the lot of them. He got an idea.

He gasped. "Hey Connor, do you know what telepathy is?"

Connor tried to say the word, but couldn't. It came out as, *telephone pee.*

"It's when people can talk without actually opening their mouths. Some of the superheroes can do it."

"Which ones?"

"Professor X and Phoenix … Martian Manhunter …"

"I don't know them. Can Batman do it?"

Orson shook his head. "No. Batman doesn't really have any special powers."

Connor looked at him like he was crazy. "Yes he does. He's Batman. Can Superman have telephone pee?"

"No. But you might be able to. Why don't you go into your bedroom and make up a story and try to send it into my brain from there. I'll come get you in half an hour and see if I know what your story is without you telling me."

Orson was fairly confident that Connor's story would be about Batman and Superman, and probably some telephone pee. His son wasn't all that complicated. Or he could be wrong, and Connor would surprise him with some random story about nothing. That had happened plenty too.

But Orson had been trying to finish an hour's worth of reading all afternoon, and he was getting closer to losing his shit and yelling at Connor. Nothing had worked so far, including the bag of saltwater taffy that Orson had bought to keep the kid's mouth moving with something other than the constant *blah blah blah.*

"Can I make the telephone pee from here?" Connor asked, obviously wanting to stay in his fort.

"Okay. But remember telepathy is all in your head. So you can't talk out loud until I tell you it's time. You're supposed to keep the story inside your brain until then."

"Okay, Daddy."

Finally.

Orson started to read. He made it a page before Connor started tugging on the leg of his 300 dollar jeans.

"Do you know my story, Daddy?"

Orson dropped his script on the table. He sighed, drew a breath, worked not to lose it.

"No, buddy, I don't, because there wasn't enough time. Remember, you were supposed to wait for a half hour. You're working on your telepathy, and I'm working on reading my script. We're a team. I can't do my part if you don't do yours." Orson turned around and gave Connor his undivided attention. "I really want to go to the park with you, and now I'm feeling sad that we might not be able to go."

Connor looked horrified. "Why can't we go?"

"I didn't say that we couldn't go, just that we might not be able to."

"Why not?"

"Because we're running out of time." He picked up the script and shook it. "If I don't finish reading this, then I can't go. And every time you interrupt me. I have to start over."

"Maybe we can go to the park now and you could read later?"

Orson shook his head, biting his bottom lip. "I have an idea. Why don't you go into the kitchen and count all the tiles on the floor. I know how many there are, so if you get the number right, then I'll give you a quarter for every one."

His eyes brightened. "Is that a lot of dollars?"

Orson nodded, then he leaned forward and in a conspiratorial voice he whispered, "It is a *lot* of dollars."

"Okay, Daddy!"

Then Connor ran off to the kitchen.

The silence was golden, and this time it lasted a full three pages, the longest today. Then it started, the worst series of sounds so far, clanking and clanging and clinking, echoing through the apartment from the kitchen. He threw the script onto the coffee table, sprang to his feet, and marched over to the kitchen where he saw Connor sitting on the floor, not counting tiles. He had all the pots and pans removed from the bottom cabinets, and had climbed up onto the counter to pull down a pair of cooking utensils, so that he had drumsticks to accompany his drums.

Orson looked at the scene and lost it. He roared, "Connor, *enough!*"

Connor stopped immediately. The spatula dropped from his right hand, though he still had a death grip on a big black spoon. He looked up at his father. His eyes started to water and his lip began to tremble.

Then he lost it.

Connor's cries weren't only deafening, they might also have been the most awful sound that Orson had ever heard. He had never been around a pod of dying dolphins before, but that would have to sound something like this.

Orson felt as guilty as he did helpless.

He crouched down beside Connor. "It's okay, buddy. You don't have to cry."

But that made him sob louder, then his cries got specific.

"I want Mommy!"

Orson put a hand on his shoulder. That didn't work either, so he scooped him into his arms.

Gallons of tears seemed to be leaking from Connor and onto his shirt, an impossible amount. How could the kid have that much moisture inside him?

Orson didn't know who he was angrier with at the moment, Connor or himself. Because *shit*, why couldn't his son just shut the fuck up for half an hour? Was that really too much to ask? Was he being an unreasonable father, even when expecting so little, and let's be honest, giving so much?

But of course this wasn't Connor's fault. How could it be? He'd lost his mother. Outside of their visits, he hadn't seen her in weeks. Clearly that was taking its toll. Orson couldn't take it personally because every child was hard-wired to want — okay, *need* — their mother.

Orson hugged him harder, petting the back of his head and rocking him back and forth until his whimpers of *I want Mommy* relaxed, then finally died.

Once the kitchen was quiet and Connor more settled, Orson said, "Would you like to go and see Mommy now?"

Connor vigorously nodded his head.

"Okay then, let's go."

He set his son on the floor, its tiles still uncounted, then took him by the hand and started walking toward the door, giving his script a sideways glance on the way.

They walked down the hall as Orson's door closed and automatically locked behind them.

Then into the elevator, his stomach upside down. All of the guilt and concern for Alexis that he had been trying to suppress were now like a thousand LEGOs poured onto the floor. His world was out of order, and until he got some of his emotions under control, he hadn't a hope of getting it back.

Every time he put his emotions into a closet, whether that meant his fretting over Alexis, his constant concern for Connor's welfare, his deep disenchantment with Jess, or his frustration with Hadley's neediness, it all made him feel like a time bomb packed with plastic, made of pressure, and his ears were filled with the ticking.

He loaded Connor into the car, the boy's tears now just streaks on his face.

Orson drove toward Gateways, telling himself that everything would be better soon.

Chapter Thirty-Five

Alexis lit up like the sun when she saw them. Not just Connor, but Orson too. He was sure of it.

"My boys!"

She didn't just look better than she had since the incident, she almost looked like her old self. The one from before all of this, the Alexis he'd fallen in love with six years ago.

"Hey, Alexis."

"Mommy!" Connor raced into the private room and right into her arms.

He covered her with kisses, and she covered him right back.

She pulled away and inspected him. "Have you been crying?"

Connor nodded, embarrassed. "I was sad."

"Why were you sad?"

"Because I misted you!"

"I missed you too," Alexis said from her side of a bone-breaking hug. She looked up at Orson. "I didn't know you were coming today. Thank you. I really appreciate it."

It was hard not to feel genuine affection for Alexis, once her defenses were all stripped and he was staring at the woman in her most vulnerable form, like an animal exposing its belly.

"I'm glad to be here. We both wanted to see you."

Orson surprised himself by walking over and giving her a kiss on the cheek, even though he only meant to leave her with a hug. She grabbed his wrist as he pulled away and gently tugged him back. He turned around, looked into her eyes, and saw something that hit him like a slap.

Alexis looked profoundly lonely.

So Orson dared to ask her. "Have your parents come to visit you yet?"

Her eyes got glassy as she shook her head and bit her bottom lip, but Alexis didn't take her gaze away, or let go of his hand. "No, not yet. But you have."

He pulled away, feeling something unexpected and not exactly wanted, at least not right now.

Of course he had thought about getting back with Alexis. Many, many times in the years since their breakup. Of course he would want to reconcile with the mother of his child. That would be what was best for Connor.

But right now she was vulnerable, and he would be wrong to act on that vulnerability. Right now he had work to do, people to please, and money to make for them, with a better than fair percentage for himself. Right now he had feelings for Jess that were like critters scampering around in the closet. Trapped inside with nowhere to go, scratching at the walls, waiting to scurry out the second Orson opened the door.

Yet another thought of Jess was a like bullet through his heart.

Not knowing was the worst. Knowing that he probably

loved her was hard enough. Dealing with her total disappearance was harder. And worst of all was wondering not just where she was and what she was doing, but who she was doing it with.

Jess is fucking Harrison Turner now, Orson old boy. You don't stand a chance.

She never wants to talk to you. Not ever again.

She hates you for ruining her life.

Jess still didn't answer when he called, and Orson was still too unsure to ask Ellis, knowing that his friend would have to blame him, even if only a little.

Alexis waited for him to speak. The only thing he had to say would sound so insensitive. But it was the one thing he needed to know, the one thing that would finally help him move on with his life. Orson loved spending time with Connor, but the kid was making his new life impossible.

Alexis sat in a chair and Connor climbed into her arms. She lay back, petting his hair.

He crouched by her chair and finally spoke. "So, how long do you think they're going to keep you?"

"Oh," Alexis shrugged. "I can go at any time. Right now I'm here voluntarily. I—"

Then why the hell are you still here?

"—just need to put myself back together."

And you can't do that at home? With shared custody? So that I can work?

"Oh," he said.

"I miss you, Mommy!"

"I miss you, too, Punkin."

Connor nuzzled into her chest, practically purring.

Orson considered his next question. He didn't want to be insensitive. She did lose her boyfriend to an OD in her house after all. But Alexis had been away for a while now, and she had responsibilities waiting at home. Life was supposed to go on.

"Is there anything I can do to help … put you back together?"

Alexis laughed, but she didn't answer the question. She asked one of her own instead.

"So how are things with Jess?"

That was the last thing that Orson wanted to talk about, at least with Alexis.

"She's fine."

"Is it getting serious?"

He couldn't believe this, or read her face, though Orson did find himself realizing, or maybe remembering, how beautiful Alexis actually was when not ranting and raving or dressing him down.

He shrugged.

"Come on," she coaxed, "you can tell me."

Her eyes were hungry for some sort of connection. What must it be like, living out your low point in a place that your parents will foot the bill for, but they wouldn't visit you while you were there? That was the story of Alexis' life.

Orson admitted defeat. "I don't even know where she is."

Alexis looked surprised. "Oh?"

"She moved out of the Brick."

"Did you ask Ellis where she went?"

Orson shook his head. "Not yet."

"Oh …" There was so much more that she wanted to say. He could see it in the way she looked up at him with wide eyes, obviously hoping that he would fill the silence with something that might make her feel better.

An invitation. An offer. A solution.

Because that was Orson's nature. He always wanted to be the hero and please everyone. He'd kept his distance from Alexis for so long because for the last few years, the more he cared, the more he hurt. And now, as circumstances had gone out of their way to soften her, he felt softer too.

But he was still fixated on Jess and his many, many commitments to the Shellys. Figuring things out with Alexis would fix the situation with Connor, and once that was solved, Orson had to believe that everything else would be well on the way to solving itself.

He changed the subject again, or at least he dragged it back to where it had been. "So, are they helping to put you back together? What do you do here?"

She looked away. Didn't want to talk about this.

There was something wrong with her eyes. They weren't just glassy, they were haunted.

Then Orson realized, there was something that Alexis wanted to say, but she wasn't just going to say it. He was going to have to pull it out of her. This wasn't new, but it had been long enough that it took him a while to recognize it for what it was.

In many ways Alexis had seemed like a different woman the last few years. Their divorce, her disappointment in Orson, and the endless demands of being a mother had changed her. Their interactions were starved of the sweetness they'd shared once upon a time, when Connor was a bump in her belly.

Right now, Orson was looking at that Alexis. The one who used to lie beside him for hours, brushing her fingers against his cheek, looking over at him with her expressive eyes.

He gave her a look, confident that she could read his expression, just like she used to: *I've got this.*

He pulled out his phone, swiped until he had Connor's favorite game on-screen, then showed it to his son.

"Hey, buddy, do you want to play some Elimigator?"

Of course he would. It was one of his favorites, and Orson kept it off of Connor's tablet for exactly this reason, only allowing the boy to play it on his phone when Orson needed him to entertain himself, which he was willing to do approximately half the time.

He handed Connor the phone and a pair of wireless earbuds, then pointed to the corner. "You can play five games. But you have to do it over there. Deal?"

"Five games!" Connor cried out, then scrambled over to the corner, sat criss-cross apple sauce, and started to play.

Alexis laughed. "Smooth."

"I've learned a few tricks."

"Clearly."

Orson took Alexis by the hand and led her to the opposite side of the room and gestured for her to sit in one of a pair of chairs with a tiny end table between them. He took the other chair.

"So, do you want to tell me what's on your mind?"

She shifted in her seat and her upper lip trembled, just a little. Orson might have missed it if he hadn't been looking. But even so, he would have definitely caught her white-knuckled grip on the chair.

"What do you think?" Alexis laughed, a brittle little thing that seemed to break in half at the end. She let go of the chair and gestured around the room. "All of this?"

"You know what I mean," he pushed. "There's something you want to tell me."

"I don't know what you're talking about."

But she did. Orson could see it in her blinking, broken eyes, her low shoulders that had lost all their pride, and even in the set of her sharp jaw that had inexplicably soft-ened. He could see it just like the other times she had wanted him to draw something out without her needing to be explicit.

Like the time she wanted to confess to all the credit card debt that her parents wouldn't cover, the time she wanted Orson to do better in bed, or the first time Alexis wanted him to know that she loved him, but vulnerable as she was in the moment, found the words themselves a burden to say.

He took her hand. "Yes, you do."

"No." She shook her head, still not meaning it.

Orson waited. He had all day.

Fix Alexis, and his life might return to the beautiful new normal he'd been trying to build.

A tear fell from one eye, then the other, and suddenly Alexis was crying without any sound.

Still he waited, saying nothing but squeezing her hand. "You can tell me."

"But I can't." It was barely a whisper.

Orson looked over at Connor, eyes glued to his game, then back at Alexis. "Don't you want to come home?"

He waited for her to nod. She did.

"Don't you want to be with Connor?"

This time a whimper followed her nod. The crying was no longer silent. Orson pulled her chair over, adjusting it so that Connor could only see his mommy's back. The boy looked up then back to his game.

"You know you're going to tell me." Orson reached out, lifted her chin and met her eyes. "So do it now."

Alexis turned away. He grabbed her chin, still gentle, but firmer than before. "Let me help you. *Please.*"

Orson felt desperate to help her. She was a combina-tion lock with one turn of the dial to go.

She started to cry harder.

He pulled Alexis against him and encouraged her tears.

She kept them muffled, both for Connor and herself.

"You can tell me anything," he whispered.

Then Alexis whispered back.

"I think I killed Tyler."

Chapter Thirty-Six

Orson left Gateways in a panic, though he tried not to show it.

He might have been lying to himself -- he had a way of doing that -- but it seemed like Alexis was better when he left.

He sure as hell wasn't.

Orson didn't know what to do. He couldn't exactly pretend like he hadn't heard her confession. From what Alexis had said, manslaughter was a best-case scenario for the mother of his child.

He needed help, had to know the best way to play this. First, tell Dominic and Melinda before they found out some other way, because if they were starting to get annoyed with him, then this would push them over the edge for sure.

Orson looked over at Connor, wishing that he didn't have the stupid *no playing in the car* rule. People were idiots behind the wheel, especially in this city, always texting instead of keeping their eyes on the road. He didn't want his son to grow up associating the car with the phone. It was one of the few parenting things that he and Alexis saw eye-to-eye on a hundred percent, which had always surprised him.

So Orson did what he usually did on those rare occasions when he had to make a call with Connor in the car.

"I'll just be a minute, buddy," he said, pulling into an empty lot and got out of the car to make his call.

Dominic answered on the second ring. "Orson."

"Hey Dominic, I have a situation."

"Sounds dire."

He took a deep breath then said, "I don't know what to do. I just got back from Gateways."

"I take it Alexis isn't doing well."

"At first she seemed better than I thought, but then …" How could he say it?

"But then what, Orson?"

"But then … she told me something."

"You're not reading from a script at the end of Act I. There's no need to ramp up the tension right now. If you have something to say, then spit it out."

"Alexis might have had something to do with Tyler's death."

After a long and painful silence, Dominic said, "Be more specific."

"She—"

"Wait. Don't. We shouldn't have this conversation over the phone … is this something that should be reported to the police? And I'm not asking if you *want to*. I'm asking if it should be."

"Yes," he said, mostly at the end of an exhale.

"Then I need you to go to the police. Immediately. You can tell me all the specifics later, but right now you need to get in front of this. It's in the wild. If Alexis told you, then she might very well tell someone else. You don't want to be an accessory. We can't afford that, Orson. Do you understand?"

No hesitation. "Absolutely. But, I have Connor right now."

"Of course you do," Dominic said, not sounding happy. "Figure something out, but do it fast."

"Okay." Orson looked over at the car, and Connor waving. He gave his son a smile that felt like a benchpress. "I'm on it."

He hung up the phone and got in his car.

"Who was that, Daddy?"

"It was my boss. Dominic. I need to run an errand right now."

"Are we going to Target?"

"No." Orson pulled into the street. "We're going to the police station."

"Really?"

Connor sounded excited, giving Orson the perfect way to play this.

"Yep, really. It's a field trip. We're going to see where the good guys catch all the bad guys. We won't be there long."

"What are we going to do there? Are we going to see the bad guys in jail?"

"No. I don't think they'll let us see any of the bad guys because that's dangerous, and they'll want to keep us safe. We'll probably just see all the desks and stuff in the place where they do all the police work."

"Oh," Connor said, sounding a lot less interested.

"But you'll get to play Elimigator!"

"At the police station?"

"Yep. Because it's a grownup place with a lot of grownup talk about bad guys, so the officers will probably want you to plug your ears. But I think we can outsmart them by using the earbuds. Then you'll get to play your game."

Everything happened so fast once they got to the station. Fifteen minutes later he was sitting across from Officer Duvall, a guy who looked younger than he probably was. It was unsettling. Orson had expected to spill his guts to some grizzled old officer who'd been taking statements since the '70s.

Connor sat in the seat beside him, earbuds in and Elimigator out. What a fucking asshole he was, doing this to his child. The boy had no idea that his father was turning his mother in right now, for murder or manslaughter or something. Whatever it was would keep her away from being Connor's mommy for a long, long time.

Maybe they could stop by Acres of Toys on the way home. Did they still have those? Orson had been buying everything either on impulse or Amazon. Going to an actual toy store would be fun. Or maybe the movies. Possibly Disneyland.

"Mind if we go over the details again?"

Orson looked from Connor to Duvall and nodded. "That's why we're here."

"So your wife — sorry, your ex-wife, accidentally made her boyfriend overdose."

Orson nodded.

"And her boyfriend is Dylan from *Greens*."

"Tyler Crane. That's right."

"Wow."

You've gotta be kidding me. This idiot kid is impressed. What would happen if I asked to speak to his manager?

"Right. Wow." Orson glanced again at Connor. "Can we speed this up? I'm not sure how much longer I can pretend that this is awesome." He looked around the precinct and added, "I'm not that good an actor."

Duvall sat up straighter, and his face looked immediately more serious. "How can you accidentally make someone OD? Either he wanted to get high, or she was trying to poison him."

Orson shook his head. "That's exactly it. She thinks it was both."

"How so?"

"Tyler was using, but Alexis didn't know that he had taken anything. She was just trying to get him to chill out, so she mashed up some of his pills and put it in his ice cream. It's this vanilla soy stuff. Apparently, he binges, and half the time he purges right after he eats, so she wasn't even sure if it would make a difference."

"But it did." Duvall looked thoughtful. "Is this how your ex-wife usually gets people to *chill out?* By drugging them?"

"You don't understand. Tyler was an asshole."

Duvall looked incredulous. It was amazing how difficult some people found it to separate a character from the person who played it, but an officer of the law should know better. Maybe he would, after he'd finished going through puberty.

"You still can't drug someone, even if they're an asshole."

Orson shook his head. "No. I don't mean like the guy was a jerk, even though he was. I mean that this was self-defense. Alexis was scared because Tyler liked to hit her."

Duvall leaned forward. "Did she ever call the police on him? Or press charges?"

"She couldn't. Tyler's press meant everything to him."

"Looks like he doesn't have to worry about that at all anymore."

"If she was afraid for her life, then isn't that self-defense?"

"Look," Duvall said, far more flip than he had any right to be, "I'm not the judge or the jury, or your lawyer. My job is to take your statement."

"Well, you're not very good at it."

The officer stared at him, then laughed.

"Here," he said, pushing a clipboard full of paperwork across his desk toward Orson. "Fill this out."

Why was the world going fucking nuts all around him?

After four aimless years, Orson had finally gotten his shit together. But here it was, all falling apart anyway.

He couldn't think of Jess without wanting to cry. He couldn't think about his work with Shellter without feeling an almost cellular certainty that Dominic and Melinda were pissed at his many failures and were always imminent minutes from letting him go.

Now he couldn't think about Alexis or Connor without knowing that in some way he was destroying them both.

Orson looked up from his paperwork. "What's next? For Alexis, I mean."

"She'll be brought in for questioning. It could get worse from there." Duvall almost sounded sorry.

Was the Universe trying to give him a lesson in being careful what you wished for? Because if so, message received, loud and clear.

Orson had wanted more than every other weekend with Connor, but he hadn't expected to be a full-time single father. That was a job he simply could not afford to take. Opportunities were slipping like sand through his fingers. He couldn't film during the day, go out at night, or party his way to the top.

The Shellys were probably talking about him right

now. Strategizing the best ways to eliminate him from their lineup while minimizing the hit to their bottom line.

Orson had become a liability.

They stopped for ice cream on the way home instead of going to the toy store. It seemed lower maintenance, and Orson needed a nap. His headache felt like the threat of a full-body shutdown. He couldn't remember it ever hurting so much. They went to Inside Scoop for the real stuff, and he let Connor order a full grownup-sized sundae. It would make him sick, but at least then they could be sick together. And if the boy got a stomach ache like he always did after eating too much ice cream, then he would probably do what he usually did and take a bear nap.

But this time he didn't get a stomach ache, even though he ordered the Marble Mountain — three scoops of the Scoop's special blend of vanilla and caramel that they called the Marble, topped with hot fudge, Heath Bar nuggets, chocolate chip cookie crumbles, white chocolate shavings, toasted marshmallows, and a healthy dollop of whipped cream.

Orson was exhausted and desperate for sleep. His son was higher than he had ever been in his life.

Orson collapsed on the couch and closed his eyes, but he couldn't ignore his Connor, squealing as he thundered through the apartment and into the upstairs loft where he slept. He shouldn't be up there, Orson really needed to get him down.

But he was so, so …

"Daddy, Daddy, it's raining!"

Orson groaned and turned over, clutching a pillow, wanting to put it over his head. "That's nice," he said.

"It's raining inside!"

Inside?

Orson bolted up in bed and took a look around. It sure as hell wasn't raining.

He lay back down.

With his eyes halfway closed he heard, "In the music room! It's raining in the music room!"

Then Orson was on his feet and marching across the apartment.

He heard it before he saw it, the heavy dripping from ceiling to floor. His luxurious bathroom was leaking. It was the left side of his little loft suite, off to the side of his bedroom. He remembered Connor climbing the stairs as he drifted to sleep on the sofa, too lazy to stop him.

"What did you do?" Orson was working furiously to not lose his shit, but he was clinging to the edge by his fingernails.

"Nothing." Connor looked away.

Orson spun around, darted toward the stairs, then raced up into the loft and over to the bathroom. The door was closed. He flung it open and wanted to explode.

Water was *everywhere.*

"Connor!" He screamed, louder than he ever had at his son. "Get in here. NOW!"

A moment later his son stood in the doorway. "I'm sorry, Daddy!"

The boy started to cry.

Through gritted teeth Orson growled, "What did you do?"

From behind his tears he blubbered, "I flushed a peel?"

Jesus Christ. "A banana peel?"

Connor nodded violently.

"How many times did you flush the toilet before it went down?"

He didn't answer. Just kept shaking his head, even harder than he had been nodding it.

"How many times, Connor?"

"Too many!" Connor cried out.

Then the dam shattered, as if this moment weren't wet enough already, and the boy began to wail.

Orson took out his phone. He had to call the plumber, of course. But there was another person he needed to reach first.

Feeling irredeemable, he made a few swipes.

"Orson," Dominic answered.

"I need the number for Natural Nurturing."

Chapter Thirty-Seven

Summer wasn't all that different from winter in LA, if you were judging by things like the weather or the apparel. The skies were blue a bit more often, and the days were definitely longer, but that was about it. Nothing at all like where Orson had grown up.

Farewell, Atlantis would start shooting in a week. So life would change yet again. But every change since he'd accepted the Shellys' offer had been an improvement.

He loved his daily routine, of walking from his apartment to the park, people watching for a bit, then reading the news on his phone, before making the short walk back to the Catalyst.

Arbor Park was new, probably about the same age as his building. It was small enough to feel cozy, but big enough that he couldn't see the whole park at once. There was a pond, with ducks that you weren't supposed to feed, although everyone did, and four clusters of three benches each circling its perimeter. Orson always chose the one that put his back to the hot dog cart. Because he wasn't about to stop liking hot dogs just because his trainer, Drake, told him that eating lips and assholes in plastic tubing made him a pussy.

The old couple sitting directly across from him, feeding the ducks and taking turns as the lookout. The teenagers under the blanket behind that tree, pretending they weren't having sex. The mom with her three children, pulling snacks out of her bags like she was doing magic tricks. The other mom, who also had three children, but made it seem easy. The old woman sitting alone, watching the moms and looking like she might cry.

Orson wondered what they might be thinking about him. Probably not much. That's one of the reasons he liked this park so much, and this bench in particular. Something about it made him feel a little invisible. And while that was cancer to an actor, every day at 2:30 or so it felt like a salve.

Orson looked at his phone. Like usual, he checked Hollywood Hunted first. And like usual, he wondered why, because it always made him feel bad, even if there was nothing to report. Just knowing that Ellis was behind those words felt like cold steel at his neck. The world didn't know who was behind the site, but Orson did, and he could feel his friend's bitterness growing, toward the city, its monstrous puppeteers, and the actors who performed like marionettes on their behalf.

He always looked, hoping that one day Ellis might mention Jess. But he never did.

Maybe he never would. Orson thought that with so much bad news circulating about her, Ellis would love to drop a beneficial bomb if he had one.

But there was nothing today.

He skipped around to a few other blogs, following his random, regular pattern, then ended by opening Melinda's daily email full of Rummage links he was required to read.

Before meeting the Shellys, Orson had used a simple Google Alert with his name. The Rummage app was a different level. He didn't understand all the filters that Melinda had entered into his personal feed, but he didn't need to. Rummage tailored Orson's news to him, and Melinda insisted that he stay up-to-date on what was being said, not because he was self-involved, but so he would remain prepared for whatever might be coming.

His feed was filled with the usual. Orson thought it sort of odd that Ellis' blog never showed up in his feed, even though it circled all the same news and seemed to be exploding in numbers and growing by the day. Ellis wrote about him a lot, and his angle was always positive, but he seemed to defy or at least disregard the stories that Dominic and Melinda were wanting out in the wild. There was nothing about Orson today, and every second on the site kept Orson thinking of Ellis, and that hurt, so he quickly moved on.

Most of the remaining articles were irritating. Stupid clickbait bullshit. The headlines were catchy, but clicking got you three insipid paragraphs if you were lucky. And so many of them were saying the same ridiculous crap -- showing photos of Orson looking sad or distraught, all of them out of context, and photos of Jess partying hard, on the arm of this actor or that one, including a couple of the feistier headline grabbers like, Vanessa Holloway and even the porn actress Dakota Sparks.

Not a single one of these writers knew Jess, and yet none had a problem calling her a whore, or implying it. How did Ellis get off being pissed at Orson, or blaming Hollywood, when he had the voice to defend her and didn't?

The thought about Ellis hurt, so Orson cast it away.

He came to a story about Alexis. He had passed

several, but this one he clicked on. Nothing sexy about this headline; it got right to the point.

Troubled Daughter of Restaurateur Desmond Belle Charged With Tyler Crane's Murder.

Orson read what he already knew, that Alexis had been charged when she got out of the hospital. She'd confessed — knowing the charge was coming thanks to Orson, which she shockingly didn't seem to be holding against him — but claimed it was self-defense. She was now embroiled in an ugly battle with both the law and the press. Fortunately, and no surprise to Orson (it was one of the things that had made it easier for him to turn her in), Alexis had documented her boyfriend's abuse and had hundreds of pictures to prove it. Once the case went public, Daddy Desmond stepped up, posting bail and paying for an attorney that probably cost more per hour than Orson used to spend on child support each month.

Alexis wasn't allowed custody of Connor, so Orson was still a full-time dad. Or at least as full-time as he could be, considering that Connor spent most of every day with Natural Nurturing and his special liaison, Armando, while Orson worked. Orson had a hard time pretending he liked the guy.

At least Orson and Alexis were getting along, and she seemed optimistic that everything would turn out. She also seemed genuinely interested in his career and how well things were going for him. There was a time when Orson would've assumed her interest was based on her desire to see Connor benefit, but Alexis was one of the people who had believed in him first, and hardest, and sometimes he thought she might actually be happy for him.

"You really did it, Orson. I'm proud of you, and I'm sorry I was such a bitch all the time."

She had said something like that every time they'd

talked for the last few weeks, and it was healing something inside him.

Same for whenever he talked to his parents. They had come out with his brother for Memorial Day, then Samuel stayed behind for an extra few days. He and Orson had the best time they'd had since before his high school graduation.

Everyone seemed so proud of him, and most importantly, Orson was proud of himself.

Except for the thing with Hadley.

After he'd told the cops about Alexis' confession, he couldn't risk being in a relationship with her. Jess seemed lost to him — even Ellis had no idea where she was, and she wasn't replying to his emails any more than she answered Orson's.

And Hadley had been so … persistent.

Orson didn't think he'd ever love her, but she was beautiful and fun and great for his career. Not to mention her determination to have sex with him as often as possible, as energetically as possible, and as inventively as possible.

As far as he could tell, the things that tabloids said about their relationship seemed to turn her on as much as he did. Which made things easy for him because he didn't have to love her, or stop loving Jess. He just had to fuck her hard and make nice for the paparazzi.

He wasn't proud of his relationship with Hadley, but it was easy, and the rest of his life was so demanding that easy was what he needed most right now.

He finished reading the garbage, wondering if he could skip tomorrow without Melinda knowing. She probably had some sort of tracking pixel that told her when he opened the email and how long he spent reading.

He sighed and opened his email, reading the one from Dominic first.

Oscar season was still months away, but his performance in *Bottleneck* already had people buzzing. He'd shot a touching father-and-son commercial for Sloppy's, and now strangers were approaching him on the street to thank him for making them cry. The Hill of Beans barista two blocks from the Catalyst had always been flirty with him, but now she looked like she was falling freshly in love whenever Orson opened the coffee shop door.

Even if he didn't land the statue, his nomination seemed like a shoo-in, and there was plenty of advancement that came with that accolade alone.

And if he wasn't nominated? Then Orson would benefit from the industry outrage of his being overlooked.

It was like being back in high school, basking in all of the praise. But it was different this time.

Logan had said, "You'll know when everything is about to change because even the air feels like it's constantly about to change. Pay attention when that happens because you'll never have that time again, and once it's over, you'll miss it."

Orson had listened, which is why he walked to the park each day. With what the Shellys had lined up for him, life would be upside-down from everything he knew. Soon he would be recognized wherever he went, and these were his last gasps at freedom.

The park was his happy place, where Orson could reflect on the horizon ahead, and all the mistakes happened behind him. He could focus on work, close his eyes and memorize lines. No distractions. No women. No child.

With school out, Orson no longer had to worry about helping Connor adjust to kindergarten. But he did have to worry about Armando. Orson had a hard time with how attached Connor seemed to the liaison. Orson wanted to spend more time with his son, but he knew it was selfish in more ways than one. Connor needed to be around other kids right now, anyway. And with him occupied all day, Orson could focus on his career.

He stood and stretched, wondering why he was feeling so low.

The park was supposed to make him feel better, but today for some reason Orson felt worse.

Was it Connor, Alexis, or Jess? Something with work, the Shellys, or Hadley?

Orson didn't know, but it picked at him, scratching like jagged nails on a scab.

His eyes caught the hot dog cart the second his nose caught the scent. He was defeated immediately.

He paid for his dog with a smile. No one had to know. The first bite of hot dog tasted like Heaven itself.

He followed enough of the rules, and he was starving. Not for food, but just for a hit of flavor and fat, one of which was in shorter supply than ever before and the other an endangered species. Orson had a done what he thought was a decent job of staying in shape through the last four years while hoping to get back in front of the camera, but now that he had a nutritionist and a trainer, he realized how much of a joke that actually was. With the upcoming shoot, and the amount of time that he'd be shirtless, the Shellys expected perfection.

He had been eating all of his vegetables for months now; Orson deserved a little dessert.

Eating his vegetables wasn't just about the food. Beyond the nutritionist and trainer, acting and dialogue coaches, the career counseling, the cleaning crew that came to blitz his place once each week, Orson regularly went in to get the pubes ripped from his skin. He hated that the most, found the whole thing humiliating. At first he hadn't minded, even liked it a little. He never knew exactly how to trim himself down there and appreciated the manscaping, but now there wasn't edging so much as a full mow, and it left Orson feeling like a little boy.

Of course, Hadley liked it. But she liked everything that the Shellys wanted her to.

"I love you this way!" Hadley had raved the first time he came out looking like a mannequin. "I hate it when I get hair in my mouth when I'm blowing you, even though I *totally love* blowing you."

Then Hadley fell to her knees.

On the bright side, Orson did feel like he could be himself around her, whether they were disappearing into the dark shadows of the darkest clubs or walking hand in hand down the red carpet. They talked and they laughed and they had mind-blowing sex. Most of the time, that was more than enough.

Sure, Hadley was a bit relentless about their rekindled relationship, but that was her business if she wanted to live in the delusion.

Okay, if he had to admit it, there was one other thing he wasn't proud of.

He was drinking too much.

And he really shouldn't be doing coke.

But it was everywhere around him, and so far it hadn't been all that much, just the occasional bump, mostly to keep Hadley happy.

When Hadley was happy, life was good. If he focused on the future and stopped trying to fix all the people from his past, it would get better.

Orson's phone rang outside the elevator. Fate testing him. A text from Ellis.

Long time. Wanna get together?

Ellis was baggage. Jess was baggage. Alexis was baggage. How long was he going to keep dragging them around?

He was about to put his phone away when Ellis texted again.

I wanna talk about Jess.

Chapter Thirty-Eight

Ellis had been both dreading and looking forward to this get-together for a while now. When Orson finally agreed to stop being a selfish asshole and meet him, he'd expected they would get together at the Litter Box, go to the Mill, or maybe even lunch or a movie. The last thing he pictured was them working out in the Catalyst. Or more accurately, Orson working out while Ellis spotted him like an asshole.

"So, you have to lift heavy shit and starve yourself every day?"

Orson didn't answer. He just grunted, benching 220 before finishing and sitting up.

Ellis was at least fifty pounds overweight and hated exercise of any kind. He also liked processed foods, despite knowing the evils of the industry, and was content to die a little sooner, so long as that meant that he was living a little more. Ironically, meeting in the gym had been Ellis' idea. Scheduling time with Orson was a major production.

So Orson was getting a workout in while the two of them finally caught up.

It was all so efficient. So impersonal. So Hollywood.

They'd already caught up on the everyday stuff, while dancing around the real reason they were both even there. Orson now knew that Lacy was filming amateur porn in her apartment, that Angus was in the hospital for old age or something, and that the kid who lived in Orson's old place was kind of a cock.

But Ellis would rather wait for Orson to ask about Jess. It was going to be a difficult conversation. The least Orson could do was start it.

"I'm done lifting the heavy shit. And I can stop starving myself as soon as I'm done in here. But I need to run before then. Wanna run with me?"

Orson pointed toward a pair of Athletatone treadmills.

Ellis followed his finger then looked down at his stomach and laughed. "How about if I walk?"

"Sounds great. I'll jog so that we can still talk." Orson pressed a few buttons and the belt started moving, but then he wasted no time. "So ... Jess?"

Ellis had been waiting for that prompt for nearly forty minutes, and still it somehow managed to catch him off guard.

For the first time, Ellis wondered if he'd be able to get through this without crying.

His throat hitched. A terrible sign.

"She moved out a while ago. It might have even been that last night I watched Connor. Hard to know for sure. She was practically a ghost by then anyhow."

Orson didn't answer, just cranked the treadmill speed up a couple notches. So Ellis continued.

"I got tired of knocking and knocking, so I finally asked Benson to open it up. Her door wasn't even locked. I felt like an idiot for never even trying it. I just didn't want to intrude. But there was nothing in there."

Orson slowed the belt, looking like he might vomit.

"She looked like hell the last few times I saw her, though she manages to keep it together on the red carpet."

"I've noticed," Orson said, looking that much closer to puking.

For nearly half a minute, which felt excruciatingly close to three, the Catalyst gym was silent except for Orson's elevens slapping the belt as it passed underfoot. He slowed the treadmill again.

"You said you had news. That sounds like no news."

"You knew that Jess moved out?"

A beat, then, "No. But it doesn't surprise me. Half the time she's with Harrison Turner, and the other half, it's some billionaire or big name of the week. I can't really see her slumming it at the Brick."

Ouch. And totally unnecessary, asshole.

Ellis crossed his arms. Orson knew more than he was saying. Probably about Dominic too. She had been talking to the Shellys a lot in the days before she disappeared. Her walls were thin, and when she was all coked up, Jess wasn't quiet. Not on the phone, and not while she was entertaining a man. Ellis had no romantic feelings toward Jess -- he'd known her way too long for that -- but still he hated that particular sound more than any other.

"What do you know about her and Dominic?"

"What?" Orson looked over and nearly lost his balance, that question a sudden rock on his road. Either he didn't know or was surprised that Ellis did.

"Jess and Dominic. They were talking a lot right before she went bye-bye. And it all sounded personal."

"What do you mean, *personal?*"

Ellis shrugged. "Hard to say exactly. But there was a definite vibe."

"Can you please be more specific?"

Orson was getting bothered. Good. Maybe they were getting somewhere.

"I don't know much," Ellis said, telling the truth, at least more than Orson. "Just that there were phone calls, and they seemed frequent enough. I couldn't hear exactly what was said, but I could hear the tone."

"How frequent?"

"Three or four times. And you can't tell me that's not like fifty for a guy like Dominic Shelly."

Orson stopped the belt.

"And what about the tone?"

"She sounded … indebted."

Now Orson seemed mad. And Ellis was sure that he hadn't known.

"I don't know what that means."

"Me either," Ellis admitted. "But you know Jess. She doesn't take bullshit and she calls things like she sees them. That's not how it sounded when she was talking to Dominic."

"But you didn't actually hear anything that she said?"

Ellis shook his head.

Orson was getting more agitated. "How do you know it was Dominic?"

"Context, I guess. I heard his name a couple of times."

"I thought you couldn't hear anything?"

"I heard *thank you, Dominic* a couple of times. That sounded clear."

Orson shook his head, emphatic. "I don't see why Dominic and Jess would be talking."

"But is it *possible* they were? Or are?"

"Dominic would have told me."

Ellis tried to be gentle. "But would he have?"

"I don't know, Ellis. But if they are talking, then I sure

as hell don't know what that would be about, and it definitely isn't my problem. It *can't* be my problem."

"Are you serious?" A few successes, and now Jess meant nothing to him? What an insufferable pig Orson had turned out to be. "Do you not realize that she wouldn't even be in this downward spiral if not for you? I mean, no offense, but you led her right there. This all started on the night that you got your invitation."

Ellis had nearly added *stupid* before *invitation.*

"How do you know this is a downward spiral? Leaving the Brick isn't a bad thing, if you're moving up and not just out. You've seen the pictures. Maybe it's not the Jess we know, but does it look to you like she's not being taken care of?"

"Honestly, that's exactly what it looks like to me. I think she's in trouble, and I think you should be more concerned."

"What do you want me to do, Ellis?"

"I don't know, man. You could start by caring."

"I care," Orson snapped as he dismounted from the treadmill and turned it off. "What else can I do?"

Ellis eyed him, then decided to go for broke. "I'd like to interview you for my blog."

"Hollywood Hunted?"

"Right. The massively successful blog that's been publishing some really great stories about you lately, that don't paint you in a depressing light or beat up on Jess? You know, that one? I'm working on a really big story, and I think you'd have some great insights. Fifteen minutes, on the record."

"How does that help Jess?"

"Trust me that it does. Even if it doesn't, it helps me."

Orson shook his head. "I can't. At least not without asking Melinda. She has to approve all of my interviews."

"She has to approve all of your interviews? What the fuck? Are you serious?"

"Of course I'm serious. Do you know how much they're investing in me? The wrong press can undo everything, even if it's the right sentence written in the wrong place."

"Sounds like some sage advice from Mrs. Melinda Shelly."

Ellis could tell by Orson's face that it was.

"I'm sorry,' he said, shaking his head again. "But I can't, not without asking. But I've never actually asked about an interview before, and I can't imagine why they would say no."

"I can. Please don't."

"Come on, Ellis. You don't have to be like that."

"I'm not *being* like anything. But I don't want you to ask the Shellys for shit."

"Why? I bet this is a slam dunk. They'll probably be thrilled to hear that I know the guy who runs Hollywood Hunted."

"No, Orson. Nobody knows. And right now, I'm sorry that you do."

"Well, okay then." Orson checked his phone. "I've got another appointment."

Ellis said, "I understand."

And he did, even though that filled him with a mournful sort of woe.

Ellis drove home, lamenting the cracks that were so clearly appearing in Orson's exterior and thinking about his biggest project yet, the one that might have enough impact to help Jess, Orson, and this entire fucking town.

Ellis was going to *destroy* the Shellys.

His phone buzzed in the center console, rattling against the edges. He looked down at the screen and felt a happy lump in his throat. It had taken forever to get here, but now it was happening fast.

Ellis pulled over and answered the phone.

"Hey man," said the voice. "It's Harrison Turner. I'm ready to talk."

Chapter Thirty-Nine

"It's really fun to prove people wrong," Hadley said to Connor.

The two of them were stacking LEGOs, though considering the sprawling plastic skyline, *architecting* might be a better word. Orson was on the couch, going over his lines, and looking up every few moments, surprised every time by how well his son and Hadley were getting along.

"What do you mean?" Connor asked.

"Jimmy said that you couldn't ride a bike like he could, right?"

"Uh-huh." Connor stacked a big blue block on top of a tiny yellow one, guaranteeing that the thing would topple.

"Well, you *are* going to ride your bike, then Jimmy's going to feel really silly. And that's going to feel good."

"Oh." He stacked another one and sent the wobbly edifice spilling to the floor.

"That's one of the things that works best for me," Hadley admitted to the five-year-old. "If Jimmy told me that I couldn't ride a bike, then I would be riding by the end of the day, no doubt about it."

"But I don't have a bike."

Hadley winked at Orson, then whispered, "Maybe you should ask your dad."

Connor spun around. "Can I get a bike, Daddy?"

"Sure."

"Today?"

"No, not today."

"Why not?" Connor asked.

Hadley said, "We have plans."

"All of us?"

"All of us!" Hadley squealed.

Orson was always surprised by how enthusiastic Hadley seemed about spending time with Connor. But it made him feel better about their not-quite-relationship. He didn't love her but was comfortable with her, and she was good to his son.

"What are we going to do?" Connor asked as he did a little dance of anticipation across the hardwood floor.

"It's a surprise," Orson called out from the couch.

Hadley smiled at him from across the room, then she planted her palms on the floor, pushed herself to her feet, and stretched. But now it didn't seem like a show for his benefit. It was oddly domestic. The sight filled Orson with appreciation — Hadley really had helped him to feel better about everything lately, and not just because of all the blow jobs, although those definitely helped.

"When do you want to go?" Hadley asked.

Orson's phone rang before he could answer. He looked at the screen. Alexis, calling from prison.

Like always, it made him feel sick to his stomach. They were getting along, but she only called because she wanted to talk to Connor. Orson didn't know what would be best for his son, but he wasn't willing to be the kind of dad who kept his son from talking to his mother, no matter where she was calling from.

He accepted the collect call, then said, "Your mom is on the phone."

Connor scampered over and took Orson's phone. "Hi, Mommy!"

Then he started shoving two minutes worth of words into that first thirty seconds, circling the couch while awkwardly holding the phone a bit too far from his ear. When he reached the other side he sank down to his butt, planted his back against the couch, and babbled away like he always did when talking to Alexis, for however long he had until her time was up.

Hadley sat next to Orson on the couch.

"You're a great dad."

"Thanks. It's hard to feel that way half the time. But if you don't mind my saying so, I think you're going to make a great mom someday."

She made a face. "No thanks."

"But you're so natural."

Hadley laughed. "That's because I'm the oldest of six siblings. My brother Jacob still calls me Mom to this day. I was always the one counting heads to make sure we hadn't lost anyone. Keeping the brood entertained when Mom was trying to make dinner. Making sure that no one fought because when they did our dad might beat the hell out of Mom. So yeah, I can do it, but that doesn't mean I want to. There's too much fun stuff to do. Like this." She kissed him long and full on the mouth, then added with a whisper and a glance at his bulge. "Want me to finish?"

"When we get back home," he said, getting slightly harder.

"Or while we're out," she teased. "So, when are we leaving?"

"As soon as he's off the call." He hesitated, not sure if he should ask. "Are you sure you wanna come?"

"Are you kidding?" She gave him a playful punch on the shoulder. "House hunting is *fun.*"

Hadley's interest was making him nervous. Going together would definitely be a lot more fun than going alone, especially considering she would almost for sure drag him into an empty room before dropping to her knees and sucking him off, once she had found a way to keep Connor occupied, which she had become expert at doing. But she had suggested this, found a bunch of houses, contacted her realtor friend Alana, and scheduled the day full of showings.

"What is it you love?"

"*Everything.* I would be a realtor, if I didn't look like this."

What had sounded like false modesty when Orson first met her was the real thing. From not getting cast in the roles that she wanted to being underestimated at every turn, looking like a super model was a major pain in Hadley's ass. It was shocking to realize that a person could be *too* good-looking.

Connor prattled to Mommy in the background, talking about LEGOs and pancakes and waffles and syrup.

"Why would you want to be a realtor?"

Hadley smiled, like they were about to talk movies. "I love looking at the houses themselves. All the rooms, ceilings to floors and all the moldings in between. Big rooms, little rooms, hidden rooms. I love bedroom and bathroom suites that are the size of the house I grew up in. Spanish tile saunas and yoga rooms with bamboo floors. I love ridiculous kitchens and pools where you can't see the whole thing at once."

"You know my house won't have any of those things, right?"

She smiled. "It'll have enough, and it will be fun to look."

Connor moved on to baseball, then Batman and Robin.

"So what should I be keeping in mind?"

She looked almost giddy. "Okay, three rules. First off, know what you're looking at. Of the four places I picked out, only one is in your price range. You want to shop with a budget and figure out how much you want to spend."

"How much should I spend?"

"Keep your max price in mind and all that, but never be afraid to look. Conventional wisdom says to ignore houses above your price point, but I say *fuck that.* Mindset matters."

"Yeah, but so does the mortgage."

"Shopping and buying aren't the same. Shopping is dreaming. We'll do that first. Second, know your needs versus your wants. Indulge your wants while you're shopping, and take care of your needs when you buy. I'm sure you'd love a theater, but you might have to settle for a gym. Third, and this is really important — take lots of pictures."

"And we're going to look at houses!" Connor cried out from behind the couch.

Despite all the times that he had wanted to rub something like that in her face, Orson wished that Connor hadn't told Alexis. It just felt … mean.

Connor ended the call with something about dinosaurs and macaroni.

"He didn't get to talk to her for very long," Hadley said. "Is that usual?"

Orson looked at his watch. "That was shorter, but not by much. She gets fifteen minutes, after waiting about twice that long to talk."

"I'm not sure she got to talk much, anyway. Did you hear your son?"

Orson laughed. "Constantly."

A few minutes later they were in his Lexus on their way to the first showing, feeling more like a family than he'd expected to.

"Are you excited?" Hadley asked.

Orson looked back at Connor in the backseat before he answered. His son was staring out the window with a mile-wide smile, studying the world as it passed, his every moment of life an adventure.

Same for Orson. He was excited about the house. Ridiculously so. He still couldn't believe it was happening, and a part of him worried that the dream might get yanked out from beneath him. This wasn't just the biggest investment he'd ever made, it was the only one. At some point in the very near future he would be committing to purchase a home that would cost him multiple millions of dollars. It was only slightly more exciting than scary.

"Yes," he finally admitted, allowing his face to split into a smile. "I am."

"What are you most excited about?"

"I guess that the house will be mine. Even though I love my apartment, the place has never really felt like *me*, you know? It's always felt like something I walked into."

"It was," Hadley laughed.

"Well, exactly. And I think about that all the time. This is a place that I get to pick out for me."

"For *us*," Hadley corrected, even though that wasn't exactly right ... at all.

But Orson said nothing, because the last thing he wanted was to start a fight.

They made small talk through two songs before they arrived at the first house. Orson felt disingenuous, shopping for a house that he couldn't afford yet, but he stopped caring about wasting Alana's time about six seconds after walking through the front door.

The place was a palace, and he wanted everything inside it.

The second mansion made the first look like a hovel, and the third was embarrassing. The trio filled him with a cavernous wanting that Hadley assured him was the perfect fuel for where he wanted to go.

"Are you tired?" Orson asked Connor on their way to the day's fourth and final showing.

He said, "Yes," through a yawn, closing his eyes and letting his head loll to the side.

There had been an awful lot of walking, and Connor had gotten lost at the second house. It was ten minutes before they found him outside in the greenhouse.

"What was your favorite thing you saw?" Hadley asked, still glowing.

Orson thought about the grand foyers with extravagant twin staircases, and the other one with one large set of curved steps to the right of the front door. He thought of the balconies and bed chambers and bathrooms; closets the size of an average-sized bedroom; cloak rooms and powder rooms behind discreet little doors; the kitchen, both the main and the seconds; walk-in pantries and sculleries; the outdoor kitchens with large, bricked-in barbecues, wood-fire ovens, bars, and alfresco dining areas; the gyms, both in and outdoors; pools, tennis courts, and stables; screening rooms, panic rooms, and — maybe Orson's biggest surprise — rock-climbing walls. His dreams were being constantly redefined, and he wasn't feeling sure about Hadley's philosophy of wanting because this much desire was starting to hurt.

"All of it," he said.

Hadley laughed and started scrolling through her phone. "Me too."

They pulled up to the last house. It looked downright modest compared to the last three, but he still would've called it a mansion when he woke up that morning.

"He is *out*," Hadley said, glancing at Connor in the backseat, before returning to her phone.

"Ugh … I really hate to wake him."

"You go," Hadley offered. "Alana can show you the place. I'll stay."

"But you love looking at this stuff."

She shrugged. "I saw it on Zillow already. And we can come back later. Just take a look and tell me what you think when you get back."

Orson took Hadley up on her offer and was already missing her one room in. And not just because he was hoping for that surreptitious blow job — not possible with Connor at their heels every step of the way, except for the time when they'd been frantically searching for him. He found himself wanting her there with him, to comment on the Viking ranges in the kitchen, the Delta faucets in the bathroom, or the crystal and steel orb chandelier in the bedroom.

The house was big, but not too big. The yard large, but not obnoxious. Orson could see himself living here, could see himself cooking in the kitchen — he'd been wanting to take lessons — and swimming in the pool. As the realtor chattered, he pictured Connor running around the yard and playing in the playroom.

He imagined fucking Hadley in half of the house.

He tried not to think of Jess. And failed.

But then he saw the price and wondered what Hadley had been thinking.

He got back in the car and closed the door. He looked at his still-sleeping son in the back before turning to Hadley. "I think you're wrong about Alana."

"No way. There is zero chance that she's gay. You're just totally not her type."

"No, I mean I'm not sure she was thrilled about all of our show and tell."

"Whatever, she'll be happy when she's cashing her commission check."

Orson started the engine. "I don't think anyone cashes checks anymore. I think money just shows up in your account. And she's not going to be getting a commission on that house."

"You didn't like it? Of course, we should look at more places first. And wait, don't drive yet."

Orson put the car back into park. "I loved it, but it's still way out of my price range."

"It's possible that you don't really know what your price range is." Then she showed him her phone. "Look."

Orson looked at the screen.

"Scroll," she ordered.

He went from shaking his head to laughing. "Wow," he said, handing it back to Hadley.

"I know, right?"

Hadley had posted the first seed, but the Internet garden of gossip was already blooming in full. She'd shared at least a handful of shots from each of their first three houses. Headlines were already screaming:

Engagement!?!

Orson Beck and Hadley Witt, House Hunting on a Saturday Afternoon!

Dream Couple Orson and Hadley Looking for Their Love Nest!

It was all fake, all for publicity. Melinda was a master and Hadley an eager apprentice.

That sort of thing from Hadley used to bother him. It was one of the reasons he didn't want to be around her, because it seemed like she was having trouble parsing fiction and fact. But lately, he'd realized that wasn't the case. The Shellys had taught her to manipulate narrative so that she could write a better reality for herself. And Orson was grateful for the lessons.

Hadley was easy to be with, in part because she was the only one in his life that truly got all of this. She uniquely understood the stress he was under. They could complain about the same things, laugh about them too. And *want* them.

Orson started to drive. "So what's next? More houses next Saturday?"

"Did you love that last one?"

"I did."

"Then that's the one that you're going to buy."

And even though he couldn't believe it, Orson knew that Hadley was right.

What he didn't know was how he was going to tell her they were never getting engaged.

Chapter Forty

Cameo was on the constant verge of partying too hard.

The club was frequented by the rich, the famous, and those willing to pay for proximity. The drinks were the price of an elegant entree, and the party was drowning anyway. The club was dark enough to disappear into, which made it perfect. After the blogging blitz of his buying a house, being invisible for the evening while still getting to celebrate his face off sounded just about perfect to Orson.

Because he should celebrate. Buying a house was a big deal, especially buying one that he technically couldn't afford. *Yet,* as Hadley and the Shellys were constantly reminding him. 2.1 million for a house sounded absurd to a guy who'd grown up in the biggest house on his block, in a great neighborhood, that his parents had paid 280,000 for at the top of the market.

Orson's new house was 2.1 million *over his budget.*

He didn't tell his parents when they asked. Same for Samuel. But they could do the math, and he didn't have to tell them. Samuel read stuff about him online all the time and shared it with their parents. Orson hated that. But it wasn't like he could get his family to stop paying attention, or for the bloggers to stop blogging. And the way it was feeding him, why would he want to?

It would all pay off. It had for Harrison and all of the proteges before him. He was overextended for now, but that was a quality problem. Nothing he was experiencing now compared to the pain he had felt while filling his miserable shifts at Provisions.

There was a tiny piece of him that wished he hadn't listened to Hadley. But he was trying not to worry, and his prospects were shining like diamonds. To celebrate signing the papers on his house and a gleaming, glittering future, he and Hadley were partying at Cameo for a night of drinks and whatever, on him.

She leaned over and whispered in his ear. "Want me to suck your dick?"

Hadley always wanted to suck his dick, and yeah, he did kind of want that. But it could wait. Right now, Orson wanted another bump more. He took it, then whispered back. "At home. I want to tongue-fuck you first."

She purred in his ear, bit his earlobe.

Orson leaned back against the soft leather sofa and took a long sip of his forty-dollar Old Fashioned.

The coke hit the spot, though he hated to admit it. Same as he hated to think about his recent dependency on Hadley, or the gallons of alcohol. His workouts were getting more difficult, and although he'd been an early riser since childhood, he'd never had a harder time saying hello to the sun.

But he could always cut back on the booze. No problem. And it wasn't like he was taking coke all the time or anything. Only when he was partying. Or after a long night when Connor wouldn't go the fuck to sleep.

But it was all manageable. He took another sip and wondered how his son was doing with Armando right now, then tried not to think about how little he liked that guy.

One more bump, then off to the bathroom.

He wiped his nose and looked around. Cameo had bathrooms everywhere -- one of the things that made the place special. Rather than having one or two communal restrooms, the place was peppered with tiny toilets in every nook and cranny. Their promotional brochures said it was for privacy, but the stalls were all ripe with the reek of fresh sex.

He spotted the nearest bathroom then leaned over and said, "I'll be right back."

"Are you sure you don't want me to come with you?"

"You can come with me tonight."

"I'm planning on it." She licked her lips and handed him the vial. "Take this with you. It shouldn't be out."

Orson dropped it in his pocket, headed toward the bathroom, and crashed into a memory. Even though it looked little like he remembered.

Maybe that was why she noticed him first.

"Hey, Orson," Jess said.

It took him a second, especially since she sounded so happy to see him. "Hey, Jess. It's good to see you."

And it was, even though he felt like someone had peeled off his skin, then kindly asked him to step outside it.

"You too. You look great."

"Thanks." He smiled. So many old feelings returning. "So do you."

But did she?

The old Jess was beautiful, though almost intentionally understated. This Jess was the opposite, working to accentuate every feature. Even in the dark, he could see that her dirty blonde hair was now brunette and a little too done, her makeup too precise, her body packaged like very expensive sausage in that skin-tight dress.

Her eyes were glassy and her smile wasn't all the way there, broad though it was. If she hadn't just greeted him, Orson might think that the person in front of him didn't even know where she was.

But still, he couldn't stop his pounding heart or convince himself in this moment, that Jess Lindley wasn't the love of his life. She was definitely the life of his longing, of his now, of his sleepless nights and fitful dreams. Hadley was his companion, but he'd never needed her like he'd needed Jess.

His heart ached too much. Jess stared at him. Neither of them knew what to say, but both of them wanted to say something.

Orson swallowed. "What are you doing here?"

It took her a moment, then her smile bent at the edges and she gestured around the club full of shadows. "This."

His heart wasn't just broken because he couldn't have her. This was all her fault. She was clearly fucked up on something.

But then again, so was he. Life was great. His career (overextended and in debt, both to the Shellys and to the bank), his relationships with Connor (who spent more time with Armando than he did with his father, while his mother was in prison awaiting her trial) and Hadley (a sham of a union that kept Orson and his dick both entertained), and his new house (that he couldn't afford). Even his celebration at Cameo (numbing himself with booze, coke, and Hadley).

He had no idea what was going on in her life, outside of the headlines and rumors. But right now, with his heart beating too hard and a lump in his throat, it felt like he was staring into some sort of psychic, spiritual mirror.

"How about you?" Jess asked when Orson said nothing.

He smiled, excited to tell her. "I'm here to celebrate. I just bought a house."

Her smile got both bigger and smaller. "So I've been reading."

Good thing one of them was. Orson had ignored his Rummage for two days. Melinda would kill him if she knew.

Booming music filled their silence and froze the time in between them. Eventually, the ice had to crack, and when it did Jess took a step closer. She put her hands on Orson's shoulders and sent a deep shiver down through his body, settling into his toes but stirring his cock on the way.

She looked into his eyes. Hers were still so far away.

"You did it, Orson. Now do you want to do me?"

He wasn't sure that he had heard her right.

But, of course he had.

Because this wasn't the Jess that had been his neighbor at the Brick. This Jess was closer to the one that he had been reading about. The Jess who dated anyone who wanted her, just for the chance to be part of the scene.

Orson was still dumbstruck. Hadley was one crowd behind them. This was happening fast, and it felt like Fate waiting to mock him. Remorse lurking with a devil's smile around the next bend.

She glanced at the nearest restroom. Maybe she'd been heading there too.

"Now," Jess said.

She was off and he followed.

Into the restroom they went.

They were on each other immediately.

Lips mashing against lips, tongues tasting tongues, paws clawing at bodies.

Orson wasn't sure if they were totally lost, or if the pair of them had finally been found, but right now he didn't care. He *couldn't* care. The blood in his veins was now pumping.

Jess, too. They were both surrendering to urges they had been suppressing for so long. Years lost at the Brick. As she reached down to lower his zipper, Orson remembered that last night at his apartment, before she drove him to the rendezvous point, and before he boarded the shuttle that would take him to the Glass House and introduce him to his new life. He wondered what would have happened if he had taken her up then. If—

No. This wasn't the time for that.

This was the time for them, because it might not happen ever again.

It was hard to believe it was happening now.

Hands were everywhere. They were grasping for each other, same as they were clinging to any connection.

"Do you know what a big star you are, Orson Beck," she whispered into his ear, using her words as much as her tongue. His cock fattened in her hand, so Jess kept on going. "Everyone is talking about you. Everywhere I go people are always asking me about Orson Beck."

She started to stroke him.

"So it's been impossible to get you off of my mind."

She kissed him hard then pulled away. "I just want to be closer to you."

Orson wanted that too. Maybe more than anything.

But that wasn't what she meant.

Jess fell to her knees and took all of Orson into her mouth.

He closed his eyes. Couldn't believe this was happening. Didn't want it to start because then it would have to end. But he placed his hands behind his head to steady himself, and lost his balance just a bit anyway.

Jess braced her hands on his thighs and sucked.

It was heaven at first. Almost rehearsed. In an odd way it reminded him of Hadley, and she was otherwise miles away from his mind. But it quickly devolved into something sloppy and surprisingly unsatisfying.

Orson had been dreaming about this for years, but the dream had never felt so sour.

The woman of his fantasies abrading her knees on the tile floor. He looked down on her, loving who she used to be and hating who she had become. But mostly, Orson hated himself.

He hated himself as he thrust.

Hated himself as they moaned together.

Hated himself as he finished.

Orson was dizzy, his head swimming. He collapsed with his back to the wall as she stood, wiping her glistening lips.

There were no words, just a look of longing to pass in between them.

Then she was gone.

Orson was already back on the couch with Hadley before he realized that the coke in his pocket was gone right along with her.

Chapter Forty-One

Orson thought he knew devastation, but then Jess had drained him dry three ways at once.

This stew of feelings threatened to wreck him. He'd slept two hours last night, after having to get it up for Hadley again, to keep her from getting suspicious. Emotions piled atop each other. There was anger, almost rage, but so was humiliation and shame, guilt and discomfort, a lot of confusion, and an unrelenting stress, like two thumbs pressing down on the center of a pencil, a second from its snapping.

He needed a vent, a place to aim his fury.

How do you know it was Dominic?

Context, I guess. I heard his name a couple of times.

It didn't make sense, but so little did. Confronting Dominic might be the worst mistake of Orson's life, but he had to know the truth. Maybe Ellis was wrong, it's not like he knew everything or had context for all he discovered. Orson knew firsthand how a photo and headline could lie and conspire, could crinkle the smoothest image.

"He isn't expecting you, Mr. Beck."

Orson stared at the receptionist. "Tell him I'm not leaving until we talk."

The intercom cut in with Dominic's voice before she responded. "Of course Orson can come in."

He nodded his *sorry*, then opened the unlocked door and stepped inside.

"Everything okay?"

Dominic was out of his chair and walking over to Orson. He rested a hand on his shoulder and pointed to one of the two chairs in front of his desk. Orson sat, but instead of going to sit on his side of the desk, Dominic made himself at home in the chair right next to Orson, a hand still on his shoulder.

"What is it?"

Orson looked at his boss, felt a flush of shame for being there, but said, "It's Jess."

Dominic's brow crinkled with concern. "What about her?"

"I saw her at Cameo last night." Orson paused, not quite sure of what he was saying.

"And?"

"She looked terrible."

"Terrible how? Did she look abused? Hungry? Depressed?"

Orson thought. He swallowed again. "She looked vacant."

A storm of sudden emotion swept in to darken Dominic's eyes. He exhaled, long and hard, shaking his head as he stood. He ran a hand through his hair and mumbled, "Fucking drugs," then went to pour himself a drink.

Dominic started mixing Orson an Old Fashioned without even asking, bringing it straight over. Then he sat, took a sip of his whiskey, crossed his legs as he set the drink on his desk, and gave his attention to Orson.

"I'm really sorry, son. I feel like I let you down here."

"How?" Orson didn't like this a bit.

"You need to know that I kept this from you with the best of intentions. Things were going well for you. I didn't want this to be on your mind, and I didn't want to make your world smaller by marring your view of someone you obviously cared so much about."

"What do you know about Jess?"

"She came to me begging a few months back, saying she was desperate to get back in the game 'by any means necessary.' I told her that she shouldn't go around putting things that way, and that people might get the wrong idea. Frankly, she was taking advantage of her former relationship with you to try and revive her career, but Jess is the kind of girl you want to help, as I'm sure you know, and she's a good person despite her mistakes, so my heart went out to her. Besides, I figured that helping her was helping you. It wasn't in either of our best interests for you to feel embarrassed, so the two of us decided to keep it mum, and I promised to make a few calls."

How could something sound so right and so wrong at the same time? Orson's head thought Dominic's story sounded logical, but his heart screamed that it was a lie.

"I had no idea it would all turn into such a fucking mess. I'm so sorry."

"What happened to Jess?"

The door opened on the other end of Dominic's office and Melinda entered the room, looking surprised to see Orson.

"Well, hello," she said. "Are we talking about Alexis?"

Dominic turned to his wife. "Jess. We haven't even got to Alexis yet."

"What about Alexis?" Orson asked.

Melinda looked at him sharply. "So I take it you haven't read your Rummage Report?"

"No," he admitted. "Not yet. I came straight here this morning."

"Obviously," she said, eyeing his unkempt state.

"So what about her?"

Melinda looked at their glasses, seemed like she was about to say one thing, but then turned toward the bar. "I guess we're starting early."

Dominic said, "Alexis is out. You were apparently too busy partying last night to read the headlines, but —"

"Or check your Rummage Reports."

Orson shouldn't have been surprised, but— "Alexis won her case?"

"She did, and—"

"Her father probably paid off the judge." Melinda was walking back to the table with a Bloody Mary.

Dominic turned and gave her a look — *Will you please stop interrupting?*

"That's good, right?" Orson asked.

"Not exactly," Dominic said. "She's talking."

"Running her mouth is more like it." Melinda scrolled through her phone, then showed him the screen.

The headline was a quote — *I've healed myself, now it's time to heal my family* — next to a gorgeous photo of a grieving Alexis. She looked well put-together for someone who had so recently fallen apart.

Orson's first reaction was happiness, that she'd gotten her life back and that Connor would have his mother back.

He looked from the screen to the Shellys, unsure. "Do you want me to read this?"

Melinda plucked the phone from his hand. "No. I wanted you to have already read it."

"It's okay, Melinda. He's going through a lot. Let's help him." Then, to Orson, "Alexis is taking this very seriously. We think she has someone coaching her on exactly what to do right now."

"Not her lawyers," Melinda clarified. "This is classic *Trust Me I'm Lying* PR. Someone is designing it for her. She went on a fucking blog tour. So your feed was full of shit you should be in the know about."

"He knows, Melinda," Dominic said, still looking at Orson. "Do you promise to be better about reading your feed?"

Orson nodded. "Of course."

Dominic turned to Melinda. "Can we move on?"

A begrudging nod and the hint of a smile, then Dominic smiled too. He turned back to Orson.

"Alexis is talking a lot about how much work she did on herself in treatment and about how abusive Tyler was. She forgave herself for what she had to do. It wasn't about revenge, it was about trying to protect her son. She's coming off great in these interviews. Compassionate, articulate, and—"

"Well-coached," Melinda interrupted.

Orson wasn't getting it. "But this all sounds good?"

"Alexis is also saying that she wants to get her family back together and that she would like for the public to respect her privacy while she does it." Dominic gave him a look that he couldn't interpret.

He was definitely still missing something. "That sounds reasonable?"

Melinda shook her head. "She made a broadcast, but doesn't have to respond. She dropped the mic. Hinted to the world that the two of you would be getting back together, then ducked into the shadows where she wouldn't have to talk about it."

"I don't think that's what she's saying," Orson said.

Melinda glared at him. "Read your links."

"Look, Orson, none of this is easy, except for the solution." Dominic took another sip of his whiskey. "All we need right now is for you to understand the importance of what we're trying to preserve. This whole thing with Alexis is unfortunate, but we have a carefully crafted narrative. We have included you in our story, so it is your job to help us tell it. Do you understand what I am saying?"

"I think so?"

"He's saying," Melinda chimed in, her glare softening, "that the world is watching you and these next steps are important. I don't know whether Alexis wants you back or not, but she is clearly taking control of the narrative. You're not to meet with her alone under any circumstances. A lawyer must be present. Do you understand that?"

Orson felt backed into a corner, shanghaied by this sudden twist in his life. "Yes."

"Excellent!" the Shellys said together.

"Good. That's settled." Dominic clapped him on the shoulder. "Now we have one last thing to discuss, some other attention that we didn't see coming, this time from Hollywood Hunted.

"You should have read your links."

Chapter Forty-Two

It had to be done. Even so, Ellis still felt sick to his stomach.

He read over his work for the eleventh time. He usually didn't do this many passes. It was so easy to lose yourself in revision, and blogs were a medium of immediacy. While Ellis liked to believe that all of his work had stakes, these posts about Orson were sharply pointed and planted deep.

For a long time, Ellis had prioritized the integrity of their friendship above all else.

But he couldn't do that anymore.

It was time for karma to have her say. Time to stop the things that shouldn't be happening, end the Shellys once and for all because he knew what they were doing, or trying to do. Even if he could only see the very edges of their scheme, it was becoming clearer, and he could smell it like a chemical taint in the Hollywood air.

Breaking Orson was the best way to injure the Shellys. They had a lot riding on him, a hell of a lot more than anyone realized, including Orson if the couple's plans were what Ellis felt ever more certain they were.

But Ellis had to be careful. He couldn't just publish what he knew and tip them off. This had to remain as the slowest of burns. The flame had to blaze once lit, without ever getting too hot, at least not at once. If he did this right, then the Shellys wouldn't understand what was happening until their world was a roaring fire around them.

That conversation with Harrison Turner changed everything. The guy wasn't just willing to talk, he was eager to blab about every tiny little thing he'd been holding inside. Once Ellis promised him that he would be off the record, using his information and honest insight only as an open door to the cellar of priceless secrets that he was sure the Shellys were guarding, Harrison couldn't stop talking.

Ellis had a theory. But without any prompting on his part or leading the witness in any way, Harrison painted a picture that justified his suspicions.

So far no one was willing to go on record, but the stories were finally coming. Mostly through email and all of them with phony addresses, referred to Ellis by this person or that one. But he was comparing the details and stringing specifics together. He was making his move, starting with Orson.

Ellis had never expected the call from Alexis, but it had made so many other things fall into place.

Of course he would be happy to help her. She was one of the few people who knew who was behind Hollywood Hunted and had never once tattled. Ellis would do whatever he could to help Alexis, especially if it helped him help Jess.

Even though she hadn't returned a single voicemail, email, or text, Ellis didn't take it personally. Jess was hurting, walking the razor's edge yet again. The warmest person Ellis knew had turned into the coldest. All it took was a few lines of snow.

The Shellys knew exactly what they were doing, just like always.

And for that, Ellis planned to destroy them.

Chapter Forty-Three

Kirsty descended the steps of her office building, passing the stone gargoyles on guard at the front, then around the corner to the old lamppost beside the bus stop.

The lamppost was ancient beneath the billboard, blinking between two ads. The first displayed a twenty-something, ridiculously pleased with his smart phone. The next showed a woman in black stilettos and crimson lingerie, the single word Tonight, *beneath her full red lips, hovering above a bottle of expensive-looking Scotch.*

Kirsty leaned against the lamppost, back to the billboard, waiting for her boyfriend, Damon.

It had been a long day. Fridays usually ended at 4:00, per her contract. That meant she was usually seeping in hot water and bubbles by 6:00, while Damon stood guard at the front door waiting on their pizza. She waited all week for Fridays — pizza from the Tomato Shack, a bottle of Coppola, and a fuckfest from Damon.

Always once and often twice.

At least it used to be.

. . .

JESS SAT ALONE in the hotel room, writing as fast as she could, almost in a fugue.

The coke was fuel for her head and her fingers, the story spilling onto the page without effort.

It wasn't always like this. Sometimes writing was hard, and occasionally even impossible, with hours lost to the bright white page, empty except for her longing. But these days, writing her new series, *Naughty Hollywood*, there was little difference for Jess between thinking and getting those words onto the page.

The more she fixed herself to the story, the less she had to think about Orson.

Kirsty glanced at her watch — 8:47. Where the hell is he? Damon promised he'd pick her up at 8:30 sharp, swore that despite her having to work late, this Friday would be like the old ones.

But the street was black and empty, punctuated every minute or so by the occasional blurring red light from a passing car and the live band in the bar a block away.

Kirsty pulled her phone from her purse and checked her messages. Fourteen emails, one voicemail, two texts, but nothing from Damon.

Asshole.

He had five minutes, not one minute more. After that,
Kirsty was calling a car.

The main character of this story had a lot in common with Jess. Both were escorts, or extremely high-class call girls was more like it. They made thousands each night. They both loved sex and felt no shame, though Kirsty was *a lot* louder about it. And they both knew that the world misunderstood what they did for a living. Looked down on it when they didn't have any right to.

Kirsty didn't have a coke habit, and Jess really didn't want to give her one because that was something that she hated about herself and wasn't ever going to stop hating.

Ever since the blowup after her show *Adulting*, Jess had been making a living as an indie author. She loved to tell stories and was an excellent writer. She'd fallen into the erotica market because those stories were the fastest for her to tell. It was always easier to be sexy on the page than it was in real life. As Lexi Maxxwell, Jess was pure confidence.

The money she made as an author now paled compared to what she was pulling down as an escort, but her expenses had also skyrocketed. She was smart enough to know that this particular train wouldn't stay on the track forever, so she was building a series with legs.

Her most popular series before as Lexi was called *Naughty USA*. Jess decided to do the easiest thing in the world, taking the old characters she'd created and adapting them to the life she was inhaling right now. *Naughty USA* became *Naughty Hollywood*, and right now it was a toss-up whether Jess would make most of her money that month from spreading her legs or writing about it.

She'd never written faster. The words had never been more exciting. This wasn't erotica, this was a series that would someday be on TV.

KIRSTY DROPPED *the phone in her purse and waited, still leaning against the lamppost. Five minutes felt like ten, waiting for the town car. Kirsty tapped her feet to the catchy rock, rolling in a wave from the bar a block away. After another five minutes passed, which felt like fifteen, a black Escalade finally kissed the curb. She figured they must have had to send the SUV because of her short notice, then wondered if they'd bill the firm extra for the luxury.*

The passenger window opened with a purr. The driver didn't look a thing like the usual silver-haired chauffeurs the transport company hired. He was young, maybe thirty-five. A full head of charcoal hair, mopped over dark, confident eyes. A strong jaw cast his light stubble in a handsome shadow.

He smiled.

Kirsty smiled back, gave the driver a slight nod, then opened the passenger side and stepped inside the Escalade, closing the heavy door behind her. The driver smiled again, then put the car in gear and pulled into the street.

"So where should we go?" he asked.

Kirsty opened her mouth, but before she could say anything, the driver said, "Never mind. I know a place. It's right up ahead."

NOW SHE WAS GETTING to the good part, but Jess had to stop writing. Poor Kirsty didn't realize that she was leaning against that lamppost like a hooker and had no idea what she was about to get into. But she would have to find out later because Jess had an appointment, and she was always ready. Just like Kirsty, Jess knew there was nothing more important than making the man who paid you feel like a king.

She checked her ranking one last time, saw that the first book in her series was still hovering just above the Top 1000 on Amazon, knew the one thing that mattered was still cemented firmly in place, then took another bump.

Jess went to the bathroom and looked in the mirror, stripped out of her yoga clothes and into her uniform. In this case, a cherry red teddy, squeezing her full breasts together, and a matching pair of panties. The set cost her more than 300 dollars and managed to make one of the her least favorite colors look elegant. The shade was on the warm side, like the darker set of her tanned skin. Or her hair, which had gone from blonde to dirty blonde to full-on brunette.

She looked exactly as ordered and was ready to follow her client's every command.

Except that this was Grady Blum, and today he would be following hers.

Grady was Jess' favorite john so far, and one of the last men she would have expected to pay for sex. Maybe that's why they got along so well because he also understood that hiring an escort wasn't about sex.

Grady was a good-looking guy in his early fifties, and one of the world's biggest directors. If he wanted to have sex, he could have dialed any number of two dozen women and had their panties past their ankles and ass in the air by the hour's end. He didn't pay for sex because he couldn't get it otherwise. Grady paid for fantasies without any baggage. Even killer sex with someone you knew came with history or an aftermath. Never so with an escort.

Whatever Grady was in the mood for, casual and meaningless, hard and pounding, elegant and sensual, or streetwalker back-alley nasty, he could pay to get exactly what he wanted, when he wanted, and never worry about the consequences. And as Grady had seemed to enjoy telling her, this way was cheaper.

"The longer the relationship, the more expensive it is. We're going from dessert to jewelry to cars. I know exactly how much I'm going to spend with an escort and exactly how much fun I'm going to have."

She always had to be on as an escort, especially for Grady, but more so today since he had apparently suffered a long week filled with too many decisions.

"I want you to do all the work, just tell me what to do. But I want you in red."

His colors were always specific, and in the last two

months Jess had dressed in every hue of the most elegant rainbow.

One more bump to ensure a better performance, and just in case Grady didn't want to when he got to his room.

She finished inhaling as he opened the door. No surprise, the man was always on time.

"Hey," Grady said, looking her over, clearly pleased with what he saw, his cock already pushing against his thin linen pants. He closed the door behind him.

Jess strode over and kissed him on the cheek. Then she unbuckled his pants, pulled out his cock, wrapped her warm hand around it, and led him over to the bed, stopping in front of the end table beside it.

Grady looked down at the coke and smiled at the three remaining lines. Then he sat on the edge of the bed and took a bump, just like Jess was hoping he would.

Her turn. She leaned over, doubled down for the hell of it, snorting one right after the other to clear the mirror. Grady wouldn't mind.

"You. Stay," Jess said on her way to the bar. She began making their drinks for later. But soon. His first time was always fast. "Get naked. Now."

She finished making their drinks — a whiskey sour for him, a shot of vodka for her — and turned around.

Grady was naked, his cock pointing up at the ceiling.

So Jess dropped to all fours and started crawling across the carpet toward him.

"Don't touch me. You're not allowed to move unless I say."

He whimpered a *yes*, already hers.

She turned around and shook her ass in his face.

He whimpered again. Then she pulled her panties to the side and lowered herself onto his throbbing cock, just to the tip until he whimpered some more.

She turned around and purred. "What do you want to do to my pussy? Do you want to fuck it? Or do you want to lick it and kiss it first?"

"I want to lick it," he panted.

"What else do you want to do?"

"I want to put my fingers inside it."

Jess fell back and stepped out of her panties, then gave Grady a lap dance, shaking her tits and ass, rubbing everything she could all over his face. She could tell that he wanted to grab her tits, twist her nipples, throw her to the floor and fuck that teasing smile right off her face.

But Grady had his orders.

Jess spent the next several minutes drawing it out because that's what he wanted, using her tongue and her lips and her hands, exploring Grady everywhere. He grabbed her hair to give himself a better view, but she slapped his hand away, wet with her power.

"It's time," he said. "I want to fuck you."

Jess lifted her head just long enough to shake her head no, before she went back to bobbing and left him moaning in protest. When she felt like she had taken it maybe a second two far, she traded her lips for her breasts.

"You like that," she purred, "having your cock between my tits?"

He moaned again.

She stopped and stood. "Do you want to see how wet you've made me?"

Then she took his hand, pushed it against her center, and started grinding against it.

This was all food for her stories. Jess could write it just as it happened, with names changed to protect the innocent, of course. Grady was an excellent lover and paid her well for the pleasure. He would finish in a few minutes, then he would talk and talk and talk, feeding her with even more stories, better than those she could conjure on her own, because truth was stranger than fiction, or at least, a helluva lot sexier.

After he vented, Grady would be ready for the second round of his extra special attention.

And Jess would enjoy that, too. She might even love all of this, think that it was all okay, if she wasn't suddenly sick to her stomach again, thinking of Orson.

Chapter Forty-Four

Orson sweated less than this when he worked out. A lot less.

He looked back at Connor in the rearview, telling himself yet again that he was doing the right thing.

Connor clapped and said, "We're going to see Mommy!"

That made it easy to feel better, but Orson's shirt stuck to his clammy skin. He'd never openly defied the Shellys before, not like this. Sure, he had skipped a workout here and there, and cheated on his diet a few times. There was the thing in the bathroom with Jess, that was a bit public and could have maybe spiraled out of control. In a different way than it had. In a way that might not have left an ugly stain inside him.

This was different. Their missive couldn't have been clearer. Orson was not to see Alexis without a lawyer present under any circumstances. But was he really supposed to tell her that when she called to ask when she could see her son again, because how could she not?

He had to do the right thing, even if the Shellys saw it

as wrong. He would be careful. Besides, the lawyers would be involved soon enough. He could sneak out and help her this one time, explain it in person. Make her understand his side. It wouldn't be good for their relationship if he had to fumble through an explanation over the phone.

So long as no one went out of their way to snitch on him, the Shellys probably wouldn't even know.

Do you really not think they're keeping tabs?

You're not that stupid … are you?

Orson ignored the voice. It wasn't like he was about to make a U-turn a block away.

He had to do this. Everything would be okay. If he got caught, he would beg forgiveness. This was the mother of his child, and he was trying to do what was best for Connor. The Shellys would have to understand.

But will they?

Everyone deserves a mental health day, not just time off work, but a break from the requirement for sound mental judgment.

Orson told himself that everything was going to work out as he stopped in front of Alexis' house. He turned back to Connor. "How excited are you?"

"Over the moon and back!"

Orson opened the back door and helped Connor out of his car seat. He took his son by the hand as he scrambled onto the grass and they both started walking.

"Am I going to live with Mommy now?"

"I'm not sure what's going to happen now. But I promise that we'll find out soon, okay?"

"Okay. If I live with Mommy will I still get to play with Armando?"

"I don't think Mommy will want to share you with Armando."

"You share me, Daddy, because Armando is my friend."

"He's not really your friend, buddy. It's his job to take care of you when I can't."

"You said he was my friend when you had to work all that time."

Fuck you, Armando.

"Okay then, he is your friend. But if we don't pay him, then he's not going to be your friend anymore, and I doubt that Mommy will want to share you if she has to pay him."

"Oh." Connor sounded both sad and confused. Orson was the asshole who'd made him feel both.

He was surprised to find himself missing Hadley. She had a way with Connor. Not only did she always seem to know the right thing to say, she made Orson sound better. He could feel himself being a better father around her.

But then again, she wasn't Connor's mom. And it's not like Orson could have invited her along. She was deathly loyal to Melinda and Dominic. He put his life on Do Not Disturb the second he left. He couldn't afford any interruptions or give himself a reason to second-guess a plan that deserved exactly that.

He stood on the front porch, drenched in a cold sweat. He looked around, wondering what he thought he might see. A white van with an artificial logo for a plumber or technician of some sort, a stakeout at Alexis', keeping tabs on Orson's every possible move. He'd seen too many movies. And if he wasn't careful, he would be in too few.

He looked down at his son, ringing the doorbell.

Connor smiled.

Alexis flung the door open and cried out, "You're finally here!" as though they hadn't rushed right over.

Connor jumped into her arms, yelling, "Mommy! Mommy! Mommy!"

Alexis exploded with glee, squeezing the kid hard enough to turn his insides to paste. She spun him in a circle, set him down to tousle his hair, then hefted him back up as if she couldn't stand to be parted so soon, this time high enough to strain her now-impressive arms, before ending with a hug that was like her limbs expressing the hope that she would never have to let him go again.

They went inside and Connor started talking, trying to fit months' worth of stories into the seconds they had in between their greeting on the front porch and fresh lemonade in the kitchen. He stopped long enough to gulp his entire glass down to pulp at the bottom, then he wiped his mouth and kept going.

The kid told his mom all about school and Armando, of course, but he was also going on and on about stuff that Orson was surprised he even knew. Like dinners at La Boca and — he really should have seen this coming — Hadley.

"She's like another mommy, but not as good."

Orson expected a flare of jealousy or worse, but Alexis just laughed and said, "That sounds about right." Then she leaned down and took his face in her hands, one cheek per palm. "I missed you *soooooo* much!"

"I missed you too, Mommy!" Connor gave her his longest hug so far.

"Do you want to see the presents I left in your bedroom?"

He didn't even answer. Just made an about-face, then ran down the hallway toward his room.

"Don't worry, I'm not spoiling him or anything. I just bought him a bunch of puzzles."

Orson made an embarrassed little laugh. "You mean you didn't get him a miniature Tesla?"

Alexis laughed too, but then she made him feel better.

"Believe me, I get it." Then she set her hand on his upper arm and started rubbing it back and forth.

But no. Alexis had that look in her eyes. She wanted more than he could give. Orson used to think that a family reunion would be best for Connor, but he didn't necessarily believe that anymore. He and Alexis had a lot of healing to do, a lot of bullshit had ripened between them. That had to be fixed before they could think about anything else. That would take work. And if Orson was being honest with himself, he had plenty to manage without adding that kind of emotional labor to his life.

The stakes were big and getting bigger, he needed to stay in the game. It wasn't like before, when Orson used to wonder if Connor would ever accept another woman in his life. Back then the constant thought was Jess, but now it was Hadley.

As if she were reading his thoughts, Alexis said, "So, how's Hadley?"

Orson shrugged. "She's fine."

"We can talk about it, you know. I'm a big girl."

"I want to talk about you. How are you doing?"

"I know you'll find this as a shock, but I'll be happy not talking about *me* for the next hundred years or so."

"That'll wear off soon," Orson said, hoping he wasn't pushing too far. "There's no way you're going to completely lose interest in your favorite subject."

She laughed and Orson exhaled.

"Seriously, though. We need to be friends. And friends talk. Tell me about Hadley."

"What do you want to know?"

"Are things serious?"

"Yes. No." He looked at her, helpless. "Depends on what you mean."

"Can we talk about why you're really here?"

"What do you mean?" Orson genuinely wanted to know. "I'm here because Connor needed to reconnect with his mother. He cries himself to sleep half the time. He doesn't understand that we have to wait for a lawyer, and he shouldn't have to."

"I know you, Orson. If the Shellys forbid you to see me and you came anyway, then it isn't *just* about Connor. It's about us. Maybe getting back together." She took his hands. "Being a family again."

He shook his head and let go of her hands. "I'm sorry. I can't do this right now. That's not why I'm here."

"Because you're fucking Hadley."

"No, Alexis. This has nothing to do with—"

"Do you like fucking her better than you liked fucking me?" Alexis stared, waiting for an answer.

"It's different."

Now Alexis was glaring. Orson wanted to go and get Connor. He never should have come.

Her face settled and her shoulders relaxed. She dared to reclaim his hands, and he let her.

Alexis looked into his eyes with a knowing gaze that froze him to the core.

"I understand where you are right now, Orson, because I was there for a long time, too. But you *do* want to work this out. Hadley isn't right for you. Both of us know it. And there's no way you're going to want to live in that giant mansion alone, all by yourself."

Oh shit. She actually believed that.

He took a deep breath. "Actually, you're right. I did come here to talk about us. You've got to stop telling everyone that we're getting back together."

"I will. As soon as it happens."

"You're hurting my career."

She dropped his hands. "You asshole."

"I mean it. I didn't want to humiliate you by letting a lawyer explain it. I wanted to tell you myself because you're the mother of my child."

"Fuck you."

He left without saying more because an angry Alexis was actually a best-case scenario right now.

And by the time she calmed down, she'd also be settled into life as Connor's mother again. She wouldn't care about Orson or Hadley — she'd realize how good she had it: a fat child support check, a new life with her son, and a chance to start over. Maybe find someone better than Tyler Crane to share her life with.

For now, the best thing for Orson to do was to sneak back to his own life, before the Shellys noticed he'd left.

Chapter Forty-Five

Orson couldn't believe this was all for him.

The house and grounds, several stocked bars, a pool that people were already jumping into, enough five-star quality food to feed the elite in abundance then scrap the remains without care, a handful of genuine A-listers, and a hundred or so people that Orson barely knew or had never even met.

And none of it had cost him a dime.

Dominic and Melinda were paying for it all and had invited every guest. This was his official coming out. His Bar Mitzvah, Quinceañera, and Debutant Ball all rolled into one big party. He'd done his job and followed all their directives. If you lived in the industry, then you had heard the name *Orson Beck*. So the Shellys had also done their jobs.

The hard part was done. They deserved to celebrate. Orson was no longer going from zero to one. He had some finished work in the can and was earning praise for his talent. His upcoming slate was better than a dream come true because just half a year ago even his more vibrant fantasies would never have dared to go there. If he continued to do the work — take things seriously, follow the rules and appreciate the opportunities that came his way, sharpen his craft, and make the best possible long-term decisions — then he had nowhere to go but up.

Unfortunately, even if it was all for him, Orson felt overwhelmed. He had never felt more *on*. It was easier to feel off-duty when the cameras were rolling. This was his party at his new house that he couldn't afford and probably never should have bought. It was his new furniture, paid for with the promise of tomorrow, like everything else in his life right now. If there were stains, he would have to pay for them. Broken furniture, yep, he would have to pay for that too.

Maybe he shouldn't worry. It wasn't like his house was full of meth heads.

Yet, he had been on the other side of Hollywood parties, when it was easy to assume that the hosts had enough money to *enjoy* throwing it away. Dominic and Melinda had shelled out plenty, but Orson still couldn't help but feel like this party would cost him. Just like everything else.

But the view was gorgeous, staring down from the hills. Orson had slipped into the shadows under the sprawling branches of a bay fig. It was time to go back into the fray, greet more guests, be more social, continue to ignore the gnawing in his gut. Stop trying to figure out what it was.

Again, he thought of Connor, because surely that was a lot, if not all of this. He was in the playroom with Armando, and Orson had made sure he was settled for the hour before the party, happy while Hadley handled everything out front. The shindig was just forty-five minutes in. Orson had already checked on his son once and was thinking about checking on him again.

When had he become so neurotic? Connor was fine. Perfectly happy. Armando was his friend, even if Orson paid him. Or rather, Dominic and Melinda paid him.

Maybe that's what bothered him most. Orson had never wanted to have this party. They wanted it for him and he had to agree. They wanted everything for him. For the most part that was amazing, but sometimes he felt like the walls were closing in.

Maybe he was bothered by the fact that he was only a few months in and already going numb. The house and grounds, the stocked bars, the pool that went on forever, filled with A-listers and hangers-on, all the ridiculously expensive food and drink they were going to shovel and drain into their mouths. None of it felt like much of anything, and being empty when his life was full was something Orson didn't understand.

But it was all an adjustment. This was still the life that he'd wanted, the life that was best for his son.

"Taking it all in?" A hand fell on his shoulder from behind. Dominic, of course. "Don't be overwhelmed."

"I'm not overwhelmed."

"You're not?" Dominic scoffed. "I would be. All of this?" He waved his hands theatrically out at the hills, sweeping the edges of the pool on his way. "It's a lot to get used to. You know what part was the hardest for me?"

Orson shook his head.

"Feeling desensitized. That does fade, and the appreciation returns."

How was it that Dominic always seemed to know what he was thinking? "I appreciate it."

"I know you *appreciate* it. But everything is happening fast. You went from nothing to everything almost all at once. A lot of that is our fault. Melinda and I want you to have everything, but not too much. We try to ride the line.

Not to be your parents or anything, but we've never had children of our own. And despite what Melinda thinks, those fucking dogs don't count."

Dominic laughed, took a long drink that Orson didn't even realize he'd been holding in his opposite hand.

"You might be worried. Now that you're here, you have to stay here. You're overextended. You owe more than you have, and by a lot. If the offers dry up then you're upside-down. No longer marquee, but not a big enough name to anchor TV. Yet. You've still got dues to pay. Believe me, we're here to help you settle everything owed, then get what's coming to you. We've given you Shellter, and that means something in this business. Do you understand that, Orson?"

He nodded. In a weird way, he absolutely did.

"The offers aren't going to dry up because we control the machinery behind them. Do you understand *that*?"

Another nod. Because he *sorta* did.

"Right now some of this all feels cold and impersonal, but that's because you're still new. A freshman. Outside looking in. You know Logan and he's friendly enough, but you've never done Cannes. You will. We've given you more than one *best and into the rest of your life* night already. Tonight is another. Eat, drink, and be merry, Orson. This is for you. Your dreams are coming true, and it's time to get used to that."

"Thank you, Dominic."

"Of course. And Orson …"

"Yeah?"

"I understand that Alexis has been working awfully hard to reach you."

"She's calling a lot, yeah. But we're meeting with the lawyer next week."

"Good." Dominic cleared his throat. "I know I don't

need to remind you, but Melinda will kill me if I don't. You can't talk to her, Orson. Not without the lawyer. Tell me you understand that."

He felt paralyzed, wondering if Dominic knew. "Yes. Absolutely."

"Excellent," he said, nothing but smiles as Hadley appeared right behind him.

"There you guys are. I've been looking everywhere."

"The place isn't that big," Orson tried to joke.

Dominic laughed. "The next one will be."

Chapter Forty-Six

Hadley was all over him, even more than usual. Like this was her homecoming too.

In many ways, Orson supposed it was.

She had been doing her time for two years longer than he had, and now — *finally* — everything was working for her. She owed a lot to Orson, at least that's how she seemed to see it, even though it was so much easier for him to see it the other way around. From sex to conversation, Hadley gave more than she took in every conceivable way. Except for the way that maybe mattered most. She demanded that he play house, even when he didn't want to.

It was such an awful thought, constant and haunting. Would they have had a relationship if it hadn't been sketched on the blueprint? It kept them from ever getting truly close, at least for Orson.

But feeling guilty only filled him with shame, because what did he have to feel bad about? Why in the hell couldn't Orson enjoy it? So he had to prance around town with a gorgeous model on his arm — *boo fucking hoo.* And that model was forever ready to fuck him, hard and fast or soft and slow or whatever the hell he was in the mood for, because Orson always came first. What a shitty hand he'd been dealt.

But the party still felt like a prison.

"You need a drink," Hadley said, rubbing his arm.

"I'm fine. I think I should check on Connor."

"Connor's fine. You just checked on him."

"Like a half hour ago."

"And what do you think has happened in the last half hour?" Hadley laughed. "Besides Connor's talking Armando's ear off."

"It's really loud."

"It's a party."

"My new neighbors are going to hate me."

"That's why Dominic invited them. So they won't."

Orson turned to Hadley. "You're right. I just need to clear my head. Get present."

"Exactly."

"So let me go check on Connor one last time, then I'll come out and get a drink. I'll have a good time. But he should be going to bed soon, and I should say goodnight."

Hadley rolled her eyes. Probably wanted to say more. "Okay. I'll wait for you out here so we both don't disappear. But please do say goodnight and hurry back."

"Thanks." Orson kissed Hadley on her cheek, feeling genuinely appreciative and eager to get out of his head. "I'll be fast."

Up the winding staircase and down the long hallway, all the way to Connor's bedroom at the end. He went in without knocking and closed the door behind him. Connor was in bed, with Armando sitting in a chair by his side, reading a pop-up version of *The Bordinary Boy*.

"You're not sleeping."

Armando narrowed his eyes. "We were trying to get there."

"The music's so loud," Connor said, or sorta whined.

It was. Not like it was in the thick of things, but still enough to feel like a violent hum, heavy enough to sit in the room like a stink in their ears.

"I'm sorry about that. I'll see what I can do."

Armando laughed. "Good luck with that."

Connor stared at Armando, suddenly angry that this man was haunting his house. Orson had never wanted him to be here. It wasn't that Armando had a bouffant hairdo that reminded him of Big Boy, or that he had a ring in his nose and two in his lip. It wasn't even that he had screamed at Orson to not assume his gender within seconds after meeting him, or that he hated himself a little for just letting that go, establishing himself as the sort of boss who was allergic to backbone. What Orson really couldn't stand about Armando was his smug, self-satisfied swagger because he knew that the Shellys were his ticket and that Orson was only a guy standing in the way.

"Are you going to read, Daddy?"

"Yeah, Daddy," Armando smirked. "Are you going to read?"

"I'm going to take care of the music," Orson said. He looked at Connor. "One more, then bedtime, all right?"

"All right, Daddy."

Fuck. The only thing that felt worse than having a party when you didn't feel like it was the guilt that came from feeling ungrateful. Tonight was supposed to be for him (or for the Shellys, he still wasn't sure). His big moment (or maybe his turn onstage, following the script like a good boy) at his house (that he couldn't pay for without the Shellys' help). His friends (acquaintances) and peers (assuming this isn't all gone tomorrow).

Orson wanted everyone to go home because the party was a reminder of the truth -- that he didn't have this under control, that he was spiraling, a slave to the strings that moved him, orchestrating his life into successes and missteps. A blueprint written in secret, equalizing his fate with predetermined dogma.

Orson no longer belonged to himself. Yes, he had always wanted the hits, but he had never asked for the excess. That had never driven him, not like the work. And the party was screaming the truth in his ear. The music was too loud, like the voices telling him what he had to do. People were everywhere, but he felt beside himself trying to remember their names, and all he kept thinking about were the nights when he couldn't stop laughing while slumming it at the Litter Box with Ellis and Jess.

Jess. Every part of him still hurt when he thought of her. What were the chances that someone would bring her here tonight by accident? Orson had considered it more than he cared to admit.

He found the DJ and asked him to turn it down.

"This your place?" he asked Orson, his head rocking hard to the beat as it faded.

Orson nodded.

"*Nice,*" the DJ said.

A few steps away, Orson heard a voice call out, "Hey, man!"

He turned and smiled. It was Berto Reyes, his co-star on *F the '90s*, and now the producer of two hit shows, and the star of one of them. "Hey, Berto!"

They hugged. Berto gestured around at Orson's house. "Dude."

Orson laughed. "I know."

"So, it's all happening, huh? How are you holding up?"

Orson laughed harder. *Never let 'em see you sweat.*

"Great, great, I mean, the schedule is something else. I'm sick of the gym and would kill for some ice cream, but that's among the very first of my first world problems for sure."

He eyed Berto, trying not to be obvious. The guy had gained at least fifteen pounds since the last time Orson had seen him, and then Berto had been five to ten heavier than in the *F the '90s* days. But Roberto Reyes wasn't paid for his body.

"Sucker." He laughed. "Write and direct something. Then you can eat whatever the fuck you want. It's brownies and pasta for me."

I can tell.

"How is everything else? I read about that stuff with Lindley and Alexis. You still smoking the Green Unicorn? And you got any?"

Berto was always fun to smoke with, and the last time they had seen each other Orson had just been gifted with some of the bud from Ellis. He'd shared it with Berto and Clementine Mears when they'd come in shopping at the end of his shift at Provisions. Orson had been feeling generous, thinking that maybe that time would lead to a next one. It never did.

"It's all good. The work, the house, the everything. I've been spending a lot of time with Connor, and that's been great. Alexis is out now, and seems to be doing well. I'm sure we'll start sharing custody soon. I haven't heard from Jess, so no idea there." Then he shrugged, missing Ellis and the old life behind him as he said, "And nope, I've not smoked any of the Unicorn in a while, though if *you* have some this time, I'd love to share it."

Berto laughed. "I wish. Wanna get a drink?

He really needed to circulate. "I will in a minute. I disappeared for a while. The Shellys want me to be social."

Berto made a face and moved his head back and forth between them. "Isn't that what you're doing now?"

"Good point," Orson said, following him to the bar.

"You ever had a Pirate Shot?"

"No," Orson admitted. "What's that?"

"It's a tequila shot, but you take it after you snort the salt, but before you squeeze the lime in your eye. It burns like herpes and forces you to close it and yell *ARGGHH!!!* You know, like a pirate."

"That sounds terrible."

"Oh, it is," Berto agreed, then took his shot anyway.

Orson settled for his usual Old Fashioned, then said adios to Berto. He made the rounds while trying not to think about checking on Connor or wondering about Jess. The Hollywood bacchanal was making him think she might appear around any corner, even though he hadn't invited her. But then again, Orson hadn't invited Berto, or anyone else.

And the revelry was everywhere.

Weed was legal so that was happening all over the place, out in the open. Coke was still very much not, but that was no less discrete. Orson had been at parties where the law had treated this loosely before, but he had always imagined that the homeowners were complicit. Weren't the penalties strict for having drugs in your house? Or for throwing what could almost be referred to as a drug party?

But Orson was more comfortable with the coke than he was with the sex. It was everywhere too, and in many various forms, enough that he had to wonder if the Shellys had a special box on the invitation.

Do you like orgies and have no problem fucking in public or enjoy people fucking in public around you? Check YES or NO!

A younger version of Orson might have checked yes, and even believed that he would have enjoyed that. But this version of himself most definitely did not. Because he couldn't escape, it didn't feel like a choice.

He was talking to the Showrunner of *Greens* — now onto his next show, *Everyone Gets Divorced* — along with some of the cast and crew, Adrian Frank and Lonnie Shroeder, the writer and director of *Parcheesi* (the worst idea to ever actually work and the year's biggest commercial surprise so far). Adrian was genuinely curious as to why Shroeder even attempted something as nuts as Parcheesi. He'd directed a dynamite indie, then a modest studio follow-up. Shroeder said that he knew it was a risk, but that if he pulled it off no one would ever doubt him again, and if he didn't then no one would blame him because who in their right mind would ever think that a movie based on a board game would work, when it had never come remotely close to working before?

Orson wanted to pay attention to Adrian's next question, and Lonnie's answer. But it was hard when Missi Evans — Samantha on *Everybody Gets Divorced* — stood from the circle, waltzed a few feet over to the sofa, lifted her long, loose skirt to show everyone her freshly shaved pussy, gleaming beneath the well-designed lighting, and started grinding herself to first one climax, then several, while everyone in the room pretended it wasn't happening. Missi barely seemed drunk. It was more that it just seemed like something to do. And inhibitions at Orson's big party apparently didn't exist.

Regina Hall was talking to Caitlin Farr when a man Orson didn't recognize came up behind Regina and softly said her name. By the time she turned around, the man had his semi-hard cock hanging out of his pants. Regina didn't blink or flinch or even seem the slightest bit surprised. She just slid the whole thing into her mouth and started moving slowly back and forth, fully engorging the guy in seconds. Orson stood there frozen, while Caitlin watched him watching Regina, until he finally walked away, aroused and embarrassed, ashamed that he wanted to see the ending of what never should have started.

A few steps away, he was back to feeling sick and wanting to check on Connor, but Melinda appeared like magic. "Orson! You're just who we were looking for."

Then Dominic was there right beside her. He looked at his wife, running his eyes up and down her body, as though he hadn't already been appreciating her framed tits, toned legs, and tight ass all night. "You found him."

Melinda took Orson by the arm and started walking. Dominic fell into step beside them, putting him in the middle.

"Are you having fun?" she asked.

"Of course."

"You don't seem like you're having much fun," Dominic said.

"I'm having fun." A nervous, grateful laugh. "It's just overwhelming, and it's loud. I'm worried about Connor."

Seriously, it sounded like the DJ had turned the music *up*.

"You do worry a lot," Melinda said.

"Is there anything we can do to help?" Dominic showed Orson his closed fist, then opened it to reveal a tiny black vial. "Here. A present."

Orson shook his head.

"I don't want to hear it." Dominic took his hand, opened it, and placed the vial inside it. "Not now, obviously. Go check on Connor, then get out of your head and into a better place."

"You're wasting your opportunity," Melinda added.

That was the last thing that Orson wanted to do. So he thanked the Shellys and headed toward Connor's bedroom, stopping only to shake his head in bafflement at a girl who might have been underage, or paid to look that way. She had her palm flat against the fish tank, crying hard enough to ruin her makeup, blubbering about how sad she was about all the little fishies in prison.

Orson opened the door, but heard his son crying a second before he did.

"What's wrong?" he asked, running across the room and sitting on Connor's bed. "You okay?"

"He's tired. The music is really loud, you know."

"Yeah," Orson said. "Thank you for telling me that."

"I want to go to sleep!"

"I know, buddy. We're going to figure that out right now." Still patting the back of Connor's head, Orson turned to Armando. "I need you to take him somewhere else. A hotel or Hadley's or—"

"Nuh-uh." Armando shook his head. "No can do. My contract is explicit. I'm supposed to watch him here, at your house, at the party that I'll be attending myself as soon as I get the kid sleeping."

You have got to be kidding me.

Orson looked at Armando in disgust. "Go. Enjoy the party. I've got this."

No argument from Armando. He practically pranced to the door and right into the hall.

Orson held his son and matched his breathing, falling in and out of time with his own, hoping he wouldn't fall asleep himself, but thinking that maybe that would be okay if he did.

Chapter Forty-Seven

Orson wasn't sure how long he had drifted off by the time he finally opened his eyes. But Connor was snoring, and the party was throbbing even harder.

He was exhausted, and now that Connor was down, he definitely needed a means to get through the rest of this party. So he took out Dominic's vial and took a bump, then one more after that.

Things were much better after that. He felt more like himself, or at least like the self that he wanted to be, bouncing from conversation to conversation as he searched the party for Hadley, finally feeling loose like his bosses wanted him to. Until he wandered into the wrong room and lost his shit.

There was Armando, balls deep in some bent-over cocktail waitress, while giving a waiter with bright white teeth a rather vigorous hand job.

Isn't anyone working?

He marched over to Armando and pulled him out of and away from the help with a slurp.

"What the fuck? I'm not working right now!"

"Or ever," Orson said. "You're fired."

"I don't work for you. I work for Natural Nurturing."

The waiter and waitress were scrambling to get themselves together and out of the scene.

"Get out of my house. Now."

"What was I doing? What, I'm not allowed to have a good time because I take care of your child when you can't?"

"No, Armando. It's because you're an asshole. Now get the fuck out of here before I make this personal and start looking for ways to make sure you never work again."

Orson wondered if he had that kind of power. Probably not, but it sure felt good to say.

Another bump after Armando left made him feel better, then Hadley appeared to help send him over the moon. Or at least she got started. She wanted more coke and preferred a private room. So they slipped into the study that he still couldn't imagine ever really using, then after a little more snow, Orson was loose enough to get grabby.

He looked over at Hadley texting and grabbed her tit.

She finished texting, then took his hand off of her tit. "Not yet."

"Why not?"

"I want you later."

"You can have me again." His hand was back on her tit, but now his lips were on her neck and his tongue was starting to lick her."

"No, Orson." But then she giggled.

There was sheetrock in his pants. Hadley never turned him down. And he wanted to fuck. So what was the big deal?

"Come on …" Orson pulled her back toward him, pressed her tight ass against his hard cock.

But then she shimmied away from him, brushing his crotch with her ass on the way.

"Are you fucking with me?" Orson laughed, but his cock was throbbing.

"Do you want me to be fucking with you?" She smiled like a siren, just out of reach.

"I want you to be doing something to me."

"Like what, Orson?" Hadley took a step back. She smiled wider. Licked her lips.

He didn't want to say it. The best part about Hadley besides her perfect, willing body was that he never had to ask, and on the rare times he did, she didn't even say yes before starting.

"Tell me what you want me to do it." Another step. "Otherwise I'll keep going backward until I'm not even here. So Orson, what do you want me to do?"

"I want you to fuck me."

She took a step toward him. "How do you want me to fuck you? With my mouth? With my pussy? With my asshole? With all three of them, and in that order?"

"Yes," he said.

He'd had her so many times before, and still she made him crave her.

Her hand was on his cock, rubbing it over the fabric. Just right, soft but with a light pinch and a little squeeze, teasing him from shaft to tip, making him picture her mouth and her pussy and her asshole, all three in exactly that order.

"What are you waiting for?"

"Am I enough for you, Orson?"

What the fuck? We're going to have this talk? Now?

"Is there anything you want that I'm not giving to you? Because I want to give you everything." Her hand was rubbing faster, her breath was heavy between her words.

"Of course you're enough," Orson assured her, if that was what Hadley really needed right now.

"Have you ever wanted a threesome?"

Oh, that. Of course he had. He would never ever *ask* for one. But yes, that was on his bucket list, and something he expected to eventually happen in the most natural of ways, once he had ascended to the top of the Hollywood temple. Was that now?

"It's a yes or no question. I know you haven't had one, unless you lied on your application or you've cheated on me since. So have you ever wanted a threesome?"

She read my application?

"Yes." Goddammit his cock was throbbing. "I've wanted a threesome."

Hadley unbuckled his pants. She took out his dick, kissed the tip, and her tongue around the head. "Would you like one tonight?" She swallowed his shaft while awaiting his answer.

"Yes," Orson moaned.

Hadley slid off his shaft, another kiss on the tip as her lips left his skin.

The door opened and she turned toward it.

"Perfect timing," Hadley said, as Melinda entered the room.

Orson scrambled to make himself presentable, shoving his dick back down into his pants, gently so as not to bend the hot meat now throbbing in his hand.

"It's okay," Melinda laughed.

"It's okay," Hadley echoed, before she batted Orson's hands away, reclaimed his cock, and put it into her mouth.

Melinda slipped off her dress.

She looked even more stunning than Orson had imagined. He'd thought that surely she had to have some sort of Spanx keeping things up. She was anywhere from forty to fifty-five; Orson couldn't tell and didn't want to ask. Her IMDB page was unclear. But he was staring at her now in a black bra and panties. All he saw was perfection.

She smiled at Orson's appreciative eyes.

Hadley started bobbing.

"Have you ever wanted to fuck me?" Melinda asked, walking toward them.

Of course.

No!

Why are you asking me that?

This was suicide. Melinda was both his boss, and his boss's wife.

"You don't have to worry," she assured him, surely reading his face. "Dominic approves. We're both allowed to have our fun, especially on a night like this. And I've been wanting to taste you for a long time. May I taste you, Orson? Would you like to taste me?"

Hadley popped off of his cock with a giggle. "You're going to want to hurry if you want to taste him."

Orson was woozy.

Maybe that's because he hadn't drawn a breath since Melinda lost her dress.

"Take him to the couch," she ordered.

Hadley grabbed him by the wrist and started to drag him. He protested a second, then surrendered in full. His body became elastic, taffy between these women and reality. He couldn't do this. Everything would be different if he did.

And he couldn't afford that.

Not with Alexis and Jess and Connor and the house and his future and—

Hadley was stroking his shaft, and Melinda was cupping his balls.

Then Hadley handed his dick to Melinda. It throbbed in her hand as she straddled him, then slowly dipping—

The door opened and Alexis marched inside.

You've got to be kidding me.

He wanted to disappear or die, whatever was faster. And still his cock refused to stop throbbing.

"What are you doing here?" Hadley and Melinda asked together.

"Armando called me!" Alexis was yelling at Orson and ignoring the whores. "He told me that you made him leave so you could get your drugs and your fuck on. I don't need to see more than one to know that both are true!"

"You're talking to Armando?" *This isn't happening.*

Melinda spun around toward Alexis. "How did you get his number? Did he call you or did you call him?" She shook her head. "It doesn't matter. He's finished either way."

Orson observed the scene while shaking his head. Hadley was still dressed, but Melinda was in her bra and panties. Even black, they did nothing to hide her arousal. He could smell it in the room. Surely Alexis could, too. He looked from Melinda to Hadley and back, his eyes pleading. "Can we have a minute?"

"Absolutely not," Melinda said. "We've already talked about this."

"Talked about what?" Alexis looked sharply at Orson, ignoring Melinda.

Hadley stepped back and off to the side, awaiting a clearer directive.

"I already told you," Orson started, nervous as shit, wondering what he should say before blurting the rest, "I'm not allowed to talk to you without a lawyer present."

"When did you tell her that?" Melinda asked.

"Why does it matter?" Orson responded, though he knew precisely why.

"Why does that matter?" Alexis echoed, asking for an entirely different reason.

"*Please,*" Orson begged.

"Absolutely not." Melinda marched over to her dress, leaned over, and dropped it over her body. Even though it was tight enough in all the right places, it still seemed to spill right down her sides.

"We were going to work everything out!" Alexis screamed, punching Orson on his chest, not hard enough to bruise him on the outside, but enough to hurt him in more permanent ways.

Hadley rushed toward them, probably to pull Alexis away from him. But Orson raised a hand to stay her.

"I've got it," he said, then gently grabbed Alexis by the wrists. "I never said that."

"You did!" Now she was sobbing. "You said that Hadley wasn't right for you, and that this giant mansion was too big to live in all by yourself!"

"*You* said that!"

"So, you talked to her without a lawyer." Melinda spoke without a hint of emotion, which was somehow exponentially more terrifying than it would have been if she'd screamed.

He ignored her. He had to for now. He shook his head and fixed his eyes on Alexis. "This isn't the time or place. I never said that, and—"

"So where is the time and place, Orson? With your lawyer around?"

"Exactly," said Melinda.

Hadley laughed.

"Fuck you!" Alexis screamed.

"Alexis ..." Orson said.

"Fuck you, too!" She stood there glaring at him, breathing hard through her nose, fists clenched at her side.

Orson wished this wasn't happening. He was sorry for all of it. That he hadn't told Melinda the truth, that Alexis had showed up at his house party unannounced, that he was so totally fucking high, and that he was still hard despite it all, and needing to put his dick into something.

Alexis marched toward the door. "I'm going to get my son!"

"You can't do that!" Orson called out, stomping right behind her, still at full mast.

She turned back. "This is no place for him, and you know it."

"I have custody, Alexis. It's the law."

From behind him, Orson heard Melinda say, "It's unfortunate that our Orson is unable to follow simple directions, so that we can help him navigate the dangerous waters that you have dragged him into. But I assure you, Ms. Belle, I have no such difficulties. If you don't leave these premises immediately, I will have you escorted out. Raise a fuss, and I will press charges. As it stands, you'll be lucky if I let you leave without making it my mission to sic every one of my lawyers into every corner of your privileged little life. Just let your daddy try and stop me."

The women glared at each other.

Orson waited for the moment to pop.

Then it did. Alexis swallowed, and still holding Melinda's gaze, said, "You have no idea what you just did."

Melinda laughed. It sounded almost girlish. "That's where you're wrong. I always know *exactly* what I'm doing. Now, good evening, Ms. Belle."

Then Melinda stared her down until Alexis finally withered and went slinking out of the den's still open door.

Chapter Forty-Eight

"Orson."

Someone was shaking him, the voice familiar.

He wanted to open his eyes, but also fuck that.

Orson groaned or something then turned over.

Whatever this was, he couldn't deal with it now. He needed another year of sleep, maybe some morphine.

He tried to remember, but that wasn't happening. At least not much beyond the tits and drugs. The smell of sex, still in the room, ripe but stale.

"Orson, wake up." More shaking.

"Grmphrumble," Orson said.

A spike through his skull and Orson remembered something he wished he didn't. Alexis storming out of the office — is that where he was now? No, his den didn't have a bed — with a threat that he couldn't quite …

Melinda and Hadley and—

Oh my god.

Orson remembered the everything that happened after Alexis left.

The sex drugs. The drugs. The goddamned rock and roll.

The women had fucked him hard. Held him down. Took turns. Burned the experience into his memory.

Then they sent him out into the crowd to mingle, with two blue pills. He swallowed them without water or even asking what they were. It was the least he could do after what they had just done for his dick, and what they promised to do again and again once the party wound all the way down.

So Orson went out and had himself the time of his life.

Bobby Lawless was at the party. At *his* party. He couldn't wait to tell his parents. Mom and Dad were impressed with pictures of the house and grounds, and they promised to come back out to California soon, but Dad would shit his khakis when he heard that Bobby had been there. The guy was a legend, and "Wrong Side of the Mountain" was the soundtrack to Orson's childhood -- strapped into the car seat in back beside Samuel while Dad sang along with Bobby upfront, knowing every word and never missing one whenever Bobby was singing about the girl with the blue eyes and the bluer tattoo. Mom was always quiet for that one.

Of course he wasn't going to refuse a round with Bobby. The singer had no interest in powder or pills, but he was a connoisseur of pot, with stories that Orson kept trying to tease out of him, both because he wanted fodder for his father but also because they had the ring of tales that were too good to be true, and therefore surely had to be. Bobby corroborated Ellis' theory about Green Unicorn going back to Humboldt and said that he'd been there himself.

Bobby had more stories, and Orson wanted to hear them all, but he had a job to do, and didn't want to let

Melinda and Hadley down. So he circulated some more, and—

"ORSON!"

WHAT THE FUCK DO YOU WANT? he thought, but said, "Grmphrumbleareubalmblebum."

So he circulated some more, then …

Fuck.

Now it was hard to remember. And that was bullshit because he'd *just had it.*

There was something, then something after that, and probably some more stuff as guests left the party like air leaving to deflate the balloon. More drugs. Then he was alone, except for Melinda and Hadley, and all the girls they were willing to share him with because they wanted Orson to know that he was important, a prince in their eyes.

He saw the king with a harem of his own, Dominic strolling up the spiraling staircase with a foursome, two dolls on either side. A voluptuous redhead with milky white breasts, a blonde waif who looked like she was auditioning for the lead in *Tinker Bell*, and may very well have been, a pale Goth with raven hair and a carnival of tattoos, and a brunette that Orson couldn't stop staring at, not just because she was a jaw dropper but because she invited images of Jess into his mind.

The last time he'd seen her.

Him looking down on her, staring up at him on the tile floor. Thrusting into her mouth. His head swimming.

Then like a thief she was gone.

But good for Dominic. That looked like a helluva time.

And it sure explained why he didn't mind his wife fucking Orson, many times, sharing him with Hadley and another rotating trio, one of whom might have been Dominic's redhead, though Orson honestly couldn't—

"HEY!" A slap across his face.

And now his eyes were open.

"What the hell?" At least that's what Orson thought he said. Because holy shit, this headache.

"Orson, you have to wake up," Hadley said. "Some people are here."

"Whu peble?"

"Orson. It's Child Services. Melinda is stalling them downstairs, but you need to wake up."

Then he was up. Lightning might as well have struck his head and burned him from the insides. He was wide awake, or at least blinking enough to turn the engine.

He looked around. Drugs out, naked bodies in a pile.

Shit.

"Shit!"

"Exactly."

"What do we do?"

"We start by getting you out of here."

She held out her hand and he took it. Then he threw on some clothes and burst out of the room.

Melinda was downstairs, trying their patience.

"Mr. Beck," said a woman at the bottom of the stairs, extending her hand as she approached him. "I'm Anna Pierce, from CPS. I need to look around."

Downstairs? Fine, have at it. The place was immaculate because the Shellys paid for the cleaning crew to take care of things both during and after the party. Details were everything to them. But the bedrooms were upstairs, and that had hosted more than one drunken, drug-fueled orgy.

"Of course," Orson said, wondering if the smile looked weird on his face.

Probably. Asshole.

"Great," Anna said, then took a step toward the stairs.

"Shouldn't we start down here?" He had to buy some time. Get the guests upstairs dressed. The drugs stashed.

Fucking Christ. How had this become his life?

He was trying not to panic, but his heart wanted to pound right out of his ribcage.

Orson was tapping his foot, obviously nervous. He forced himself to stop.

"We've already looked downstairs," Anna said. She glanced at Melinda and added, "Thoroughly."

Then she walked past him and onto the stairs, fast enough that Orson didn't know what to do.

"Wait!" he called out, now three steps behind her.

Anna kept walking. "Yes, Mr. Beck?"

Melinda was at his heels. She growled into his ear, "*This is why we have rules.*"

His world fell apart at the top of the stairs, because what was he going to do, *lie?*

Anna found Dominic's room, though he was already cleaned up and sharp enough that he might have gotten away with it. If not for the pesky starlets in their birthday suits and the powder that wasn't from Dunkin.

But that wasn't even the worst of it.

That came when Anna opened the door to Connor's room.

His son was bawling his eyes out. His eyes were red enough that Orson had to admit that he might have been crying for hours.

What time is it?

"Daddy! Daddy! Daddy!" he bawled.

Anna let Orson comfort his son, but that didn't mean she was anywhere close to letting this go.

"I'm going to have to take him into custody."

"You can't do that," he begged.

Neither Melinda or Hadley tried to help him. Dominic was surely worthless, cowering in his suite with the celebrity sluts in training — and no, that wasn't the same redhead, but they might have been sisters.

"You can see the problem that Child Protective Services would have with an environment like this, don't you, Mr. Beck?"

"It looks worse than it is," Orson said. "I can explain."

"I'm sure that you can."

"This was Alexis, right? You realize that makes this a setup, don't you?"

Anna just looked at him.

He took a breath and tried again. "I'll be right back."

Fuck the lawyers, they had ruined everything. The only thing that worked with Alexis was talking to her like a human. He'd threatened lawyers — *Melinda* had threatened lawyers — and Alexis came back with two smoking barrels. This was his fault. He should have seen it coming, shouldn't have listened to the Shellys.

Not about this.

Or maybe he should have listened to them all the way.

It didn't matter. The damage was done.

Orson left everyone wondering as he stepped out into the hallway and dialed Alexis.

"Gee, I wonder if I would be getting a phone call right now if you didn't have a little Won't You be My Neighbor at your house right now," Alexis said instead of hello.

"This isn't cool. Why are you doing this?"

"Why am *I* doing this? I wasn't the one who was about to have a threesome with my boss and my boss's whore, while my son was sleeping a—"

"Are you kidding?" Orson cut her off, trying not to yell. "Are you telling me that you've never had sex while—"

"That's not the point, Orson. You said you were there for me, then you threatened me with lawyers."

"I didn't threaten you with a lawyer, Alexis. I said that I

couldn't talk to you without one because my employers were afraid of something happening, *exactly like this.*"

"The employers that you're fucking?"

"Come on, Alexis …"

"What do you want from me, Orson? This is *your fault.* Not mine. I've done everything I was supposed to do. I screwed up and I told the truth. Then I paid the price—"

Hardly.

"—and now I want my life back. That starts with Connor. It could have included you, but you decided you wanted to live on my Fuck You List instead. Congratulations. It's not a long list, but it is a devoted one. You have my full attention. Anyone on that list has earned my full wrath for the rest of their natural lives. You could have had everything, but instead I'm going to make sure you have nothing. I can't talk to you without your lawyer present? Fuck you, Orson. I can't have my son? Fuck you, Orson. Then neither can you."

"That's so selfish, Alexis. You don't have to do this."

"I'll tell you what, why don't I hang up right now, and that will give you a nice head start on thinking about all of the things you didn't have to do, that you went ahead and did anyway."

Then she hung up.

It wasn't just the phone. Something inside Orson disconnected.

He begged Anna to understand, to listen, to give him another chance. But according to Anna, it wasn't for her to decide. This was the first step in a long and miserable process, and she was just doing her job.

"No, Daddy!" Connor called as Anna ripped him out of his house and his father's life.

Why is this happening to me?

But that thought was instantly chased by, *Because you let*

it. This is all your fault. Your life is spinning out of control because you were drunk behind the wheel.

The front door closed and Connor was gone.

The Shellys promised that they would do everything they could, reminded him that there were reasons for their rules, and, looking on the bright side, suggested that this little hiccup now would save them a world of headache later.

Hadley promised to make him feel better, with a salacious wink that was like wearing red to a funeral.

"I just need to be alone right now," Orson said.

He went into his room and took out his phone, not meaning to torture himself when he checked his Rummage Report for the day, more curious than eager to get what had to be done over and finished with.

But then, as was his habit, Orson checked Hollywood Hunted and read something that he wished that hadn't.

Ellis obviously wanted his attention.

Well, now he had it.

Chapter Forty-Nine

"How are you this fine afternoon?"

Orson waved as he strode past Angus and up the front stairs into the Brick then six dozen flights to the top.

Orson pounded on the door with three hard knocks, then thought *Fuck it!* He turned the knob without waiting for an answer and stepped inside.

Ellis was at his small living room table, where he ate nearly every one of his meals alone and spent a wide majority of his days and nights hunched over his laptop.

He looked up from the screen with a smile and said, "It's good to see you, Orson."

"Bullshit! Why would you write that about me?"

Ellis shrugged and shook his head. "What else was I supposed to do?"

"What are you talking about?"

"You're here, aren't you?" Ellis looked around his shit-hole apartment, but Orson wasn't getting whatever he was trying to say. Then he did.

"So you wrote that shit about me to what, get my attention?" Orson was trying not to yell and mostly failing.

Ellis stood, then started walking toward the still-open door. "Look man, I didn't want to send out this kind of smoke signal, but it's all your fault. You were ignoring me. Again. You promised not to after the last time, but -- emails, calls, and texts, man, you didn't respond to any of them."

No way. How dare he. Orson wasn't going to let Ellis put the blame on him. So what if he hadn't answered a text or two? He had a lot going on, with his life both imploding and exploding at the same time. Ellis couldn't see that? Couldn't be a better, more understanding friend?

Well, *fuck him.*

Ellis closed the door behind Orson, mumbled, "Make yourself at home," then went back to the table and sat, starting to type while Orson continued to stand there, dumfounded.

It took him a moment to find his voice. "You have no idea what I've been going through."

Ellis kept typing, not looking up. No acknowledgement, not even a twitch of his head.

Orson was rolling to a boil.

"You know it's not easy, just because the money is there. Life has been a fucking nightmare lately. Alexis is out, but I'm not allowed to talk to her without a lawyer, I still have no idea about Jess, although everybody thinks I want to hear every little rumor, and the truth is that I do, even though they always tear me apart. And everything with Hadley and the Shellys, it's not like it seems from the outside. It's—"

"That's what *I've* been trying to tell *you*," Ellis said, finally looking up.

But Orson shook his head. "It's not like that, not like you're saying. But it is different, and it would be nice if you showed even an ounce of compassion."

Ellis laughed, but this laugh was sad and brittle. "An ounce of compassion? Buddy, I've been working with buckets of the stuff and can't even get you to fill a glass."

Orson was still shaking his head, but now he wanted to cry. He was careening past his breaking point. The one friend in his life who wasn't at least partly responsible for what his world was becoming, and he didn't have a single shit to give for Orson.

His voice hitched and cracked. He was splitting from the inside.

"I can't believe you would do this, Ellis, you of all people. My life is falling apart right now. I'm at the end of my rope, and you're publishing shit about me? I just can't—"

"That's a bit dramatic, isn't it?" Ellis shook his head. "And that's the thing that you're not getting, man. Your life *will* fall apart. That's why I'm trying to help you—"

"Fuck you, Ellis! THEY TOOK MY SON AWAY FROM ME!"

Now the tears were streaming, hot on Orson's face.

Ellis said, "Are you done?"

Orson stared at his friend — *is he my friend?* — while collecting his breath. "Why did you write that about me? You had to know how much it would hurt."

Ellis nodded. "I had a good idea. And don't get me wrong, you totally deserve it for being a dickbag to Jess, but that's not why I did it."

"Then why did you do it?" Orson asked through gritted teeth, angry at Ellis but somehow unable to hate him, knowing that his old friend — and yes, he was definitely that — somehow had his best interests at heart, and was about to tell him exactly what that meant. "Why am I here?"

Orson sat on the other side of the table, waiting for

Ellis to talk. Ellis knew something, or maybe a lot of some-things, judging by his expression and posture. Orson wondered what was on the computer screen, just out of sight.

"Not that you've bothered to ask lately," Ellis began, "but Hollywood Hunted has been doing well."

"I didn't need to ask, Ellis. I read it every day. I can see that."

It looked like Ellis swallowed his response to that one. He glanced at the screen then turned his laptop around.

"Take a look."

But Orson had no idea what he was looking at. Some sort of spreadsheet with enough colors to make him dizzy. There were names he recognized, like Logan White, Harrison Turner, and Hadley Witt, with a few dozen others. Then it got more personal, with Jess Lindley, and Orson himself.

Each name had a row of boxes, each one filled with text.

"What am I looking at?"

"Would you like to know what your bosses are up to?"

Chapter Fifty

Orson couldn't decide if Ellis was brilliant or demented.

"What is this?" Orson finally asked.

"It's six months of work. So take your time catching up."

Orson asked a few more questions, but Ellis just kept encouraging him to *keep on looking*.

The mind map was massive, and a much more colorful version of the data available on the spreadsheet. Orson was looking at something that resembled a family tree. He could see the roots and all the countless generations of chaos sired by the Shellys. Their lineage looked like it could strangle the industry, or maybe give it cancer, seeing as how they controlled so many cells inside the body.

Orson clicked on boxes of interest, each one leading deeper into a series of questions without answers, puzzles in dire need of solving, dubious circumstances, impossible coincidences, and unfortunate outcomes. But also plenty of fame and fortune, death and destruction, and successes bought and sold like souls to the devil.

"How many of these do I have to click before you'll

start telling me what in the fuck this is?"

"We can start any time. But we're starting with Jess."

His stomach curdled. "Of course."

Orson had clicked on a lot of boxes, but he'd been avoiding that one.

Ellis tugged on his big red beard, which was longer and fuller than the last time Orson had seen him. "You sure you're ready?"

No.

He nodded and Ellis clicked.

"Jess is an escort."

An ice pick of horror stabbed him through one ear and came out the other side. "How do you know that?"

Orson wasn't questioning whether Ellis did because if Ellis wasn't sure, they wouldn't be having this conversation.

Ellis pointed at a picture of Harrison Turner. "I've had my eye on the Shellys for a while. You know that."

"I never really got it, but yeah."

Ellis narrowed his eyes. "Enough with the bullshit, man. You did know, and we're not going to get very far right now if you don't knock that off. I understand why you turned a blind eye, but you can't do it anymore. Do we understand each other?"

Orson looked at Ellis and knew from the set of his mouth that he wasn't getting a choice.

He nodded. "We do."

Ellis pointed at the screen. "I had a lot of suspicions, and I'd heard a few stories about the Shellys, just like you. But no one was ever willing to go on record. Until Harrison."

Orson sat straighter, the hair on his body bristling.

"I've still not heard from Jess, and she won't answer my calls, no matter what message I leave on her voicemail. But she was part of Harrison's story, and I find it hard to doubt a word that he said. He gave me some names and a trail to follow. I am going to publish this, Orson. I'm going to tell her story. Jess deserves vindication, and so do all the other people who have been used and abused so that the Shellys could—"

"It's not that simple," Orson said, shaking his head. "A lot of people would look at that list and wonder if maybe you have some sort of vendetta. Because that's also a list of people whose dreams have come true."

"At what cost?" Ellis looked incredulous.

"One that all of them are willing to pay."

But Orson wondered if that was true. His stomach right now was a bucket of acid, so that suggested *probably not.*

"Not true, man. I've talked to a lot of people. There's a distinct pattern of manipulation that—"

"They're Hollywood producers! *Of course* there's a pattern of—"

"Not like this, Orson." Ellis glared at him. "Do you want to see what happened to Jess or not?"

He wasn't sure if he did, but if Jess needed him, could he walk away? "Tell me."

He could barely breathe as Ellis told him Harrison's part of Jess's story, about how Dominic had got her hooked on coke, then Melinda had opened the door to her whoredom, practically planted a foot on her back and shoved the woman he was in love with right across the threshold.

It couldn't be true, but it was.

Dominic and Melinda had done this to everyone. They had ruined countless lives in pursuit of their own goals. Orson knew about Jess, and Ellis knew about all the names on his mind map — Orson couldn't count them all, but there were at least fifty, maybe a hundred or more.

How many more were still in the shadows?

Chapter Fifty-One

Orson was drowning.

This story was bigger than him, bigger than Ellis. Looking at the mind map, it appeared bigger than Hollywood and ran the gamut from drugs to back-channel deals. The Shellys seemed very interested in changing legislation around sex, and Shellter Productions either owned, operated through a middle-man, or was heavily invested in a sprawling web of sex and success, the two spun together like fibers in a strand of yarn.

It was hard to understand, and Ellis was still untangling so much of it, but the Shellys had a stable of girls that they moved in and out of some of the world's highest production porn, lucrative escorting contracts, and for the best of the best among them, stardom in whatever flavor the Shellys could imagine. Their creativity, like their ambition and the endless supply of fresh meat, grew in leaps and bounds by the day.

But it was clear that the Shellys always got what they wanted because they had what everyone else was willing to step over their own mothers to get. They weren't interested in creating more of what everyone already had. They were making something new, something brilliant that the world had never seen, something the planet would be working overtime to catch up with for a while.

Why create another product when Shellter Productions could create a whole new market?

"Do you see it?" Ellis asked him.

Orson nodded his head. He didn't want to, but he was certainly starting to.

"Do you see why they need to be brought to their knees?" He waited for Orson to respond. A barely perceptible nod, but that was enough. "Do you see how much deeper this goes than Jess?"

Orson nodded, stronger this time. He swallowed and realized that his throat was on fire.

"You have to do something for me, Orson. You can help us hold them responsible."

His heart started beating faster. He shook his head, even though he didn't mean to. "There's nothing I—"

"You can make a difference."

"What do you need me to do?"

But Orson couldn't possibly do a thing. He thought of Connor, of the mortgage, of all his many signatures staring up from the bottom of contracts that he'd signed but had never read.

"I want a tell-all interview. No holds barred. I ask and you answer. Completely unscripted."

"I *can't* do that. They'll—"

"You have to, man. You're the only one who can. I don't have a story I can run. I have pieces, but I need something — *someone* — to help send this thing over the edge. I need you to help me out. I need you to do the right thing."

"You don't understand. I just bought a house."

"You can buy another one."

He shook his head. "No, I'll go bankrupt."

"That happens all the time."

"They'll ruin me. I'll never work again."

"No. You will never work for the Shellys again."

"I'll never work in Hollywood!" Orson's voice had clawed its way up a couple of desperate-sounding octaves.

"Bullshit!" Ellis was practically growling. "There will be a line of people willing to hire you for both your talent and balls!"

He stood there, staring at Orson and exhaling through his nostrils like an angry bear.

It was all so easy for him to say.

Ellis wouldn't have to give everything up. Take everything that he had worked and waited for, then just chuck it all into the ever mounting pile of *fuckme.*

It wasn't just that his star was continuing to rise and that Dominic and Melinda were both yanking hard on the opposite end of the pulley. They had done everything they said that they would, delivered on a hundred percent of their promises, acted only in his best interests so far as he could tell.

He was the one who had not always honored his end of the bargain, done things that he promised he wouldn't, violated the oaths that he had offered his name to.

But what had his best interests cost the people around him?

Every hit leveled on Jess had ostensibly been in Orson's best interests, from those first "candid" shots on his balcony to the coke that she stole from his pocket — an act whose DNA could be traced back to an impromptu (yeah, right) lunch in Dominic's office.

Orson had lost so much along the way, as had some of

the people who had been there for him, both before and after the monster he might have turned into.

He wondered how deep this could possibly go. If maybe Tyler's tragedy wasn't an unforeseen misfortune at all.

Or maybe he was being paranoid, fed by a muckraking Ellis.

Because could the Shellys *really* be responsible for Jess' descent into madness? Couldn't there be a simple explanation for all of this? And didn't he owe his employers a chance to explain, given that they'd changed his life not just once but several times and seemed to be on his side even when he defied them?

Or is that the argument that Robert Johnson made to himself, walking away from that dusty fork with a weathered guitar, now playing licks like the thing had been picked up from the holy carpenter's floor?

Was Orson just like any other fool who had found himself on the wrong side of a deal with the devil?

A clueless sucker who had sold his soul and taxed everyone in his life who had ever bought into the lie of loving him?

Was he worse than cursed?

Orson looked from Ellis to the screen, thinking. Ellis gave him plenty of time. The two of them shared the silence, inhaling and exhaling together, circling the edge of a life-changing resolve.

Then he took the deepest breath of his life. Then, both resenting his friend for being Jesus and Judas, he shook his head and said, "Sorry, man. I just can't."

Chapter Fifty-Two

Sorry, man. I just can't.

Orson had regretted those words the second he said them.

He didn't blame Ellis for kicking him out. Or for the things he'd yelled before he had.

But what was he supposed to do? Doing that interview would be an act of suicide on multiple levels. Going against the Shellys was like making a targeted strike against Hollywood itself. It would show anyone and everyone that Orson might ever work with that he was a turncoat who could not be trusted.

He'd worked too hard to climb the mountain. He couldn't afford to meander into the abyss of oblivion. He had Connor to consider. His career. The house. Things with Hadley, whatever they were.

His allegiance to Dominic and Melinda because no matter what, the whispers said they had done, the Shellys had always appeared to put Orson first.

So no, he couldn't help Ellis. At least not like he wanted him to, and not right now. But he could definitely help himself, and he would. Orson was getting his shit together.

Because the one thing he could fix was how Connor would see him for the rest of his life.

How Jess would hopefully see him, if he could ever find a way to rescue her.

How Orson would see himself.

He wanted people to know what he was about without having to think about it, like people knew his parents and brother. The Becks did the right thing, every time, and everybody knew it.

That had always been at least seventy-five percent true.

Orson had been thinking about his family a lot. Mom, Dad, and Samuel. What did they always say?

Sometimes it's better to lose and do the right thing, than to win and do the wrong thing.

He couldn't call his parents or Samuel to ask for advice because Orson already knew what they would say.

He couldn't talk to Ellis because that was who he was failing.

He couldn't reach Jess because he'd already indirectly ruined her life and now she wanted nothing to do with him, unless she could distract him long enough to pilfer his coke.

And he couldn't meet with the Shellys because he wouldn't even know where to begin, even if he was sure that it was worth the risk of ending up with little in life and less in the credits.

But he could have a conversation with Hadley, so that was where he started.

She was home when he got there. *His* home, the one she'd sort of cajoled him into buying. But she was sitting on the sofa in a silver teddy, despite not being invited. Most of the times these days she simply assumed. For a long time, Orson had pretended he didn't mind, that his casa was her casa and all of that shit. But the other half of the time he hated it.

Hadley looked up as he entered, lowering her magazine. A copy of *Oh the Humanities!* with Orson smiling on the cover. It made him feel even sicker. She was probably reading that article now, or looking at the picture of her and Orson together, a candid shot from *Bottleneck*, where she was half-finished with her makeup and laughing hysterically, much to the crew's mounting frustration, and Orson stood beside her, laughing just as hard.

That was a good day. This one wouldn't be.

"We need to talk."

She rolled her eyes and tossed her copy of *Oh!* onto the coffee table. "Great. I can already tell that this will be fun."

"Why are you here?"

She laughed and looked down at herself, like that was an answer.

"Did I forget that you were coming over?"

Now she looked insulted. "Do I need an invitation?"

"It's the polite thing to do."

Hadley was up in a flash, her eyes narrowed. "Polite? What are you doing, Orson?"

"I'm not doing anything." Except that he was.

"Yes, you are. You're picking a fight."

"I'm not picking a fight ... I just ... we can't do—"

"No, Orson. We're not breaking up."

Hadley sat back on the sofa.

He looked at her dumbfounded. "I'm serious."

She picked up the magazine. "Actually, you're not. You just went for a drive or something and got all moody. That's not—"

"No. I mean it. We're done. I mean, as a couple."

"Were we ever *really* a couple, Orson?"

He stared at her without knowing where to take this. Then he guessed. "You were always acting like we were something more than I thought we actually were. I figured that's what you wanted."

Hadley laughed. "It is what I wanted. What I *do* want. What you want too, so knock it off. I mean, get it out of your system, obviously, but then knock it off after that."

Orson crouched next to Hadley, not wanting to sit on the sofa, but needing for her to take him seriously.

She took his hand and put it on her tit. "Why don't we talk about this after you fuck me?"

He pulled away from her and stood. "You don't get it. I really am serious."

"That what? You want to 'break up' — why Orson? This is the perfect relationship. We—"

"It isn't a relationship!"

"That's where you're wrong. It's a more honest relationship than most people have. Look at where the world is going, Orson In a few more years we'll all be able to know our perfect match because LiveLyfe or Forage or Amazon will have all the data they need to tell us. And we'll still all be clamoring to know more. Until then, you and I are lucky enough to have the Shellys. We're together, Orson. If you need to get something on the side, I understand. But don't embarrass me. And I promise to do everything I can to make myself more than enough for you. There's nothing I won't do for—"

"But it's not real. Doesn't that matter to you?"

Hadley was back on her feet, the first arrow to finally pierce her armor.

"What's not real about it? What are the best parts of any partnership? The friendship? The shared friends and interests and goals? The sex? They're as real as anything in this world."

But Orson couldn't let this go. He'd promised to do the right thing, starting with Hadley, and now he was standing in front of his chance. So he said the one thing that he knew would end this for good. The one thing he had been so careful not to say.

"I don't love you, Hadley. And I never will."

It hit her like a slap. She fell back onto the couch, so vulnerable with barely anything on, her limbs all akimbo.

"Hadley …"

"Don't." She was back on her feet and circling behind the couch, her eyes darting around the room, probably looking for whatever clothing she had carelessly cast off on her way to the sofa. She spied it and marched over.

Orson approached her as she put on her dress.

"You can't do this," she said.

"I'm not trying to do anything."

"Exactly!" Hadley leaned forward, as though she wanted to march back toward him but wasn't willing to grant him the steps. "I'm going to tell Dominic and Melinda."

I'm going to tell Mommy and Daddy on you!

"I understand. Do what you have to. But what exactly are you going to tell them? That I don't want to be a fake couple anymore? That I'm looking for something more real in my life?"

Another slap, but this one was miles from what he meant. Orson wasn't trying to say that Hadley wasn't real, but that's surely what she heard.

It took her a moment, but then she found the words to cut him off at his knees, said the thing he'd been afraid of all his life, especially these last couple of months.

"What a waste of my time," she said. "You were never worth the effort."

Hadley turned back at the door. Orson was stupid

enough to think she might be trying again, but then she added, "I slept with five guys this month, and the other four all fucked me better than you."

Then she was gone. And Orson didn't get to say what he wanted to tell her the most.

I hope you take better care of yourself.

Chapter Fifty-Three

Alexis was next on his list.

Orson called and called and called, but she refused to answer.

He went by her house, knocked on the door, rang the bell, even peeked through some windows, but he was pressing his luck and knew it. Had to get out before someone called the cops. It wasn't like he could be incognito much these days. He had to settle for leaving Alexis a message while sitting in his Lexus staring at her house.

"Hey Alexis, I really didn't want to do this on the phone, but you won't answer. I'm pretty sure you're home right now and are ignoring me. I get that, I understand all of it. But we need to work this out, for Connor's sake. This isn't fair to him, and it isn't what's best for any of us. I'm sorry for whatever I did to make you think I wanted things to work out between us. Wait. I didn't mean it like that. Of course I want things to work out. I mean romantically … I'm still working on myself. I'm not even with Hadley right now. We both know she's a mess. I'm really trying to do the right thing here …"

He drew a deep breath, then blew it out away from the receiver before he finished.

"Just … please … let's talk. You can call me any time."

He tried to call Jess again, but that was just for the hell of it. There was zero percent chance that she'd answer, judging by the number of times that she'd answered so far, but it wasn't like the number was disconnected, and he still got to hear her voice every time, even if he had long ago tired of leaving his in return.

Orson almost left a message this time, vowed to do it the next time, then hung up a second before the beep and longed for long-ago days wasting away at the Brick.

He checked his email and feeds, a few breadcrumbs scattered in a meandering trail online, but found only gossip as usual, the kind that cranked his stomach like a stalling engine. He gave up and put the car into drive, heading for Provisions and the next stop on this tour of his own bullshit past.

Orson was walloped by an odd nostalgia the second he entered the store. He hadn't stepped foot inside the place since his indentured servitude and had only thought of it with scorn. But he had started to warm on the way over, knowing that he'd be speaking with Lester and wanting to get in the right frame of mind. You never wanted to feel sorrow going into a scene where you'd have to be laughing, or smiling into one where you were required to cry.

So he turned to some of his fonder memories, and there were some. Many, once he started digging.

Going toe-to-toe with Ivan over their IPMs — items scanned per minute — and winning $132 in the pool.

Trying to detain the woman who was clearly stealing an entire turkey in her otherwise empty stroller, and chasing after her three children. She'd dumped it out onto the sidewalk, then ran with her children over to a battered-to-shit Toyota Previa and peeled away. Orson and Amanda had laughed for twenty minutes straight. Amanda's first day on the job.

Learning to bag items better than anyone else had been something that he found both more fun and more rewarding than he'd ever imagined. He had even filled in for a few of the bagboy shifts, just because, playing Tetris with produce and meat.

He walked right in and asked for Lester.

Orson's old manager sauntered out with a chip on his shoulder a few minutes later, looking him and down and surely assuming the worst.

"Hey, Lester."

"Orson." He nodded. Looked for a second like he might be pleasant, but then said, "What brings you down here with all the little people?"

Orson smiled, he deserved that. "I just wanted to come by and say that I was sorry."

"Oh?" Lester said, looking surprised. "For what?"

For being a dick and thinking I was better than everyone who worked here.

For thumbing my nose at all of our customers, mostly because I couldn't be one of them.

For not giving my best when I worked here, even though it would have been easier than giving my worst.

"For everything."

Lester regarded him, then offered Orson his hand. They shook and the Lester's smile seemed genuine. "Thank you for saying that. I always thought you were better than you were."

"Thanks ... I think." Orson laughed, to let Lester know that even if that was a knock, it was okay. He bought a tub of guakalemole for the hell of it, then climbed into his car and headed to his final destination.

He wanted a drink. Or a handful of drugs. Most any kind would do. He could use some uppers to elevate his mood because those amends were only the batting of an eyelash and meant nothing in the face of what he still had to do.

Or maybe downers would be better, since he felt jittery as fuck, about to beg for what was right.

Or maybe he needed some spirits to raise his spirits, if he couldn't have the drugs to drown his doubts. At least drinking was legal.

But no. Orson had to go in there clutching a cold turkey by its gobbly little neck. He couldn't let them so much as *think* he might be wanting to want the things that he shouldn't ever be wanting again.

He killed the engine and double-checked the address, even though it was unnecessary. It said *Social Services* right there on the building. Orson got out of the car, swallowing hard and already sweating. He wondered if he was being reckless. If maybe he should have brought his lawyer.

The Shellys' lawyer.

Dammit. That's how deep he was in.

Orson checked in and made small talk with the receptionist. She seemed all too pleased to meet him, and even though it turned his stomach, he was willing to play along if his participation in the exchange promised to even remotely improve his chances of seeing his son sooner rather than later.

He took a seat and waited an eon.

His heart pounded when he was finally called, and he made his way down a long corridor to a small office at the end. He opened the door and saw the woman who had taken Connor away, Anna. She gestured for him to sit.

Orson didn't waste a second. "When can I see my son?" he asked, as soon as the seat was kissing his ass.

"It isn't that simple, Mr. Beck."

Then Anna Pierce proceeded to tell him all the reasons that Connor was not yet ready to go home with his father.

"I'll do anything," Orson begged. "Just tell me what I have to do and I'll do it."

"I told you, it isn't that simple, and I'm not the one who can make this decision. There is a lot of paperwork involved."

Yes, the paperwork, the very important paperwork.

"The important thing is that right now, Connor is safe."

"Says who?" Orson felt like spitting. "Just because he's with her parents, doesn't mean that he's in a good place. They raised Alexis and she ended up trying to kill someone."

Anna blanched, then she stared until Orson said he was sorry.

"I didn't mean that. It's just—"

"I understand, Mr. Beck," she said through tight lips that begged to disagree.

Then she excused him.

He wandered back to his Lexus, defeated.

What he was doing wasn't enough. Orson needed to reevaluate every decision that had led him here to this moment. An iceberg stabbed the horizon of his life, and he had to find a way to turn his ship around.

So he dialed the phone.

Ellis answered on the first ring.

"What do you want to know?"

Chapter Fifty-Four

This was a different kind of sick to his stomach.

Orson poured himself a drink, to soothe his nerves, not get him drunk. He wanted to stay miles away from shit-faced for a while. But this was big, and he felt a new breed of butterflies in his belly. Just as colorful, but with bigger and more delicate wings. He was afraid he might tear them.

This all felt so fragile. He was a puppet onstage with nothing to complain about.

Life was amazing, except for all of the stuff that mattered.

Sitting in the limo with only Hadley and his thoughts for company, headed for the first screening of *Bottleneck*. The buzz was off the charts, at least outside of the limo.

"Are you going to say anything?" she asked.

He looked at Hadley, but didn't want to fight. "What do you want me to say?"

"I don't know. Maybe that this is a dream come true. Put a fucking smile on that second-rate face of yours. So I don't look like an asshole by association."

"You'll do fine by yourself." So, he supposed they were fighting. "And don't worry about me. I know how to act."

"Fuck you, Orson."

"Never again."

"You wish you could."

"Not in the least. I don't pay for my pussy. Or share it with four other men in a month."

"Maybe you should have done a better job pleasing me."

"I pleased you plenty."

He did, and she knew it. Just like she probably knew that he did want to fuck her right now. She was the best he'd ever had, and they were good enough together.

The limo pulled up to the theater. Otherwise they would have ended up doing what much of the crowd probably assumed they did anyway, one final hate fuck for the road.

He opened the door and stepped onto the carpet.

Let its gravity sink into him.

Orson closed his eyes to inhale it, then exhaled and held out his hand to Hadley.

Beaming, she took it, and together they walked down that carpet as though it were an aisle on their way to betrothal.

Cameras flashing, crowds waving their hands and arms, some holding signs — *We LOVE you, Orson!*, *Hadley + Orson = The Perfect Ship*, and, absurdly, *Beck will be better than Welles!* — and others clutching their cameras and phones.

Yelling and screaming, too many voices at once, but all of it sounding like praise and compliments, applause and roaring pats on the back, lionizing him in ways he didn't deserve and that felt so wonderful and terrible at once, like acid rain in the desert.

He was walking with Hadley, instead of Jess, and he'd rather be walking alone.

But the Shellys wouldn't allow that, and Orson couldn't blame them. They'd invested a lot with him, and he understood that in a way that he couldn't before, while riding that shuttle up to the Glass House, oblivious to the ways his life would change, both subtle and sledgehammer-loud. He had a job to do, and part of the job meant taking Hadley by the arm, and at least for the length of the red carpet, black as it scratched at his insides to pretend that he loved her.

The press had been unfair, giving him all of the credit and none of the doubt. Dumping buckets of disparagement on important people in his life. Ruining their lives for clicks. Jess was a victim and they painted her like a harpy, same as they painted Orson as a victim of Alexis and the state. When it came to Connor, he had all the sympathy. It's what he'd always wanted, until he had it undeserved, and so it sat like a splinter of glass still inside him.

He wanted all of this Ellis stuff over with, sooner rather than later. He'd agreed to say nothing, to be a good boy. That worked out for both of them. Because while Orson played nice he could be stashing money and paying down his house, getting a few steps ahead so that he didn't trip too hard when the rug was inevitably yanked from under his feet. In the meantime, Orson would be Ellis' eyes and ears, on the ground and behind enemy lines.

It made him a traitor, but Ellis kept telling him that it would make him a hero, and even if that was a lie, it felt better to believe. So at least for tonight that was his mantra. He was doing good work that needed to be done, and taking the benefits of what he had earned along with it.

Orson! Orson!

"Orson," a microphone floated in front of his face, "Do you see yourself as more of a Tom Hanks or a Tom Hardy."

Tom Hanks, he thought.

Hardy, he heard the Shellys in his head.

Another mic. "Are you excited for tonight?"

Ridiculous question. Even with everything else on his mind, of course he was *excited.*

"Yes, but also nervous," Orson admitted.

"How do you feel about the movie?"

Like I was cast for a movie that wasn't yet written, after passing an audition I didn't know I was on.

"It's really fantastic. I just feel so grateful that I've had the opportunity to make this film." He looked at Hadley, smiling even wider than he'd promised. "And I'm lucky to have a costar like Hadley. People will be talking after they see this film. If they're smart, they'll be talking about her and not me."

Hadley beamed beside him. A third mic sailed her way.

"What was it like working with Adrian Frank? We've heard that this movie's sex scenes are smoking? Is that true, and if so, how do you keep the intrigue in a world where so much porn is available with a swipe?

"Oh …" Hadley touched her chest. "Adrian would have been a dream come true to have as a director at any stage in my career, but to have him so early … I'm truly blessed." Then she giggled self-consciously and looked over at Orson. "And *yes,* the sex scenes in this movie are as hot as you've heard, but they're not over the top. What you're seeing on the screen is natural. Organic. Because Orson and I were in a relationship, we were able to pour ourselves into the performances in a way that wouldn't have been possible any other way."

Orson agreed, then they ascended the stairs and made their way into the theater.

There were more people inside waiting to kiss his ass, to glad-hand him, to treat Orson like the Prince of Hollywood that he sure as hell hadn't been, and probably never would be.

He couldn't help but feel that he had done nothing to make that happen. That he had been chosen for some criteria that he still didn't understand, and moved along like a piece on the Shellys' board.

But you did earn all of this, they kept on reminding him.

And yet where was the proof?

Maybe he was about to see it on-screen, in a room full of his peers, and people who offered their narrative to the public. Perhaps the applause would tell him all that he needed to know, and Orson would be sure in his heart of what he could not reconcile in his head.

He was itching under his tux, uncomfortable in his skin despite the sea of friendly faces.

Orson was surrounded by well wishes and affection, but he was also alone, missing a lot as Hadley clasped his hand, squeezing it tight and making him long for Connor's small digits in his, wondering if there was a version of this world with all the glitter and lights where Jess was dressed in red beside him, instead of Hadley in her usual white.

Ellis was the one person in the world right now who could offer the most solace, and the one who couldn't be anywhere near the event.

But that didn't mean he couldn't send him a text, let Ellis know that everything had gone as planned, and that the show was about to start.

Ellis texted back, asking Orson to hit him after the movie was over. He sent a thumbs up, then dropped the phone in his pocket.

"Who were you texting?" Hadley asked.

Orson looked at her, shaking his head. "Are you kidding me?"

An usher led them down to their row, right up front with the Shellys, already seated and waiting. They stood, traded hugs and greetings, then waited for Orson and Hadley to sit before taking their seats just a second behind them.

"Congratulations again," Dominic said, patting Orson on his knee. "This all turned out as well as I had hoped."

"You mean the movie?" Orson asked. He could feel Hadley rolling her eyes beside him.

"He means all of it," Melinda said. "Enjoy tonight. It's another one you'll want to keep up here for the rest of your life." She tapped at her temple.

Dominic smiled and the lights dimmed.

Adrian Frank took the stage.

Orson tried to slow his breath. The Shellys were right. This did deserve some congratulations, and this would be a night to remember for the rest of his life. If there was a time to relax and start enjoying the ride, that time was right this second, as *Bottleneck* was being introduced.

The movie started with that perfect opening shot, and Orson was hooked from the very first second, awed that what he had read on the page so many times was now vibrant with life right before him. The overturned motor-cycle, that bright white moon, blinding in the background, and the vintage Chrysler cutting through the fog.

His heart beat in a whisper, afraid to disturb this perfect moment.

Because *this* was what it was all about.

He had helped to create this beautiful thing that everyone was staring at now.

And it would awe them, as it had awed him.

Orson inhaled the room's energy, sinking into that first gorgeous act, all the way up until Hadley's character first stuck that needle into her arm. The audience was loving it. So were the Shellys, soaking up the film, which they had surely seen before, but also the temperature of the room. Hadley owned that scene, until Orson walked on to gently take it away.

Someone was crying softly behind him. A sniffle echoed, then another.

And they hadn't seen anything yet. In the next—

The phone buzzed in his pocket.

Dammit.

The Shellys had to have heard that. Hadley, too, but Orson didn't care.

Then it buzzed again, and again and again and again.

He kept hoping it would stop, praying almost, but after a sixth buzz he pulled it out of his pocket and dared to look at the screen.

911

SOS

Need you, man.

Red alert.

Jess is in the hospital.

Doesn't look good.

Fuck. Fuck. Fuck.

The phone was already back in his pocket, but now both Dominic and Melinda were eyeing him. Hadley had crossed her arms, acting like he was standing in front of her sun.

Now he was fidgety. The movie still had more than an hour and a half to go, and Orson was worried that those ninety minutes might feel like a day.

He'd been worried about Jess for months, trying to track her down, willing to do anything to straighten out what had gone so horribly wayward. And now she was in trouble. She needed his help and Ellis was asking for them both.

Orson looked up on the screen and saw the man he was playing, then doubted the man that he was.

He had to do the right thing, even if it ripped out his guts from the inside.

But how could he? Dominic and Melinda were both giving him the look: *shut up, behave, and keep your eyes on the screen.*

Orson was right when he said that he didn't have any choice, but wrong about exactly what that meant.

Because he didn't have a choice. If he did the wrong thing now, then he'd regret it forever.

He leaned over to Dominic and whispered, "I've gotta go."

"Where?"

Orson couldn't afford to answer. If he paused, even for a moment, he might not have the fortitude here that he was full of on-screen.

So he stood from his seat and scurried down the aisle, back down the empty red carpet, and into a taxi.

Without looking back.

Chapter Fifty-Five

Orson thanked his driver and got out of the FASTr, looking up at the hospital entrance with a feeling of impending doom. Ellis met him in the lobby.

"Thanks for coming," he said, pulling Orson into a hug.

They collapsed against each other. This was the closest he'd been to Ellis in a while. Maybe ever.

"No. I mean it. Thank you. I know what a big deal this is, that you left the movie. And honestly, I didn't think you would. This could have waited a couple of hours, but then you would have been partying, and I don't know, I hate to admit it, but maybe I was testing you. Either way, I guess I'm glad you passed."

"Me too," Orson said. "So what happened? I didn't want to ask any questions over text. I just wanted to get here."

"I figured. *On my way,* doesn't invite much discussion."

Orson felt one nudge from tears. "I just couldn't deal."

"I know, man," Ellis said. "I know."

Then he put an arm around Orson's shoulder and led him over to the elevator.

"So what don't I know?" Orson asked, alone with Ellis.

"A friend called me after finding Jess at the edge of death."

Orson expected more, but Ellis stopped talking. "And …?"

"That's really all there is to it."

"There's more than that," Orson said. "Who was your friend?"

Ellis looked uncomfortable. "I don't want to say."

"Tell me, Ellis."

"I can't, man. People trust me for a reason."

"Fine. What does 'at the edge of death' even mean? Did she OD? Try to commit suicide?"

The elevator dinged and the doors opened.

"No, I don't think it was suicide, but this person did find her in a bad way. She was choking on her own vomit. Sounds like they got there just in time."

"Who was she with?"

Ellis shook his head. "It's not going to happen, man. I'm sorry."

Orson sighed. "Okay, then take me to her."

Ellis led him down the hall and two right turns, then they walked into her room and Orson felt a sudden *THUNK! THUNK! THUNK!* inside himself that was very much like the final nail getting pounded into the top of a coffin.

"Can she hear us?" Orson asked, feeling like an idiot.

"No. Not right now. Unless she's faking. And honestly, I don't think she's in the mood."

Orson laughed like he was supposed to, but it was raw enough to hurt his throat.

He looked at Jess in the hospital bed with her closed

eyes and her wan complexion, thin hair and eyes that were obviously hollow even when closed. Sunken cheeks and well-used lips. A chin that had sharpened to cut him like so many other things in his swiftly moving life.

Something shattered inside him.

There would be no one to blame but Orson if she died. He would hold himself responsible, even if the world refused to. His world would be gone. And who could he cry to?

Woe is me, with my millions. I killed the woman I love, and now I miss her.

The worst part of all? He had done it for the money.

If each win equaled a loss to his *self,* then that math was a weapon against him. If success only came at the cost of his soul, then Orson could no longer pay. The tax on his family and friends was too high, the levy against his life no longer worthy of dreams that he had suckled too long.

He started to sob. For a while, Ellis let him, until his friend could no longer take it and pulled him into a hug, even deeper than before as Orson soaked his shirt.

"It's going to be okay," Ellis said. "We can fix this."

Orson pulled away, shaking his head and wiping his eyes. "What if she doesn't wake up?"

"She will. She already has. She just has some healing to do. But she has friends. We're going to help her, you got it?"

Orson nodded.

"This all leads back to the Shellys, and their greed. You're in a unique position to help. You can stop what happened to Jess -- and a lot of other innocent people -- from happening to anyone else."

"What do you want me to do?" He was too vulnerable to be asking that question.

And sure enough, Ellis asked Orson for the one thing

he couldn't give. "An exclusive with Hollywood Hunted. You, on the record, about the Shellys. Everything you know, right there on the page."

Orson knew it was suicide, but he said *yes* anyway.

Chapter Fifty-Six

"Are we recording already?" Orson asked.

Ellis looked at him, his eyes kind and his smile patient. They were sitting in his apartment, hunched over the same table where Ellis did most of his work for Hollywood Hunted, about to change Orson's life. It was still a debate whether that was for the better or not.

"Yes, we're recording, but like I said, I want you to relax. You don't have to worry about every little thing you say. I don't want you to be on guard. Don't think of this as an interrogation, it's a conversation."

"And I can read everything before you publish it, right? I mean, my part."

"Man, I promised you could read all of it, the whole thing, and I meant it. But yeah, this conversation won't be posted as is or anything. It's just me and you talking. Be as honest as you can, and remember that I'm your friend. You ready?"

"Yes." Orson said it like he meant it.

"Can you tell me what it's like, working for the Shellys?"

Orson had to think about that one because Ellis hadn't told him what questions would be coming, even though he had asked plenty. Ellis didn't want him sounding rehearsed.

"It's fast. You never really know what's happening until it's already happening." He gave Ellis a nervous little chuckle. It would be a while before he was comfortable.

"What do you mean?"

Orson shrugged. "Things were always moving and changing and just going-going-going, right from the start."

"You mean once you were hired by the Shellys?"

"Even before that. Back when I first got the invitation. It seemed like life was barreling forward."

"What about the invitation? What was that process like?"

"That isn't my place to say." Orson shook his head. "It's a private process, but I will say I feel fortunate to have been a part of it."

"Okay, so take me through what happened next. You got the invitation and started working for the Shellys? Did you meet them that night, at the event?"

"No. I went to their house the next morning."

"Alone? Did they send you a second invitation?"

"No. I had a ride."

"A ride?" Ellis sounded surprised. Orson wondered how much he knew, didn't remember what he'd told his friend back in the days when he'd first landed the gig and couldn't stop bragging. "Who drove you to meet them?"

"Hadley Witt."

"And she'd been there before?"

"Yes, definitely."

"So you went to their house and they hired you? Was there an interview?"

"No. Not exactly."

"But they offered you a job?"

"I guess?"

"What do you mean, *you guess*?"

"Well, I sort of suppose I already worked for them."

Ellis looked genuinely confused, but Orson was familiar with both acting and his friend. "What do you mean?"

"They cleared the way and made it easy for me to start immediately. I had some personal debt and a few obligations, but the Shellys made that all go away so that we could get to business."

"The business of making you a star?"

"I suppose," Orson said, shifting in his seat.

"How were you treated by the Shellys, from that first day until now?"

Again, Orson wasn't sure what Ellis was after because the Shellys had been his guardian angels. They gave him a place at the Catalyst before he could afford one of his own. They paved the way for his success and paid for every stone on his path out of their purses and pockets. They even set him up with a generous allowance to draw off the promise of his glowing future and gave him a warm body who promised to love him in all the ways she knew how.

"They treated me well."

"Well? Can you be more specific?"

"They gave me a lot of chances that I wouldn't have otherwise had. Like I said, they took care of some debt and helped set me up, but there were a lot of other things they just sort of took care of."

"So that you didn't have to?" Ellis smiled, reminding Orson that they were friends.

"Right."

Silence. Maybe Orson said something wrong.

"Were they ever unkind to you in any way?"

Orson thought. Shook his head. "No."

He wondered when he was going to get to the good

stuff and stop throwing softballs. Ellis had said that he wanted to bury the Shellys, not put them up on a pedestal.

"So, they let you make all of your own decisions?"

The question caught him off guard. After a second Orson said, "I can make my own decisions, but there are a few rules to follow, of course. Same as any other job."

"Right. That makes sense. We'll get to those. I just want to follow this thread for a moment, if you don't mind."

Orson nodded. *Go ahead.*

"Okay, so the Shellys treated you well, but how would you say they treated others? People not being groomed to perform in their stable?"

How could he not think of Jess, especially the way Ellis was looking at him?

But there were also plenty of people that the Shellys weren't conditioning for stardom or infamy who they still took care of like family. Orson had hated Armando, but Shellter still took care of everyone at their branch of Natural Nurturing, same as they took care of everyone at Pretty Pretty Pussycat. They spent millions of dollars a year on making other people's dreams come true. They were generous tippers and indulgent with their praise with just about everyone he had seen.

And still there was Jess.

This was harder than he'd thought.

"The Shellys believe in abundance, and I saw them prove that over and over. But they are also businesspeople, and they can be shrewd. So yes, I also saw them ... step on some heads to get where they wanted to go."

"Stepped on some heads? Can you be more specific?"

Orson looked at Ellis. *No.*

"I'm not sure that I can be."

"Go ahead and give it a try. We're just having a conversation."

Orson couldn't flinch, he had to talk. "There were times when maybe the Shellys pulled some strings to get what they wanted, and those strings might have hurt some of the people in my life."

"Ouch. I'm sorry to hear that. But you do believe that the Shellys always had *your* best interests at heart, right?"

"I do." He thought he did.

"I mean, as long as you were working out. Did you ever think about what would happen if a couple of your movies bombed, maybe the first two right in a row? Do you think the Shellys would have your best interests at heart then?"

His heart was pounding and his skin felt cold. Was this almost over, or had it just started? He looked at the wall and wished for a clock. Taking his phone out to look would be too obvious. *Fuck.*

"It depends what you mean by best interests. I don't think they would do anything to hurt me, but if their investment hadn't paid off, it would be fair for them to stop supporting me like they have."

"Do you think they would hurt you if maybe you were in the way of something they wanted? What if you were up for a role against someone they plucked from next year's Onyx List? What then?"

Orson looked away. "I don't know."

"Did the Shellys ever engage in blackmail?"

Blackmail? That one surprised him too. No, he had never seen the Shellys blackmailing anyone, but if Orson heard that accusation he wouldn't have a hard time believing it. He could even imagine Dominic telling him that it was no big deal, boisterous in his delivery, definite in his conviction and booming in his command, making Orson feel like everything was alright, with Melinda like a minstrel singing the ballad behind it, or probably more likely, writing it herself.

Could he imagine the Shellys engaging in blackmail? *Yes.*

Had he ever seen such a thing with his own two eyes? *No.*

"Uh-uh," Orson shook his head. "No."

"No for sure, or not that you know of?"

"What's the difference?"

Ellis shrugged. "You tell me."

"Not that I know of."

"Are the Shellys ethical?"

Now Orson knew why he hadn't been given a heads-up on these questions. They were all full of traps. How could he answer a question like that? It wasn't even a matter of wanting to protect them. The world wasn't that black and white. They were building a billion dollar business; Melinda had reminded him of that several times. Nobody did that without having to make some harsh decisions. Orson knew a lot of ethical people who had done unethical things. He liked to see himself as one of the good guys, and if the Shellys were bad, then maybe he was too.

"I think they're as ethical as most people in their situation would be."

"Can you elaborate on that?"

Ellis was looking at Orson, and Orson was eyeing the phone on the table between them, recording every word.

"It's like what they say about politicians. You know, about the only honest one is the one who will stay bought? You get to where you get by maybe doing a few things you don't really want to do, then those things become the way of doing business, and the only way you can keep your doors open. I'm sure it applies to a lot of situations, but for sure with something like what the Shellys are trying to do, building all of that something from nothing. They've probably cut corners and hurt some people along the way, but I think they believe that the ends justify the means and that they always *mean* well."

Orson exhaled. He had barely drawn a breath through his answer.

"If the ends justify the means, what do you think the Shellys see as their ultimate end?"

That was the best question so far. Orson chewed his lip and settled into his chair.

"I don't know, but it's big. Like Disney or Apple or Coke."

"Those are three very different companies," Ellis said.

"Exactly."

"What is the relationship dynamic between Dominic and Melinda?"

"You mean who wears the pants?"

"Not exactly. Just, what is it like between them?"

Orson wasn't sure what Ellis meant, or exactly what he was looking for with any of this, so he just started talking.

"They're best friends. You can tell how much they love each other just by watching them. It's actually sweet, and I saw it from the second I met them that first Sunday morning at their house. It's one of the things that captured me. I'm only realizing it now as I'm saying it out loud, but watching the two of them together, it's easier to believe that you can have it all. The money, the fame, and the love." Orson swallowed hard because it hurt to realize. "And I think that last part is what I've always wanted most."

"I know, man," Ellis said, taking a moment away from his role. "I'm sorry."

"Dominic makes you feel more at ease, but I think Melinda really makes most of the rules. It's not that

Dominic does whatever she tells him, but he respects her opinion, and I've never seen him defer to anyone else. I'm not sure that Melinda defers to anyone."

There was a lull, and Ellis was ready to move on, but Orson found himself wanting to add more, surprised now that he was having to think about it, how fascinating the Shellys really were. "And they're always eye fucking each other. Like I said, they love each other. But they also like to …"

Never mind. He shouldn't have said that.

"Like to …?"

"Sorry," Orson shook his head as though he had baffled himself. "I lost my train of thought." He laughed. "Not sure where I was going with that one."

Ellis smiled. *Of course.*

"Were you ever coerced or pressured to do anything that you didn't want to do?"

Waxing my balls, eating quinoa, taking regular psych evaluations, the endless exercise.

"I mean, I had responsibilities. Again, like any other job. It's not just about how well I can carry a scene, my physical and emotional health are important, so I need to give them a level of attention I might not give them if I was all on my own. But I wouldn't say that that's the same as coercion."

Hadley. The house. Armando.

"So, you never felt like you were going along with something against your better judgment?"

Well, that was a different question. And one that was a lot less comfortable for Orson to answer.

"Hindsight is twenty-twenty. Everyone makes mistakes in this business, on both sides of the camera. Part of my job is to get better at recognizing what I'm good at and what's going to cost me in the long run, then navigating through my best possible choices."

Ellis nodded, acknowledging the bullshit. "How far will the Shellys go to achieve their goals, whatever they might be?"

This one he considered deeply because in his heart Orson wasn't even sure that he had a problem with his answer. Wasn't the American dream built on folks who would stop at nothing to plunge their shovel deep enough to hear the striking of metal on treasure?

"I think they'll go pretty far. They're big thinkers. They see a symphony where I can see only the notes. So I try not to question what I don't understand. But when you can hear all the music, I imagine you'll do what's necessary to fill your orchestra."

"Even if that hurts other people?"

"Yes," Orson said, his answer less surprising than his total lack of hesitation.

"And you really don't have any thoughts on what they might be planning? What the Shellys' ultimate goal might be?"

"I don't," Orson admitted, suddenly wondering harder.

"What would you do, if you were the Shellys? What would you be trying to build?"

"A new studio system."

"Obviously," Ellis said. "But there's more to it than that. What *kind* of studio system?"

"I don't know ... but they want to control all the pieces."

"What do you mean?" Ellis leaned forward. A smile raked his face.

"They're putting a lot of stuff together. The stars, the projects, and I don't know, I guess the news that makes it all happen? I don't know exactly. It's something I feel more than I can actually say. Can we go to the next question?"

"Of course." Ellis settled back in his chair, the smile still there but lighter. "What has surprised you the most about working with them?"

"I like them," Orson admitted, not expecting that answer at all. "They're real people, and they're very direct, especially Melinda."

"So you trust them with your career?"

"Yes. Of course."

"But do you trust them? As people?"

Orson needed time for that one.

Dominic gave Jess coke when he knew she was an addict. Only a monster would do something like that.

Except he did it for you.

No, asshole. He did it for himself. And Melinda.

"I guess I'm not sure."

"What do you mean by *real people?*"

"You know how sometimes you meet people and they're obviously full of shit? Just trying to please everything, working too hard to be all things to all people?"

Ellis nodded.

"Well, that's like leading someone on. Because even if they like that person, which a lot of people won't because that kind of personality reeks, they're going to think that person is someone they're not. And that's bound to fall apart. The Shellys are who they are. I've seen a few things, sure, but I never feel like they're putting on pretenses. And honestly, I respect that."

"Fair enough. Do you feel that working with them has helped or hurt your career?"

That was the easiest question anyone had ever asked him. "They've helped, of course."

"Is it fair to say that you could have never done this without the Shellys?"

It hurt to admit it, but over 6,000 hours at Provisions made it impossible to believe anything else. "Yes, that's fair to say."

"So is it also fair to say that you feel indebted to them?"

"Absolutely. Of course. Without any question."

Ellis filled the next empty moment by crossing his legs. He let the silence settle. Then he ruined it. "What about your personal life?"

Orson swallowed. "Can I get a glass of water?"

"Of course." Ellis disappeared, then reappeared a minute later with two glasses of water. He set Orson's on the table, then started sipping his as he sat. "So, your personal life?"

Orson took a sip of cool liquid and gathered his thoughts. "That's a more difficult question. I've had a lot of hard things happen in the last few months. It's not like that's all the Shellys' fault."

"But some of it is?"

"I don't know that any of it is. Sometimes things just happen."

"Things like ..." Ellis prompted.

"I lost custody of my son."

"Would you like to talk more about that?"

"No." Orson reached for his water.

"Will you?"

"What are you asking?"

"How did you get custody in the first place?"

"There was an overdose in the house, Alexis' boyfriend. She wasn't really fit to take care of him after that."

"Were you happy with this arrangement?"

"I wasn't happy with how it happened, but yes, I was

happy that I could finally spend so much time with my son."

"And how did you lose custody?"

Orson took a breath. "There was a party at my new house, and things got out of control. Child Protective Services dropped by the next morning and didn't like what they saw."

"And who threw this party?"

"Well, it was my house."

"Right, but was the party your idea? Who paid for it? Who called the caterers, or wrote the guest list?"

Orson started to stammer.

"Who paid for the drugs? There had to be drugs, right?"

Still stammering, Ellis saved him. "You know what, let's change the subject."

Thank God.

"Even if they had your best interests at heart, it still meant quite a few obligations and some rules, right? Do you care to elaborate on those rules?"

"Sure, I mean, they were all perfectly reasonable. Right of first refusal and NDA stuff, showing up for work, weekly grooming sessions, diet and exercise like we talked about."

"You're right. That all sounds reasonable. What about more personal stuff?"

"Like?"

"Like, what about your sexual partners? Don't they need to be approved if 'photographed in your company?' And aren't all unauthorized sex tapes the sole property of Shellter Productions?"

Orson had forgotten about that one because it didn't matter. It's not like he had a sex tape out there.

"Yes, but I'm sure that's just to protect us. They want to

own the tapes to preserve our images. They weren't trying to profit off of the sex tapes themselves."

"Were there ever any consequences for breaking any of these rules or not doing something you were asked to do?"

Orson had to think, but no, there hadn't been. "The Shellys were always understanding. There were times when I skipped out on the exercise or the grooming or my diet, or did something else that they didn't exactly love, but they were always chill about it, and we always figured a way out together."

"What about unauthorized interviews?" Then a wry smile. "Surely you don't have permission for this one. Do you think there will be any consequences from the Shellys for this?"

His blood ran cold. It wasn't like he didn't already know that he was skirting the line, at best.

"No. I'm sure they won't be happy."

"Do you think there will be consequences?"

"I don't know."

Orson wished that he did.

Ellis took another sip. "Since we're talking, can you give me an example of something the Shellys wouldn't necessarily want to share with the public?"

Orson smiled, thin as it was. "I don't think I can, at least not without violating my NDA. But I imagine any business would have things they wouldn't want the public to know, that might make sense in context, even if it might look terrible from the outside looking in."

"Did you ever see anything like that? A situation where the public saw one thing, but it looked totally different from the inside?"

Jess. Alexis. Hadley.

Everything, in its way.

"Yes."

"Would you care to elaborate?"

"No."

Ellis nodded. Must be thirsty -- he went for his water again, then finished and said, "Did the Shellys ever engage in any illegal activities?"

Orson looked at him across the table. *What the fuck, man?*

He couldn't answer that question. He'd already skirted around the drug question; this was bullshit.

And actually, other than the drugs, *had* he seen them engage in any illegal activities? Ellis had suggested that maybe they were involved in blackmail of some sort, in his saying-shit-without-saying-it way, but Orson hadn't seen anything to corroborate that. Had he seen anything illegal beyond that? Or something that he didn't realize was even against the law?

"You know what? I take that back. An unfair question. NDAs and all that. What drew you to work with the Shellys initially?"

"Honestly, they chose me, and I was just so grateful to be noticed finally, you know?" Orson sighed, remembering the ache of wanting, having nothing and seeing so much of everything each and every goddamned day. "So what drew me to want to work with them was that they wanted to work with me."

"What had you heard about them before that?"

Orson shrugged. "The rumors. Same as anyone. Or at least anyone who reads this blog."

"Did you believe those rumors?"

"Yes and no.

"And were the Shellys like you expected," Ellis asked, "when you finally met them?"

"Yes and no. You know how it is."

"But I don't, 'know how it is.' So can you tell me?"

"They're larger than life, like I expected, but they're also more …"

"Down to earth?"

"Yeah, I guess. Like I said, they're real people."

"How did your original vision of the opportunity compare to the eventual reality?"

This felt more like a therapy session than an interview.

"It's the same … but different."

"Yes and no, same but different — come on man, you can do better than this. You were promised nirvana. Tell us what you got. Did your dreams come true?"

"Yes."

"And were there also nightmares that you didn't expect?"

"Aren't there always? Doesn't every dream have its cost?"

"I don't know, does it?" Ellis shook his head. "I guess it depends on the dream."

"Don't judge me."

"I'm not judging you, man."

"Except that you are." Orson wanted to stand, maybe even storm out. Instead he rooted his feet. "You promised a conversation. This is feeling like an interrogation."

"I think I'm being gentle." Ellis let the moment settle, then after a deep exhale, he added, "I think you know it. I'm sorry this is hard, but you'll be glad after you did it. For Jess and for you and for Alexis, and for Connor most of all."

"Yes, my dreams came true. And yes, there were some nightmares. But no, I would not like to elaborate on anything in particular."

But Ellis pressed. "Is there anything you regret doing during your time working with the Shellys?"

Why did he have to keep saying their name like that? Each time like a cough.

"I regret hurting a few of the people closest to me. I think that can happen when everything is moving so fast. That doesn't make it okay, but hopefully I can use what I've learned to do better next time. Every time I read the script, I get better at knowing my lines."

Orson laughed and it broke the tension.

Ellis smiled. "I understand. Every time I dig into a story I know it that much better. These people you hurt, are they people you're still talking to now?"

"No, not really." Orson shook his head, which weighed about twice as much as it should on his shoulders. "That's part of the problem. I mean, *I'm* part of the problem. But I'm getting better. Trying to fix things."

"I think that's why we're here." Ellis smiled.

That was a relaxant to Orson. He felt it in his shoulders. With a sigh he said, "Yeah well, what else do you wanna know?"

"If you could get into your DeLorean and take it eighty-eight miles an hour back to just before all of this started, what would you do differently?"

"Depends what you mean by 'all of this'."

"Let's say, the day you received your invitation for the Onyx List."

Orson was thinking, but Ellis cut in.

"Did you ever wonder about the other people who got invited to the party?"

He had, of course, but Orson wasn't sure what Ellis was getting at. "Sure. What do you mean?"

"The idea is for Hollywood's elite to pluck talent from obscurity, right?"

"Yes."

"How many of the Hollywood elite are outside of Shellys' stable?"

Orson had never thought about it. "I have no idea."

"Okay, back to our regularly scheduled programming. If you could go back in time to before you got the invitation, what would you do differently?"

That was a bulls-eye of a question, and Orson was grateful for the extra moments to consider his answer, because in truth, there was a lot he would have done differently. But if there was one thing more than all else, it was the anything and everything having to do with how he'd shit the bed with Jess.

He had so many chances to get things right and yet he managed to get them so perfectly wrong.

I agreed to dinner. I didn't know I was getting dessert.

She couldn't have been throwing it out any harder. Everything could have been different in those moments before he'd boarded the shuttle. That would have changed things with Hadley, his circuit cut before the connection was made.

Did that mean that the Shellys would have chosen someone else?

It didn't matter. Orson had plenty of opportunities to be better to Jess after that, but he'd failed and failed, every one of those chances, until he had failed her right out of his life.

"I would have been better to my friends."

Ellis said nothing while Orson guzzled his water, then he asked him if his priorities had shifted.

Orson thought back to his days taking inventory and how much he had wanted for just three things: a brilliant career, more time with Connor, and perhaps someday, if and once he really truly deserved it, a relationship with Jess.

But was that the order he had set them in? And was he paying the price for that arrangement now?

Had the first warped the second and soured the third forever?

He had never dreamed about a Lexus or a mansion, or sex with a supermodel. At least, not really. Orson had imagined all of that, but they were the sorts of things pictured with closed eyes, or maybe a handful of his manhood.

"Yes," Orson admitted. "I think maybe they have …"

Ellis waited. No hurry.

"My dad always said that success was getting what you want, but that happiness was wanting what you got. I think I wanted some of the stuff that I got so bad that it made me forget about all the stuff that really made me happy. And sure, it hurts to admit it, but at least I'm seeing it now."

"I think that was Dale Carnegie."

"What?" Orson said.

"The happiness quote. I think that was Carnegie. Your dad was probably just borrowing it. Sorry, you were saying?"

"Just that at least now I can see where my priorities have been in the wrong place. I know better, so I can do better for the people who love me."

A strange expression found Ellis' face. A pregnant beat preceded his question. "Did you fall in love?"

Orson flinched. That wasn't the question he had been expecting. Even the way it sounded, like syllables shot from a gun. And did he mean Jess, or Hadley?

He looked at Ellis to read his eyes, but the irises were emerald and still, and in their silence said nothing.

"Yes, I think I did."

"Are you in love now?"

"Of course."

Orson wondered how long it had been since he blinked.

"Who?" Ellis finally asked what Orson hoped that he wouldn't. "Who are you in love with?"

"It's not a who, it's a what. It's all of it. This thing I'm trying to do, this life I want to build. I just went about it all wrong. I stopped putting the right things in front of me. But I'm done with that. I'm in love with acting, and I'm in love with bringing stories to life. I'm in love with my son. And yes, I'm in love with a woman I didn't do right by. Maybe one day I'll have the chance to make amends."

"I'm sure you will." Ellis nodded, his face serious. "Do you mind if we finish up with just a couple more questions?"

"Of course."

"There were a lot of stories involving you with Jess Lindley and Hadley Witt. Hollywood Hunted was light on the coverage, abstaining from all of it with the exception of a few newsworthy facts. But the stories were everywhere. Can you comment as to the veracity of the narrative as reported?"

When did Ellis turn into Anderson Cooper?

"To be honest, I read a lot of stuff that was bullshit, especially about Jess. She's one of the best people I've ever known, and the press destroyed her with their lies. That's why I'm here talking to you, because Hollywood Hunted never did that."

"What about—"

"And things with Hadley are different in real life. I never read a single article that had a clue what it was talking about."

"Have you ever wondered where those 'news' outlets are getting their sources?"

Orson shrugged. "Not really."

That's too bad." Ellis sighed. "You're not really giving me much to work with in the expose department."

"You wanted me to tell the truth, didn't you?"

"More than anything." He cleared his throat. "One last question?"

"Shoot."

"What's next for Orson Beck?"

I have no fucking idea.

You're an actor. Act.

Or tell the truth.

"I'm not sure. I only know that I'm sick of spending money I haven't earned to buy things I don't want. And that I'm going to make things right, starting with Jess Lindley."

Chapter Fifty-Seven

Jess looked up from her bed, blinking.

She was lost. Trying to remember, where she was, how she got there, and what catastrophes she might have left in her wake. Jess heard voices in the room, and had for a while, but her world was a fog of sights, sounds, and smells, all of them blurry enough to keep her from making much of anything out.

The scents were mostly antiseptic, except for one, which was familiar and wistful, and smelled almost like home.

That one she recognized immediately.

She opened her eyes all the way, and sure enough he was there, looking down at her, his smile glum, edging on tragic, but also full of hope, with every ounce of it so obviously devoted to her.

"Is it really you?"

She knew perfectly well that it was, but Jess wanted to hear his confirmation. She might have even needed it.

"Yes." He took her hands, first one, then the other. It

was a minute or more before he finally added, "I missed you."

"Why are you whispering?"

Orson shrugged. He looked seconds from tears. "Maybe some things are easier to believe when they're whispered."

"What do you want me to believe?"

Jess wondered if she already knew, if that's what she was seeing all over Orson's wounded face. Whatever he wanted to say was apparently stuck in his throat. And she was just waking, so naturally this still felt at least a little like a dream.

"Say it," she prompted.

He whispered. "*I love you.*"

Jess didn't know what to say. Not while she was lying in the hospital, only now remembering the broken road that had brought her here to such an ugly place. A lot like the man who'd just declared his love, and was still holding her hands, Jess was also near tears. But hers were born and bred in a disparate hell.

"How did your premiere go?" It was the safest question she could think to ask.

Orson laughed. The sound was surprising, not just because the merriment didn't match the room's otherwise sterile atmosphere, but because his cackle was so rich, it was surely born somewhere deep and unpleasant.

"Is that good?" Jess said, uncertain and timid, maybe even a little scared by the way he was still laughing.

"The movie or the premiere?"

"What's the difference?"

"*Bottleneck* is great. I was lucky to land a project like that. The film itself is exceptional, and I think it's going to do great. But the premiere was sort of a bust, seeing as how I walked out before the movie was over."

She gasped, had to pull her hands away from his to cover her mouth. "Why would you do that?"

He looked down at Jess, only a few minutes awake in her hospital bed. "I had more important places to be."

She wanted to respond, but that made her voice hitch. She choked, recovered, then managed to say, "You didn't …"

"I did."

"So what's going to happen now?"

"I have no idea." Then he laughed again, as though he were going as batshit as the last couple of months had apparently made her. "Whatever happens, happens. It's all okay. And you know what, Jess? *You're* okay, too. All of this is. Everything is going to get better. This is our rock bottom, okay?"

He reached for her hands again.

She let him take them, but then she shook her head. Sure, she wanted to believe, but life, especially over the last few months, kept kicking her whenever it wanted, and the few things that were going great, well, he couldn't possibly know about those.

Then, looking both stern and sorry, Orson said, "I called your parents."

She snatched back her hands. "What?"

"I got their information from Ellis. It—"

"Why would he give it to you? Why would—"

"Because I made him, Jess. He even offered to call them himself once he realized I was serious and wasn't going to let it go. But your parents deserved to know, and it was my penance to tell them."

"Your penance?" Her mood had been roughly shoved from uncertain to rankled. "So you're making this all about you."

"No," he calmly replied. "I'm making it all about us."

A tear slid down his cheek, the tax for telling her a truth that was so clearly painful to say, and that she obviously didn't wish to hear. "I'm just so sorry, for everything. I wanted to pretend that I didn't know how you felt about me because that meant that I wouldn't have to step up or put myself out there. I let you go because I didn't have the balls to keep you close. But I won't let that happen now. I'll do anything to save you, even if it means sending you away."

She didn't know what to say. Words she'd been hoping to hear forever, but also, he wanted to send her away?

"This place isn't good for you," he finally continued. "At least not right now. Maybe you can come back when you're better, but—"

"I left Skokie for a reason." And even Orson wasn't going to send her back. "You don't get to decide what's best for me, or where I live, or who should be taking care of me. That's not your—"

"Jess," he interrupted, his voice grave. "There's something you should know."

She looked right into his eyes. "What is it?"

"The Shellys. Dominic and Melinda have been using you from the beginning, and—"

She laughed, loud enough to cut him off.

"Why is that funny?"

"Do you think I don't know that they were using me? Do you think I'm that dumb or naive? Of course I know when I'm being manipulated."

"But you can't—"

"Did it ever occur to you that I was using the Shellys too? That I was getting what I wanted? Or needed? Or that maybe I finally had the chance to capture some of the things I had been either dreaming about for so long, or pretending that I wasn't? Maybe I'm the one who made terrible choices with the chances I was given. It's not like they put a gun in my mouth and told me what to do."

Orson stared at Jess, dumbfounded. Clearly that wasn't the reaction he had expected at all.

But it wasn't like she could tell him about *Naughty Hollywood* and how it had taken off last month. Could she?

Jess wanted to be with Orson Beck more than anything else in the world.

But what she wanted didn't matter. Not right now. Even though meeting him was like listening to a song for the first time and knowing it would be her new favorite. Maybe they had the right love at the wrong time. Maybe it wasn't meant to be, and maybe Orson wouldn't be their happily ever after she always hoped and even secretly believed that he would be.

Then again, maybe he would.

But it couldn't happen right now.

"How can you be okay with all of that?" Orson finally asked, after staring at Jess forever, with what it hurt her to realize was pity, or something uncomfortably close. Yet another reason why their time wasn't now.

"Aren't you okay with a lot of things that we both probably wish that you weren't?"

Of course he was. She could see it all over his face.

They weren't much different. So much sadness between them, when a different tilt to their world would have made them so happy.

But then Jess thought of something that made her smile. "Where's my phone? Do you know?"

Orson shrugged. "It's probably dead."

"Can I use yours? I'll be fast."

"O-okay." He didn't love the idea, but he handed it right over anyway.

Her thumbs danced on the glass. She looked up. "You

shouldn't stay logged into your email like that. I'll log you out." She did, then logged into hers, scrolled down to the message she had been dying to get and desperate to see, opened the email with a stab, and closed her eyes with relief.

"What?" Orson asked. "What is it?"

Exactly what I need.

"A way out," she said.

Chapter Fifty-Eight

Orson stepped out onto his balcony, inhaling a view that he didn't deserve.

Ellis needed a moment. He'd join Orson outside in a few minutes, then the two of them could leave together.

He loved what Ellis had written. It wasn't what he expected at all. He'd been nervous. Worried that it was going to destroy something good. But denying his friend was obviously the wrong thing to do. A touching piece of writing, painting Orson as a phoenix, rising again despite all odds on the Hollywood scene. A resurrection from Provisions to production.

Honest and vulnerable, not just revealing the Orson underneath the photogenic smile, but a glimpse into the author and curator of Orson's story. It cut through the hype. Debunked all the shit that had been said about Jess in the press.

Orson had a newfound understanding of how the ups and downs of his climb to the top made him want to stop more often. Hold onto one rung before reaching for that next one. It wasn't just his job to claim responsibility for his destiny and actions, it was his calling.

Ellis hadn't cried as he read his article out loud, but he had gotten misty. He paused when he needed it, but otherwise kept going until he got to the end. Then he pretended like he needed the bathroom. Good for him. Ellis' vulnerability was one of the things that made him such a great guy.

"So, what did you think?" Ellis had asked him, after he came back from the bathroom, looking fresher, less like he'd been crying.

"I loved it," Orson said. "Of course."

"Even the shitty things I said about you?"

"I'd be pissed if you left those out. They were the best parts. Except for the line when you said I was like a well-aged River Phoenix."

Ellis finished the quote. "But one who has a long and exciting career in front of him."

"Thanks for that. How are you? Is it what you wanted?"

"Nah," Ellis shook his head. "Not even close. I mean, I love it for what it is. But that's not what I set out to write. There's something there, and I want to know what it is."

"Let me know when you do."

"Are you kidding? I'll be using you to get answers as often as I can."

"How about I just pay for everything, and you stop endlessly asking me questions instead?"

"Deal," Ellis agreed. "But only for now."

Orson looked over the balcony, squeezing the railing in thought.

He used to look up from the bottom, wishing upon every star that he could be looking down from the top of these hills instead. Now he'd made it to the top, but feeling inside-out, if not entirely empty. Orson preferred the simplicity, the companionship, the open arms of a life now lost, a time and a place that, once forgotten, he could never have back.

But maybe he could recover something like it, earned instead of designed. He'd get there someday. Orson felt certain of that in a way he never had.

Yes, Orson was broken, but no more so than he had been when he'd been working at Provisions, desperate for momentum and dying for anyone to notice him. Back then, he didn't demand enough from himself. Not with Connor and Alexis, or with Ellis and Jess. He'd been sitting around, waiting for life to happen. So how could he be surprised that it made a left instead of the right he'd been so desperately wanting?

If he hadn't been damaged, the Shellys wouldn't have been able to pluck his pieces from their neat little pile and arrange them so fastidiously onto the board of their ambitions.

This wasn't their fault. They didn't *do* this to him — *Orson had allowed it to happen.*

Manipulation wasn't a terrible thing when taken by itself. Wasn't that his job? Same as the writers, directors, editors, composers, and anyone else who worked on a film, Orson was supposed to make people feel what he was feeling every minute he spent on screen. And that wasn't always easy. The gauze between his real self and his on-screen persona grew thinner with every new article about him, whether posted with or without his permission.

Performing on film was hard, but doing it for the public even harder. It took its emotional and physical toll. Inhabiting the mind and mannerisms of an adopted persona had been both the blade he carried and the one that gutted him.

But manipulation, fueled by good intent, was the sort of thing that changed the world.

Something told him that the Shellys were trying to do exactly that.

He could take the risks and reap the rewards, but Orson would no longer allow Dominic and Melinda to manipulate him, not like they had been. Now he would demand to be part of the plan. He deserved to know the game and understand his part in it. He wasn't going to let them take his dream away. He'd worked too hard and sacrificed too much. But that didn't mean that he couldn't move forward with integrity and deliver on the promises he had made to all of the most important people in his life.

Maybe it was his father in his head.

Victim or victor, it's all up to you.

Orson wondered if that was Carnegie, too.

But it was hard to see himself as the victim, when he knew that he had been blinded by his ambition and had allowed the Shellys to destroy Jess, not caring a wit if her life fell apart, so long as it served their almost elegantly nefarious aims.

Orson did care and would do everything he could to right his wrongs and get back on top of his life. All Orson wanted was what he already had. A clear idea of who he was, where he had erred, and how he could inch closer each day to who he wanted to be.

Would he have a career going forward?

Yes, absolutely. Orson was sure of it. He hadn't done much in the last few months, but he had still finished some significant work, and his resume was enough to get him some indie gigs for a while. He had his non-compete with the Shellys, but he would figure that out. Worst-case scenario, maybe he would move to Mexico and make some telenovelas. Orson didn't care.

He still wanted to be the best of the best, but it was time to start worrying more about being his best *self.*

Orson thought he had reasonable insight into what the Shellys ultimately wanted — his mind had been turning on little else since his interview with Ellis had ended — and saw no reason why they couldn't all be friends. Allies. Confederates in this great game of life.

Same for Hadley.

The last several questions from Ellis had hit Orson with a wallop, but the ones might have smacked him the hardest were:

Did you fall in love?

Are you in love now?

He'd done a lot of thinking since — impossible not to — and realized that he'd been denying something obvious. He did love Hadley, although not in a way that he could put a name to. He didn't love her like he loved Alexis, as the mother of their child, or like Jess, whom he loved with all the fire inside him.

He loved that she actually wanted to play with Connor. He loved that she'd wanted to be a realtor. He loved that she gave everything to the role she'd chosen to play, even when it meant doing something she didn't like.

He loved that she was smart and funny and driven, just like he was.

She deserved so much better than he'd given her, and he was going to make that right too. He actually missed her.

Because now it was obvious that Hadley was his friend.

Hopefully that's the way the Shellys would see things with him.

Orson didn't want to blow it, but he wouldn't do anything to maintain his standing with them.

When Dominic called, he even picked it up on the first ring and answered with a confident *Hello.*

"Bold move," Dominic said.

Orson could hear Melinda saying something in the background, but not exactly what. Shockingly, she didn't sound angry. He waited for Dominic to continue.

"I'm sure you're shaking in your shit kickers, but you don't have to be, son. We have big plans, and would love to have a conversation. But none of it has to happen before you're ready. Melinda and I understand that things are in flux right now. Just give us a call after however long it takes you to feel better, assuming you'll be feeling better in no more than a week."

"Uh—"

Dominic hung up before Orson had a chance to apologize. Or protest. Or say any of the things that had been swirling around in his head.

And that was okay. Orson didn't need to live out the drama of a fallen Hollywood idol.

He'd had enough drama to last him a lifetime.

Now he wanted to live out a love story.

And a buddy movie.

And a touching story of fatherhood and redemption and second chances used wisely.

Ellis joined Orson on the balcony, carrying his tablet and smiling wider than he had in a while. Maybe ever.

"Good news?" Orson asked.

"Couldn't be better. Hollywood Hunted has officially blown. Up. The tips are pouring in. I haven't had time to vet a tenth of what I've seen so far, but oh man, have I seen some shit already. Like—"

"Don't tell me, Ellis. You promised. If you don't follow the rules, then this isn't going to work. Only tell me things that *directly* impact me, got it?"

"Got it," Ellis agreed again, then changed the subject. "The site is finally profitable. The *New York Times* linked first. Everyone linked after that, and I still haven't caught up. Makes sense since this is the biggest story to hit La La Land in a while. I don't even have to take ads. I've found a few clever ways to monetize, but it's a done deal; this is now my full-time gig."

"Congratulations!" Orson gave Ellis a hug.

"You too." Ellis pulled away from the hug, adjusting his tablet after nearly dropping it in the middle of Orson's surprise embrace. "Jess texted. Seems like she's doing okay."

"We spoke this morning. She's doing what she has to, and that's good. I have to let her go, at least for now, because right now, the only thing I can control is myself. Same for her. The best next step is deciding that we're not happy where we are, and we've both already done that."

"True that," Ellis said, looking like he wished he had something to toast. "And what about with Connor? How are things there?"

"He's still with Alexis' parents, but there's a hearing next week."

"And Alexis?"

"It's actually getting better. We're talking."

"I'm happy for you." Ellis looked at his watch. "Same time next week?"

Orson nodded. "Same time."

Ellis turned from the view and nodded toward the house. "You gonna miss this place?"

Orson laughed. "Not even the teeniest, tiniest bit. Already moved my stuff out."

"You ready to say goodbye then?"

"Saying goodbye to this is me saying hello to everything else."

Ellis tapped his watch. "Go ahead and call. We can leave when you're done."

Orson smiled and nodded, dialing as he did.

Connor picked up on the first ring. This was his favorite time of day.

"Daddy!"

"Hello, Connor."

"When are you coming to get me?"

And in that moment, without a red carpet, black tie attire, or anything other than the squealing excitement of his number-one fan, Orson knew that his world had been righted.

"Right now."

Natalie hasn't thought about her sorority sister, Olivia, since she slept with — then married — the love of Olivia's life. Now Olivia is back with some very bad news and an indecent proposal Natalie can't bring herself to refuse.

A Quick Favor ...

If you enjoyed this book, please take a moment to write a review on favorite bookselling site so other readers can enjoy it too. It would mean a lot to me.

Thank you,
  Nolon King

About the Author

Nolon King writes fast-paced psychological thrillers set in the glitzy world of entertainment's power players with a bold, insightful voice. He's not afraid to explore the darker side of human nature through stories featuring families torn apart by secrets and lies.

Nolon loves to write about big questions and moral quandaries. How far would you go to cover up an honest mistake? Would you destroy your career to protect your family? How much of your soul would you sell to get the life of your dreams? Would you cheat on your husband to keep your children safe? Would you give in to a stalker's demands to save your marriage?

Also By Nolon King

Cold Vengeance

Cold Vengeance

Cold Reckoning

Hidden Justice

Hidden Justice

Hidden Honor

Hidden Shame

Hidden Virtue

No Justice

No Justice

No Escape

No Hope

No Return

No Stopping

No Fear

Once Upon A Crime

Once Upon A Crime

Twice Upon A Lie

Three Times a Murder

Dead For Good

Dead For Good

Left For Dead

Dead Of Night

Wake The Dead

Dead For Life

Stand Alone Novels

Pretty Killer

12

Blown

Miserable Lies

The Target

Secrets We Keep

Close To Home

Heat To Obsession

A Simple Kill

Tell Me No Lies

Red Carpet Black

Fade To Black

Victim